Criti...
Catherine Li...

FOLLOWING THE WRONG G...

'A wonderful love story with ... ...eeling of
Singapore and traditional att... ...wards life. Yin and Vincent are
very real characters and it is a splendid piece of storytelling'

Publishing News

THE TEARDROP STORY WOMAN

'A tender Malayan tale of superstitious families and lovelorn siblings'

Marie Claire

'Movingly tender ... A beautifully written exploration of the meaning
of love, giving a fascinating insight into a culture worlds apart from
our experience of being a woman'

Woman's Realm

'If you loved *Wild Swans*, you'll adore this book'

Company

'A beautifully written tale of forbidden love alongside a fascinating
insight into Singapore culture. Unputdownable'

B magazine

THE BONDMAID

'A powerful and moving saga ... fascinating and skilfully related'

Daily Mail

CATHERINE LIM
The Song of Silver Frond

Marshall Cavendish
Editions

Cover art by Opal Works Co. Limited

First published in 2003 by Orion Publishing.

This edition ublished in 2011 by Marshall Cavendish Editions
An imprint of Marshall Cavendish International
1 New Industrial Road, Singapore 536196

All characters appearing in this work are fictitious. Any resemblance to real persons, living or dead, is purely coincidental.

Other Marshall Cavendish Offices:
Marshall Cavendish International. PO Box 65829 London EC1P 1NY, UK • Marshall Cavendish Corporation. 99 White Plains Road, Tarrytown NY 10591-9001, USA • Marshall Cavendish International (Thailand) Co Ltd. 253 Asoke, 12th Flr, Sukhumvit 21 Road, Klongtoey Nua, Wattana, Bangkok 10110, Thailand • Marshall Cavendish (Malaysia) Sdn Bhd, Times Subang, Lot 46, Subang Hi-Tech Industrial Park, Batu Tiga, 40000 Shah Alam, Selangor Darul Ehsan, Malaysia.

Marshall Cavendish is a trademark of Times Publishing Limited

National Library Board Singapore Cataloguing in Publication Data
Lim, Catherine
  The Song of Silver Frond. – Singapore : Marshall Cavendish Editions, 2011.
  p. cm.
  ISBN : 978-981-4346-23-8

  1. Singapore – Social life and customs – Fiction. I. Title

PR9570.S53.L477
S823 — dc22   OCN703135839

Printed by Fabulous Printers Pte Ltd.

To my family, with much love

CONTENTS

PART ONE
The Child Woman

1
The Truth Cockerel

In the months following the end of the war and the devastation left by the hated Japanese, the people in the little village of Sim Bak, instead of starting on the massive work of repair and rebuilding, began to interest themselves in a sordid little family quarrel. It was none of their business, for the family was not even one of their own, being from a neighbouring village.

Besides, the quarrel was not even remotely scandalous. A father had accused his son of stealing some money. But when the people of Sim Bak heard that it would be resolved by no less than the ceremony of the truth cockerel in the Yio Tok Temple in the town of Nam Kio, they knew they could not miss that spectacle of high drama in which the gods themselves would be called upon to bear witness to human veracity.

A child had reported seeing the cockerel that the accused son had bought for the ceremony – a pure white bird, without even a speck of colour in its feathers. The purer, the more potent. Also, the more expensive. The child said breathlessly he had seen the young man take out a lot of money from his pocket.

Soon, details about the other requisites for the ceremony were also reported and spread excitedly – a brand new chopping knife, which would remain in its paper wrapper till the moment of use, to prove its newness, and the special yellow trousers and white headband, borrowed from a temple medium, which the accused would wear when he performed his act.

Silver Frond, aged thirteen, a girl soon to be visited by first blood and therefore not welcome at a holy place, asked her father to take her to witness the ceremony that everybody was talking about. By then, she was already showing the unusual beauty that would be both promise and danger, sorrow and joy to herself and others.

Her two younger sisters, Silver Flower and Silver Pearl, as unlike her in appearance as raw earth and shining sky, rough weed and delicate blossom, as their own father would say with poetic unfeeling, stood by grinning, not daring to join in the request, content to get the story from her afterwards.

'Of course! Of course!' said Ah Bee Koh, with hearty affability, wheeling out his bicycle. The bicycle had no pillion, so his daughter would have to sit across the bar in front, which was wrapped thickly with gunny sack, to ease the bumpy, half-hour ride to the temple in the hot morning sun.

'Mad! Mad! Both of you are mad!' shrieked his wife. 'You want to get into trouble?' Gods were averse to the desecrating presence of females in the uncleanness of parturition or monthly flow, and could punish severely. Some years ago, an unclean woman had gone to worship in the Bright Light Temple during the festival of the Nine Emperor Gods and had been struck down.

Ah Bee Soh wanted to make sure that her daughter, with breasts already beginning to bud under her blouse, would stop going to places visited both by gods and men, to avoid annoying the first and arousing the second.

But her husband and daughter had already left.

A large crowd had gathered at the courtyard of the Yio Tok Temple. The accused, a young man in his thirties, wearing only a pair of loose yellow trousers and a white clothband, which was tied tightly round his head, stood facing the crowd, barefoot, his head bowed in grim, silent prayer to the gods. In his hands, clasped tightly together and raised to the level of his chin, he held a large cluster of lit joss-sticks, sending up clouds of smoke. The smoke rose heavenwards towards the gods with the message: Get ready to bear witness.

On one side of the man stood a temple priest in a saffron robe; on the other, his assistant, in the same ceremonial trousers and headband, struggling to hold down a furiously flapping and squawking cockerel. On the ground at his feet lay a brand new chopping knife, its blade glinting in the morning sun. At the back, against a red pillar, stood a large golden urn with a giant joss-stick spuming huge billows of pungent smoke, which stung human eyes to tears and sweetened the path for gods' arrivals and departures.

When the man finished his prayers, he looked up, turned and walked to the urn to arrange the joss-sticks in it. He walked back slowly, with deliberation, to take his place once more between the priest and the assistant. He stood very still, his cheekbones standing out in cold white fury amidst the dark shadows of his face. Once again he bowed, this time to acknowledge the presence of witnesses, both mortal and divine. Throughout he maintained total silence. Words of denial and protest were no longer needed, neither was the presence of the accusers. The man's family, it seemed, had refused to come.

The appointed moment, which everyone was waiting for, had come. But the man, relishing his central role in the high drama, would delay it further. He continued to stand very still,

as the crowd watched in total silence. Now he was murmuring
something, and the crowd strained to hear. Suddenly, with a
piercing cry, he dropped to the ground on his knees. Then, with
another cry, he seized the cockerel from his assistant, pressed
it to the ground with one hand, picked up the knife with the
other and, with one mighty blow, struck its neck.

The cockerel gave a last angry squawk as its head flew
up, together with a powerful squirt of blood, both making
a graceful double arc in the air before falling with a plo*p* at
the man's feet. The crowd murmured with satisfaction. Then
they laughed with delight as the cockerel's headless body, with
blood still gushing from its neck and splattering its pure white
feathers, sprang up, ran hither and thither with lunatic frenzy,
before finally collapsing in a heap by the man's feet.

It was said that, in the old days, the gods struck dead those
who had dared to abuse the ancient rite of the truth cockerel.
As the blasphemer's knife fell, so would he, struck by a lightning
bolt hurled from heaven to shrivel up his lying tongue. The
gods seemed less recriminatory now; perhaps they were waiting
to visit the retribution upon later generations.

The man stood up and wiped his hands on his trousers with
a theatrical flourish, leaving long red streaks. He was panting
heavily, as he gazed reverently upon the bloodied knife, head
and body on the ground, noble instruments of justice.

Now a roar of admiration and support rose from the crowd.
The man smiled and waved, a temple celebrant in full glory.
Thus he stood vindicated by gods and mortals. Henceforth, he
was free of all taint of shame. He had sought in vain to convince
his family by protests, pleas, tears. His father had persisted in the
accusation. In desperation, he had even sworn on an ancestral
tablet. But the gods were more powerful than ancestors. He

could go back home now, completely exonerated, and silence his accusers for ever.

As soon as Silver Frond returned home, her sisters ran to her, demanding to be told. But the truth was that she did not like what she had seen, and was sorry for the poor cockerel. How it had clung to life, down to the last breath thrashing about so desperately inside the headless body! She felt sorry for all mutilated creatures. If she were one of the temple goddesses, she would have given the cockerel a new head and set it free.

Goddess Pearly Face, the kindest and most powerful goddess in the Yio Tok Temple, could surely have intervened? It was not at all a comfortable feeling – disappointment with a deity. Silver Frond had gazed at the goddess on each visit to the temple with her mother, and been struck both by the kind look on her face and by her beauty, especially her skin, which had the translucence of pearls. Perhaps even gods and goddesses could be forgetful and careless.

Disappointed wish combined with fervid imagination to produce a compensatory flow of sparkling narrative, making up for the remissness of gods. Silver Frond's eyes shone, her cheeks glowed as she sat cross-legged on a mat, facing her giggling sisters. 'The truth cockerel's white feathers had turned all black from taking on the man's lies – for indeed he had really stolen his father's money. Then I saw the Goddess Pearly Face come down and scold the man. She was not at all afraid of what he would do to her, for she was a goddess. She said, "You liar! The poor innocent cockerel has died for nothing. You ought to be ashamed of yourself !" Then she directed her powerful fingers straight at the head lying on the ground, and it shot up and attached itself back to the cockerel—'

Her father laughed and said, 'My daughter is not only beautiful but a clever story-teller! She is even better than Liang Por.'

Few could match that weaver of glittering tales on Singapore Redifussion who had thousands glued to their radios every day. It was said housewives neglected housework to listen to his magical tales of long ago and far away.

'Enough, enough!' cried her mother and hurried Silver Frond to the well, where she washed her hair and face with water purified by scented flower petals.

2
Pah Bor Chai

'Once upon a time, a very long time ago...' Liang Por would begin, and instantly Silver Frond would stop whatever she was doing – sweeping the floor, feeding the chickens, separating the good grains of rice from the husked ones, collecting eggs from the henhouse – to listen spellbound.

Once upon a time, a very long time ago, there lived a man who was less poor than many others in his village, so that occasionally he would spend a little more money on food for himself and his wife, though pork, chicken and large prawns were only for very important occasions such as the New Year, and abalone and dried black mushroom were of course out of the question.

One day, the man went to market and saw a very leafy, succulent-looking vegetable that he liked very much. Moreover, it was affordable. He bought a large bundle to take home to his wife to cook for their dinner. Now, unfortunately for the wife, the vegetable was the kind that shrank to a tiny fraction of its size when boiled or fried. It was just the nature of the vegetable; no skill in cooking could prevent the shrinking. So when the wife placed it before her husband on a plate, he saw only a very small portion of what he expected.

He stared at it. 'Is that all?' he asked incredulously.

'That is all,' said his wife.

'You're lying!' shouted the man. 'I bought a huge bundle!'

He demonstrated the size with his arms encircling a huge amount of space.

'I'm not lying,' said his wife.

'I know what you did,' said her husband. 'You took half of the bundle and either secretly sold it for money, or you slipped out and gave it to your parents for their dinner.'

'I did not!' protested the wife. He did not believe her and began to beat her soundly. He used his fists and then a stick. *Whack! Pok! Krak!*

'Help! Help!' she screamed, as he chased her all round the house.

From that day, the vegetable became known as *Pah Bor Chai*, Beat-the-Wife Vegetable, which, on principle, no man should buy, even if it is cheaply and abundantly sold in the market.

Silver Frond said, 'I'll never eat that horrible vegetable as long as I live.'

Silver Flower said, 'Even if you are very hungry? Even when you don't have a single mouthful of food for dinner?'

Silver Pearl, enjoying the hypothetical situation, carried it to its extremity. 'Even if you are starving and don't have a single grain of rice for the whole day?'

Silver Frond replied loftily, 'I told you I would never ever touch it. And I'll never marry a man who goes to market to buy it.'

Her mother laughed and said, 'We can't afford it anyway.'

3
Fortune's Fluxes

Ah Bee Soh said that her greatest relief, when the foreign enemies came to invade and stay, was that her eldest daughter was still a child. It was a special protection from the gods that Silver Frond's beauty manifested itself only after the barbarians had left. It was miraculous, but true. One day she was this ordinary-looking child, no different from the other village children, and the next, she was in first bloom, with promise of much more to come. A beautiful child-woman, in that intriguing in-between stage when people could not tell where innocence ended and seductiveness began, and were charmed by both. The period would be brief, but it shimmered with possibilities, and stirred expectation and hope.

The people of Sim Bak Village and the town liked to stop and look at her, commenting on her eyes, skin, hair, mouth. They said she looked like the famous actress Ling Ling in her younger days.

'No, no,' Ah Bee Soh would protest laughingly, deflecting all compliments as modesty and decorum required. If the special ardour of a compliment called for some balancing criticism, she would say, 'Ah, but what's the use of having a pretty daughter if she is stubborn and wilful and talks back to her mother? I scold her with one word, and she answers with ten!'

The kind gods had covered the growing bud with their hands, delaying awakening. Then when they saw that the evil foreigners were truly gone, they touched it into instant bloom. The brutal conquerors could so easily have extended their rapine to beautiful child-women.

As it was, they had only been interested in the farm produce of Sim Bak Village. At that time, the village boasted some of Singapore's best vegetable gardens, worked by men and women who had made the long journey by ship from the ancestral country in search of fortune and ended up on farms even more demanding than the ones they had left behind, because the sun in the new country blazed all the year round and made their skin as hard as leather. Ah Bee Soh's grandparents, who had come from southern China, had been among these hard-working and hardened farmers; her own parents fared only slightly better.

Ah Bee Soh remembered very clearly the day the Japanese plunderers made their first appearance. The rapacious troops rolled up in a truck along the dirt road leading to the village, jumped down with their guns and bayonets and summoned the frightened villagers to make their demands. *Hak! Hak! Hoik!* They were quick with the conquerors' language for rounding up the conquered, but did not know the local word for 'fowl' and so went through a comical routine of clucking, quacking and flapping their arms. A child laughed out loud and was instantly silenced by his mother's hand clamped upon his mouth. An hour later, the men rolled off, with a full truckload of vegetables, fruit, chickens, ducks and even a pig, which they had made the pig farmer Old Ah Song slaughter before their eyes.

'Better our livestock than our sons.' The conquered sought solace in a lesser loss. Old Ah Song reminded all of what had happened to the nearby village of Chu Tian. The Japanese, seeming to know where sons could be in hiding, had searched under beds, behind doors, in cupboards, then had gone out to the pig-sties, woodsheds, even the lavatories and wells, and had hauled out the terrified young men. The men, whimpering, pleading, were taken away in trucks, thrown into jail or put to work on massive, cruel building projects and never seen again.

Old Ah Song had been instantly and severely silenced. Such loose talk! Such foolish tempting of fate! If indeed, the Japanese soldiers had returned for the young men of Sim Bak, he, the oldest and the most respected person in the village, would have stood accursed for the rest of his life.

When she heard that the war was over and the enemies properly vanquished, Ah Bee Soh spat on the ground, rubbed the spittle into the dirt with a triumphant heel, then went to wash her hair at the well, with water freshened by flower petals, to signify the beginning of a new life of hope. She grew a jasmine bush beside the well, to provide the sweetness in water both to wash away evil and attract good. She said that at last they could all think of bringing up their children in a decent way.

Their farm produce should bring good money. Besides selling it in the mornings at the market, they could sell it in the late afternoons to those families who happened to need fresh vegetables for the evening meal. Soon she and the more enterprising of the villagers began a competition for the business patronage of those families in the town who had somehow not only survived the war, but had benefited from it, thus having ample money to spend on food.

The Wee family, for instance, had managed to run a small groceries shop very successfully. Just months before the war ended, they had the foresight to use the profits, wads of Japanese currency notes tied up with rubber bands and stuffed into six canvas bags, to buy up whatever articles of worth the townspeople were selling in order to buy food for their children. The five members of the Wee family fanned out, paying three times more than usual for small gold ornaments that were the last to go, such as newborn babies' First Month good luck anklets, bracelets and rings, old women's jade hairpins, sewing machines, radios, gramophones, clocks, solid pieces of furniture, good quality *batik* sarongs, which the proud *Nyonya* women sold only in the stealth of night, chilli grinders, a rice pestle and mortar, even a child's wooden rocking horse. The Wee family accepted anything, anxious to get rid of the six canvas bags of money.

When victory was finally declared and the enemy's money became useless overnight, fit only for burning or for wiping backsides in the most vivid demonstration yet of the people's hostility, the Wee family laughed, celebrated, and soon prepared to sell back the entire stock of their new possessions. Expensive roasted suckling pig for celebration meals was a rarity in the restaurants in those early post-war years, but the Wee family bought one to offer to the temple gods, then took it home to carve out for the most joyous family meal ever.

The Bong family claimed a greater ingenuity for the preservation of assets against war's devastation. His wealth, Ah Bong Chek said, lay entirely in his two bright sons who ran his charcoal business. It would only be a matter of time before the Japanese came to take them away. When they went to Ah Bong Chek's house, they found the two young men in ragged clothes, covered with charcoal dust, grunting like beasts, sitting on the floor and playing with their own urine. Ah Bong Chek tearfully explained that they had offended the chief god in the Bright Light Temple and had been struck insane in consequence. They had even tried to set fire to their mother's hair. As the older brother stood up and lurched forward, a whiff of faeces hit the visitors' nostrils. They fled.

Ah Bong Chek said that a fortune teller had told him this would be the last hurdle for the family to clear on the road to prosperity. Even as they washed the filth from their bodies, his two sons were casting off all the bad luck of the past. The gods would bless them with enormous profits in their business, and ever true to their promise, they did, as soon as the business was extended to include kerosene and cooking oil.

Ah Bong Chek's ruse had certainly worked better than that of the town barber, who had managed a very convincing and grotesque limp, until an alert Japanese officer spotted him one morning in the marketplace agilely climbing up and down a lorry, unloading crates.

The fluxes of fortune touched the village people only much later, many years after the war, when the government in its urbanisation and development programmes cleared the villages of the farms and turned them into industrial sites or housing estates. Some of the villagers were actually able to rise to prosperity through wise use of the compensation money, setting up modest foodstalls, which later grew into thriving restaurants. Others were not so fortunate, living out their days in misery in crowded, highrise flats, and missing even the smell of pig and chicken dung.

Ah Bee Koh, and many of his neighbours in Sim Bak Village, died years before the compensation scheme was even thought of by the government. But that year, when the war had just ended, he was still in good health and spirits, which made him talkative and disposed to make fun of those townsfolk like the Wees, who had become rich by dishonestly foisting useless Japanese currency on innocent people.

'The gods have eyes,' he said ominously. 'The Wees will eventually know that the gods see and punish.'

'Meanwhile, they live in a big house, and their children go to school and do not have to sell vegetables and eggs,' said his wife with a bitter laugh, for she had already put her daughters to the ignominious work of selling their produce from door to door, and tolerating the insolence and unreasonable behaviour of some of the buyers. Silver Frond had come home one afternoon, her eyes filled with angry tears, because one of the buyers had brutally tried to bargain down the already low prices of all the vegetables, and then had flung the money into her basket.

'You think I'm a failure,' said Ah Bee Koh cheerfully, preparing to go out and spend another idle day in the coffee-and-beer shop, 'but one day I'll be a wealthy man, and buy a big beautiful house in town for you.'

It was more malice than prescience that made his wife say, 'One day, you'll still be a failure, but your daughter Silver Frond will be wealthy and buy me a big house to stay in.'

Better to depend on a growing daughter's beauty than a husband's luck at the lottery.

Meanwhile, Ah Bee Soh had to send Silver Frond and her sisters out every afternoon, to the homes of well-to-do people like the Wees and the Bongs, with baskets filled with succulent beans, bittergourd, chillis, yams, brinjals, *chye sim* and *kangkong*, but not tapioca, as people had had enough of that ubiquitous war food and never wanted to look at it again. It was said that some people had gone soft in the bone and in the head from eating nothing but boiled tapioca.

4
Silver Frond and the Venerable One

Ah Bee Soh was lucky to have secured, almost from the start, the business patronage of the Great House, which belonged to the Old One. It was actually a row of four connected shophouses in a long row of twelve that faced King George Road in the town, with the dividing walls torn down to form one continuous building for the necessary accommodation of the Old One's three wives, their children, their children's children and an assortment of relatives and servants.

In the ancestral land, the houses would have been sensibly grouped around a courtyard, for more effective control, but the Old One, moving up and down the long chain of houses through a series of tastefully connecting moongates, managed effectively enough and was able, it was said, to give equal attention to the wives.

Such a large household required a large daily supply of vegetables and eggs. After a while, Silver Frond's family became the sole supplier of the eggs.

Nobody, of course, would have guessed at that time that the lives of the Old One, then already sixty-five and Silver Frond, then only thirteen, would become so strangely, so extraordinarily intertwined. Neither gods nor demons could have planned anything like it.

Once a week, Silver Frond, not yet fully showing a woman's body so that it was still safe for her to go to the town on her own, went to the Great House and always managed to sell the entire basket of eggs. She came back with the money securely tied in a corner of a handkerchief, which was then folded into a small square and put inside an inner blouse pocket, safely hidden from view.

It was an unvarying routine her mother had taught her: begin with First Wife, as a sign of respect for her status, and let her have first choice of the eggs; then go with the rest to Second Wife and Third Wife. Apologise politely if there are not enough eggs left and promise to bring the rest the next day. Receive the money with both hands and say thank you very respectfully. Once out of the house, tie up the money in your handkerchief and put it away quickly. But make sure first that nobody is looking. If the Bad Brothers are watching, just clutch the money tightly in your hand, pretend you have not seen them, and walk away quickly. And don't linger to watch the *sinseh* teaching the Old One's granddaughters unless they allow you to.

Silver Frond had told her mother enthusiastically of those visits to the Great House when she had heard sounds of teaching and learning coming from a part of the house sectioned off as a classroom for the numerous granddaughters of varying ages. The Old One, following the ancestors' practice of sending sons to school but keeping daughters at home, privately believed in the value of education for girls, and compromised by employing a well-educated *sinseh* to come and tutor his granddaughters.

Silver Frond had actually been allowed, on a few occasions, to watch the impressive *sinseh*, long-faced, with a straggly beard and glasses perched on his nose, reading from a book and making the girls repeat words of wisdom after him.

He taught them to write the characters for divinely appointed virtues such as right conduct and right thinking. He taught them to repeat after him poems of astonishing beauty written by classical poets and he listened with pain as the poems came back, emptied of all their beauty by the Old One's dull, droning granddaughters.

She had watched, with envy, the granddaughters bent over copybooks with their pencils, the tips of their tongues poking out in intense concentration. One of them, the oldest and the most stupid, was always having either her head or knuckles rapped with a wooden ruler by the strict teacher, whose reputation was enhanced with each reported act of strictness. Sometimes one or more of the wives would look in and smile with approval at each rebuke or thwack of the ruler.

Oh, how she wished she could have a *sinseh* teaching her too! She would not at all mind her head or knuckles being rapped, as long as she was allowed to hold a book and write in a copybook and recite those wonderful poems.

'*Their* world is there,' said her mother, pointing to the far distance, 'and *our* world is here,' pointing to the hard earthen floor of their house, unswept as yet of the daily chicken droppings. Watching rich people's granddaughters being taught by a private tutor was not part of Silver Frond's routine at the Great House. She was to concern herself only with selling her eggs to each of the wives in order of status, and then coming straight home.

Fortunately, she could deal with First Wife and Second Wife simultaneously and save much time, because the two women did everything together, including buying eggs. They were in fact sisters. Second Wife was said to be simple-minded, leaving all decisions to her older, more capable sister. Silver Frond had observed that she was totally incapable of ascertaining the quality of an egg by its size, shape and colour. She only watched placidly, like a contented child, as First Wife tested each egg by rolling it gently on the cheek. Every week, with rare exceptions, the eggs passed the cheek test.

Third Wife, who lived in the last of the four houses forming the Great House, never did any testing of the eggs. She merely asked Silver Frond, in a rather surly voice, 'Are they fresh?'

As for the Old One himself, Ah Cheng Peh – sometimes called the Venerable One because of his generous donations to the town's temple and the death home for the destitute elderly – Silver Frond seldom saw him. Indeed, he was rarely seen in the women's quarters, preferring to keep himself apart and aloof in the front portion of the first house where he and his assistants conducted his business of managing several land holdings and coconut plantations, and renting out rows of shophouses, as well as a fleet of lorries that plied the roads all over the island.

It seemed that the enormous wealth was built upon the sweat and remarkable entrepreneurial acumen of a single ancestor who came from China in the last century, as a boy of thirteen, with nothing but the shirt on his back. This forbear's business skill rolled down the generations undiminished; by the time it came to the Venerable One, it had combined with a canny understanding of the local politics to ensure family prosperity even amidst the disruptions of war.

During the Japanese Occupation, he had allowed the Japanese soldiers to make use of some of the shophouses, instructing his assistants to give them whatever they wanted, in order to avoid trouble.

'They are wrecking the place,' reported the assistants in frightened whispers. 'They bathe in huge, round, wooden bathtubs, splashing water everywhere and making the women servants scrub their backs and private parts.'

The Venerable One frowned, put a finger to his lips and shook his head several times, signifying the need to maintain peace at all costs. He gave instructions for all repairs to be done to the houses, if requested by the Japanese occupants.

Beyond that, he had nothing to do with them, thus maintaining a commendable balance between resistance and cooperation. When the town authorities, guided by the British advisers, rounded up suspected collaborators as soon as the war was over, they never thought of questioning the Venerable One.

It was calculated that he owned as many as six rows of shophouses, making him the town's biggest property owner. All were rented out to shopkeepers and small retailers, except one, which was reputed to be haunted.

It was the ghost of a woman who had hanged herself, a long time ago, from a rafter on the ceiling. Many of the townspeople claimed they had seen her, always in a long robe, with long hair that fell over her face like a thick black curtain, which she parted with both hands to peer out at people who had not even been born when she died. On cold, moonlit nights, dogs heard her low sobbing and howled in their turn. In front of the house, just by the entrance, somebody had placed a placatory joss-stick, stuck in a cigarette tin.

Food would have been better, some people said. For the ghost had gone hungry all these many years. Even during the Feast of the Hungry Ghosts, when others were treated to rich feasts of suckling pig, steamed chicken, roasted duck, noodles and the sweetest pomelos and oranges, this ghost had nothing to eat.

No, it was not food the ghost wanted, said others. It was a man. This very lonely and lovesick ghost had been wandering the earth for a hundred years.

The Venerable One, in his steady aloofness, had no time for

such nonsense. He despised idle chatter, and the women in his household fell into a respectful silence as soon as a brief, stern cough announced his approach. He rarely spoke to his wives or daughters, married and unmarried, and never to the female servants. He had four sons-in-law, who were happy for their wives and children to stay for long periods in the Great House, and for themselves to come for meals or simply to look around, and be impressed by the wealth and influence of their august father-in-law. They were always reminding their children not to make too much noise when the Venerable One was taking a nap.

The grandchildren were of course all afraid of him. He never spoke to them either. He deigned to speak occasionally to his senile mother, ninety years old, still talkative, moving around energetically on her little bound feet with the help of a servant.

The One with Gold in the Mouth, First Wife called him, but of course, not in his hearing. Those with gold in their mouths never spoke, for fear the precious stuff would fall out and be picked up by others.

The Venerable One had an adopted son, actually a distant cousin, who did all the accounts for his numerous rented properties, having successfully competed with one of the sons-in-law for the coveted job. After the war, many of the townspeople were eager to rent shophouses for this or that business. The Venerable One gave instructions to the adopted son, who was called Black Dog, to try harder to find a tenant for the haunted house, perhaps an Indian goldsmith or barber or money-lender, who would not be bothered by a Chinese ghost. If the Indian tenant insisted, Black Dog should get a monk from the Bright Light Temple to cleanse the house of the ghost by leading her gently home to the abode of her ancestors, to end a hundred-year exile this dreary side of eternity.

The Venerable One had much respect for the spirits of ancestors, resting in well-tended tombs, honoured daily at the ancestral altars and forming a continuous line of family unity with those living and those yet to be born. But he had no idea how to deal with homeless, hungry female ghosts. He did not like the thought of a long-haired, sobbing spirit residing in one of his shophouses.

The Venerable One never smiled. When he took his daily walk through the town, in his familiar white cotton vest and black silk trousers, impeccably uncreased, a small towel laid across his left shoulder, impeccably folded, sometimes carrying a long stick in his hand to shoo off sniffing, smelly stray dogs, he merely nodded at those who greeted him, or gave a short grunt of acknowledgment.

'Good morning, Ah Cheng Peh.'

'Errmm.'

'Are you well, Ah Cheng Peh?'

'Errmm.'

'Have you eaten, Ah Cheng Peh?'

'Errmm.'

The first time Silver Frond saw the Venerable One in the Great House, she greeted him nervously.

'Good morning, Ah Cheng Peh.'

'Errmm,' he said, without looking at her, and walked to the table where his breakfast of hot steaming rice porridge and pickled vegetables was waiting for him.

Exactly six months later, he would notice and speak to her for the first time, setting in motion the chain of remarkable events that even many years later, people still talked about.

That fateful encounter would not be in the Great House.

5
A Strategy of Laughter

Ah Bee Koh, who smoked, drank coffee, and engaged in gossip the whole day long, scratching his armpits and guffawing loudly, while his wife did all the work, made ribald jokes about how, despite his austere taciturnity with his wives, the Venerable One had sired a total of eleven children – alas, all female, except a sickly imbecile son, now twenty-five years old, who stayed locked in a room because his father was ashamed to show him to the world. 'My dear husband, it is my turn to sleep with you tonight.'

Ah Bee Koh could mimic convincingly the slow, thick accent of First Wife who, it was rumoured, no longer wanted sex, having been long ago exhausted by it, and had suggested her sister, twelve years younger, as Second Wife.

'Errmm.'

'No, it is my turn! How am I going to bear you the healthy son you've always wanted if you never sleep with me?'

Ah Bee Koh had never heard Second Wife speak, and assumed she had the same dull, heavy voice of her sister. He gave her a liveliness she did not possess, for she was known throughout the town for having no brains at all, being content to echo her sister's every opinion. She was never without a small packet of dried melon seeds in her hand, which she could unhusk inside her mouth, several at a time, with expert clicking movements of tongue and teeth, spitting out the husks and keeping back the tasty flesh inside. The children in the household tried to imitate her, but unsuccessfully. It was the only thing she was good at.

'Errmm.'

'Come to me tonight! I have the breasts of the actress Lai Kwang and legs that spring apart at a touch!'

Ah Bee Koh always eagerly anticipated this part of his act, for he mimicked perfectly the shrill, strident voice of aggressive Third Wife, who was the youngest and most attractive. The whole town gossiped about Third Wife. She was the only wife who dared perm her hair and wear lipstick. She also called herself Molly. Last in the hierarchy of wives, she made sure her power exceeded her status. It was well known that First Wife disliked her intensely, and avoided her as much as possible, though they invariably met at least once a day in the large common kitchen with its common stove and rice-grinding millstone.

Their hostility was shared by their respective servants, who loyally spied for their mistresses. They whispered behind cupped hands, twisted their mouths into sneering smiles, made loud insinuating comments to empty space, bribed lower servants and small children, peeped through keyholes or cracks in window slats, and were able to report on the Venerable One going in and out of wives' bedrooms. The idle townspeople titillated each other with speculations about his arrangement of giving equal time, and wondered whether Third Wife, being the most attractive and possessing an impressive store of rare herbal potions for restoring male strength, actually got the greatest share.

Second Wife, of course, sided with her sister against Third Wife, and showed the amazing skill, in addition to multiple melon seed de-husking, of contorting her features into an expression of amazing malevolence each time Third Wife passed by.

'Errmm. All right. But make haste. And take a bath first. Then clean my ears.'

Ah Bee Koh acted out the delicate task of ear-cleaning. The Venerable One's meticulous hygiene, down to his toenails, was well known. Third Wife possessed a fine set of gold earcleaners, inherited from an ancestor in China, and not available in any of the goldsmith shops in Singapore, with which she gave excellent service.

The truth was that the only reason the Venerable One did not get rid of her, despite his exasperation with her permed hair, lipstick, Western name and habit of bantering with his male assistants, was his supreme satisfaction, not with her effective herbal potions, but with her ear-cleaning.

Nobody could do it like her. He required her to clean his ears once a week, sometimes twice, for the sheer pleasure of the sensation, reclining in a chair, and forbidding any of the grandchildren to play around and make noise. Third Wife peered, probed, dug. She did it all most skillfully, making sure she did not go in too deep and cause pain. She held, between thumb and forefinger, the exquisitely crafted instrument, slimmer than a toothpick, with a tiny bowl at the end for the miniature excavation. She always wore it in a small cylindrical locket on a chain round her neck, to be at the ready.

Ah Bee Koh said, with a snigger, 'The old patriarch would rather she opened her locket than her legs.'

The daughters, Silver Frond, aged thirteen, Silver Flower, aged eleven and Silver Pearl, aged ten, giggled and covered their mouths with their hands.

Ah Bee Koh picked up salacious gossip and liberally embellished it for his clowning, to forestall criticism from his wife, or simply to drown that out with laughter from his daughters. It was a good strategy.

Ah Bee Soh, washing or ironing huge piles of the townspeople's clothes, muttered, 'The fool. Talking like this in front of his daughters. Doesn't he have any sense of decency?'

'Come here, all of you,' commanded the father. In his effort to look severe, he looked comical, and his three daughters let out another burst of giggles behind their hands.

'Now, you listen carefully to me. If anybody is rude to you or gives you trouble, you come home at once to tell your father. I'll show them!'

Ah Bee Koh pointed to a tattoo of a flaming dragon's head on his right arm, which signified the hope of, rather than actual membership of, the most feared triad in town. He repeated darkly, 'They insult my daughters and they know what's coming.'

His wife, fanning the coals inside the clothes-iron, while the perspiration gathered on her forehead, muttered, 'The braggart. The fool. Instead of talking so much, why doesn't he go out to work?' She grew bolder in her irritation and said loudly, 'Why can't you go to collect the clothes instead of letting Silver Flower and Silver Pearl do it? They can't manage the heavy bundle and they get teased.'

The little sisters no longer sold vegetables. Instead, they went out every day with a long pole and a large basket between them to collect the laundry from a dozen houses, and every few days returned the clothes, freshly washed, ironed and folded. It was said that Ah Bee Soh ironed so well the shirts gleamed like mirrors and the trouser pleats cut like knives.

It would be years before Silver Flower and Silver Pearl became women and showed breasts, but still there were bad boys, like Ah Lau Chek's awful sons, who went round teasing and frightening young girls. In much less that time, Silver Frond would be a woman, and would have to stop going round selling eggs. Men and boys were only too quick to smell first blood.

'If she is so pretty as a child, what more as a woman?' said some of the neighbours.

But others disagreed. 'It will only be for a few years. Then her body will become thick with childbearing, her face old with worry, her hands coarsened by work.'

Ah Bee Soh, whose hands were as hard as wood with the daily washing and ironing of clothes, cried fervently, 'May the gods grant her a better fate!'

There was a framed photograph on the wall of Ah Bee Soh as a girl, a sad reminder of cheated youth.

She told the neighbours that if she had given birth to a dozen more daughters, they would all be as plain-looking as Silver Flower and Silver Pearl – the poor things, with their broad, flat faces and dark rough skins! – because the first-born had used up the entire quota of beauty allotted by the gods.

In the time of the emperors in the ancestral country, Silver Frond would have been spotted and plucked out of her village, like a tender flower, to bloom in the imperial court, and, for the rest of their lives, her parents would have been well provided for.

'You are special, so don't let anyone in the Great House insult you,' said the father earnestly. 'They are rich and we are poor – so what? They eat good quality white rice every day; we eat broken brown rice. The Old One drinks Hennessy brandy; your father doesn't have money for a cheap beer. His wives and daughters go to Poh Seng Goldsmith to buy thick gold chains and bangles; your poor mother here has to wash people's dirty clothes for a few miserable dollars. So what?'

Poverty's grievance was by turns mocking, abusive, self-pitying. It could be magnanimous, for Ah Bee Koh got up from his chair, walked to where his wife was ironing clothes on a pad of old blankets laid on the floor, squatted down close to her and said kindly, 'One day, when your husband strikes first prize in the lottery, he'll go to Poh Seng Goldsmith and ask for the longest, thickest gold chain and the heaviest bangle. They'll come running to him with cups of steaming tea and say, "Oh, how are you, Ah Bee Koh? Are you well? Have you eaten?" I'll say, "Hurry up, you fools, because I'm going to Sin Hin Goldsmith next, to get my wife the jade and diamond crab-claw hairpin she's always wanted."'

Ah Bee Soh gave a little laugh of derision and did not look up from her ironing. It was exactly this kind of cheerful boasting from her husband that provoked a bitter lament of his terrible dereliction of duty as provider. 'Idling all day, while your daughters walk for miles with a load they can hardly manage, spending money with those useless people in the beer shop, never contributing a single cent ...' She could have gone on and on, and elicited no more than laughing remonstrance and a wave of the hand in playful dismissal.

Ah Bee Koh told his daughters that their mother's angry words were like the knives, swords and spears, hurled by the enemies of the great Feng-yu. The lethal weapons flew through the air, over roofs and tree tops, towards the resplendent warrior as he rode away on his horse. Feng-yu stopped, turned his horse to face them, then raised a hand majestically in the air. *Whooosh! Shooosh! Splat!* The weapons came up against the cool raised palm and dropped uselessly to the ground. The next moment they were up again, screaming all the way back to jab the fleeing enemies' buttocks, while Feng-yu smilingly continued his journey.

Silver Flower and Silver Pearl screamed with mirth. But it was Silver Frond's laughter the father would have preferred to hear.

'You are a useless husband and father.'

This was too hurtful an accusation, in the daughters' presence, for even Ah Bee Koh's easy affability. If it needed a provocation to flare instantly into pure hostility, this was it. He could have got up and slapped her face, pulled her hair or pushed her to the floor. But Ah Bee Koh prided himself on the fact that never once in their marriage had he raised a hand against his wife. Fights between husbands and wives were messy and unproductive, as he could see by the many examples in the village – Bah Bah broke his wife's nose, went into hiding to elude angry in-laws, then spent a punishing week visiting his wife in hospital and bringing her food – whereas it cost much less simply to humour his aggrieved wife. He had perfected the art.

'What? What?' cried Ah Bee Koh. He immediately walked up to his wife and administered the mock punishment of boisterous, teasing love-play. He locked her in his arms and began nuzzling her face, neck, breasts, roaring with great ferocity, 'What? What? You dare make fun of your husband? Take this, and this and this!' He kissed, tickled, pinched, squeezed, watching to see his daughters giggle.

And when their mother finally struggled free and cried out, 'Stop it, you crazy fool! Can't you see your children are around?' pushing away his hands from her crotch in a burst of embarrassed, helpless laughter, he knew that he had won once more. A hardworking wife who nagged harmlessly and earned good money was truly a gift of the gods. Ah Bee Koh was a very contented and grateful man.

6
Egg Girl

'Silver Frond, tell me, what will you say if the people at the Great House call you Egg Girl? "Egg Girl, come here. Egg Girl, go there. Egg Girl, are your eggs fresh?" '

'I will say, "My name is Silver Frond." '

'What else?'

'"I may be poor, but I earn an honest living."'

'What else?'

'"I may not be in school, but I am cleverer than any one of you. I may be poor, but everyone says I am prettier than any one of the Venerable One's granddaughters. There can be no comparison. We are like sky and earth."'

'What else?'

'"One day I, Silver Frond, will marry the richest man in the whole of Singapore. I will live in a house bigger than the Great House. The Venerable One will stand in front of it to admire it and I will invite him in, and ask a servant to serve him tea and buns. The Venerable One's granddaughters will come knocking on my door selling eggs. I will say, "No, I have plenty of eggs already, but here's the money for them. I have enough money to fill your basket."'

Ah Bee Koh gave a hoot of pure delight. This was the girl's own bright answer, over and above what he had taught her. Even her mother smiled.

7
How a Goddess Got Back Her Good Name

Silver Frond turned round and her worst fears were confirmed. It was the Bad Brothers. She walked faster. She would be safe in the Yio Tok Temple. They would not dare follow her there.

They followed her right inside, to the small inner enclosure where Goddess Pearly Face stood on a table, surrounded by offerings of joss-sticks, fruit and cups of tea. To her horror, she noticed that no one else was around. The Bad Brothers had been quick to see an opportunity and seize it.

She had no choice but to go through with her errand for her mother. She took out a bunch of joss-sticks from her basket, lit them and stuck them in a bowl of ash in front of the goddess. Then she took out a batch of rice cakes and two hard-boiled eggs stained a bright red, and presented them as additional offerings.

From the corner of her eye, she watched the Bad Brothers, who were watching her with anticipatory glee, their arms folded across their chests, their mischief temporarily suspended. But that was the only concession they were prepared to make in a holy place. She knew that as soon as she stepped out of the sacred precinct of the temple, they would pounce on her.

She would gladly have diverted the propitiatory gifts of the rice cakes and hard-boiled eggs from the goddess to these evildoers in order to save herself, but this time it was not food they wanted. The eldest brother, who was sixteen, had a savage gleam in his eye, like a predatory animal about to spring. All three would tease her and try to touch her, or force her hand to touch them in their secret places, in the brief moments before her shouts brought help. Then they would run off laughing, and wait for the next opportunity.

In her imagination, she had already consigned them to the Tenth Pit of Hell, where they would be starved for all eternity, with not a grain of rice to eat nor a drop of water to drink, for ever excluded from the annual Feast of the Hungry Ghosts, when even hell was allowed to open its gates for its inhabitants – but not those from the Tenth Pit – to come to Earth for a proper meal.

She looked around in mounting panic. Now she could see two very old women praying before a warrior god, and an old barefoot beggar, with sore-covered legs, leaning against a pillar, trying to brush off a small swarm of flies buzzing around his sores. They would be no help.

She decided she would stay in the temple as long as possible. Let the Bad Brothers wait! More people would come in, and they would have to slink away in defeat.

Silver Frond began her ceremony of strategic delay, taking the cluster of joss-sticks out of the urn one by one, praying with each in slow, deliberate movements, then sticking them back, again very slowly, one by one, glad that there were at least twenty sticks that her mother had put in her basket that morning.

Seeing her ruse, the eldest Bad Brother got angry. 'So you think you are so clever?' he snarled and moved aggressively towards her. His brothers followed him and made similar threatening sounds.

They would have circled her and teased her in their brutal way right there and then in the sacred territory of the Goddess Pearly Face, if the goddess herself had not intervened.

It was a very convincing intervention, a loud crashing sound, which sent the Bad Brothers scampering out in fright.

Silver Frond laughed to hear their shrieks of fear as they fled, the eldest and worst Bad Brother actually stumbling and falling down in mid-flight through sheer terror.

She later saw that it was an improvised altar, a short distance from the goddess's own, made up of an old table covered with a piece of cloth, which had suddenly collapsed. No fellow deity was allowed to be hurt by the act of intervention. A brass statue of the Monkey God had simply rolled off harmlessly.

The least Silver Frond could do to show her gratitude was to pick up the statue and place it respectfully beside the collapsed altar until one of the temple keepers came to put it up in its proper place again.

The Goddess Pearly Face, perhaps ashamed she had not been assertive enough to save the poor truth cockerel, had tried to regain her reputation. Her good name was saved.

8
A Dream of Love and Heaven

In the cold of the night, Silver Frond, curled up on her mattress on the floor, was shaken awake to help chase away the Sky Monster.

'Hurry, hurry! It's come!' yelled her two sisters, who then dashed off, not wanting to wait for her and miss the monster's advent.

Silver Frond rubbed the sleep out of her eyes, threw off the blanket, and went to the kitchen to get a pail or a pan. The floor felt very cold under her bare feet. It was dark and the kitchen was lit only by a small lamp on the table, with the wick turned very low to save on kerosene. She found a small rusty tin pail used for washing vegetables, and decided it would do.

Outside, the village children were already energetically beating metallic objects with spoons and ladles. *Bang*! *Clang*! *Bang*! The sounds filled the night air, and were answered by similar sounds, faint but audible, coming from a neighbouring village whose children had also been awakened by their parents to chase away the Sky Monster. The sounds met joyously in mid-air, a conspiracy of children, entrusted with the supreme task of winning a cosmic battle.

Heady with the novelty of being encouraged by adults, who only earlier in the day had tweaked their ears or smacked their heads for rowdiness, the children entered into ferocious competition to see who could make the loudest noise. Still usable pots, pans, pails and spoons would be badly dented, but the adults would cooperate with tradition, as indeed they should, to preserve the wisdom of forefathers in the eternal fight of good against evil. Gods and monsters – the forefathers had laid down precise rules as to how they should be dealt with by mortals.

By the time Silver Frond went out to join her sisters, the Sky Monster was already halfway through its swallowing of the moon. Everyone gazed up into the night sky, and held their breath as the dark shadows of the monster advanced, covering the moon's brightness.

Soon the moon would be in total darkness. The children were told they could shout but not point; the moon did not like being pointed at, whether in victory or defeat, and could punish the culprit by cutting his ear while he slept. A disobedient child could wake up with one ear or both ears flapping loose.

Silver Frond watched in fascination as the moon disappeared, first into the Sky Monster's mouth, then down its throat, like a piglet or calf being swallowed whole by a giant python, travelling down the entire length of the beast's body in a long unbroken undulation. 'Help! Help!' cried the moon, in little squeaks of terror, but first it had to go through the ordeal of capture and imprisonment, as ordained.

The Sky Monster twisted and turned, working the powerful muscles of its body to propel the moon more speedily towards its tail. At last the moon, frightened and shivering, reached the tail where it stopped struggling and quietened down, a huge round lump, a second head, only twice as large. The Sky Monster smacked its lips and gave an evil laugh.

'Help! Help!' cried the moon again from deep inside the monster's body, and now it seemed that it was directing its frantic calls to Silver Frond. The Heavenly Ribbon Princess will not fail you, she said, and instantly, she came out of the Heavenly Garden where she had been amusing herself twirling her one hundred ribbons of silk amidst flowers and butterflies. One of the ribbons fell to the ground and became a long, shining sword. She bent down and picked it up. Then with one mighty blow, she sliced open the Sky Monster's tail, and out popped the moon, safe and sound.

'Oh, Heavenly Ribbon Princess, what reward would you like for saving my life?' said the moon, and she answered, without the slightest hesitation, 'Wealth, health, prosperity and long life for my parents.'

Filial piety decreed parents came first in any supplication. Her father should no longer have to go to graveyards and conjure up ghosts to obtain winning lottery numbers. Her mother should no longer have to wash other people's clothes till her hands were as hard and cracked as the washboard she used. Any remaining largesse should go to her little sisters whom she loved dearly and pitied for having had their share of beauty stolen from them. Silver Flower and Silver Pearl could kick away the long pole and large clothes basket they carried between them, and be given money for new clothes and shoes and toys.

Money would always figure large in any humble petition to heaven. 'For myself, plenty of money, enough to fill a basket, so that I won't have to go to the Great House any more.'

The moon said kindly, 'Your wish shall be granted,' and added, 'Yours was a very brave act indeed. What second reward would you like?'

Silver Frond said, 'To have a good husband when the time comes for me to marry. He must not have a face covered with pock marks. He must not be a cruel man who beats me for no reason.'

The first fear had come from her mother; the second from Liang Por, the story-teller on Singapore Redifussion.

'Eat up everything on your plate!' her mother would admonish. Rice grains left on plates by untidy, fastidious little girls meant they would grow up to marry men with ugly, pock-marked faces.

'Young women, I have serious advice to give you. Pray to the gods that you don't marry a *Pah Bor Chai* man!' Liang Por had urged at the end of his tale. 'If you are so foolish as to ignore my advice, then make sure you never buy that dangerous vegetable when you go to the market!'

The moon once again said, 'Yours was the bravest act of all. Make a third and last wish.'

Silver Frond, emboldened, took entreaty to the highest level of urgency. She said, 'For the pain in my body to stop, so that the Bad Brothers will not follow me and disturb me.'

She was too shy to mention her breasts, and the sharp little spurts of pain she was experiencing, which seemed to be pushing them outwards and making them swell, for all to see. She had taken a little mirror into the bathroom one day and looked at herself in dismay and embarrassment. Walking with her shoulders hunched to keep them out of sight as much as possible, or holding her basket against her chest helped a little, but soon she would not even be able to do that. Defiant things! The more she tried to hide them, the more they pushed out.

Sometimes she wore two layers of clothing. Men and boys stared at her, and she knew it had to do with the fearsome changes in her body. Once a young man stood by, idling under a tree, watching her draw water from the well. As soon as she was alone, he walked up and boldly stared at her body, at the same time pointing to his own, to the bad hard thing pushing against the seam of his trousers. He unbuttoned his trousers, and the thing sprang out. When she looked down, her face reddening in shame and disgust, he laughed, then walked away.

She hated her recalcitrant body.

Her sisters came running to shake her awake and rouse her to action. 'Quick, why aren't you banging on your pail, they say the Sky Monster is specially fierce this time and we have to make more noise.'

A sadness had come into her heart, which took away all mood for play. The Sky Monster, the moon, the Heavenly Ribbon Princess – all had faded into a pale irrelevancy in the brute reality of bad men and her renegade body.

She attempted a feeble knocking on her pail, and Silver Flower, with much impatience, snatched it from her and banged it deafeningly against an old tin kettle.

A roar of delight arose from the children as the moon, after being completely shadowed, began to emerge in light again. The noise had done its work; the Sky Monster had begun the unswallowing. First a faint sliver of light, then a clear, distinct disc, then a plump half crescent, and finally the fully regurgitated moon was whole again, intact and bright as ever.

The Sky Monster, defeated, retreated into darkness. The children beat on their pails and pans and kettles, this time to announce victory. Good had triumphed over evil once more. The battle would be played out in the vast cosmos, again and again, till the end of time, even when children grew sophisticated with learning and enterprise, adopted a foreign language and foreign ways, and relegated the traditions of their forbears to a bygone, no longer needed dreamtime.

The thoughtful widow Ah Lan Soh, who had lit three joss-sticks and stood them in an empty bottle in full sight of the moon, passed round rice buns and peanuts.

'My mother is an idiot. Sim Bak Village is full of idiots.'

Ah Lan Soh's only son, fifteen years old, full of sneering knowledge because he was one of the few who went to an English school, stood nearby, idly chewing a blade of glass. He looked at Silver Frond through his long, narrow, languorous eyes, not excluding her from the condemnatory remark. She looked down uneasily and edged closer to her sisters, who were eating buns and still talking excitedly about the Sky Monster's defeat.

'Why are you afraid of me? I'm not going to swallow you up, you know!'

The youth had approached her on a few occasions before, always with a jaunty swagger to mark his superiority of intellect. Between the open contempt and the secret desire as he watched her in the moonlight, he became somewhat confused, so that even as he stared fiercely at her, his voice quavered and his mouth twisted into an awkward smile. He moved closer to her. A hand brushed her side. Still she looked down. Silver Flower and Silver Pearl, to her alarm, had moved away and gone off somewhere.

'I have a lot of books. I could teach you to read and write. Here, take this.'

It was a book. Buns, sweets, pieces of fruit, a hairclip, a hair ribbon – these would not tantalise as much as a book. A quick side glance told her it was a good, new book, full of words and pictures. She sometimes passed a school where children sat on benches with books in their hands and shouted out words, one by one, after their teacher. Some of the children wore patched clothes and slippers almost falling apart. Some had sores on their legs and mucus trickling out of their noses. But they were in a school! They read loudly from their books, wrote in their copybooks and were allowed to write on the chalkboard with pieces of smooth, white chalk.

Silver Frond cast another glance at the coveted gift. The cover showed a mountain and trees and very large characters. She could read one or two of them. But no, there was danger in a gift from a man. A man offered a gift and then when you stretched out your hand, he directed it to the bad thing between his legs. It had happened once to her, and once to her sister Silver Flower, who was as stupid as she was plain, allowing her hand to be led there.

She had to think quickly, to avoid the shameful contact. She wanted the book badly.

She said, 'Show me the book.'

This was precisely the moment the youth was waiting for. 'Come here,' he said. She moved towards him, cautiously. He held out the gift to her. As soon as she stretched out her hand for it, he lifted it high up in the air, beyond her reach. She jumped to get it, and he moved it to his other hand. She jumped again. He passed the book swiftly back and forth, while she leapt frantically and tried to grab it with increasing frustration. By now the surly youth was laughing.

So he only wanted to tease her with play. That was all right, so long as she got the precious book.

'Come.' He was inviting her to follow him to a dark spot under a tree, away from the other children, still talking and playing under the moon. She could no longer see her sisters.

'Come,' he said impatiently. So he was going to do bad things to her, after all.

'No,' she said vehemently, 'I don't want your book. It's a useless book anyway,' and began to walk away quickly.

The youth shouted angrily after her, 'Egg Girl! You're only an egg girl! Do you know why they buy your eggs at the Great House? The Old One wants you to be the wife of his idiot son! And also to take care of his old mother and wash her smelly bound feet every day, because the servants won't do it!' And he laughed loudly and walked away.

Silver Frond had seen the Venerable One's son only once, on one of her weekly visits to the Great House. He had been born to First Wife, after several daughters. He was a strange-looking, misshapen young man who wore several protective jackets over his pyjamas and mumbled to himself. That day, he had walked up to her, frowning, grunting and scratching his side, exactly like a monkey. Two small grandchildren stood nearby, gleefully watching her growing alarm. But the strange-looking man did no harm; he merely squinted painfully into her basket, as if laboriously counting her eggs, then shuffled away. Some of the townspeople whispered that the more the Venerable One prospered in his business, the more daughters he would have, and the crazier his only son would become.

The old mother she had seen many times. She was a very tiny old woman, bent and wrinkled and garrulous, who would always hobble up on her bound feet to inspect the eggs, chuckling delightedly like a child if allowed to take them out one by one. She rather liked the funny little old woman, but was repelled by the thought of her smelly feet.

One week, two weeks, three weeks. Silver Frond waited nervously, and still no matchmaker appeared from the Great House to make the offer. She was safe.

9
Song and Dance At A Cemetery

In 1945, when the Venerable One was sixty-six and Silver Frond fourteen, they met and spoke for the first time, not in the Great House to which she had been going for a year with her eggs, but beside a seldom used path, next to the Hokkien cemetery, just outside the town.

The Venerable One was taking his daily morning walk. Silver Frond was on her way to the Great House but had decided, since she had plenty of time, to sit down on a comfortable slab of stone, a fallen headstone from long ago bearing an undecipherable name, and play with her dolls. A cemetery was best for play; the Bad Brothers never ventured near cemeteries in their relentless daily rounds to do mischief to other children, because they were afraid of ghosts. In any case, they had been routed by Goddess Pearly Face.

Silver Frond took her dolls out of a cloth bag, and laid them in a row on the stone slab. The grandchildren at the Great House would have scoffed at the presumption of calling these things dolls – they were just pathetic little sticks of tightly rolled white paper, tied together with white thread into crosses that sufficed for heads, arms and torsos, and with little square bits of cloth with holes cut for the heads, for clothes.

But as soon as Silver Frond unleashed the dazzling power of her imagination, her tiny paper dolls became flesh-and-blood beings and played out the fullness of their vitality and power and greed before her very eyes.

All the three wives at the Great House were represented, together with someone who clearly aspired to be the fourth – Mee Mee, the long-haired, powdered one, of indeterminate age, who lived in a rented room above a draper's shop, and who was said to have the Bad Woman's Itch. While the three wives stood together, Mee Mee allied herself with Matchmaker Auntie, known for the high rate of success in her profession, which took her as far as the villages in Malaya, a whole day's bus ride away.

All five women, active players in the business of making their men happy, whether driven by profit or duty, magnanimity or self-interest, got together in close consultation for that supreme task.

A mangy dog that had appeared from nowhere sniffed the ground nearby; an ugly black bird, which could be the dreaded one announcing the death of infants, landed on a branch overhead. But Silver Frond was unperturbed, intent on enjoying her play. She held the dolls in both hands, making them face each other and bob up and down in animated conversation.

'So you are now looking for a fourth wife?'

Like her father, Silver Frond was a good mimic. Matchmaker Auntie had a loud but indistinct voice, because she was never without a wad of *ceray* in her mouth, her lips and gums permanently stained by its bright red juice. When enough juice had gathered, she spat it out expertly in a thin red arc, which always fell to the ground well away from her neat slippers.

'Yes. My three wives are useless. Errmm. They have given me only daughters and one sickly son, who is also weak in the head. Errmm. But do not matchmake me with Moi Choo, who is too old, and Kim Choo, who is too fat and has a large mole on her forehead. Errmm. Errmm.'

She could imitate the Venerable One's surly grunt to perfection. Never having heard him speak, she gave him the clear voice of Liang Por, the masterful story-teller, with all its skilful inflections for drama or comedy. There being no doll to represent him, she used a waggling thumb wrapped in a handkerchief.

'All right. I will find you someone whose beauty all men desire. Mee Mee, come here! Show the Venerable One your big breasts.'

She held up Mee Mee, the only doll to have a necklace, a few tiny glass beads strung on a piece of red thread. Seeing that she was truly alone, Silver Frond unhunched, pushed out her chest and cried out, in convincing imitation of a shrill falsetto, which her mother said gave Mee Mee, in addition to the Bad Woman's Itch, the Bad Woman's Voice, to draw men to her like flies: '*Oooh, oooh, oooh*, you must love me a lot, and speak often to me, oh One with Gold in the Mouth! You must come to my bed many times a week! *Oooh, oooh*! You can go to First Wife only once a month, and Second Wife only twice a month, and Third Wife only when you want her to clean your ears. She and Black Dog laugh immodestly together when you are not around.'

'Is that so? Then I will give her the beating of her life!'

'Now I shall sing you a song.'

It was a passable rendition of a popular Hokkien love song, sometimes heard on the radio. It told of true love, of the sadness of parting and the lovers' willingness to climb mountains and wade through rivers to reach each other. At the end of it,

Silver Frond bowed, laid down the dolls to free her hands for enthusiastic self applause, then picked them up again.

'So you will take me to be Fourth Wife?'

'Let me think carefully first. Matchmaker Auntie, who else do you have for me to consider?'

'What will you give me if I succeed in finding you a fourth wife?'

The hard bargaining had begun. Matchmaker Auntie began every serious negotiation with clearing her mouth of the famed *ceray* juice. Silver Frond gathered her lips tightly to eject an arc of spittle, which landed neatly on the ground.

'Fifty dollars. And a pig's leg.'

'Fifty dollars, and a *whole* pig *and* a bale of good quality cloth *and* a pair of slippers *and* a bag of oranges *and* a basket of betel nuts for my *ceray and* six tins of Ovaltine.'

Silver Frond, one hand holding up the Venerable One and the other the matchmaker, turned them round to face each other, foreheads almost touching, in the heat of their negotiations. They circled each other jerkily, pugnaciously, like two fighting cocks. All the rumours and gossip about the Great House, which she had absorbed as she listened in on whispered conversations, were being shaped by her lively imagination into a merry tableau for her own enjoyment. In the unclear world between childhood and adulthood, she benefited from both.

'You are a greedy woman, asking for so much.'

'You are a bullying old man! Everyone's afraid of you, but I'm not!'

'You matchmade poor Old Sai Por with a woman who has a vile temper!'

'You are proud and vain, and want everybody to kowtow to you as if you were an emperor! You are also mean and stingy!'

'All right, all right. I give up. But you had better make sure I get my money's worth. Fourth Wife must be able to dig my ears better than Third Wife. She must cut my toenails better than First Wife. She must rub my stomach with Windy Oil better than Second Wife.'

Silver Frond, not sure about the precise functions of First Wife and Second Wife, had assigned to them different parts of the Venerable One's anatomy. One after another, the three wives protested against the insinuated insults.

'Nobody cleans ears better than me!'

'Nobody cuts toenails better than me!'

'Nobody rubs windy stomachs better than me!'

They were silly women, not worth speaking to. The Venerable One disdainfully turned his back on them and spoke only to Matchmaker Auntie.

'I have a son. Can you find a wife for him too?'

'There is one, Venerable One! She is Old Ah Song's granddaughter. She is eighteen years old and will make a very good wife. She will take good care of your old mother and wash her little feet every day. She is not at all afraid of smells.'

'Very good.'

The second part of the matchmaking was quickly and firmly concluded, because Silver Frond wanted to lay to rest, once and for all, the terrible fear that the widow Ah Lan Soh's son had instilled in her on the night of the Sky Monster.

And now, being in a very happy mood, she heard music, as if coming from the sky, and got up to dance her favourite ribbon dance, waving myriad pink and white ribbons in the bright morning sunshine. They swirled like a flock of birds. She was so happy! The humiliation of the routine at the Great House, of the growing breasts defying the hunched shoulders and the layers of clothes, was as far away as the offensive mangy dog and the black ominous bird, which were now nowhere to be seen or heard.

Ghosts did not come up from their graves till the onset of darkness; if there were ghosts now silently watching her, she was not afraid and would have invited them to join her in her joyous dance. No Bad Brothers, only benignly watching ghosts – she could not be happier.

A slight cough, the sound of slippered feet on gravel told of the encroachment of a mortal, not a spirit. She stopped, swung round sharply and saw the Venerable One standing a short distance away, looking at her, a stick in his hand.

10
A Stained Truth

'Do your parents teach you manners?' So he had heard and seen everything. How had he managed to stay hidden while he watched? Even in the paralysing terror, her mind grasped clearly the horrendous implications. The Great House would never buy her eggs again.

She could only stand very still and stare at him, not daring to utter a word. He looked at her more closely and asked, 'Are you Ah Bee Koh's daughter?' He confirmed her identity in stages – 'Are you the egg-seller from Sim Bak Village? Are you the one they call "The Egg Girl?" as if preparing for a formal accusation, denunciation and delivery of punishment.

She was truly doomed. Her mother would be in a rage and beat her, for losing not only the money for the eggs, but also for the laundry. With one act of folly, she had reduced the family to penury. For the Venerable One had enormous influence. The next time her little sisters went to collect the clothes from the shophouses he owned and rented out, they would be told to stop coming, and have the doors slammed in their faces.

Every one in the village and town, including the temple keepers, did obeisance to the Venerable One and received his grunts of acknowledgment with gratitude; she, the daughter of the wastrel Ah Bee Koh and the washerwoman Ah Bee Soh, who could be evicted anytime, with hundreds of others, from their huts allowed all these years to stand on his vast land holdings, had dared to make fun of him. That would be the ultimate punishment from the wealthy man; the immediate one would be to order his wives to stop buying her eggs.

Silver Frond was seized by a spasm of pure hatred. Her active imagination came to her aid once more, this time to present a dark, bitter tableau of revenge. Accompanied by her mother, who was decked out in gold chains and bangles, she flung her basket of eggs at the Venerable One and his wives, who were all dressed in rags, and watched them scrambling among broken shells and spilt yolk to save whatever they could for their next meal.

But the active imagination had no power over the hot morning sun, which caused little beads of sweat to appear on her forehead, or the rumbles of fear, deep inside her stomach. She continued staring at the Venerable One standing before her in judgement, a presence as intimidating as any of the temple gods her mother prayed to.

'How old are you?' he asked, and when she said, 'Fourteen,' he said, even more severely, 'Then all the more reason for you to have good manners. You are no longer a child. You cannot go round showing such disrespect. You must be punished for the disrespect.'

A slap, a beating, a whack with the stick he was always carrying in his walks – anything would be better than the decision to stop buying her eggs. She waited, holding her breath. He did not raise his hand, and her hopes sank in a cold fear that chilled her hands and feet. Her dolls were lying on the ground in disarray around her feet. How she wished she had never taken them out of their cloth bag!

He said, looking very sternly at her, 'How shall I punish you, you bad, rude girl? Let me think carefully.' The man who disdained to speak more than a few words to his wives and daughters and none whatsoever to female servants, was speaking his thoughts aloud freely in full utterances. 'Let me think carefully,' he repeated, seeming to enjoy his new volubility.

She watched him tremulously. Still in his hand, his stick remained unraised. The approaching punishment must be all the greater for the delay. Would she go home to find her mother and sisters crying, already thrown out of their home by his men?

The Venerable One said, 'I want you to do exactly what you were doing just now.' Silver Frond shifted slightly and looked at him in frowning puzzlement. He pointed to the paper dolls on the ground and repeated, 'Do exactly what you were doing just now. Every word. Every movement.'

She continued to look at him in wondering incomprehension, and he said irritably, 'Are you deaf or stupid? I say do exactly what you were doing just now, with those playthings.' He pointed to the dolls again, and added, 'Everything. Don't leave anything out.'

It was an astonishing turn of events. Glad to be spared the unspeakable punishment of the family's eviction, she was only too glad to go through the much lesser one of performing with her dolls. Was the Venerable One mad?

There would be no pleasure this time, replaying her imitation of six different voices loudly raised in argument, and poking fun at them, watched closely by her accuser, the chief target of the fun. Her mouth had gone very dry and her lips very pale. But it would be over quickly, this mad punishment from an old rich man, who could afford any degree of madness and command people at will to clean his ears, cut his toenails, rub his stomach and act for him despite their distress.

The Venerable One sat on an old tree stump, his towel carefully spread on it to protect his clean, black silk trousers. He always carried the towel, to ensure that not the tiniest bit of dirt, not the smallest drop of perspiration remained an instant longer on that clean, well-tended body. An audience of one, he sat while she went through the entire performance, nervously, expecting him to stand up to interrupt, scold, hit her with the stick.

For that must be part of the mad punishment. Now she understood. It would be his special pleasure, in the course of her performance, to stand up and hit her for each disrespectful portrayal, saying 'Take that! And that! And that!' like the rhythmically punctuating gong in an opera stage play. 'So I am a bullying old man?' Thwack! 'So my wives are ugly and scheming?' Thwack! 'So I like women with big breasts?' Thwack!

Then when his anger had been completely spent, and his respectability restored, he would rise, fold up his towel, lay it across his shoulder once more, and continue his walk.

Her hands, though trembling, held the dolls firmly; her voice, though quavering, was clear and distinct. She reenacted the entire performance perfectly, leaving out nothing. By this time, her blouse was soaked in sweat.

'Louder! I can't hear you!' 'No, that wasn't what you said. I told you to say exactly what you said. Don't change anything!' 'Do that again!' 'Yes, what a brainless lot of wives I feed!' 'So I have gold in my mouth? Ha, ha, ha!' 'What an insult to associate me with that filthy, *ceray*-chewing matchmaker!' 'The bitch! I would cast her off tomorrow if not for the ear-cleaning!'

The one who rarely spoke was scolding, encouraging, cheering, revealing the secret thoughts in his proud, erect head, the secret resentments in his aloof, closed heart. They came pouring out in a stream, surprising himself. He frowned upon laughter and silenced it as he paced the long floors and corridors of his great house; now he was laughing, richly and heartily, surprising himself. At one point, he actually slapped a thigh, threw back his head and roared.

Silver Frond thought, This is a good sign, and her fear vanished. Laughter always dissipated anger – she thought of her father's strategy to pacify her mother – and when the Old One's laughter ended, the punishment would too. The little cigarette tin in the hiding place on top of the kitchen cupboard, known only to herself and her mother, would continue to receive its part of the weekly egg money. Her mother had told her she was saving to buy a gold chain, so that she would no longer have to borrow one from her foster sister in the next village, each time she had to attend a wedding.

'Now sing that song.'

She sang, tremblingly, of lost love and parting. Clearly he too knew the song well, for when she stopped, he said sternly, 'It's not finished yet. You have left out that part where she sits by a stream to weep.' He would not be cheated of any part of her act of expiation.

The punishment was over, yet he would not let her go.

'Is that what people say of me?' She looked warily at him. He continued, with a softening of tone, to ease her fear, 'I know people talk about me. Is that what they say?' She nodded. 'Tell me what else they say.'

The people of Sim Bak Village gossiped endlessly about the Venerable One, the most hostile comments coming from her own parents. She hesitated to repeat them, in case pressed for their source.

'Tell me.'

His voice had softened further with the urgency of his need to know. The old, rich, handsome, venerated one, as he went about inspecting his many properties, heard only compliments and respectful greetings. But there was an honesty and forthrightness in his nature that made him, deep down, hunger for truth. His favourite story was that of a prince who went in disguise among his people and discovered, to his dismay, that all the praises heaped upon him were nothing but lies.

The Venerable One wanted to hear nothing but the truth about himself. He had heard part of it from the village girl and he was hungry for more.

The girl delivered it in a long, continuous speech that shocked him.

'They say that you may be a good and respected man, but you are proud and cold, with no love in your heart. You are the town's biggest property owner, but that is because you let the Japanese soldiers stay in your shophouses during the war, and secretly sent them gifts of food and women. Your guilty conscience never allows you to smile or laugh. The gods have given you enormous wealth, but they have also put upon you their greatest curse. For you have only female children. Whatever male children you have will be useless. You will die without any son to carry on the family name. All your donations to the temple and the death home are in vain. Your seed is cursed.'

Silver Frond was trembling throughout, but managed to keep her voice steady. In her head she stored fragments of adult gossip, mainly of poverty's malice against wealth, expressed in the impressively powerful language of curses formally delivered in the presence of the gods themselves. At a moment's notice, she had gathered them all together and stitched them into a seamless speech, the powerful language intact.

She had unrolled before him the stained tapestry of his entire life, past, present, future, each carrying its own stigma.

11
Confrontation

The Venerable One was aware of a distant barking, and the faint caw of a bird as it took flight from the topmost branch of a tree. For a moment, the sounds distracted him from his confusion. It was strange how, in the onslaught of a hundred screaming voices in his head and the spread of a searing heat over his face and neck, he could pause to listen intently to those far-off sounds and try to identify them.

He was now aware of the girl standing before him. He shifted about uneasily on his seat on the tree stump, looking around uncomfortably, avoiding her eyes. He saw the tombstones around him stretching endlessly into the distance, in silent accusation with this child. For truly, she was no more than a child. Yet she had stood in judgement over him, speaking in the language of adults, a mouthpiece of the gods, with one thousand silent witnesses in their graves. He must have been led to this spot by them that morning, for this strange encounter.

The confusion gave way to a feeling of anger, then shame and finally a sadness of heart such as he had never felt before. Wave upon wave of sadness swept over him. Such a heaviness and turbulence of heart! He discovered, to his shock, that he was actually crying. They were as yet just tiny hot tears prickling his eyes, that nobody would notice. He had wanted truth and it had stung him to tears.

He could have struck the girl; after all, messengers sometimes bore the brunt of the displeasure their messages caused. The girl's words had caused something much worse. It was the overpowering sadness of loss and despair, futility and terror, as when the firm ground under one's feet turns out to be crumbling earth after all, or the perilous edge just before the plunging precipice. He wanted to get away as quickly as possible from this village girl, this bearer of dark secrets and ill omens. Yet their encounter, strange as it was, could not end with that horrible, fearful judgement. It should not go unchallenged, yet he was afraid of saying anything, for fear that the girl would respond with another, even more fearful accusation.

The Venerable One paused for a while, to compose himself. Then he said to her, with a return of severity, as if he too could be an actor whose face and voice adjusted to a hundred different emotions at will, 'Don't say a word to anyone. You must not tell anybody what you have just told me. Is that clear, Egg Girl?'

Her secret relief at having escaped punishment vanished, swamped out by a sudden surge of anger. It fired her cheeks and eyes. She jerked her head up to glare at him and said sharply, 'My name is not Egg Girl! My name is Silver Frond!'

'Eh?' he said. Her spirited response pleased him, for it galvanised him into a new line of attack and defence. Suddenly he felt a surge of energy. A smile appeared with slow deliberation on his face, the contemptuous smile of the rich upon hearing the poor call themselves by presumptuously illustrious names.

'Egg Girl,' he said again, looking with mischievous provocation at her. She had caused him distress; he would do the same to her. He had entered fully into the role of the perverse adult teasing an overwrought child. 'Egg Girl, Egg Girl,' he chanted spitefully, once more surprising himself. There was no end to the strangeness of the morning, which, like a relentless current, carried him further and further from the staid propriety with which he had started out on his walk. He was no longer himself.

He watched her reaction. She stamped a foot and shouted, 'My name is Silver Frond!'

The one whose position as patriarch in a large household brooked no contradiction from wives, much less from the lower order of females, found himself actually enjoying this confrontation with a village girl. The women in his house tiptoed timidly around him; this adversary, who was female, young and poor, and hence thrice condemned, had risen to face him squarely and challenge him.

His eyes sparkled with the novelty of the situation. The sadness had gone, replaced by a keen sense of adventure.

'Do you know who I am?'

She would not give him the satisfaction of hearing the sound of his importance. She said nothing.

'I say again, you have no manners. Go home and ask your parents to teach you manners.' He could see she was now trembling with rage. He smiled.

Looking boldly at him, she said slowly and distinctly, 'I may be poor, but I am prettier than any of your granddaughters. Your Ah Nooi Kia has goldfish eyes and crooked teeth, and people call your Ah Pin Kia "Pork Bun". I may not be in school, but I am cleverer than any of your grandsons. Your Ah Kow Kia gets the lowest marks in his class. His teacher says he has cow dung inside his head.'

'What?' he said incredulously.

His grandchildren had never interested her enough to feature in her play-acting, but the gossip she had heard about them was useful ammunition against his insufferable pride and vanity.

The morning, with its strange, tumultuous happenings, was making her giddy with recklessness. She hated the old man and his entire family. She never wanted to see any one of them again.

'What?' repeated the Venerable One. The village girl was impossible! She had stripped him bare. It was as if she had yanked off his staid black silk trousers, clean white vest, properly folded towel, then replaced them with clown's gear and led him to stand in a public place, for all to gaze and laugh at.

This time she had gone too far. He moved forward threateningly with his stick. But she had picked up her basket of eggs and run off.

12
How Silver Frond Got Her Name

When Silver Frond was born in 1931, the midwife came out of the room to apologise to her father, on behalf of her mother. At that time, Ah Bee Koh had not yet developed the very useful strategy of distraction through horseplay. 'A girl-child,' he echoed with a surly laugh, and left the house to drown his disappointment in a beer with his friends at his favourite coffee-and-beer shop in the town.

He did not come home for three days. While Silver Frond's mother waited for his return, she gave the baby a temporary name, which was really no name. '*Char Bor Kia*,' she said sadly to the newborn sleeping in her arms. Female Child. For a whole week, name and sex were the same, each reflecting the other's unworthiness.

Then Ah Bee Koh returned, and his wife said, 'Where have you been? How can a man leave home and go drinking with his friends when his wife is giving birth?' He was to do that twice more, returning a few days later on each occasion, so that Silver Flower and Silver Pearl too began life simply named Female.

Births, sickness, poverty, quarrels, irate creditors and loan sharks at the door – Ah Bee Koh disliked having to deal with them, and over the years had learnt to leave everything to his efficient wife. By the time Silver Pearl, the third and last daughter was born, he had already acquired the jocularity of the carefree man at ease with the whole world.

But when he looked at his firstborn for the first time that morning, and his wife said, 'What name would you like for her? We can't be calling her *Char Bor Kia* for the rest of her life,' he said with a sarcastic laugh, 'Since you are so efficient, why don't you choose the name yourself?'

His wife waited three more days, and when it was clear that he wanted to have nothing to do with his baby daughter, much less give her a name, she decided on the most illustrious female name she could think of. Golden Frond. Kim Heok. The gold of health, wealth, prosperity, paired with the delicate beauty of natural vegetation.

The village was full of children, both male and female, whose futures were gilded with promise. Kim Leong. Kim Hock. Kim Siew. Kim Seng. Kim Chwee. KimSan. The gold was usually coupled with more than the simple beauty of nature favoured by Ah Bee Soh – it was indissolubly linked, for the entirety of life and beyond it, with the splendour of dragons, the luminosity of virtues, the strength of wind, water and mountain, the attributes of gods and goddesses. These resplendent names would be the names only of the birth certificates and school registers if the children made it to school. In daily life, the names would be wisely kept humble and self-deprecating, in order not to offend the gods or attract the jealousy of evil spirits – Bad Smell, Little Pig, Deaf, Little Bun, Fat Bun, Dumb, No Teeth, No Hair.

So Ah Bee Soh settled on the formal name of Golden Frond for her firstborn child, which the evil ones would never hear, and the everyday, unprovocative one of Little Duckling, which they would hear, and ignore.

(Ah Bee Soh lived long enough to witness, with some dismay, grandsons and granddaughters giving themselves and their children names, which, being foreign, not only lost the resonant grandeur of tradition, but betrayed it shamefully. In her old age, she struggled to pronounce names such as Sharon and Alvin and Melissa. In 1983, the year before her death from old age, one of her granddaughters, who had married an Italian American, had a baby girl named Alessandra Victoria Marchini. When Ah Bee Soh was told the name, she cried out, 'Enough! Enough!' and called her first great-granddaughter *Char Bor Kia*).

'Golden Frond. She will be as beautiful as her name,' said Ah Bee Soh, as she looked at the newborn baby girl in her arms.

All would have been well except that Ah Bee Koh, having relinquished the right to name his daughter, had suddenly been seized with the desire to reclaim it for future sons. He envisaged a line of sons – how else could he take his revenge on those laughing at him now? – and he wanted himself, and only himself, to choose their names.

His wife had already appropriated the illustriousness of gold for daughters. That would not do! It should be reserved for sons. Ah Bee Koh dreamt of three sons in a row, on whom he would confer both the nobility of gold and the mighty power of the three great cats – the lion, the tiger and the leopard. Kim Sai, Kim Hor, Kim Pah.

Ah Bee Koh pronounced each name slowly and reverently, rolling it on his tongue, very pleased with both sound and meaning. He would walk everywhere proudly with his three magnificent sons. If he should be blessed with more sons, he would go beyond warrior beasts to the august forces in nature – ocean, wind, sky. Kim Hai, Kim Hong, Kim Tee.

Ah Bee Koh was rapt in the contemplation of such a glittering harvest of male progeny.

His wife said, 'There is no more rice in the bin, nor oil in the pot. Naming sons not yet born! You would do better to pay attention to a daughter who already is.'

But Ah Bee Koh continued to fret over the theft of what should have been held in sacred trust for sons. He would not give his wife any rest. At last in great weariness, Ah Bee Soh said, 'Enough! Enough! The child's birth has not been registered yet. Go change her name and don't annoy me any more!'

He rewarded the capitulation. He told her she could continue to exercise her right of giving names to daughters, as long as she did not invest them with the shining lustre reserved for sons.

'Silver, then,' she said with a sigh, and the baby girl was renamed Geen Heok. Silver Frond. Geen Heok, Geen Hua, Geen Choo. The three daughters could still claim the beauty of leaves and flowers and pearls, but they were entitled only to a secondary precious metal.

Silver Frond. Of course! The Venerable One recollected the Egg Girl's name suddenly, as he tossed about on his bed, unable to sleep.

'Egg Girl, Egg Girl,' he had taunted, and it was then that she not only told him her name, but flung at him words that had so profoundly disturbed him, like rough sticks thrust rudely into the clear tranquil waters of a pool to stir its muddy hidden depths and rob it for ever of its tranquillity.

13
Bearer of Secrets

Silver Frond said resentfully, pointing to a bruise on her arm, 'See, she pinched me here,' and to another on her leg, 'and here.'

The Goddess Pearly Face, now her secret friend and confidante, looked down from her altar with sympathetic understanding, and said, 'She shouldn't have done that. She shouldn't have tried to force you to go back to the Great House to sell the eggs. Not after the way he treated you. Mothers must not treat their daughters unkindly.'

'I hate my mother,' said Silver Frond bitterly. 'I hate her for scolding my father and me and my sisters the whole day.'

'Do you hate your father too?' asked the goddess.

'Yes, but please don't tell him. That will upset him, and he will kick up a fuss and give trouble to everybody.'

'Do you love anybody?'

'Only my sisters. But sometimes they behave so stupidly they make me angry.'

'What will you do now?'

'I will not go to the Great House again, even if my mother pinches me all over!'

'Do you think she'll do that?'

'No. She says I have to help her with the washing and ironing now. If only Silver Flower and Silver Pearl could take the eggs to the Great House now! But my mother says they are such silly girls. They won't know how to behave there.'

'Do you know your mother has an illness?'

'Yes. She has a lump in her left breast. She has shown it to me.'

'Does it cause her pain?'

'Yes. She puts some black paste on it, which she makes with herbs from Ah Yong's medicine shop. But it does not stop the pain.'

'And she is still doing the huge amount of washing and ironing despite the pain?'

'Yes.'

'And the skin of her hands is hard and split in many places, and the beauty of her youth all gone?'

'Yes.'

'And once, when she cooked a chicken for your dinner, she pretended that she enjoyed eating chicken head and feet and entrails so that you, your father and sisters could have the best parts of drumstick and breast?'

'Yes.'

'And she never uses any of the money she earns to buy better medicine for the lump in her breast, because she wants to make sure that there is always rice in the bin and cooking oil in the pot?'

By now, Silver Frond's eyes were filling with tears. 'I don't hate my mother,' she said sadly. 'I hate only my father.'

'Did you know when you were five years old, you nearly died from an illness, and your father saved you? He promised the Nine Emperor Gods that if they cured you, he would do penance during their festival. You recovered, and your father came to this temple, fasted for three days and walked barefoot in the procession through four streets, with his tongue pierced by a skewer, and six metal hooks hanging from his chest?'

Silver Frond said nothing.

'And did you know,' continued the goddess, who appeared to have a good store of mortals' secrets, as well as a ready tongue for divulging them, 'that when you were eight years old, he took you to town on his bicycle, and you cried for a pair of pretty plastic bangles you saw at a roadside stall? He had only fifty cents left in his pocket, and he bought the bangles for you.'

By now, Silver Frond was sobbing loudly. The goddess, bearer of secrets and dispenser of solace, allowed her to cry for a while. At last she stopped and said, 'My father and mother say I will bring them good fortune one day.' Even kind goddesses were not supposed to divulge the future, but Silver Frond asked with sly persuasiveness, 'Could you please tell me when that will be?'

'Ah!' said the goddess. 'You must not tempt me. You will know soon enough. *Very* soon, I may say.'

But Silver Frond was not to be fended off that easily. 'Will I marry a very rich man and have plenty of money to give my parents and sisters?'

'Do you want to marry a very rich man?'

'Yes!' cried Silver Frond eagerly. 'But he must be a kind man who will not scold or beat me.'

'Then you won't want a *Pah Bor Chai* man?'

'No! Of course not!'

'Even if he's very, very rich, with so much money that he keeps it in baskets?' Goddesses could be teasing too, like her mother in a rare good mood.

'No. Not even if he has one hundred baskets of money.'

14
Hunger

The Venerable One tried not to think of the incident. In the later years, he would admit that more than any incident in his life, it had lodged itself in his memory, simply refusing to be shaken off, and then had taken deep root, affecting thought and action. Who would have thought of it! An encounter in a cemetery, with a mere child who stood over him in shocking judgement.

The Venerable One did not believe in ghosts, but this surely was a ghost-child, an ordinary village girl whose body had been temporarily taken over by a spirit that wanted to talk to him. The proper body for this purpose was a temple medium's, but sometimes messages came unsolicited, through innocent children possessed in the middle of play. He had heard, many years ago, of a three-year-old child, hardly out of infancy, who suddenly fell into a trance and spoke with the deep, sonorous voice of an ancestor who had died a hundred years previously.

The evil in the hearts of people who smilingly received his gifts of charity but laughed at him behind his back or, worse, sought to blacken his name. The sad fate of never having a son to carry on his name and the name of the ancestors. The bitter disappointment that he was to that most august forbear who came from China at the age of thirteen.

This was the dire message from the ghost-child.

Yet it was no ghost and no child. It was a young girl, solid in the flesh, bearing the unmistakable earthiness of village life, the crude cunning of its nurturing soil, who had spoken to him with a boldness never seen before. She had moreover insulted his family name. She had dared to step out of her world to confront him in his. Sometimes villages threw up such rebels to threaten the universal order.

The proper thing to do, to rectify this unspeakable insult, was to punish the whole family, as the ancestors would surely have done, for the slur on the ancestral name. He could throw them off his land without so much as a day's notice, and laugh to see this girl, this sudden bane in his life, cast into lifelong poverty with her entire family.

The least he should exact was a formal apology from the father, kneeling in humble entreaty for forgiveness for his daughter, whom he should already have thrashed properly.

But revenge was no longer part of the inner tumult of those days following the incident. Indeed, it had lasted only very briefly. Something else had replaced it, which grew stronger with each day. It was the wish, almost desperate in its urgency, to see the Egg Girl again.

Her face appeared constantly in his mind, her sharp words in his ears. Her sharp words! He would never forget them. They were like little thorns sticking in his skin, which only she could pull off one by one, and restore him to peace of mind once more.

Suddenly he understood why he wanted to see her again so badly. He needed closure for a bad experience. Right now there was confusion – dark clouds of doubt and uncertainty filling his mind, cold mists of apprehension chilling his heart. For the first time in his life, he felt unsure about himself. He could live with anything but self-doubt, which, like a dark, secret rodent, would gnaw away at his self-respect, leaving him an empty shell.

Closure and certitude. He needed not only to put the incident behind him, but to claim back the sense of sureness and steadiness of purpose that had been the mainstay of his existence.

He wanted her to stand before him and listen to a carefully worded speech that would answer her accusation, point by point, and thus negate it. Only then would he be able to nullify that terrible accusation, to chase the evil beast right back to its dark lair. It would be as if she never spoke to him, as if they had never encountered each other that day at the cemetery. Resenting her, he would yet speak gently so as not to frighten her, and firmly too, to make her realise the gravity of the situation she had caused.

He would say, People have misunderstood a lot of things about me, which unfortunately you have picked up and repeated. I do not blame you because you are only a child, but even children must be taught not to go around repeating falsehoods. No, I did not betray the townspeople by secret deals with the Japanese. I only allowed them to stay in my shophouses without paying rent. No, I am not a joyless old man who never smiles or laughs. There are many things that make me happy, but I don't have to grin like a fool to show the world! No, I am not a cold, unfeeling old man with no love in my heart. I love my wives, my children and grandchildren. But I don't have to go around announcing to the world that I do! I make good provision for them. They will always have a comfortable house to live in and good food to eat and the best medicine when they are ill. No, the gods have not cursed me. They are only testing my patience. I am an old man, but not too old to be unable to father more children, including many sons. I will fulfil this dream before I die. I will have sons, many sons, to carry on my name! My ancestors, whom I have always respected, will not let me down. One of them fathered a son, after six daughters, at the age of seventy-two. So I want you to cast out of your mind all those things you have said, as utterly false. If I hear about them again, I will know they have been spread by you.

Thus, through patient explanation, firm refutation and stern exhortation, he would convince the girl to retract those words that had caused so much vexation of spirit. His speech should be no less lengthy and confidently delivered than hers, on that unforgettable day in the cemetery. In the reassuring familiarity of his home, sitting on his chair of authority, against the background portraits of ancestors, he would put things right once and for all.

He had hungered for truth, but it had to be his own.

He could almost see her now, standing before him, her bright intelligent eyes staring at him, receptive and respectful where before fear had made them hard and insolent. Do you understand? he would ask. Yes, I understand, she would say, or more likely, nod assent.

A child's nod of acquiescence to make his world whole again! But that was because she had caused its damage in the first place.

He would never venture near that cemetery again.

15
The Good Wife

The Venerable One, in the darkness of a cold, rainy night, turned on his bed and gave a groan, for his spirit had never been so agitated. He heard his door being softly pushed open, and saw First Wife stand in the doorway. It was amazing how the woman whom he had ceased to call to his bed these many years had kept the fine instincts of the immeasurably caring and loyal spouse, sensing his every need, waiting to serve hand and foot at all times. She had grown fat and slow over the years, yet seemed to have the astonishing ability to be present anywhere in the vastness of the Great House, to witness a cough, a sneeze, a groan from her husband, and to swing at once into devoted service. Second Wife and Third Wife, no matter how hard they tried, could never match that dedication. First Wife said, 'Are you well? Can I get you some hot tea?'

He turned away from her, not wanting any witness to his perturbed state, but felt the ungraciousness of his action, and so turned to face her once more.

He said, 'I am well. Go back to sleep. It is a cold night. You must not catch cold.'

The kindness from the normally tight-lipped man gave First Wife the courage to speak further: 'You did not sleep well last night either. I heard you tossing about. May I fetch you some ginseng tea?'

Excluded from her husband's bedroom, she knew the other two wives were too. Something was causing the sleepless nights. First in the hierarchy of wives, she was also first in duty and responsibility, and would get to the bottom of the unease, to restore her husband to well-being again.

Every day she made sure his porridge had a fresh egg beaten into it, or finely minced pig's liver, and every week, she made him a special nourishing soup of black chicken and herbs, which she brewed for long hours in an earthen pot over a slow fire. For a while, Third Wife, that aggressive, crafty one, had competed with her for that privilege, but had given up, withdrawing into sullen defeat. She spared no expense, buying the most expensive ginseng, herbs and birdsnest to ensure her husband's good health. Men who enjoyed longevity and fathered children into their eightieth year had their wives rather than the gods to thank.

She was not prepared for what he said next: 'Ah Bee Koh's daughter – the one who comes to sell eggs – why has she stopped coming?'

First Wife had an imperturbability of expression and voice whether listening to or making the most unexpected statement, as when she announced to her husband, many years ago, that she was arranging for him to have a look at her younger sister, to see if she suited him as Second Wife. ('My sister who is young and healthy comes tomorrow. If you agree, the most appropriate time for union will be the fourth day of the next moon.') Now, deeply puzzled by the question, she asked in the same flat voice, as she stood by the door, 'Why do you want to know?'

His strange question could have been no more than the incoherence of a man having a silly dream and talking in his sleep. But her husband was wide awake and very alert. Someone – a female – was part of the new trouble besetting her husband. Moreover, it was a female from the alien – and potentially dangerous – world of the poor and deprived. Worst of all, it was a female with considerable power over him, to be causing all those groans in his sleep.

By now, the alarm bells had started ringing in First Wife's head. The threat to her secure and ordered world was as yet unclear, but it was definitely present, and had to be watched closely. Suddenly she was all alertness. Her dull plain face and thick, slow speech were unchanged; all else was geared for fight and defence.

She continued standing by the door, patiently awaiting his reply, while one part of her mind tried to recollect what dealings, if any, her husband had had with that good-for-nothing father of the Egg Girl, who was known for sponging off others for his beer and lottery tickets. He and his washerwoman wife would be quick to pick up the smell of money and opportunity. The rich had always to be on their guard against the poor.

If her question had discomfited him, its repetition exasperated him to an unwonted brusqueness. 'Nothing,' he said testily. He regretted asking the question, for now he had set in motion a whole mess of suspicion and alertness. If there was anything he disliked intensely, it was the inquisitiveness of women. First Wife was sure to share her thoughts with Second Wife, who, being brainless, received and repeated gossip easily. Third Wife, with her network of spies, was the most inquisitive, alert and ruthless of all. The women would continue to tiptoe timidly around him, but their taut faces and sly exchange of glances would reflect a conspiracy of anxiety and intrigue.

First Wife said matter-of-factly, 'The Egg Girl has not been coming for three weeks now.'

'Did she give a reason?'

Once again, he regretted his question as soon as he asked it. But it had come spontaneously, urgently, for he needed to know. The sharpened alertness of First Wife was almost palpable in the darkness. She said, 'No, she gave no reason.' She paused, then said slowly, with great care, 'Shall I find out?'

Unbelievable! Her husband, the Venerable One, most respected patriarch, and she, First Wife, head of the entire household of the Great House, were discussing, with all seriousness, a matter apparently centred on the whim of a mere village girl, a seller of eggs. It was the greatest of absurdities, which should have no place in their respectable world. The alarm bells rang louder.

'No,' said the Venerable One. He felt a rising tide of irritation. The matter he had wanted to keep exclusively private was getting out of hand. He grunted 'Errmm,' and turned away from First Wife, signalling to her to leave at once. She was a good wife, and he had turned away from her. He would always suffer pangs of guilt with regard to her.

On his own, he stayed awake a long time. When he fell asleep at last, he had a dream in which once more he saw the young face, not opening her mouth to accuse but to apologise: 'I am sorry for being so disrespectful, and I promise not to repeat the shameful gossip I hear.'

He said, 'Then will you continue to come to the Great House to sell your eggs?'

The child answered, 'No. I don't wish to go to the Great House ever again.'

He said, smiling, 'I know your name. It is Silver Frond.' She was unimpressed. He pleaded, 'Please come.'

She said petulantly, 'Nothing can make me go to the Great House again.'

'Then how can I see you?' he asked. But she had disappeared.

16
Madness and Disgrace

On a visit to a friend's house, the Venerable One saw one of the friend's small granddaughters playing with a doll. It was a large and beautiful doll, with long hair and big eyes, dressed in fine clothes, such as would belong only to privileged children. He had never seen such a doll before. Indeed, he never noticed children's playthings before, except that day at the cemetery, when he saw the clutch of paper sticks, which were supposed to be dolls.

He watched the small girl playing with it, rocking it in her arms and feeding it with a bottle. He asked where a similar doll could be bought.

In the later years, whenever the subject of the Venerable One's strange change in behaviour came up for whispered discussion among family and close friends, the interest shown in the doll was mentioned, together with a dozen other peculiar episodes, as clear evidence of the beginning of an obsession. At a stage in life when all the respect and regard he had earned should have gathered into a single, supreme peak of blessedness and fulfilment, the Venerable One had suddenly turned crazy.

'He even picked up the doll to look at it closely,' the friend had said, in an awe-stricken whisper. 'He asked many questions.

How was I to know about that village girl? I had naturally assumed it was for one of his granddaughters.'

The Venerable One had decided, as soon as he saw the doll, to buy it for the Egg Girl.

The need to punish her had receded so far into the distance that he would have been surprised to be reminded of it. It was strange, being there one moment and gone the next, like a flame that shot up, roared, then sizzled and died.

Gone too was the need to persuade her to change her poor opinion of him. He had worked himself up to a pitch of anxiety rehearsing a long speech of refutation, and then that too died. In the end only the desolate ashes of a returning confusion remained.

As the days went by and it became clear that the Egg Girl was truly determined to stay away from the Great House, the sense of desolation gave way to a mounting anxiety. Suppose he never saw her again! Suppose the only thing that remained, for both of them, from that fateful meeting at the cemetery was the memory of an angry face and the sound of bitter words.

Something akin to longing had entered his being.

For truth of fact now mattered less than truth of feeling. He had ceased to think about the matter, and had begun to feel deeply about it. The feeling had become almost a tenderness of need, flooding his entire being, making him desire not just to see her again, but to see her smiling and at ease with him.

In a dream, the reconciliation had already taken place. She was back at the Great House, with her basket of eggs on her arm. She waited for him to come back from his walk, and said brightly, 'See, I'm not angry with you any more!' And he, grateful for the new goodwill, smiled in his turn.

He wanted her goodwill so badly that he racked his brains to come up with some plan of conciliation to bring her back to the Great House. A gift was best, and as soon as he saw the beautiful doll, he knew there could be no better present.

He remembered the crude little paper dolls in her hands with the little bits of cloth for clothes, and he smiled at the thought of her face lighting up when the real doll, in its full resplendence, was placed in her arms. She would be grateful for such a beautiful, expensive gift, and never harbour unkind thoughts about him again. A young girl's kind thoughts, like the cool sparkling waters of a spring, to flood an old man's arid soul!

He recollected snatches of the girl's song at the cemetery. The words of the song came back to him. He remembered that, as a boy, he had liked it very much. He had sung it one day, very loudly, when he thought he was alone, and made a servant giggle. His father had later rebuked him for levity of behaviour.

He recollected the girl's dance, her very imperfect imitation of the stage opera actress's movements of arms, hands, fingers. But the fullness of the joy and laughter throughout the dance! No actress could ever experience that.

He was hungry for her joy and her laughter.

There was no question of his personally delivering the gift. For years, he had not set foot in Sim Bak Village, on the vast tracts of land he owned, leaving all necessary business activities to his dependable adopted son. His presence in the house of the wastrel Ah Bee Koh and his wife, the washerwoman, would provoke intolerable curiosity and rude speculation. Therefore he would present the gift through an intermediary. Black Dog would take the doll to the girl and then come back to tell him of her excitement and joy.

He had to be content with that imperfect contact for the time being.

Black Dog could manage an imperturbability of face and voice even greater than First Wife's. He received the order to buy a doll and take it as a gift to the eldest daughter of Ah Bee Koh in Sim Bak Village, as if it were an order to rent out this property or go after that tenant who was behind in his payments. But the muscles on his face tightened and his eyes blinked repeatedly behind his thick glasses, with the sheer effort of concealing his utter astonishment at the nature of the task before him and his distaste in carrying it out.

When he came back home that evening from the village, he told his wife, who instantly slipped out and went to the Great House to tell First Wife. First Wife told Second Wife, both of whom were overheard by Third Wife's servant. By morning everyone in the Great House knew about the patriarch's expensive gift to the Egg Girl. Unbelievable! Such a thing had not been heard of. Whatever could it mean?

Third Wife, the cleverest and quickest of all the wives, was waiting for Black Dog as he was approaching the Great House on his bicycle that morning. As soon as he got down, she dragged him by the hand into the kitchen, where First Wife and Second Wife, with some of their daughters, were already waiting. Contemptuous of the two senior wives, Third Wife readily joined them in sisterly solidarity against a common threat.

Everyone questioned Black Dog closely. What? Where? When? How much? The why was a matter of serious thinking and discussion, that could be seen to at a later time, but the rest of the questions needed immediate clarification. How much? The value of the gift was the first concern. Everyone gasped. Black Dog also told them about the shabby house the Egg Girl lived in, and her shabbier parents.

She is still a child, they mused together, who has probably not even seen the first advent of blood. It must be her mother's doing. Or her father's. It could be the beginning of a cunning scheme of the family to enrich themselves.

If the gift from the Old One had been a gold chain or bracelet, they would have understood. An old rich man was once again availing himself of the right to look for another wife, even a very young one no older than his granddaughters. Fifty, sixty years' difference could only add to an old man's lustful anticipation and generate an unending stream of rich gifts of clothes and jewels to the new object of the lust.

But a doll? A child's plaything? He was, in effect, acknowledging her extreme youth and unsuitability. Therefore, he could not intend her to be the desired fourth wife. So what could it mean? Adoption? That made no sense either. She was female, and he already had ten daughters and many granddaughters.

The noisy speculations swirled around Black Dog, getting noisier. He grew more and more uncomfortable, suddenly realising he should never have told his wife in the first place.

Now the Venerable One was going to be very displeased with him. So when the women crowded round him and asked the all-important question, 'Well, how did the Egg Girl receive the gift? What did her parents say?' hoping to hear something to support their conjectures, he frowned and grunted impatiently, 'All right, all right, that's enough. No more is to be said about the matter,' and got up to go.

He reserved the description of the girl's response for the Venerable One's hearing alone. The old man was too dignified to show his curiosity, but listened with obvious gratification as Black Dog said, 'She was very happy with the gift.' The terse brevity reflected Black Dog's secret resentment at being given such a demeaning task, but did not suit the Venerable One's curiosity. He wanted to know more. He was actually asking, to Black Dog's well-concealed disgust, 'Was she smiling? What did she say? Did she start playing with the doll? How did she play with it?'

Her parents' reaction was irrelevant; all he wanted to know was if he had managed to secure her goodwill.

Black Dog said, 'She was shouting with delight. She held the box tightly and kept staring at the doll. She described its hair, eyes, clothes to her parents and sisters, as if they could not see for themselves. I have never seen a child so happy.' Black Dog had never made such a long and reluctant speech, and still the patriarch wanted to know more.

Later that day, Black Dog whispered to his wife, 'It was the first time I saw the Old One smile.'

Years later, First Wife was to say that of all her husband's acts of folly, the buying of that expensive doll for the Egg Girl was the worst, for it had set in motion all the others. Foolish and mad! A disgrace to the ancestors! He donated large sums to the temple and the death home, and was tight-fisted with his own family, giving each wife a carefully calculated monthly sum to spend on household expenses, and never spending any money on his children and grandchildren beyond the Lunar New Year *ang pows*, and the fees for their tutor. That was all in order. But to buy a costly gift for a village girl, and to send it to her home, as if her parents were people of note, to risk gossip and idle speculation – that was unpardonable.

If First Wife had to assign a specific year to the onset of the madness, and the subsequent disruption to their lives, it would be the year 1945.

17
Toxic Gift

As soon as the messenger from the Great House had left, Silver Frond, in a burst of uncontrollable excitement, got ready to tear the cellophane from the box and reach for the treasure inside. Her father screamed, "Don't open it! Don't touch it!" She almost dropped the gift. She turned to stare at him in astonishment.

Ah Bee Koh said, his face reddening with the effort to prevent a catastrophe, 'Can't you see? The rich and the powerful are not to be trusted. Their gifts are a poison and a trap. The more expensive the gift, the more toxic.'

'Then why did you let her accept it in the first place?' demanded her mother. 'For goodness' sake, don't start all your nonsense! Let her play with it. I tell you it's nothing but a present from an old wealthy man to a child whose father can't ever afford it.' She folded her arms against her chest in smiling disdain. Locked into his failed life, she could still mock it.

Ah Bee Koh ignored her and said to his daughter, 'We are poor, but we have our pride. Who knows what the wealthy one's real intention is? Who knows what he'll ask for in return?' Into Silver Frond's mind suddenly came the image of the imbecile son who needed a wife and the old mother whose smelly feet no servant wanted to wash. Her father continued, 'The rich never give the poor something for nothing. We have to be ever so careful.'

Silver Frond said resolutely, 'I don't want the doll. They can have it back.'

Her father laughed, giving her an approving pinch on the cheek, 'You have your father's spirit! In a few days, Black Dog will be back with a demand and I shall hand back the gift, untouched, and say, "Forgive us. We are poor people, and my daughter is not used to such an expensive toy. So please take it back and let the Venerable One give it to one of his granddaughters who deserves it more." You mark my words. He'll be back tomorrow!'

But Black Dog did not make a second visit the next day, provoking her mother to say once again to her father, 'For goodness' sake! It is a gift. Nobody takes back a gift. Let the girl play with it.'

In Ah Bee Soh's mind, the gift was a precursor of greater largesse. It was clear that her young daughter was being singled out for special favours, whatever the reason, however extraordinary the motivation. These could be dealt with accordingly as and if they arose. Meanwhile, the one thing that should matter for the moment was the certainty of gain, and here was her crazy husband making unnecessary fuss.

The controversial gift stood in solitary isolation for several more days on the table, an appendage of privilege incongruously set amidst poverty's starkness. A chicken flew in through the window and landed squawking and flapping beside it. Silver Flower and Silver Pearl chased it away, before it could desecrate the magnificent gift with its droppings. They never passed the doll without stopping to gaze at it in awed fascination. But she, for whom it was meant, assiduously avoided sight of it.

Yet oh, how she yearned for it!

There was a secret hope, nursed to burning desire. It had come from her mother.

'Listen, Crazy One,' Ah Bee Soh had said to her husband. 'If no one from the Great House comes to reclaim the gift after one week, it will prove that you are wrong. Then the girl can open the box and play with the doll. Really, you are kicking up a lot of fuss over a simple gift! I say one week, and no more.'

Silver Frond had failed only once in her resolution not to look again at the gift, while waiting for that fateful seventh day. On the third day, she got up from her mattress in the silence of night and tiptoed to where it stood on the table, and stared at it. In case Black Dog came to take it back, she wanted to remember every detail about it – its round, rosy face, its red lips, its long wavy hair, its red silk dress, its matching red shoes. Silver Frond had never seen a doll with shoes; this one had shining gold buckles, too.

It was the most magnificent trap. Her father was right; she must be wary and guard against being enticed by a doll into marriage with the ugly, slobbering son, and servitude to the old, smelly mother.

Four days, five days. The doll continued to stand in its box, in its ambiguity of gift and poison, desire and fear. On the sixth day, Silver Frond fell ill. She felt so unwell that she lost interest in the present.

18
It Is Fate

Her mother said it must have been the harmful influence of a ghost from the Hokkien cemetery. How else could Silver Frond, healthiest of her daughters, suffer this illness? The harm, like some dark poison, must have stuck to her clothes or hair and followed her all the way home. Determined demons were prepared to traverse mountain, sea and forest. They could lie low for a long time, then strike with the full force of their malignant power. She should have bathed in water purified by flower petals as soon as she got home that day from the cemetery. Now it was too late. Who knew how long the fever and sore throat would last?

Her child-woman's body, about to erupt in first flowering, prancing on the hallowed ground of the dead! No wonder they were annoyed. No wonder the family was punished with the loss of the egg business at the Great House, and now this illness. Who knew what else would follow?

Ah Bee Soh said wearily, looking at the daughter who was so different, and who would bring so much fortune as well as misfortune to her family, 'You have got your madness from your father. How many times must I tell you never to play at a cemetery?'

Ah Bee Koh, coming in after an afternoon of idling with his friends, said in alarm, 'What? Is my daughter ill? Is my precious daughter ill?' and proceeded instantly to give loving attention.

'Let your father take care of you,' he said and went into a bustle of activity. He sat by her mattress, put a hand on her brow and yelled to his wife, 'Come and see! Our daughter looks prettier in illness than other people's daughters in health!' The fever had indeed given a preternatural brightness to Silver Frond's eyes, and spread a luminous glow on her cheeks.

'Your father talks nonsense,' said her mother. 'And now he's rushing off somewhere. Hey, Crazy One, where are you going?' But he had already rushed out on his bicycle, still in high spirits.

He came back a short while later with some potatoes and a packet of dried herbs, which he gave to his wife to brew.

'Where did you get the money to buy this?' she asked suspiciously, for the herbs were of good quality and excellent for fever. Her husband was permanently without money. Sometimes he came back waving a fistful of dollars from occasional odd jobs or questionable activities; most times, he idled around the coffee-and-beer shop or at home with his pockets empty and his head full of wild dreams of wealth.

Her fate had led her to this man, and to this failure. Even as she raised her head in bitter remonstrance, she bowed it in weary submission. Her mother, and her mother's mother, too, had said in their time, 'It is our fate,' submitting to a decree from heaven on high, rolling inexorably down the generations, that said to women, 'Endure.'

The fool could even turn misfortune into play to amuse his children. He would gather them round him, then put a hand into a trouser pocket, struggling to pull out imaginary wads of money with much panting and grimacing. Finally the hand came out empty, and went back in to pull out, in slow melodrama, the pocket, also empty. Empty hand and pocket flapped desolately against each other. The clown would sometimes pretend to cry, then poke a hole in the pocket through which he waggled a finger to make his daughters giggle.

The noisy attention to his sick daughter now was probably a ploy to forestall all questions about the smell of beer coming from his breath. Ah Bee Soh watched her husband with casual disdain as he carefully cut a potato into thin slices, put them on a plate and carried them to his daughter lying ill on her mattress. He laid the slices on her forehead, spreading them out evenly and pressing them down gently.

After a while he examined the slices and said, 'See? They have your fever now!' He removed the now blackened slices very reverently, one by one. A vegetable had nobly taken upon itself the ailment of mortals, and merited respect and gratitude.

'You are so clever, Doctor Ah Bee,' said his wife with heavy sarcasm. 'Will you be able to cure her if she gets worse? Will you be able to cure my illness?' The lump in her breast was getting bigger, and here was her daughter getting ill on purpose to escape housework, and her husband making a big noisy game of it.

In the stillness of the night, her fever gone, Silver Frond lay quietly on her mattress, thinking, while beside her, Silver Flower and Silver Pearl slept peacefully. She looked at them and thought generously, 'I'll share the doll with them.' Unclaimed for almost two weeks now, it was rightfully hers. She would let her sisters play with Moon Princess – that was the name she had already given the doll – for as long as they liked.

Silver Flower and Silver Pearl, lacking her imagination, made clumsy, ugly paper dolls representing no one in particular, inspiring no interesting stories. They made the dolls do shameful things to each other, like the squawking fowls and stray dogs they liked to watch. They also collected rubber bands, rubber seeds and small pebbles with which they played endlessly. In their visits to the town to collect laundry, they kept a sharp lookout, as they passed rubbish dumps, for still usable toy teacups and plates, which they happily added to their collection of playthings. They would not even know how to begin playing with Moon Princess.

Silver Frond thought, as she watched her sisters curled up against each other in deep sleep: When I grow up and become a rich woman, I will buy them all the most beautiful dolls in the world. I will have money flowing out of my hands, like water.

Silver Pearl had a harelip, which caused cruel village children to yell, 'Split Mouth! Split Mouth!'. It made her cry. Her mother had said that the clever doctors in the government hospital could cure her, but only very rich people could afford the cost.

Dolls, beautiful clothes and shoes, boxes of biscuits and sweets, then the cost of the operation for the harelip – she would be able to afford all when she became rich. Meanwhile, she would share with them the magnificent gift.

In the night's deep silence, Silver Frond got up from her mattress and went outside.

Through an open window she could see the moon shining in the sky, but it shone on an empty table – the doll was no longer there. The thought that it could be somewhere else in the house, unintentionally left there by her sisters after surreptitious play, never occurred. She was aware that her father was not at home, and she immediately connected the doll's absence with his. He had betrayed her trust in him.

With a heavy heart, she returned to her mattress.

19
The Useless Father

She should have guessed. Going into the kitchen the evening before, she had caught a glimpse of her father standing on a stool placed beside the kitchen cupboard, trying to reach something on top. When he heard her, he had hurried down and pretended to be searching for something inside the cupboard. Later, by herself, she sought and found painful confirmation.

Yes, there it was, right before her eyes. She peered into the cigarette tin that she had taken down from its hiding place on the cupboard top, and saw only a dollar note and some coins left. Even these were in danger of disappearing. The money from the eggs, so carefully saved by her mother, was all gone.

As she lay on her mattress, and the tears flowed silently, she saw in her mind where her beautiful doll was. It sat among an assortment of old watches, clocks, rings, radios, crockery, bales of cloth, *batik* sarongs, even babies' cradles, for the Lian Guan Pawnshop accepted almost anything, building a profitable business on desperation and heartbreak. Her father must have got the equivalent of three evenings' worth of beer from her beautiful doll.

Suddenly Silver Frond was very angry. She hated her father for the plunder, hated the Venerable One for starting it all. Two men with two gifts – the healing potatoes and the magnificent doll – the first making her well only to suffer the loss of the second. They were the noxious gifts of a conspiracy, which she should have shunned in the first place. Her mother was no help against the onslaught of so much power. Her mother talked much and scolded loudly, but did nothing.

It only needed a question, timidly uttered, for the father to break into an outburst of protest and grievance. 'Father, have you seen the doll?' she said, pointing to the empty table, and he immediately went into a paroxysm of outraged innocence, 'What? What? You are accusing your father? What did you say?' He fixed shocked, aggrieved eyes on her.

Ah Bee Soh said with a laugh, 'He pawned all his wife's jewellery; is it surprising he's pawned his daughter's doll as well?'

Ah Bee Koh said, 'You shut your mouth.' Then directing his grievance solely at his daughter, he said, 'You call your father a thief? You call your father a thief when all he wanted was to make you well again? Do you know how much good medicine like that costs? Do you know how much trouble I had getting it?'

Inflamed by the eloquent description of his fatherly concern, he came to believe it, moving swiftly from fiery rhetoric to abject self-pity: 'My favourite child looks down on me. I am nothing but a thief and a beggar.'

He dashed away a tear with a fist, sorrowfully walked out of the house and rode away on his bicycle. Silver Frond cried out miserably, 'Father, don't!'

He was stopped, not by his daughter's plea but by the sight of Black Dog once more walking towards their house. So the man had come on another errand from the Great House. What did the Venerable One want of them this time?

Ah Bee Koh turned and rode back. In the house, he saw his wife and daughters facing the grim-faced visitor with nervous expectation.

Black Dog said to him, 'The Venerable One would like to see you. At once.' The next moment he was gone. It was the terse command of the rich to the dependent poor, dispensing with all need for explanation, and it conferred authority even upon the messenger bearing it.

As soon as Black Dog was gone, Ah Bee Koh exploded with righteous rage, 'Who does he think he is? I will not go!' and immediately allowed himself to be persuaded by his wife.

'Go,' she said. 'Beggars cannot choose. Go! What have you got to lose? Maybe he has a job for you on one of his many coconut plantations. Maybe he is mad too. That will be our good fortune!'

It turned out that the Venerable One was displeased, not mad. He had found out about the shameful pawning of his gift. Black Dog's wife, who liked to go to small obscure pawnshops to pick up unredeemed items of inexpensive jewellery or household goods, had seen the doll and rushed home to tell her husband, who quickly warned her not to tell anyone. He then hurried to the Great House, told the Venerable One, watched the rush of displeasure on the old stern face, and waited to carry out any consequent errand. He would do it in utmost secrecy this time, anxious to repair the mess and hullaballoo of the last errand, which had earned him the patriarch's displeasure.

'You have done a shameful thing,' said the Venerable One severely, as Ah Bee Koh stood before him, with downcast eyes. 'Do you intend to redeem the gift?' He relied on the severity of his tone to limit the meeting with this contemptible man, who lived on the miserable earnings of his wife and daughters, to a purely business transaction. Any insolent questions from the despicable creature would be instantly repulsed. Failing in his duty as father, he had forfeited all respect due to one.

Ah Bee Koh's dire situation – the remaining meagre money in the cigarette tin had already been removed by his wife – left him without that last shred of dignity, which would have prevented abject confession, shameless flattery and desperate request all rolling out of his mouth as one utterance: 'I have no money. I only hope that your great kindness, which is so well-known in the town, will help me out of my trouble.'

'Give him the money,' said the patriarch coldly to Black Dog, still looking at the wastrel with undisguised contempt.

Black Dog counted eight dollars and placed them before him with equal contempt. Ah Bee Koh's hopes rose, only to sink once more when he realised that the offered money was the precise amount for the redemption of the doll, no more. Then the old man got up, gave a small grunt, and the interview was over.

20
The Useless Father Is Not So Useless After All

Cursing his bad luck as he cycled home, Ah Bee Koh was rewarded with its sudden and amazing reversal, almost as soon as he entered the house.

'Look!' said Silver Frond excitedly. She had been going through the pockets of the shirts and trousers, prior to putting them in the washtub, as was the practice, so that personal items such as keys and combs as well as money could be returned to the owners, as testimony to the total honesty of their washerwoman. Ah Bee Soh had kept scrupulously to the routine, scolding Silver Flower and Silver Pearl into surrendering the small coins dishonestly retained in their fists.

But Silver Frond was not holding out small coins for all to see. She had a roll of notes, tied up with a rubber band. Her mother and sisters rushed over to see and count. The rubber band snapped to release a large number of notes, which unrolled and spread out in a spectacular fan in Ah Bee Soh's hands. Sixty-two dollars. They gasped. They began talking all at once.

'What's all the fuss?' said Ah Bee Koh as he came in, and was told, with much excitement. He took over the money and held it in his hand, staring at it. He had not seen so much money for a long time.

It had come from the pocket of Ah Hoo Chek, who lived in a shophouse on Muthu Street and played mah-jong all day. It must have been his day's or week's winnings. Soon he would discover the loss and come rushing over.

Ah Bee Koh said, 'We didn't steal this money; we just found it,' and settled, once and for all, the moral right of its retention. The poor, despite their poverty, never stole. If the gods chose to put into their very hands the money of the rich or the undeserving, who were they to resist?

Ah Bee Koh repeated firmly, counting the money a second time, 'We never stole this money. It came to us.' His wife was silent and looked anxiously at him. She was thinking of an angry Ah Hoo Chek, who was probably already on his way to reclaim his money, and of his wife, a thin, frightened-looking woman, who had probably already borne the full brunt of his anger.

The principle of honest living inculcated by upright ancestors stayed strong when the money was but a few paltry coins; it wavered in the face of a glittering pile.

'It's a lot of money,' said Ah Bee Soh slowly, and this time she was thinking of the concrete reality of Ah Hoo Chek's wrath. It would be in proportion to the amount lost. The man would never accept any explanation. He would insist on a thorough search of the house. Worse, he would tell everybody about the incident, and eventually destroy the family's laundry business and livelihood. Would it be worth it?

The abstractions of moral principle had given way to the solid calculations of an abacus starting to click-click-click in Ah Bee Soh's brain.

'He'll be here any minute,' she said anxiously to her husband.

'I have an idea,' said Ah Bee Koh. He was actually quivering in the mounting excitement of his plan. He asked to see Ah

Hoo Chek's trousers, and inspected them closely. He said to Silver Frond, 'Can you remember which pocket you found the money in?' and whistled with eager relief when she said promptly, 'The right one.'

'Good. You are a clever girl who remembers important things,' said Ah Bee Koh, and now there was no stopping his frenzied energy. He drew the pocket out, inspected it and said to his wife, 'Quick, get me a pair of scissors.' She looked at him quizzically and was shouted into immediate compliance. 'I say, get me the scissors at once! I have no time to lose!'

The scissors were not for cutting but for picking out the row of machined stitches at the bottom of the pocket. Ah Bee Koh set to work, expertly loosening and snipping the stitches, one by one, watched by his wife and daughters. Finally he slipped three fingers through the hole. It should be big enough, he said, and raised it to show his family.

'The money fell out,' he said and laughed with self-congratulatory pleasure. 'Could any of you have thought of this? Ha! Not even you, my clever, pretty daughter!' he cried, pinching Silver Frond's cheek.

'Useless husband, eh?' he said, pinching his wife's cheek. 'The next time you want to call me useless, think of this.'

He was totally in charge. He could be assured of his family's cooperation. He banished the two younger daughters, who were silly and given to too much staring and giggling, to their room from which they could not emerge till everything was over. He and his wife would do all the talking, and Silver Frond would simply have to nod assent or shake her head in verification, if appealed to.

Ah Hoo Chek came looking for his money, as expected. He was pale and incoherent with the shock of his discovery. Ah Bee

Koh said amiably, 'Sit down, sit down. Now what brings you here? Would you like some tea?'

It was with great calm that Ah Bee Soh went to get the trousers, and Silver Frond stood by, not daring to look directly at the man, who was wild-eyed and making odd little noises.

In the end, it was Ah Bee Soh who excelled. She calmly handed the trousers to Ah Hoo Chek, who began searching his pockets frantically. His fingers went through a hole in the right pocket and he squeaked, 'I remember I had put the money here!'

Ah Bee Soh took over the trousers to look at the hole herself and exclaimed in amazement, 'Why, there's a tear! Was it there before? I never even noticed it!'

She had begun well, and would not stop. She turned to Silver Frond and asked, 'Did you notice a tear?' and waited for the girl to shake her head. Then she began to examine the tear very closely, clucking her tongue, and shaking her head. 'Such a big hole. Strange that you hadn't noticed it before, Ah Hoo Chek. Shall I look in the washtub and laundry basket? The money could have dropped there. Come, Silver Frond, help me look!'

Mother and daughter did a meticulous search of a huge pile of the unwashed clothes and an equally huge pile of the already washed but still unironed ones, in the presence of the bewildered Ah Hoo Chek, who wiped the perspiration from his face and said miserably, 'The money wasn't even mine.'

Ah Bee Soh, launched on the path of her husband's dishonesty, was propelled along by her own fear of its consequences. She carried the pretence to amazing heights, exclaiming with convincing solicitousness, 'Let me mend the tear for you, Ah Hoo Chek. You can't go around with such a tear in your pocket.'

Her husband tried to out do her in the deceiver's elaborate show of concern for the victim. 'Would you like me to go back to your house with you and do a search? Do you remember the places you went to when you were wearing these trousers? The market? What about under your mah-jong table? What about ...'

That evening, Ah Bee Koh, in a sudden act of generosity, gave all the money to his wife, except for a few dollars. He handed her the money with a flourish and said magnanimously, 'Go buy yourself a gold chain. Get some new clothes for the girls.' He had a slight change of mind, took back the wad of notes from her, pulled out three dollar notes, gave one each to his daughters, and returned the rest, repeating, 'Go get yourself a gold chain.'

Ah Bee Soh thought, the fool. Talking big. He'll be asking for money tomorrow. Wisely she decided to save all of it. A cloth bag deep inside the girls' mattress was a safer hiding place than the cigarette tin on top of the kitchen cupboard.

In a very happy mood, Ah Bee Koh took out his bicycle and rode to the pawnshop. He came out, smiling. He put the doll still intact in its box, in a paper bag with the top of its head clearly showing, then cycled to the front office at the Great House where Black Dog was sure to be sitting at his desk, doing the accounts. Casually swinging the paper bag in his hand, he took the eight dollars out of his pocket and placed them in front of the startled man. If he had dared, he would have said cheerfully, 'I was going to wipe my backside with them.' He left, still smiling broadly.

21
A Bad Dream

That night Silver Frond had a dream. It was not of the reclaimed doll, now out of its box, and jointly owned with her sisters, but of Ah Hoo Chek's wife. In the dream, Ah Hoo Sim, a tiny, timid woman, was hit again and again by her angry husband who was shouting, 'Why didn't you mend the tear in my trousers? It's all your fault!'

Ah Hoo Sim cried, as the woman in the *Pah Bor Chai* story must have cried, when her husband saw the shrunken vegetable on his plate, accused her of theft and beat her.

The reality was much worse. They heard, some days later that Ah Hoo Sim was beaten so badly by her husband, not in direct blame for the loss of the money, but for something she had said, which had inflamed his anger, that she had to be admitted into hospital. He had used a piece of firewood to hit her on the head, chasing her up and down the stairs in his rage.

It's all the fault of the doll, thought Silver Frond sorrowfully, and would have nothing more to do with it. She put it back in the box and in a cupboard, out of sight. Her little sisters did not dare to ask to play with it.

In the later years, when Silver Frond actually became a woman of wealth and had money to give away – though not like water flowing from her hands, as she had once fancifully described – she sought news about Ah Hoo Sim, who had left the town. The old woman had become blind and destitute after her husband's death and had gone to live with a relative in a village in Malaya, rather than stay with her sons whose wives did not want to bear the burden of her blindness. Silver Frond immediately sent money and food, and later even made a visit to the poor woman herself. Ah Hoo Sim groped for her hands, and felt the rich solidity of gold bracelets and rings. She said tearfully again and again, 'You are a kind woman.'

In the coming years, it would be kindness received and given that would bestow meaning and joy to her life, kindness given and paid back with malice that would almost destroy it. Buoyed by one force and buffeted by the other, she was saved by a third, and it was love.

She was only a child-woman when the Venerable One first met her and became so enamoured of her that for years people in the town talked and wondered about it. Some said that it was a perfect love that was rarely seen and therefore all the more to be commended. Others said it was an improper love, because it was too much and too public and she was too young. Everything, to be right, had to be in proportion and conducted with decorum. When a man loved a woman so much that he no longer cared what other people thought, or, more importantly, whether his ancestors were being dishonoured, then the love was improper.

That year, when she was fourteen, and the arrival of the doll had set in motion the extraordinary events shaping her destiny, Silver Frond could only think of how much trouble the gift was causing her. It gave her the bad dream about Ah Hoo Sim, and shortly after that, a bad dream about her mother.

In the dream she saw her mother unbutton her blouse to show a bandage on the lump in her breast, and heard her saying mournfully to her father, 'You were right. The doll is poison. Since its arrival, the pain has got worse.'

As soon as she awoke, she ran to her mother who was pounding some herbs to make into a paste to apply on the lump.

'Come,' she said to her surprised mother and dragged her to the mattress that she shared with her sisters. 'Now get out that cloth bag,' she said. She was in command and her mother stared at her, unused to the new assertiveness. 'Quick,' she said urgently, 'before Father comes back.'

Ah Bee Soh pulled out a small cloth bag from its hiding place deep inside the coconut fibre stuffing of the mattress.

'How much is there left?' Silver Frond knew that her mother had been making secret withdrawals in response to the demands of her father. But there should still be a lot left from the little fortune stolen from Ah Hoo Chek's pocket.

There were only seven dollars.

'Mother,' said Silver Frond firmly, 'I want you to take this money and go to Ah Liang's medicine shop to get the proper medicine. Don't go to Ah Yong's any more. His cheap medicine doesn't work.'

Her mother stared at her. This daughter was ever full of surprises. 'Gracious! Since when have you started talking in this way? Who taught you?'

'Will you go, or shall I get it for you?' She had had a bad dream, and she had awakened, transformed and strengthened by purpose.

'Why, Silver Frond, you are talking like an adult! Whatever's happened?' A smile of real pleasure came over Ah Bee Soh's face. 'You really care for your poor mother. You are concerned about her suffering.'

She was so touched that she took her daughter's hands, young, soft and smooth, and held them affectionately in her own, work-worn and weary. She then held them up and laid them against her face. Silver Frond, in no mood for sentimentality, pulled her hands away.

'All right. Shall we go now?'

Ah Bee Soh's pleasure gave way to the mournfulness of reality. 'Your father will be asking for more money soon. I have to keep this for him.' She put the money back into the cloth bag.

Silver Frond began shouting in her exasperation, 'You don't *have* to keep this for him! I don't understand you, Mother! You talk and scold, but you don't do anything to help yourself.'

'It is fate,' whimpered Ah Bee Soh, and once again, the efficient, sharp-tongued woman crumbled before the inexorable force, whichhad borne down on an entire line of female ancestors that stretched back endlessly into the mists of memory.

By now Silver Frond was shouting and crying in anger. 'It is *not* fate! Mother, you don't have to be *this* miserable. You don't have to go through *all* this suffering!'

At some point in her marriage, Ah Bee Soh, railing against misfortune, had suddenly embraced it and made it her own, feeding on its pain and humiliation as if they were her very sustenance. Like the labouring ox in the field, she not only refused to come out from under her yoke, but made it a permanent bondage, actually thriving on the pity that came her way. She had become the consummate self-made martyr. Perhaps it was the victim's best revenge against the oppressor.

Silver Frond felt hot tears in her eyes. She knew what she was going to do. And this time, she would make sure the toxic gift was well and truly disposed of.

22
The Devouring Tiger

A child came to tell Ah Bee Koh that he was urgently needed at the house of Ah Hoo Chek. Would he come at once?

'Eh?' said Ah Bee Koh nervously, thinking of the sixty-two dollars, by now all spent. He broke into a smile of immense relief when he found out that he was needed to cure one of Ah Hoo Chek's sons. The boy had mumps, which had caused his cheeks and neck to swell horribly.

'Of course! Of course!' he said amiably and immediately got on his bicycle.

As soon as he arrived, he set to work diligently. The boy was whimpering in pain. Ah Hoo Sim, who still had a piece of plaster on her forehead from the injuries inflicted by her husband, was trying to comfort him. She quavered, 'How kind of you to come. It was a lucky thing that someone told me that you cured Ah Kian's son last month.'

Born in the Year of the Tiger, Ah Bee Koh was in a position to perform this worthy task. He said it was his good fortune not to have been born under any of the eleven other, lesser animals of the zodiac assigned by the gods to determine the fates of mortals. Proud of the association with the mighty beast, he had had a tattoo made of it, in its full glory of sinuous, striped body, long tail and ferocious whiskers, all the way down his left forearm.

'Ah, let's begin!' he cried eagerly, rolling up his sleeve to reveal the magnificent beast. But it was only for show, no image being necessary for the healing process learnt from ancestors to combat disease and pain.

Ah Hoo Sim placed before him the requisite bowl of indigo dye. He dipped his fingers into the thick liquid, stirred it vigorously, then smeared it liberally on the swollen parts of the boy's cheeks and neck. The boy grimaced, now a clown with a blue face. Two children who stood by watching, giggled and were shooed away by Ah Hoo Sim.

Ah Bee Koh next wrote, with a firm forefinger, the character for Tiger on the smeared surface. The word stood out in all its potency. This was the most satisfying part of the ritual, for at the same time that he was unleashing the mighty tiger to do its work, he was exhibiting his own zodiacal power. 'Devour the disease!' he commanded, and the beast would do exactly that, so that in a few days, the boy's swellings would have completely subsided.

Whether with potatoes or tigers, Ah Bee Koh revelled in his power over the vegetable and animal kingdoms to cure suffering fellow humans.

Ah Hoo Chek offered a small *ang pow* for the noble service, wrapped in the requisite red paper of the grateful recipient of a favour.

'No, no, no,' protested Ah Bee Koh with amiable magnanimity. Happy to receive small gifts of money in his special, ordained role, he had decided to dispense with it in this particular case, thereby banishing, once and for all, any unease there might still remain from the incident of the sixty-two dollars. Indeed, so magnanimous did he feel that there and then he made up his mind to similarly waive payment for future services for other mumps-infected children of Ah Hoo Chek.

To his dying day, Ah Bee Koh saw himself as a major benefactor of Ah Hoo Chek's family. On his deathbed, in reminiscences, which could even be sporadically cheerful, he recounted his good deeds to family, friends and neighbours, turning to his favourite daughter Silver Frond to apologise sincerely for not having done more. To his wife whom he had throughout his life blamed for giving him only daughters, he apologised, as death drew near, for not giving her sons, in a last dramatic gesture of magnanimity. The man who, in good health, had generously promised his sick wife that he would never leave her bedside, would have been shocked by the foreknowledge that she would survive him by thirty years.

But that year Ah Bee Koh was in the best of health and spirits, and ready to ride his bicycle to help any family in distress.

'First your husband's kindness, now yours,' murmured Ah Hoo Sim the day after the devouring tiger ritual, when Ah Bee Soh came with a gift of a tin of Jacob's Cream Crackers. She would come, three more times, with these gifts of guilt's expiation. She was accompanied each time by Silver Frond, who would in her turn, unknown to her parents, continue the visits of reparation.

'Is this your eldest daughter?' cried Ah Hoo Sim. 'How pretty she's grown.' And Silver Frond, looking at her thin, drawn face, and the piece of plaster hiding the gash on her forehead, thought, I have a plan.

23
A Visit To the Great House

The whispers in the Great House, as wives, servants, daughters and granddaughters moved swiftly to keep each other informed, gathered into a general buzz of excitement, and finally into one united voice: We are right about the Egg Girl. Something is afoot. We must be on guard.

Silver Frond, carrying a large box wrapped in newspaper, which could only have been the gift of controversy, stood on the kitchen floor, while more and more of the women gathered around her. Curiosity mixed with hostility, as they stood around the Egg Girl in her new role as interloper and potential usurper, waiting to hear what she would say, watching to see what part the doll would have in the unfolding drama.

Silver Frond said, with a defiance that both intrigued and provoked them, 'I want to see Ah Cheng Peh.'

The sheer brazenness of the village girl took their breath away. In demanding to see the Venerable One, she had exalted herself immeasurably above all those present, including the three wives, none of whom had ever made that demand. For that alone, she should be pushed out and have the door shut in her face. But they understood that she had returned to the Great House under changed circumstances. She stood in a charmed circle, protected by patronage, and they had to move cautiously around her.

First Wife said gravely, 'The patriarch is out on his walk and never sees any visitors in the morning.'

Second Wife, in between her melon seed de-husking, giggled, looked at her sister and repeated, 'He never sees anyone in the morning; he eats his porridge as soon as he returns.'

Third Wife, dismissing both responses as totally inadequate for the situation, moved forward, thrust her face close to Silver Frond's and hissed, 'Why do you want to see the Venerable One? You, of all people.'

She would have liked to put a hand on the village girl's shoulder and given her a violent shove for her unspeakable insolence. But for now she had to restrain herself.

'Does it have anything to do with the doll in that package?' asked First Wife. Her dull stolidity often compared unfavourably with Third Wife's vivacity, but she more than compensated for it by a shrewd native instinct for saying the correct thing and asking the right question.

The girl's silence told her she had made a correct move. She continued to ask questions, watching the girl's reaction keenly for clues, probing for points of entry into that hard, wilful resistance, so astonishing in its departure from the timid deference of only a month or so ago, when she had received the money for her eggs with both hands and asked for permission to watch the *sinseh* teaching the granddaughters. It was amazing how an old man's favours had transformed the girl.

First Wife next said, 'If you want to return the gift, you can leave it here, and we will tell the patriarch when he returns.' She had cleverly articulated the purpose of the visit to see if the girl could confirm it by silence, or refute it by protest.

The girl was craftier than she thought, and could not be enticed into giving anything away. 'I can't tell you,' she said simply, clutching the box tightly, and continuing to stand in resolute defiance amidst her circle of hostile inquisitors.

'Leave the doll here,' said Second Wife, her sole concern being to open the box and satisfy her curiosity about its appearance as soon as the girl had left.

Third Wife, exasperated beyond restraint, turned to address First Wife, 'I say we all go away and leave her here. The more we try to persuade her, the more arrogant she gets! Let her stand here till night if she wants!'

Somebody touched Silver Frond on the shoulder and she almost jumped.

'Why, you're here again! We haven't seen you for a long time!'

The old demented mother had brief bursts of lucidity throughout the day, and she was making use of the first one that morning to be kind. She had tottered up without anyone noticing and now held Silver Frond's hand in her old gnarled one. 'Why, yes, you are our little Egg Girl, and you've come again!'

Silver Frond turned to face her, lips quivering with the terrible anxiety under the defiance. The old woman touched her face gently, still exclaiming, 'Why, it's our little Egg Girl and she's come back!' And it was at this point that Silver Frond, the anxiety building up to an unbearable point, burst into tears.

'Cry all you want!' said Third Wife spitefully. 'Maybe after the crying, you will stop being stubborn and tell us what all this is about.'

'Oh, oh, you mustn't cry!' cried the little old woman. She made little clucking noises of genuine concern and said, 'You need a handkerchief. Does someone have a handkerchief?'

24
The Venerable One Almost Runs Out of Ideas

'What is going on?' Nobody had heard the Venerable One's approach. His voice startled everyone, and gave his wives, as they moved away from Silver Frond and shifted about uneasily, the appearance of guilt. But that was only a fleeting feeling. Guilt vanished in spirited self-defence, and the next moment they were all speaking at once.

'She came to see you, but we told her you were out.'

'She wouldn't listen to us. She said rude words.'

'We didn't make her cry. She cried on her own.' Second Wife, roused to great anxiety, could take a line of defence independently of her sister.

The Venerable One dismissed everybody with an impatient wave of his hand and turned to Silver Frond. He wanted to make his voice sound firm and authoritative, but it came out anxious and gentle: 'Sit down, and tell me why you have come.' He waved her towards a nearby table.

He would have preferred the privacy of a room far away from the prying eyes and ears of the women, who had already scattered but were clearly plotting some way to eavesdrop and satisfy their curiosity.

'Tell me.' This time, his face and voice were kind.

The girl pushed the box, wrapped in newspaper, towards him on the table. She said, her eyes still filled with tears, 'I don't want the doll. I want the money you paid for it.' She had thought of secretly going to the pawnshop, but decided that selling the doll back to its donor would be more profitable. Distress gave her voice an abruptness she did not intend, for all the way to the Great House, she had rehearsed only the most courteous expressions.

As she spoke, she looked down, not daring to see the Venerable One's reaction. He would probably be angry with her. But she had thought carefully about the risky enterprise and would not go home till it was accomplished, and she had the money securely in her pocket. She was prepared to settle forhalfprice in there-sale.

She attempted a quick glance at the Venerable One's face and saw, to her relief, that he was not angry. Indeed, he seemed pleased to see her. A surge of new confidence filled her.

The Venerable One called for a servant to bring tea and cakes. Eating and drinking would calm the child in her highly wrought state. A servant – probably Third Wife's – appeared from nowhere, casting sharp furtive glances at the girl. Within minutes, a cup of Ovaltine and a plate of peanut biscuits were put before her on the table.

'Eat,' said the Venerable One. The girl shook her head. She repeated, 'I want to sell the doll back to you.' The tears were gone, but her face was pale and taut.

The purpose of the visit, whatever it meant, was less important to the old man, than the concreteness of its reality. Here was the girl who had been appearing regularly in his troubled dreams, whom he had longed so much to see again, now actually sitting with him at a table.

She said, for the third time, 'I want to sell the doll back to you.'
'Why?'

It was a question he would have avoided except that the situation warranted it. He understood enough of the over-charged heart to want to avoid giving the impression of any obtrusive probing for reasons. He asked his question quietly, matter-of-factly, resorting to the small irrelevant action of rearranging the folded towel on his shoulder, to defuse any perceived threat. But the girl was forthcoming in her response, probably because she had become impatient to complete her mission that morning and go home.

She said, 'The medicine from Ah Yong's shop is useless. I want my mother to go to Ah Liang's shop instead. And I don't want any more bad dreams about Ah Hoo Sim.'

The girl's agitation had made her totally incoherent; her reasons would need some patient unravelling. Even the incoherence contributed to the general sense of pleasure the Venerable One was experiencing as he looked steadily at her. Right now, his only concern was to make sure she did not run away again, as she had done that day at the cemetery. To have her leave him in anger once more, and run the risk of never seeing her again! That would be unbearable. He would meet her present distress, no matter how unintelligible and puzzling, with all patience, kindness and gentleness.

He would sit at the table all morning with her if necessary. He was actually quivering in the excitement of the unexpected scene he had walked into, straight from his morning walk. He had forgotten all about his breakfast of rice porridge, and nobody of course dared to remind him.

'Sure,' he said reassuringly. That was to reduce the distress. To his surprise, it vanished instantly, and the young girl's face was suddenly bright with hope. 'You will buy it back?' He remembered that day in the cemetery, when he had witnessed the swift changes of expression on her face as she played with her dolls. Now he wondered, with some amusement, at so much expressive volatility both in her make-believe and real existence.

Her eyes were sparkling as she asked, 'How much?'

He told her and she gave a little gasp. It was a princely sum, larger than the amount taken from Ah Hoo Chek's pocket. It was enough to be shared by her mother, Ah Hoo Sim and her sisters. Her head was not used to such a large figure. There might even be something left to buy flower petals, fruit and joss-sticks to take to the Goddess Pearly Face.

She asked again, 'How much?' for confirmation that she had heard correctly, and he repeated the sum, watching her reaction keenly. He thought, this is an unusual child.

He said, while she was still pondering the size of the fortune, 'Perhaps you will tell me about your mother and her medicine, and about Ah Hoo Sim. Clearly you are giving them this money. That shows you are a very kind-hearted girl. Perhaps I can help them too.'

The delaying manoeuvre, coated so abundantly with the sweetness of assent, praise and promise, worked. The girl, by now in a very happy mood, was prepared to talk about the intended recipients of the money.

The Venerable One listened very carefully.

The girl had become more than just a name, a voice, the presence he needed to restore his peace of mind and heart. She was a real flesh-and-blood being, living in a real village, which in his grand scheme of charitable giving, had been no more than a shadowy, squalid presence on the periphery of his world. She was a being far too bright, sensitive and delicate for the squalor that included a thoroughly odious father. Into his head had suddenly come the idea of rescue.

When she finished talking, he said, 'I carry no money with me. You will have to come with me to the office in the front part of the house, where I keep my money locked in a drawer. Bring the doll with you.'

It was a further delaying move, a necessary one, too, to ensure that what transpired next would be out of the hearing of the spies, one of whom had already betrayed her presence by a shuffling sound behind a screen.

'Now you take the money, and you take the doll back. It's yours,' said the Venerable One.

The girl looked startled. She said, 'I can't, I've just sold it back to you,' but her eyes widened and shone in the prospect of such a rich double haul from the Great House that morning.

'Take it,' said the Old One, and was forced to speak a massive untruth: 'My granddaughters have many dolls like this. They wouldn't want another one.'

She smiled and said, 'Thank you very much, Ah Cheng Peh, you are very kind. People say you are cold and selfish, but I can see that it's not true.'

Suddenly she bent her head and looked shame-faced. She said, 'I'm sorry I said all those things that day.'

'That's all right,' he said kindly.

Now she was getting ready to go, and he might never see her again. He had to think of something quickly. He was running out of ideas! In the few brief moments, as she was putting the money in her pocket and picking up the parcel, he was able to come up with two ideas, the first instantly dismissed, the second seized on eagerly. No, he would not continue to send gifts to her, as these would only be absorbed into the messiness of her miserable village life to benefit others, especially that scoundrel of a father. Yes, he would make an offer – the idea had come suddenly and would shock everyone in his household – that would ensure her regular presence in the Great House.

'Would you like to join my granddaughters and be taught by the *sinseh*?'

The girl's immediate reaction was to give a little scream of delight. 'You mean to teach me to read and write and recite poetry?'

It delighted him to watch her eyes grow large at the prospect. The presence of this child-woman was more pleasing by the minute. Her next reaction was to subside into such deep and anxious silence that he asked, with some alarm, 'Why, what's the matter?'

Silver Frond decided that to speak the truth was the best. The patriarch had shown himself to be kind and gentle and was not likely to take too much offence if she presented the truth politely, without any of the biting malice of the widow Ah Lan Soh's son.

'I hope you will not mind if I say that I will not marry your son, or wash your old mother's feet.'

While he had had some difficulty unravelling the strange references to her mother's medicine and to a woman called Ah Hoo Sim, he understood instantly the statement about his son and his mother. The thought that this engagingly innocent, generous-hearted girl could put such a cynical interpretation upon his proffered gift, surprised, then amused him. He threw back his head and laughed uproariously.

'Of course not! My son is not capable of taking a wife, and my mother already has a maidservant to take care of her needs. Whoever gave you such an idea?'

'I'll have to get my parents' permission.' The initial excitement over this best of gifts was being tempered by the sobering reality of her father's general suspiciousness about gifts from the rich. But at least this one could not be stolen and pawned.

'Of course. Now you must go home. It looks like it's going to rain.'

The Venerable One summoned a servant for an umbrella.

25
Inferior Wombs

Four different people – one daughter, one granddaughter and two servants – had been commandeered for the all-important task of listening in and observing the extraordinary events of that morning. They were all adept, even from difficult spying places behind doors, windows and massive furniture, at gleaning the most valuable information. The most shocking bit had been the Old One's offer to buy back the doll at three times its cost. Three times! Almost the cost of a solid gold bangle.

Collectively, their evidence formed a good enough picture of the interloper's schemes. The chief conclusion was that the Old One had become completely infatuated with the young village girl, and something had to be done to save him from self-destruction.

First Wife, sitting in a chair and shaking her head, said, 'No good will come from this. He is acting as if an evil spirit has possessed him.'

Second Wife, awed by the image of a demon inside that clean, handsome, respectable body, could only make little agitated noises of shock. She asked a servant to get a cup of hot water each for her sister and herself, and pointedly left out Third Wife. No amount of common interest could dilute the malice that provided the only animating force in her uneventful existence in the Great House.

Third Wife chose publicly to ignore the insult, which the servants were sure to talk about among themselves, but saved it privately for future recrimination. She allowed the arsenal for revenge to build steadily, and when it reached a certain point, she would discharge it, and laugh secretly at the devastation. Meanwhile, she could wait.

She said, putting her hands aggressively on her hips, and looking only at First Wife, 'We can't let this go on. We can't let a mere village girl do this to us.'

First Wife shrugged her shoulders briefly, and said, 'When a man chooses the path of folly, do you think he will listen to a woman?'

The son, grunting and shuffling, chose to make his appearance at this point, flapping his arms about and saying something incoherent to his mother. It was not just First Wife's failure alone. All three wives fell silent with the weight of so much defeated hope, which must ultimately explain the Old One's strange behaviour. Only Third Wife dared to voice the common shame.

'Who told us not to give him healthy sons? Who told us to have such weak, useless wombs? The labouring village women have strong wombs that produce abundant male offspring, like their pigs and fowls. We are therefore inferior to the Egg Girl!' She burst into angry tears.

'Stop all this noise and snivelling,' said First Wife impatiently.

'Stop crying, you look like a pig when you cry,' said Second Wife, and she laughed shrilly.

'You stop behaving like a child.' Now it was her turn to be rebuked by First Wife. She subsided into low, mirthless gurgling, and covered her mouth with a hand.

First Wife rose. 'I'm tired,' she said, and might as well have added, 'Not just of an errant husband, but all of you who are no help with your noisy, childish quarrelling!' She said, more wearily than ever, 'This is not a good time for us all. I will go to the Bright Light Temple tomorrow.'

The conference of the wives had ended most unsatisfactorily.

Back in her own quarters, Third Wife continued to vent her rage in the presence of her most trusted servant, a young maid, who had been given the nickname of Tali-gelem for having a telegram's amazing speed in conveying messages.

'Tomorrow, go to the market and get more of those bean paste buns. And the peanut candy. And the lotus seed candy,' she ordered Tali-gelem, her eyes narrowing with malicious intent. Third Wife, who took good care of her looks, spent an inordinate amount of her housekeeping money to scatter the good sweet stuff on the tables throughout the Great House, ostensibly for the grandchildren, in reality for Second Wife, an acknowledged glutton growing fatter and more repulsive by the day.

Tali-gelem had told Third Wife about the last and failed attempt of Second Wife to get into the Old One's bed. And she was not even that fat or repulsive then.

Having disposed of Second Wife, Third Wife was ready to concentrate on the more dangerous enemy.

'"Of course." "Sure." "Of course." Would he have been so generous with his wives? In all the years I have been his loyal third wife, cleaning his ears as and when he wants, I have never heard a thank you, never received a gift. "Of course." "Here's an umbrella. I don't want you to get wet." "Sure, you and your whole family can leave your miserable village with its chicken and pig dung and come and live at the Great House. All I have to do is kick out my wives! If you like, I'll make them your servants!'"

The hyperbole of grievance stretched to great heights and induced much hysterical acting, as Third Wife imitated the Old One's laugh of pleasure in the presence of the village girl. "'Ha! Ha! Ha! I put on an angry face for my three wives, but you have made me so happy that I can't stop smiling and laughing. How my old body will rejoice to be on your young one! Ha, ha, ha!'"

Third Wife, exhausted, fell into a chair and lay slumped there for a while. Tali-gelem said in a whisper, 'They say she is not yet a woman.'

Third Wife said tearfully, 'Why is all this happening? I feel a headache coming. Bring me my Tiger Balm.' Tali-gelem, ever caring about her mistress's needs, began, instead, to pinch a tiny square inch of skin on her forehead, just above the nose. She pinched steadily and systematically for a full five minutes, plucking the skin sharply, like the strings of a lute, until a bright red patch at last appeared. She had become almost as good at relieving stress through forehead pinching, as her mistress was at giving pleasure through ear-cleaning.

Third Wife roused herself with a plan of grimmest resolve: 'Black Dog may know even more. We'll need his help.'

26
First Wife Offers and Seeks Help

The Venerable One would have locked his bedroom door, except that it would have been ungracious rejection of the hot tea, ginseng, embrocation oil, and warm blankets that continued to come in a solicitous stream from First Wife. Her devotion to her husband was in no way diminished by his indiscretion. Indeed, it ennobled itself by combining with heroic courage, which none of the others in the household would have been capable of, to bring a foolish, besotted old man to his senses. 'Everyone is gossiping about your behaviour.'

With the village girl, he had spoken easily and playfully. With his wife of forty years, he remained the One with Gold in His Mouth. He said 'Errrmm,' and turned away from her.

'At your age, you should not be doing such things.'

First Wife, once more a shadowed figure at the doorway of her husband's bedroom, was referring to the whole cascade of favours following the gift of the doll. Black Dog had, under pressure, reported a virtual cornucopia, including tins of biscuits, bottles of F&N Orange Crush, watermelons and good quality mushrooms, which village people had never seen in their lives and would not know how to cook. The Old One would have preferred the girl to be the sole beneficiary, but at this stage, there was no bypassing her contemptible parents. Black Dog had winced with ill-concealed disgust at the greedy delight with which the father and the mother had received the gifts.

The greatest favour had been the installing of the village girl in a classroom of her own, a small upstairs room where, twice a week, she had the exclusive attention of the *sinseh*. He was paid extra just to tutor her alone! The reason given by the Venerable One was that the girl's brightness was holding back the granddaughters; in the first few lessons, she had overtaken them all in reading, writing and poetry recitation. It was the *sinseh* himself who had mentioned it and advised the new arrangement.

So not only were the wives being humiliated but the granddaughters as well. Some of the granddaughters were puzzled by the arrangement; all were resentful. They complained that the village girl had better quality pencils and copying books. In a household of respectable women, an upstart from a village was queening it over them.

The *sinseh*, embarrassed by the frequent presence of the Venerable One himself during the lessons for the village girl, when he had never once shown the same interest in his granddaughters, privately frowned and shook his head with dismay, but refused to be drawn into the controversy. He taught conscientiously, collected his salary politely and was able to report, in all truthfulness, that the girl was one of the brightest and most enthusiastic pupils he had ever had.

Once the Old One dropped in when the girl was learning to write, and he asked her to write her name for him to see. 'Silver Frond,' he read, and wrote it himself, happy as a child.

'I have never seen an old man so enthralled,' said the *sinseh* in confidence to First Wife when pressed for his opinion. It seemed that everyone was describing the Venerable One's strange transformation in terms of a first-time observation: 'I have never seen him smile so much.' 'I have never seen him eat porridge that has gone cold. Remember how he would push away his bowl in disgust if it didn't steam?'

'Even the *sinseh* is scandalised. I can tell by his looks. You should not be doing such things.'

Still there was silence.

'You have become a laughing stock.'

The room was so silent that for a moment First Wife thought her husband had fallen asleep.

She said, a little more loudly, 'People say you have developed a thick skin. You cannot feel the loss of face any more.'

It needed a succession of provocative statements to break through the perverse silence. He said testily, as he lay very still on his bed, his eyes fixed on the ceiling, 'I can do anything I like.' It was the arrogant claim of every spoilt person, and was meant to stop all argument.

These days, he thought, he never felt happier, carried along on a tide of pure self-gratification, which should be justification enough for his actions. *I can do anything I like.* For the first time, he experienced the thrilling sensation of making his own decisions. He had always stayed very close to the safe shore of duty and tradition, but now he had struck out for blue water. He liked the new, heady feeling!

Twice a week, he watched the girl at her lessons; twice a week, he drank Ovaltine and ate buns with her, and talked and listened to the sparkling stories spilling out of her lively mind. As a young boy, he had loved listening to the tales and legends told by his grandmother and the maidservants in the household, but his father had said story-listening and storytelling in the company of females was not proper behaviour.

Through the bright village girl, he was reclaiming some portions of a lost boyhood joy.

Silver Frond told him the story of the truth cockerel. By this time, she had changed the ending three times, making the Goddess Pearly Face give it two heads instead of just the one it lost, so that the thieving and lying young man would be haunted by a two-headed cockerel for the rest of his life.

Everyone in the Great House, including the three wives, tiptoed around a village girl suddenly exalted to unimaginable prominence by a patriarch in his dotage. It was an untenable situation that clearly could not last. At some point, it would break, like a bad egg, and carry the evil odour of gossip even further.

First Wife thought, How is it possible that he can be so indifferent? Only a short while ago, this meticulously clean-living man would have sought to avoid any slur on his good name, as he would have brushed off the tiniest speck of dirt from his white vest, or pushed away a bowl because of the faintest stain on its rim.

She said, 'You cannot do as you like.'

He became angry, sat up on his bed and said, 'What is all the fuss about? I am just helping a bright girl get the education her parents cannot afford for her. Everybody knows I give donations regularly to the poor. Why should this be different?'

But this was different, and he knew it. The generosity to the girl was only part of the truth. If only the women in his household and the town's idle chatterers would just accept this part and leave him alone to enjoy the rest. The rest was *his* truth, and his alone. It had brought a strange joy. As yet, he did not understand this joy fully, except that, having been visited by it, he could not let it go.

A new world had broken in upon him, and he rather preferred it to the old.

'The ancestors will surely disapprove.'

He could dismiss idle gossippers with disdain; he could not do that with ancestors. The Old One fell into an uneasy silence, as the stern face of the August Ancestor from China loomed before him.

First Wife went on: 'Today we sought help in a temple. We shook the sacred sticks three times. Three times we had the same message. The ancestors are displeased.' By 'we', of course, she meant only herself and her sister, never Third Wife. From the start, he had been aware of the undercurrents of hostility beneath the surface civility in his large household of women.

So it was not only the endorsement of the ancestors that this crafty woman had sought, but the endorsement of gods as well. She had mobilised all the forces of heaven to help her turn him from his wayward ways. His simple rescue of a village girl from poverty and ignorance had started a cosmic battle. Would he be prepared to fight?

The Venerable One thought, with a shuddering *frisson*, I will and I must.

To his wife, he said curtly, 'It is late. I have no wish to talk any more,' and waved a hand of dismissal.

But First Wife was not done yet. Her voice softened slightly. She was trying a new tactic. 'A man must have what he wants, and his wives must understand that,' she said. 'Old male blood must be fired and flow strongly again, if there are to be sons. Ah Kiong Chek's daughter is nineteen years old. She is healthy and has some beauty. She comes from a respectable family. If you agree, I can arrange for a meeting ...'

Exactly twenty years ago, when she sensed her body was no longer capable of giving her husband the satisfaction that was his due, she had made the same arrangement for her younger sister to be brought into the household as Second Wife. This dour, dutiful, loyal woman was doing everything wrong. He wanted to shout, 'Leave me alone! Let me make my own decisions! Let me make my own mistakes!' But always, the sheer selflessness of this woman, whom he had ceased to desire so long ago but not to respect, was the mirror to reflect his own selfishness and make him feel ashamed.

He would always be kind to her. Indeed, on her deathbed, she would be able to say, with full conviction, 'Of all his wives, my husband had highest respect for me. He defied ancestors and gods during all those crazy years, but his last act of repentance and his return to them was on my account.'

27
Third Wife's Turn

During the time of the upheaval caused by the Egg Girl, the Venerable One either forgot or refused to call Third Wife to clean his ears. His single remaining pleasure of the senses was her consummate manipulation of the little gold excavating instrument deep inside the cavities of his ears, and he had foregone it. That was the measure of the hold that the girl from Sim Bak Village had on him. It had never happened before! It was intolerable.

Each time Third Wife thought of the Old One's infatuation with the little witch, she flew into a rage, which was the greater for its suppression. The bottled fury tightened Third Wife's eyes and mouth, and actually brought about a skin rash, which the loyal and attentive Tali-gelem treated with soothing rice powder. But it was clear that any opposition would only be to her detriment.

The worst was yet to come. The infatuation would soon become a full-blown passion and the little witch would be brought into the Great House as Fourth Wife. Scheming as she was, she would in no time usurp even First Wife's position.

Third Wife knew about First Wife's failed plan to bring in Ah Kiong Chek's nineteen-year-old daughter. It would appear that the Old One was by now so bewitched that he could walk past a hundred eligible young women lined outside his bedroom, for a mere nobody, a child-woman, a seller of eggs, whose fingernails picked up the dirt of chicken coops, whose clothes would never shake off the smell of chicken dung.

Third Wife did not at all share First Wife's concern with the violation of ancestral respectability. That was a mere abstraction compared with the reality of an impending humiliation. To be obliged to receive the intruder with smiling courtesy! The Venerable One, mad with passion, might insist on the three wives' observance of the tea ceremony and the *ang pow* giving to please his bride. How could they bear this supreme insult to their position?

Third Wife's mind did several more alarming prospective leaps. She saw a reallocation of quarters and servants to suit the whims of the usurper, her monopoly of the old man's nights and the total banishment of all the three wives to the margins of influence in the Great House. It was a prospect that brought angry tears into her eyes.

The Venerable One heard the door of his bedroom softly opening and groaned inwardly at the thought of yet another tiresome visit from First Wife. But it was Third Wife.

She came with no complaint or rebuke. She only said, with a humility of submission that would have been most ungracious to reject, 'I have come to clean your ears. I could not sleep with worrying about how long your ears have not been cleaned.'

He grunted something about it being very late, but she was already by his bed, the ear-cleaner in its little cylindrical locket dangling from a chain round her neck.

Her neck was bare, as were her shoulders and arms. Third Wife's beauty, far greater than that of either the senior wives, had for a few years been the old man's delight. She had come into the Great House when she was twenty-four and he was fifty-five, and he had bestowed upon her a far greater share of his nights than had been fair to the other wives. But he had soon grown tired of her, and had been indifferent to those soft foreign nightgowns she had bought to enhance a woman's beauty in the bed. In the end, his contact with her was limited to the ear-cleaning.

Now, entering his room in her best foreign nightgown and the ear-cleaner, she was intent on reviving both pleasures.

The Old One's appetite had lain unsatisfied all these long months; the last time he had called her to his bed must have been at least a year ago. First Wife and Second Wife had been completely relieved of that role, as her maidservant Taligelem could confirm. Her best hope was that this appetite, surely only quiescent, not extinct, could be revived with a little effort.

She put some scented oil on her palms and began to massage his back, then his shoulders, then his legs. She did it slowly, sensuously. He lay very still, breathing heavily, and that was all the encouragement she needed for a start.

She said softly, 'Would you like me to clean your ears now?' For answer, he pointed to a nearby table lamp. She got up, turned on the lamp, then returned to his bed, sitting close enough for her thigh to press gently against his. She unclasped the little cylinder round her neck, and brought out the tiny, delicate instrument of pleasure. All her movements were executed smoothly and gracefully.

The straps of her nightgown had fallen over her shoulders, revealing her breasts. She made a mound of pillows for him to lay his head on, making sure that the breasts, still smooth and firm, brushed against him lightly. 'Here, lie here.' She gently adjusted his head on the pillows, turning it to one side, for the light to be focused on his exposed ear, once more making sure there was contact with the breasts.

She remembered a time – oh, too long ago! – when he stole from his time with First Wife and Second Wife to slip into her room and feast his eyes on her naked beauty, coming to her in the middle of the night with the truant's delicious sense of wrongdoing. And now here she was, a woman still beautiful, still attracting the attention of men whenever she went out – she was aware that Black Dog stole sideways glances at her behind his thick glasses – reduced to sexual beggary at her husband's table.

'Ah!' Third Wife exclaimed, peering into the cavity of his ear. 'Such a lot! I'm surprised you didn't feel uncomfortable.'

Deftly, expertly, she went to work, showing him each little curl of wax as she brought it up carefully, in the tiny bowl of the instrument, taking care not to break it, because she knew he liked to see every picking intact. 'See, such a lot, and so long!' She watched to see him smile, but there were only the closed eyes and tight mouth of concentration.

'Ah, when you marry the Egg Girl, I will teach her to clean your ears in the same way!'

It was the forced playfulness of one resorting to banter to extract information, but it was no use. The Old One ignored her and continued to remain very still.

'Everybody is talking. I suppose you will send for her parents to make an offer?' Third Wife was becoming reckless. And still she could not provoke her husband to a response.

Suddenly it occurred to him – and he almost smiled at the thought, despite his determination to remain stern-faced throughout the ear-cleaning – that both First Wife and Third

Wife were using the same tactic of eliciting a response from him by taking their questions to higher and higher levels of provocation. It was familiar female strategy, but it would not work with him. A gratifying sense of mischief stole over him, and he laughed inwardly.

Thinking of the two wives made him wonder about the middle one, whose brainlessness least merited any thought. Second Wife was, of course, not capable of making a similar nocturnal visit of exhortation. It was amazing how in the years following the birth of the third and last daughter, he had hardly noticed her, or only noticed her enough to be secretly repelled by the enormous layers of flesh piling on chin, neck and arms, and the habit of always having something in the mouth to chew or suck. He remembered a visit she had made daringly to his room one evening, probably prompted by her sister, and he had turned her away politely.

The old phase in his life to which all three wives belonged was fast receding and giving way to a new one, rich in its promise, in which they would no longer have a place. It belonged to a child-woman, and it would be the greatest challenge in his life to put her there, with the ancestors' blessing, however grudgingly given. The Venerable One meant to wrest this favour from them, no matter how difficult. He was already planning how to go about it. He saw the greatest opposition coming not from First Wife, but from Third.

He lay very still, his suspicion aroused more than his passion, the pleasurable sensation of the ear-cleaning in no way affecting either.

'Her father will demand no less than a house or a coconut plantation, her mother no less than a stack of gold bangles and a whole roasted pig. Then there's a sister with a harelip, who may need an expensive operation. You will say, "Yes, yes," because you love her so much. Everyone sees that, even the servants! Well, you can kick me and my daughters out of our quarters and let her and her family have them!'

Third Wife, in her frustration, was losing all control of herself. The playfulness had become a hysterical mix of mounting panic, angry rebuke and self-pity. Her voice had become a shriek.

The Venerable One sat up on his bed and said tersely, 'That's enough. Go back to your room now.'

'Forgive me,' she said, beginning to cry. There had been just a moment of quick thinking, which said, 'Stop! Change course at once!' She had obeyed it in time. Now she was once again the humble, submissive wife. 'Forgive me for not being able to give you a son all these years.'

Privately she put the blame on him, citing the example of her four sisters, all of whom produced male children. Men with poor seed blamed their wives. The secret resentment did not in any way affect the open contrition: 'I am ashamed of my inability. But I have been taking nourishing herbs these past few months to strengthen my womb, to bear sons for you.'

He said nothing and she waited. Like the spiralling hysteria, her pledged devotion now spun to a higher level of selflessness: 'I will do penance in the Bright Light Temple if it restores divine favour and gives you a son.'

The reference to the temple gods was unfortunate for it irritated the Old One, who had of late heard too much about the wishes of gods and ancestors. 'Forgive me,' said Third Wife again, and he replied stiffly, 'There's nothing to forgive. I do not blame you. I have never blamed any one of you. You know that. Now go back to sleep.'

Third Wife, with the straps still fallen over her shoulders, continued to linger in the bedroom. 'I did not manage to do your other ear. Would you like me to do it now or come tomorrow?'

The Venerable One was more comfortable dealing with First Wife, with her honest, forthright ways, than with Third Wife, the snake turned dove, offering its little head for the slaughter as soon as she was cornered. But only the most hard-hearted or the most uncouth could respond harshly in the face of so much meek submission. He had always behaved with gentlemanly courtesy towards his wives. Most of all, he wanted to be rid of her presence.

'I will call you if I need you.'

Those were the hardest words to hear. Third Wife thought with bitter despair: I have lost my husband to that little she-devil from the village.

One thing was clear now. The extent of his obsession could not be explained in terms of ordinary human need, even that of an old man lustful beyond the capacity of three wives. It could only be accounted for in terms of some supernatural force. The Old One must be possessed by the most potent evil spirit allowed to roam the earth and create havoc in the lives of men and women. There were many stories, past and present, of such possession.

In this belief of their husband's victimisation, the three wives were soon readily united. As to the strategies of rescue, they would go their different ways.

28
Second Wife and Food With Feet

'Sssh, don't make so much noise,' whispered Second Wife to her maidservant, in the silence and darkness of night, as they both walked down the stairs and into the kitchen. She would have preferred to dispense with the company of this clumsy girl, who made odd noises with her throat and teeth even during sleep, except that she was scared of ghosts.

She had heard stories about the lonely, long-haired ghost in the shophouse at Choon Kiah Street. Although the ghost had never ventured beyond the shophouse, which was several streets away, who knew when she would decide to wander out?

No ghost had as yet been seen in the Great House, but there was a portrait of an ancestor in the altar room, an elderly woman with a dark complexion and deep-set eyes, whose gaze was believed to follow anyone who looked at her, no matter where they were in the room.

When she first came into the Great House, Second Wife had plucked up enough courage to test the belief. One morning, as soon as she had finished the daily ritual of obeisance and stuck the joss-sticks into an urn of ash in front of the portrait, she looked up and met the gaze boldly, then walked to a corner of the room, still keeping her eyes on the fearsome ancestor, as if challenging her. Then she reversed her steps and walked back, finally doing a turn of the entire room, all the time making sure her eyes were fixed on the ancestor's. Yes, it was true. The old, glittering eyes had never left her face. From that day, she avoided looking at the portrait.

That one independent act of curiosity and adventure was all that Second Wife had been able to claim in her life in the Great House. And with the years had grown a real fear of ghosts, whether wandering about or fixed for all time within the frames of their photographs on the walls.

The night was full of dangers, and Second Wife would avoid them at all costs. If she needed to go to the lavatory at night, she woke up the maidservant, who was required to wait outside on the stone steps of the outhouse for the entire duration. A mother of three grown daughters, Second Wife remained a child when it came to the night's terrors.

'Sssh,' said Second Wife again, as she made her way towards the food cupboard. The cupboard, holding bowls and plates of food remaining from one meal and re-heated for the next, was well protected against non-human marauders throughout the day and night. It had finely meshed doors to keep out flies, its four legs stood in earthen containers of water to deter ants, and around it were placed three mousetraps to catch the rodents on their way to the plunder.

But it was never locked and had no protection against maidservants who suffered hunger pangs in the middle of the night, or against mistresses who were on an abstinence diet of vegetables and *tofu* and secretly yearned for pork and duck and chicken.

Second Wife had been forced by her older sister to be on such a diet, as penance for the wrongdoings of the Venerable One. The Old One had sinned, and his wives must pay for it.

First Wife knew that such self-inflicted punishment in the name of wifely duty was pleasing to the gods and might still glean enough merit to turn the Old One from his folly. Advice had failed; if the penance too failed, there would be nothing left to do but submit. She would buy a cageful of doves, take them to the Bright Light Temple and release them into the sky. Doves were usually for petitioning or thanking the gods; hers would be a sad acceptance of their will: I have done my best. I accept the fate that Heaven has ordained for me.

From the start, Second Wife, who had great admiration for her strong and noble sister, had shown her willingness to take part in this enterprise of storming heaven. The release of the doves was nothing to fear; the hard part was the vegetarian diet, in effect, a cruel subsistence, over thirty long days, on plain white rice, soya sauce, and steamed or boiled vegetables and *tofu* not even allowed the slightest redeeming touch of lard. 'You don't have to, I am not forcing you to,' First Wife had said, well aware that the prospect of good food in the Great House had been the main enticement for her younger sister to come in as the Old One's second wife.

As she took her last meal of rice, minced pork fried in sesame oil, vegetables fried with shrimps and pig stomach soup, poor Second Wife was filled with dismay at the bleak prospect of one bland meal after another in the days ahead.

At night, in her dreams, she saw herself at the market, passing a stall selling sausages, red, hard, oily, hanging in tantalising bunches, and another stall selling steamed chickens, glistening in their own oil, hanging by their necks on hooks, and yet a third stall selling rice dumplings cut open to show their fillings of minced pork, mushroom, lotus seeds and boiled egg yolk retaining every bit of its bright orange colour.

Second Wife realised that hunger and desire made her dream in the most vivid hues. She woke from each technicolour dream with little moans of self-pity.

On the sixth day of the abstinence, Second Wife, unable to sleep, wept with anguish. At lunch that day, she had looked bleakly at the bowls of plain white rice placed before herself and First Wife, with small bowls of steamed beans and pickled leeks, and glanced with vexed envy at a large bowl of pig trotters with sliced ginger, a plate of fried prawns and a tureen of cabbage and pork ball soup placed in the centre of the table, for the others. The delicious smell invaded her nostrils and made her sick with longing. But there was no question of stretching out her spoon or chopsticks for them. She had never once risked the disapproval of her formidable older sister.

Second Wife, in her pyjamas, tiptoeing in the darkness towards the food cupboard, was guided in her resolve by a gnawing hunger. It was driving her crazy! She tremblingly opened the cupboard doors. Very carefully, she took out a bowl containing the leftover pig trotters and a plate with at least six remaining fried prawns. There was no time to heat the food on the stove; in any case, the risk of waking up light sleepers with noise and the smell of food would be too great.

Watched by her maidservant, Second Wife ate quickly and greedily.

'Don't tell anyone,' she warned. Her hunger assuaged, she was able to pay attention to a question buzzing around in her head like an annoying fly. The food would be missed the next morning; what should she say, if asked? Once she had taken a packet of peanut biscuits bought by one of First Wife's daughters for her small son, and when asked, had promptly put the blame on the maidservant. The girl was extremely useful to have around, for she smiled goodnaturedly through any amount of scolding for sluggishness and blame for theft. Everyone suspected Second Wife when food went missing, but to preserve the household peace, nobody said anything.

Only Third Wife had been provoked enough to remark loudly, to no one in particular, 'Food in the Great House has feet. It walks away from cupboards and tables!'

Second Wife had been sufficiently provoked, in her turn, to make an equally loud comment, also to no one in particular, 'At least I don't perm my hair and put powder on my face, give myself a foreign name and laugh with Black Dog and the other men!'

The vicious one was sure to make more comments once Tali-gelem whispered to her about the vanished pig trotters and prawns. For the second time that evening, Second Wife had an idea. She would announce simply, first thing in the morning, 'The food had gone rancid. Such an awful smell! I had to throw everything away.'

In the next few days, no leftover food was stored in the cupboard. It would appear that a general malice had taken hold of everyone in the Great House, depriving her of her secret nocturnal sustenance.

Second Wife's dreams became even more frantic and colourful. On the thirteenth day of the abstinence, desperation drove her to the most dastardly deed.

'Just what do you think you are doing?'

Later, Second Wife, her mind greatly sharpened in those desperate days, understood it had all been a scheme of spiteful Third Wife. But at the time, caught trying to steal a slab of roasted pork from an ancestral altar in the silence and darkness of night, she could only give a little gasp and say the first thing that came to her mind, 'The pork has gone rancid. I came to throw it away.'

A thief of the worst kind, stealing food from the mouths of the gods themselves, Second Wife stood uncertainly in the dim light coming from a small lamp on the altar, her mind working very fast to meet any number of questions. I was supposed to throw the pork away, but forgot, till just now. I had a strange dream just now that told me to remove all offerings from the altar and replace them with fresh ones.

Third Wife, in her pyjamas and hair in curlers, leaned against the wall and folded her arms across her chest in gloating satisfaction. 'Go ahead, eat it,' she said. 'I won't tell anybody tomorrow. I'll just say that the roasted pork grew feet in the middle of the night and walked away!'

Second Wife never hated her so much as then.

29
A Happy New Year

Silver Frond said sharply, 'Don't touch it!' and her sisters sheepishly moved away from Moon Princess, still pristine in her box behind the cellophane. The doll stood inside a cupboard, untouched since the day it was brought back from the Great House, untouchable, because it had survived both a sordid pawnshop transaction and an attempted re-sale to its donor. It stood in the cupboard, no longer just a toy, but a potential instrument of power.

Silver Frond still had a lot of the money left from the amount brought home from the Great House, even after buying her mother's medicine, another tin of Jacob's Cream Crackers for Ah Hoo Sim and cloth for her mother to sew a dress for each sister for the coming New Year. She had never had so much money in her life. For safety she kept it in her pocket, always remembering to take it out when she changed clothes and to re-pocket it. She had never felt so happy or excited in her life.

By herself at night, in the dim light of the kerosene lamp, she bent over little scraps of paper, salvaged from old calendars, to do her sums, unwatched by her father or mother, who were sure to ask questions, or her sisters, who were sure to peer over her shoulders and laugh senselessly. She did the sums with meticulous care and came to the thrilling conclusion that even after giving her father some money for his beer – she could not avoid that pleading, pitiful look in his eyes any more – she would still have enough to make it the happiest New Year they would ever have.

Normally her mother killed one of their own chickens for the New Year's Eve dinner, bought some cheap New Year cookies from the market and gave *ang pows* that contained only a coin or two each, so that she and her sisters, feeling the hard edges through the red paper, looked with disappointment at each other. There was one year when there were no new dresses, no dinner and no gift money, so that they put their heads down in shame as the other village children, dressed in bright pink or red, deliberately stood before them to munch New Year cookies noisily and count *ang pow* money loudly.

This year, with her new wealth, she made sure that things were different.

'This duck is the best,' her father pronounced at the important eve dinner, ladling out a large portion of the delicious soup on to his plate. He looked round proudly at the other unaccustomed luxuries on their table – a bowl of chicken curry, from a large chicken bought from the market, larger and fleshier and tastier than any of their own, and plates of pork fried with ginger, steamed pork sausages that dripped oil so tasty every drop had to be mopped up with rice, shredded turnip fried with squid, fried prawns seasoned in tamarind juice, a platter of expensive vegetables.

Everyone turned to the source of all this largesse and showed their appreciation by taking turns to heap the good stuff on her plate.

'Enough! Enough!' cried Silver Frond. With an expression of deadly adult seriousness, she transferred a chicken drumstick,

glistening in oil and spices to her mother's plate and said
sternly, 'Mother, I want you to have this.' If her mother, from
sheer selfless habit, helped herself only to the head, neck or
feet, she was ready to seize these unworthy items and remove
them from the table.

'No, no! You must take that yourself. Or let your father
have it.'

'No, Mother! I insist you have it.'

And there ensued a lively family squabble as the contentious
drumstick was passed around.

Both Ah Bee Koh and Ah Bee Soh looked at their daughter
in awed admiration, in her new position of authority. Money
had given her an adult's confidence, but she remained the
generous-hearted child, dispensing it freely, to make others
happy. Poor child! She had no idea the money would soon be
gone, and she would slip once more into the obscurity of her
position.

Ah Bee Koh and Ah Bee Soh, in the privacy of conversations
at night after the child was asleep, spoke in hushed whispers
about how that obscurity could be changed into vistas of bright
promise.

'Don't touch Moon Princess!' Silver Frond was ever on the
alert, sometimes slapping down a disobedient hand. Her sisters
were always watching for the opportunity to lift the cellophane
and touch the doll's hair or clothes or shoes, if only for a few
moments.

'You promised you would share Moon Princess with us,'
they complained.

'Things are different now,' said Silver Frond. 'It's no use
explaining to you because you won't understand.'

She protected the doll in its new role as potential source of immense wealth. She waited for more money to come from it. Her mother took her aside to explain the untenability of her plan.

'You cannot go to the Venerable One again,' she said patiently. She knew of her daughter's plan to offer to sell the doll a second time, accept the Venerable One's generous counter-offer, return with both doll and money, and repeat the procedure at least a dozen times.

Years later, Ah Bee Soh, more relaxed, more capable of laughter of the happy, uncynical kind, was to remind her daughter about the staggering naivety of those days, and both laughed heartily together. But in that year of strange happenings started by the gift of the doll, she was far from relaxed, and had to guide her daughter carefully along the remarkable, perilous path that fate seemed to have opened up for her.

Ah Bee Soh said, 'He will be very displeased. He will think you are extremely greedy, and lose his good opinion of you.' The loss of the present favoured status of her eldest daughter was one thing she wanted to prevent at all cost.

Thus ended Silver Frond's scheme for a regular source of income.

She was by no means dismayed, being more absorbed by that larger favour of the exclusive tutoring by the *sinseh*, which was giving her untold joy. Nothing could compare with that!

It had even banished, once and for all, her fear of the Venerable One's strange son. One morning, when she was left alone by the *sinseh* to do some copying, she felt a breathing over her shoulders and looked up to see the son, grinning and frowning by turns, staring at her. Her first impulse was to run; her next was to protect her valuable copybook and pencils from the destructive energy, like a naughty child's, which she was sure he was about to unleash. She put her hands over her book, and forced herself to stare back at him, feigning a boldness she did not at all feel.

The young man, still in the layers of jackets over his pyjamas, still smelling horribly of dark, airless rooms, merely sat down docilely beside her. He pointed to her book, with a child's curiosity, and she opened it and read some words to him. From that moment, all fear of him vanished.

The two presences in the Great House that had frightened her more than ghosts – the strange son and the old mother – had become benign. She would never have believed, if anyone had told her then, that, in the later happy years of her life, she would actually draw them into her circle of generous giving and loving, and that, in the tumultuous years of her pain and grief, they were among the few who would offer solace.

At home, she told no one of the incident of the strange son in the classroom.

She no longer played with her paper dolls, which she had given to her sisters. An old phase of her life had been left behind; a new one was beginning. She spent her time, when she was not helping her mother with the laundry, practising her reading and writing. One day, she had the bright idea to turn tutor herself to her sisters, and enjoyed it so much that she conducted regular classes for them.

'Say that again! Say it correctly! Take that, and that! It will knock your brain into greater activity. It will wake your brain up from sleep!' She had a wooden ruler, like the *sinseh*'s, and imitated him in his most irascible mood, but not in the harshness, so that the ruler never touched Silver Flower's head or Silver Pearl's knuckles, or only very lightly. The girls would pretend to cower with fear, and hold their hands over their heads, laughing merrily. After each lesson, she took out two coins from her pocket, one for each sister, and said with a great show of severity, 'Go get yourself some brain-food; otherwise I'll have to knock your head harder at the next lesson!'

She dispensed fistfuls of coins; her money seemed unending, kept safely in her pocket. It made her so happy to see her younger sisters run to put the coins in their money-boxes, two cigarette tins with slits cut in the lid.

The supreme joy of the giving was on the morning of the New Year, when they stood before their parents to receive the New Year *ang pows*. Silver Frond watched with much gratification as her sisters tore open the red packets, and saw not coins but dollar notes. The girls' excitement had already begun when their fingers felt for the usual metallic hardness and settled on the flatness of paper instead. It burst forth in shrieks of joy when they pulled out the notes, one by one. There were two dollars in each packet from each parent. Silver Flower and Silver Pearl jumped up and down in wild joy, waving the unaccustomed fortune in the air.

Her mother was about to say something when Silver Frond put a finger to her lips. Revealing the truth might spoil the sisters' pleasure. She had, the evening before, after the New Year's Eve dinner, actually gone to her parents and asked to see the *ang pows* they had prepared for the next morning's presentation. As expected, there were just the coins. Silver Frond tore open the packets, took out the coins, and replaced them with the notes. 'You can give me whatever you like, but these are for Silver Flower and Silver Pearl.' She had grown up; she could dispense with New Year gifts for children.

Her parents had looked in amazement at her, then uneasily

at each other. The child had violated tradition in usurping her parents' role as *ang pow* givers. Done spitefully, it would have been an intolerable act of impiety, involving an unspeakable loss of face. But the child had acted from generosity and largeness of heart.

Their eldest daughter, on the threshold of womanhood, beautiful and pure in body as in spirit, singled out for extraordinary favours by the town's richest man, was a treasure they would have to protect and nurture to its full promise.

30
No Less Than a Shophouse

In the darkness, Silver Frond heard low voices coming from the kitchen. She knew her parents were talking about her. She crept out of her mattress, and tiptoed to a well-concealed spot behind a cupboard.

'At least a shophouse. Or a coconut plantation.' She heard her father tell her mother about a very rich old man in Malaya who had given the family of his young bride a shophouse *and* a coconut plantation. 'Biscuits and F&N Orange Crush and dolls and copywriting books. *Tchah!* My daughter is worth much much more.'

'You are talking as if the Venerable One wants to take Silver Frond as his fourth wife.'

'Are you blind? Can't you see? The gifts, the exclusive tuition from the *sinseh*, who I hear charges the highest fees. No man, however rich, will do that for a woman unless he wants to make her his wife.'

'She is only fourteen. She has not even had her first flow.'

'She will not be fourteen for ever! He will wait.'

'No man waits for a woman.'

'I tell you he'll wait! He is totally besotted with my beautiful daughter.'

'She is so naïve. She knows nothing about the ways of men. Even her younger sisters know more.'

'It will be your duty as mother to tell her.'

'These things need not be told. They will come naturally.

My real worry is that she will be eaten up by those wives in the Great House. I hear Third Wife is merciless.'

'My daughter may be naïve in the ways of men, but let me tell you this. She has a good brain! She will learn very fast and will know how to deal with those wives. My Silver Frond will be the favourite wife, you mark my words. I can see her now, with gold bangles stacked right up to her elbows! But she will take off all those bangles, at a moment's notice, and sell them for money to help her poor father and mother and sisters, and others besides. I know my daughter too well. The gods have given her not only beauty but a heart full of kindness.' He allowed himself a moment of humbling truth. 'How could I, poor wretch that I am, produce a treasure like this?'

Her mother said anxiously, 'I hope she never has to sell her jewellery to help her family.'

'She will not need to. An old man's love will put money in her pockets for her to give away as she pleases!'

'I heard that the Old One gave a shophouse to the family of Third Wife.'

'That's what I've been telling you! No less than a shophouse for our Silver Frond. *Plus* a coconut plantation.'

31
The Ancestor Who Could Not Be Bribed

The Venerable One did not need the mediation of temple priests to speak to dead ancestors. They came to him in dreams to advise, cajole, console, warn.

The huge ancestral altar in the Great House, which had a room to itself, comprised not one but three tables, a large central one and two smaller side ones, covered with richly embroidered cloths edged with long silk tassels. On ordinary days, the altar tables carried urns of joss-sticks, cups of tea, plates of oranges and sweetmeats and vases of sweet-smelling flowers; on special days, such as the New Year and the Feast of the Hungry Ghosts, they creaked under the weight of massive offerings of food, including whole steamed chickens and roasted suckling pigs, and enormous pomelos and watermelons.

On the walls hung the large framed portraits of the ancestors, both male and female, serious-faced men in Chinese suits and women in dark *samfus* with their hair pulled severely from their foreheads into tight sleek buns at the back, and their ear-lobes bearing tiny jade or diamond studs, modest signs of their wealth and privileged position. These portraits were replicated on their tombstones, those of husband and wife side by side, enclosed in oval settings, their dates of death sometimes revealing an amazingly long wait of decades before a spouse was laid to rest beside the other.

The August Ancestor who came from China had the largest portrait and urn of joss-stick offerings. The photograph in faded sepia showed an austere-looking man with a thin face and a straggly beard. He had had four wives in a strictly maintained hierarchy of importance in the household, but only the first, of course, was buried beside him in the Hokkien cemetery, the others being relegated to plots whose distance from this central tomb corresponded precisely with their official position in the hierarchy, though not necessarily with their private position in his affections. He was said to love his last wife best, whose proximity to him was least.

The Venerable One lit a joss-stick and stuck it in the ash of the porcelain urn in front of the August Ancestor's portrait. It was the first act of the day, and if accompanied by a silent, earnestly asked question, could merit an answer to the question that very night.

In his dream, the Venerable One was sitting at a table facing the ancestor. He did not repeat his question, which would have been an insult to the ancestor's retentive memory. Moreover, he was known during his lifetime as a very practical person who hated wasting time and beating about the bush.

He said, 'Have you considered the consequences of your decision? Have you considered what a laughing stock you will be?'

So the ancestor was taking the side of First Wife right from the start.

'I won't be a laughing stock. I am just taking as my fourth wife a young girl. She may be a poor village girl, but she is bright and of good character.'

'You can know nothing of her character. She is only fourteen. Besides, she does not come from a respectable family. Your marriage will link you with a good-for-nothing man with a bad reputation. His wife is a washerwoman who may be consumptive. One of her sisters has a serious physical defect.'

The ancestor had prepared all his reasons and was systematically laying them out, as if he had been in consultation with First Wife, who indeed was the one in the privileged position of attending to his altar and ensuring that all the grandchildren lit a joss-stick of respect every day.

'I am marrying the girl, not her family.' The Venerable One was becoming assertive, but only in intention, not in word. The intention had expanded into a plan to offer the parents a large sum of money in exchange for the promise that they would not show themselves at the Great House, except on necessary occasions, such as the first day of the New Year. The daughter was a precious gem, and they were the crude rocks in which the treasure was still embedded. He would do the disengagement very carefully and meticulously.

He was himself involved in the much larger disengagement from the stern tradition of his forbears, which would require the same care.

At this stage, he allowed himself the boldness of argument, which, as a young man, he had secretly desired whenever he stood before his father to be told of major decisions made for him. He said to the August Ancestor, 'Poverty and a humble family background should not be a setback.' He was tempted to remind the ancestor that one of his own four wives had been a village girl too. The ancestor could obviously read his thoughts, for he said, a little testily, 'Your Third Grandmother was seventeen when she came into the household. This girl is still only a child-woman. People will talk.'

'She is healthy. She will bear me many sons.'

'You can have far more suitable women who will bear you many sons.'

The Venerable One wanted to shout out loud, 'Actually, right now, I'm not thinking of sons! I want this girl for herself! I love her very much!' The truth had surprised even himself. That paramount need – to have male heirs carry on his name – had receded in the face of his passion.

Filial deference had to be preserved. So he remained silent. Even in dreams, the visits of the dead had a time limit, and the August Ancestor said sternly, 'Don't cause embarrassment to your ancestors. None of them was as crazy as you over a woman. Have you lost your head?' Then he was gone.

When the Venerable One woke up, he suddenly remembered a small incident about this ancestor that he had heard when he was a boy. The August Ancestor had made a lot of money in his lifetime, but had kept extremely frugal habits, eating simple rice porridge, wearing cheap sandals, and living in a small, modest shophouse, until his acquisition of wives forced him to move to a larger one. His greatest pleasure had been opium, but his frugality prevented him from enjoying a certain high quality grade of opium, which he could have easily afforded in his later years. It was supposed to be the very best, the ultimate dream of the opium connoisseur, taking him to the Tenth Court of Heaven. Yet he, with all his money, had never enjoyed it even once.

On his deathbed, it seemed he had expressed a wish for this foregone pleasure, but nobody had taken him seriously. His family had spent a small fortune on a magnificent ghost paper house for his funeral, the size of four sedan chairs, complete with paper furniture, paper servants and huge stacks of ghost money, to burn at his grave and thus provide him with a good life in the next world. If they had remembered the dying wish for the opium, they would have provided a paper simulation of it as well, possibly with a set of ghost opium pipes, also made with the finest paper.

As it was, the August Ancestor got neither the real thing in life nor its simulation in death.

The Venerable One had an idea. Nowadays, he was often inspired, and it made him as excited and happy as a boy.

Once again, Black Dog was summoned for a special errand. He was to purchase the opium, whatever the cost, however great the risk of illegality. Once again, the adopted son desisted from asking questions. First a doll, now opium. As long as the Venerable One continued to attend ably to his business and make money, these eccentricities were tolerable. The rich were entitled to all the quirks it pleased them to come up with, so long as they continued to accumulate wealth for progeny, including adopted sons.

Obviously the latest quirk of the opium was connected with the young enchantress from the village, but in a roundabout way rather than the straightforward gift of the doll. Black Dog surmised that it had something to do with the demands of the village girl's father, who must be exploiting the old man's infatuation to the full.

This time, Black Dog did not tell his wife. But he did tell Third Wife. He sometimes met up with her for tea and idle talk, usually out of sight of the other wives' prying servants. He was rewarded for this sharing of information, as usual, with a frenzied bombardment for more, for nowadays Third Wife lived on a knife-edge of anxiety and vexation. 'Why? Why the best quality opium when he's never touched the stuff in all his life?' But Black Dog was himself equally puzzled about the purpose of the strange purchase. Third Wife sulked and pouted, looking very attractive with her curled hair and rouged cheeks. She pinched and nudged Black Dog with playful energy, but he was not able to tell her more.

All her life, Third Wife puzzled over the mystery, one of the few annoying gaps in an efficiently assembled picture of what was going on in those days. She had tried her utmost to extract information from First Wife, whom she suspected of knowing far more than she did, and had been regularly repulsed by that dull-voiced, dull-faced woman. In the end, she had given up, and concluded that the stuff must have been requested by the young witch herself as part of a potent charm to hold the old man in thrall for ever.

By himself, one dark night, the Venerable One slipped out of the Great House, got into a trishaw and made his way to the cemetery. The trishawman was told to wait, and sworn to secrecy with a generous amount of money slipped into his hands.

There, in the darkness, before the tomb of the August Ancestor, on behalf of the neglectful forbears, he made the offering of the desired pleasure, fifty years late, but not too late, for ghosts kept their unfulfilled desires alive, and lingered for a long time on the face of the earth, hoping their living descendants would remember.

The Venerable One lit some joss-sticks and clasped them in both hands as he bowed three times with great reverence. The slab of expensive opium, laid on the ground before the tombstone, crackled and hissed in the flames, sending up a pungent odour, and was finally no more than a blackened heap on the ground.

The Venerable One said softly, 'Give me a sign.' He was being a little presumptuous, in demanding proof that the valuable gift had reached its intended recipient, and was being received with appreciation. He stood still in the darkness, waiting. A sudden cry from a nocturnal bird, a sweep of wind, a flash of light in the sky. Any of these would have been reassuring. But the ancestor chose to remain unresponsive.

The Venerable One gave up waiting, and got ready to return to the waiting trishaw. He realised, with a start, that it was the first time he had ventured out alone at night. An exhilarating sense of adventure filled him as he sat in the trishaw and let his thoughts wander. How happy he felt!

The August Ancestor came again in a dream, some days later. But he remained unmoved, despite the expensive gift. During his life, he had allowed himself to be both a giver and receiver of bribes, arguing that business could not be done otherwise. But in death, he had achieved a noble immunity to them.

He presented the same arguments against bringing the village girl into the Great House as Fourth Wife. His position remained unchanged.

32
Urgent Consultations

The Goddess Pearly Face was, as usual, most patient. She looked as beautiful as ever, but the paint on her face, and on the lower part of her robe, was beginning to peel a little. It suddenly occurred to Silver Frond that when she became rich, she would pay a very skilled craftsman to restore the goddess to her full beauty.

She had brought two oranges and a small bunch of flowers for the goddess, together with the usual joss-sticks. Normally, there was only a handful of petals, instead of a full bunch of blooms. She had been spending money freely, but there was still some left in her pocket. The joy of buying things for her parents and sisters was fast disappearing, and a great fear, like the chilling touch of a night wind, was taking its place.

She wanted to consult the goddess about a lot of things, and thought she might as well begin with the fear.

'My parents want me to be the Venerable One's fourth wife.'

'So? Many parents want their daughters to be the Venerable One's fourth wife. Or fifth. Or sixth. Remember, he's the richest man in town. They say he is a very good husband and provides well for all his wives. Are you afraid he will not provide well for you?'

'No.'

'Are you afraid he will treat you badly? Scold you, beat you like the *Pah Bor Chai* man?'

'Oh no! The Venerable One is kind and gentle. He will never scold or beat me.'

'Are you afraid he is marrying you on a pretext? Is his real reason to get you into the Great House to be his son's wife, to teach the poor thick-headed fellow to read and write, since no *sinseh* will do it, and to be his old mother's maidservant, since no servant will wash her smelly feet?'

'No, no. He's already told me he'll never ask me to do that. I know he always speaks the truth. Besides, I'm not afraid of the son and old mother any more.'

'Are you afraid that his three wives will be cruel to you? Scold and pinch and slap you when he is not around?'

'He'll never allow that. No, I'm not afraid of any of the wives. Third Wife always looks at me with angry eyes. Once she spat at me. Another time I found one of my copybooks torn, and rat droppings in my shoes. I think she got her servant or one of her daughters to do that. But I don't care.'

'Are you afraid that once you become Fourth Wife, the Venerable One will stop the tuition with the *sinseh*?'

'No. He says I can have the tuition as long as I want.'

'Then why are you still afraid of becoming the Venerable One's fourth wife?'

The hard part was now. Even to a goddess who had become dear friend and adviser, it was very embarrassing to talk about such things. She would never have dared ask her mother, and now she was blushing to have to consult a goddess.

'They say when you marry a man, you have to sleep with him.'

'Surely your mother has told you that?'

'A man does bad things to you.'

'A kind husband will not do bad things to his wife.'

'A painful thing then. He pushes his hard thing into you and causes you to bleed. The bedsheet is full of blood but he does not care. He will keep pushing his thing until you faint from pain.'

'Who told you that?'

'Silver Flower and Silver Pearl.'

'Your younger sisters told you that? How do they know?'

'They know a lot, but they won't tell me everything. I know too, because of the Bad Brothers. They like to stare at my breasts. Once the oldest brother thrust his hand into my blouse. Luckily I managed to push him away. I told my mother. She says all males are like that. I should just avoid them. Another time, a man came to me while I was drawing water from the well, and showed me his thing. That night, I had a horrible dream. I dreamt that he came to me with his trousers unbuttoned and his thing poking out. He pushed me to the ground, opened my legs and put his thing there. It turned into an ugly, hairy animal that burrowed deep inside me. It was so painful! There was blood everywhere.'

'Has your mother told you that you are still not a woman? You cannot marry yet because you have not had your first flow.'

'My mother brews good herbs from Ah Liang's shop. She says they will make my body strong and prepare it for the first flow.'

'Do you know whether the Venerable One has asked your parents for your hand in marriage?'

'I know something is happening. The Venerable One has asked me to stop going for the *sinseh's* lessons for a while. He did not look as if he was angry about something I had done. Rather, he looked very pleased. He even asked me to eat *tong yin* with him, and fed me spoonfuls from his own bowl.'

'Did he ask you to be his fourth wife?'

'No, he just fed me the *tong yin*. Yesterday, someone from the Great House paid a visit to my mother. I know she is a relative of the Venerable One. She brought a gift of biscuits and fruit and looked very serious. I know the visit has something to do with me, from the way my mother was behaving. I also overheard her talking to my father later in the evening.'

'What did they say?'

'My father said, "A shophouse, no less."'

'Did your mother want something too?'

'No, she didn't say. She only said she wanted me to have a very good life, and to be able to take care of my sisters when she is gone.'

'Is her illness getting worse?'

'We got better medicine from Ah Liang's shop. She told me the pain is less.'

'Now let's consider everything very carefully,' said the goddess. 'Everything depends on you, you know. If you don't want to be the Venerable One's fourth wife, even your parents can't force you. First question: Do you love him?'

'He's been very kind to me. He's given me many things. I can't even name them, they're too many.'

'But do you love him?'

'He treats me much better than he does anyone in the Great House. Everyone is afraid of him, even First Wife, but I am not afraid of him. He asks me to tell him stories, and sometimes he laughs at the stories.'

'But do you love him?'

'You mean that I have to sleep with him and let him touch my breasts and put his hard thing into my secret part?'

'Yes. Every night if he wishes, because you are his wife, and it is a wife's duty to make her husband happy. And you cannot scream, even if it's painful. That may annoy him. You have to show that you like what he's doing. That pleases him. And then after a while, you must bear him a son. That will please him even more.'

'I won't sleep with him, but I'll bear him a son.'

'You can't bear him a son unless you sleep with him. Hasn't your mother told you that?'

'I can learn to cook his porridge the way he wants it, and clean his ears better than Third Wife.'

'But you still have to sleep with him to make him happy.'

'Then I won't marry him. I won't marry him or any man!'

'How foolishly you talk! Every woman must marry.'

'I don't want to marry. I don't want a man to—'

'Then you will be poor all your life. You will lose your beauty, and one morning, you will wake up and find that it's all gone and no man will look at you. You will be a disappointment to your parents. You will have no money to help your sisters. They will have to sell eggs and wash people's clothes for the rest of their lives.'

Silver Frond fell into a deep, worried silence, pondering her options. On one side were stacked a man's wealth and his generosity, allowing her to use his money freely to make her family happy, and help unfortunate people like Ah Hoo Sim. On the other, was this dreaded prospect of the physical shame and pain of a wife's duty. She had heard an awful story about a young girl who did not even survive the wedding night.

Suddenly a thought occurred that brightened her face with hope.

'The Venerable One is a very old man. Maybe he isn't as strong as the Bad Brothers or that man at the well. Maybe he wants me as his fourth wife because he likes hearing my stories, as he says—'

'I wouldn't count on that,' said the goddess. 'Don't you know of Ah Hoo Chek's uncle who fathered a son at the age of seventy-five, and Matchmaker Auntie's old, lecherous husband whose hand is always you-know-where whenever he looks at the *ronggeng* girls swaying their hips? Would you say that sometimes the Venerable One looks at you like these old men would look at a pretty young woman? Has he ever tried to touch you?'

'He has stroked my hair and touched my cheek.'

'What else?'

'Once he held my arm and said I was too thin, and needed to eat more.'

'What else?'

'He said I am a very pretty girl who will grow up into the most beautiful woman.'

'What else?'

'That's all.'

'Were you upset by what he did?'

'I was afraid someone would come in and see.'

'But were you upset?'

'No. His touch was kind.'

'When you become his fourth wife, he will do much more than all that. A man always does much more to a pretty woman, even if he is old enough to be her grandfather! Your mother should be telling you all this.'

The situation was getting very serious. Silver Frond knew she had to make a decision quickly. She said with a worried frown, 'What do you think I should do?'

'Listen to me. Your father will never win that first prize in the lottery he's always dreaming about. He will die with no money in his pockets and his friends' scornful laughter in his ears. Your mother will die from hard work, like an ox in a field that simply collapses with the plough on its neck, if she does not die from her disease first. Silver Flower may find a husband, but he will be someone from the village who will not give her enough money so that she has to sell eggs or wash people's clothes like your mother. Silver Pearl will never get married because of her harelip, and she may eventually jump into a well or hang herself from a tree. Remember the story about the ghost with long hair in the Venerable One's shophouse in Choon Kiah Street?'

'Yes?'

'Well, she hanged herself from a rafter in the ceiling because she had a harelip or some such disfigurement that turned all men away. Her mother taunted her for not being able to get married, and being a burden on the family. In the end, she decided to kill herself. Her ghost still roams the earth, looking for a husband. Do you want Silver Pearl to end up like this?'

Tears had come into Silver Frond's eyes. She felt a special affection and responsibility for the youngest sister. She said sadly, 'Tell me what I should do.'

'Do you want to help your family?'

'Oh yes. Especially Silver Pearl. I want to have money to pay for the operation.'

'Then agree to be the Venerable One's fourth wife.'

'But I am still afraid—'

'Answer this question. Suppose the Venerable One decides that you are not worth all his attention and decides to take as his fourth wife a young woman that First Wife has recommended. In fact, there are already about three or four young women eagerly waiting. Would you prefer that?'

'Oh no! Oh no!'

'Suppose the Venerable One wakes up tomorrow morning and says, "Yes, my wives are right. Silver Frond is far too young for me. I will forget her and look for somebody else to be my fourth wife."'

'Oh no! Oh no! That must not happen!'

'That proves that you like him. He is old enough to be your grandfather, but you like him.'

'I like him because he's given me so many things—'

'But you are still afraid to sleep with him?'

'Yes.'

'You will get used to it. Every woman gets used to it. Now tell me, do you love the Venerable One?'

'I could learn to, once I get used to it.'

'It's easy to love a kind man.'

33
Tong Yin

The Venerable One's porcelain spoon, containing a perfectly round, white *tong yin* swimming in a little pool of sugar-water, approached Silver Frond's lips, which parted slowly, hesitantly. But realising it could be too big for the girl's small mouth and delicate throat, he withdrew the spoon, put the *tong yin* back into his bowl and searched for a smaller one. He finally scooped up the smallest, stained a bright red, and once more offered it to the girl. It slid effortlessly into her mouth. The Old One watched her chewing slowly and finally swallowing the *tong yin*, the little movements on the skin of her throat giving him a rare pleasure. She was probably not enjoying those balls of boiled rice flour in syrup, but was responding delightfully to his overture of affection. 'Does it taste nice?'

She nodded her head. It occurred to him that the girl had suddenly gone shy. A slight flush was spreading over her cheeks.

'Here, have another.'

He had never spooned food into a woman's mouth with so much pleasure. The intimacy of the action filled him with a warming glow. One put food in a child's mouth for sustenance, into a woman's mouth for love. The only intimate moment during a long wedding ceremony when a man and his bride stood stiffly side by side was when he was allowed to feed her with soup in a spoon or a piece of meat on his chopsticks, to seal his love.

From now onwards, the annual *tong yin* festival would have a greater significance beyond the roundness of family unity, the red of prosperity, the sweetness of happiness, that the gods promised. The threefold blessing would be superseded by a fourth, the excitement of a growing passion. Gods and ancestors left that out as an irrelevance or something that grew naturally from the first three, and therefore did not deserve a special category of its own in tradition's grand scheme.

This girl was turning into a woman before his eyes. How beautiful she was! How he loved her!

'I love you so much.'

A man never voiced his love for his wife or the woman he was planning to make his wife, in this direct, explicit way. A woman would have blushed and not wanted this breach of tradition on her account. Thus, the words stayed shyly unexpressed in the Venerable One's heart that clearly had still a long way to go in the ongoing secret battle with ancestors. Before long, he would say, to justify his behaviour to the disapproving ancestors, 'Times have changed. The heart must move with the age.'

'Here, let me wipe it off.' The girl's mouth had moved a little, causing a small spill of sugar-water down her chin.

He could have used his handkerchief, but chose the intimate contact of flesh. He gently wiped the small trickle off with his fingers. Then he laid a forefinger on her lower lip. The girl looked down, still blushing. He saw that she was not discomfited by the touch. He traced, very slowly, the entire outline of her mouth with the forefinger.

'You are very beautiful,' he said. He heard the sound of footsteps, and instinctively withdrew.

34
Of Doves and Secret Blood

The imbecile son, to First Wife's great relief, submitted himself to the process of being washed, put into new clothes and having his hair combed and fingernails cut. His unpredictability of behaviour had necessitated a series of bribes – a new abacus, a calendar with bright pictures of women in long, sleek *cheongsams*, a glass paperweight filled with water, a handful of money. He liked the calendar best, and while he was exclaiming excitedly over a picture of a curly haired woman in a pink *cheongsam*, smiling coyly from behind a fan, his mother pulled off, one after the other, his three jackets, then his pyjamas, all smelling horribly, and led him to the bathroom.

The son had been First Wife's most bitter disappointment. Born after several daughters, he was the gods' blessing only to become a curse. For in infancy, he had had a strange illness, which left him cruelly deformed in body and mind. There followed a period of real sorrow such as only a failed wife can feel.

'You have my blessing to take a second wife,' First Wife had said with mournful magnanimity to her husband. But he was kind. He assured her that it was not her fault, and he could wait. When the waiting grew too long, and her womb too anxious to bear any more children, much less a son, she made arrangements to bring in her younger sister as Second Wife.

Over the years that followed, First Wife had stood shamefaced at the head of a line of wives incapable of providing the desired heir. She, her sister, younger by twelve years, Third Wife, supposedly sensuous, with a body that should awaken an ageing man's appetite – all had only daughters thereafter. Their daughters were free of the cruel incapacity, but what was the use of grandsons only on the daughters' side, who did not bear the ancestral name? The Old One's seed would be lost for ever.

But to save it at risk of destroying himself! The Old One did not know what he was doing. He would be cold in his grave before his new wife's body was ready to bear children! She, First Wife, would have to save him from himself. The ancestors had not been exactly helpful. The gods in the Bright Light Temple were the last resort, and this time, the son's presence was needed.

After his bath, the son was put in new clothes and his hair carefully combed with hair cream. Black Dog took a full two hours to make the young man presentable. First Wife, who did the cutting of the fingernails and toenails, was panting and sweating with the effort. By this time, news of the strange activity had spread throughout the Great House. Nobody dared ask any questions, but everybody, on the pretext of doing one thing or another, came near enough to watch, and carry away enough information for speculation. Tali-gelem, as usual more efficient than any of the other spying servants, was able to tell her mistress a great deal.

Whatever was going on? Again, the guess was that it had something to do with the astonishing developments of the last few weeks. The Egg Girl, in one way or another, was turning life upside down for everybody in the Great House. Everything that the Old One and his wives did must be connected with that young sorceress.

The next stage of the very difficult task confronting First Wife was to get the son out of the house and into a trishaw. Here Black Dog once again proved indispensable. He asked the trishawman to wait while he mobilised all his powers of persuasion. Contrary to the general rumour that the Venerable One was too ashamed to show his son and kept him locked in a room, it was the young man himself who chose to remain indoors, contentedly prowling around in his layers of jackets. Once he cut his forehead in a fall, and was forcibly put into a trishaw to go to the hospital for the gash to be stitched up.

Black Dog remembered the son's fascination with a turtle, which a grandson had brought into the house one day. 'Turtle,' he now said to the young man whose eyes lit up immediately.

'Turtle,' he repeated with delight.

Black Dog said, 'If you get into the trishaw with your mother and me now, we will take you to see one hundred turtles.'

'One hundred turtles,' he repeated, and allowed himself instantly to be led to the waiting trishaw. All the way to the Bright Light Temple, he sat docilely, muttering to himself, and clutching the calendar of beautiful women.

Black Dog, shuttling between the Venerable One and his wives on secret errands, promising discretion to all, was least discreet when talking to Third Wife. He always went to her with the intention of saying little, and left wondering whether he had revealed too much.

'Now, hold these joss-sticks, like this,' First Wife instructed her son, who, unused to the brightness of the outside world, had not stopped blinking. They were standing in the temple courtyard before a giant joss-stick urn, which belonged to no one god in particular, and could be used for all purposes. 'Now bow three times.'

The most important part of the day's ceremony came when Black Dog brought in a large cageful of doves. There were at least twenty of them. He had bought them on First Wife's behalf from the temple keepers; they were the most beautiful doves and had cost a lot of money.

First Wife and Black Dog, between them, managed to get the son to go through the entire ceremony with the doves, reminding him, at each step, of the hundred turtles, to get his cooperation. As soon as he had stuck his joss-sticks into the ash in the urn, they got him to open the door of the cage. The doves emerged excitedly, flapped their wings and soared up into the blue sky in a beautiful white flock.

'Whoa!' cried the son, clapping his hands with delight at the sight. For a moment, the sounds from the fluttering wings filled the air, and made him clap with even greater joy. He was no longer blinking but staring out into the vast blue void.

His mother looked at him, and her heart was heavy with sadness. She knew it was right to involve him in this final supplication to the gods. For the poor imbecile son, through no fault of his own, had started this terrible family tragedy, and should have a hand in its closure. His fingers had fumbled clumsily at the cage door, but with the release of the doves, he should also be released from all blame. She too should be freed from all taint of the whole sorry business, and be able to hold her head high. 'My last plea for help,' she would be able to say. 'If none comes, nobody should blame me, neither dead ancestors nor living relatives.'

There would be no closure for the crazy Old One persisting in his madness, but for her, loyal wife of nearly forty years, and for him, unfortunate son for twenty-six years, their work was done, and the gods were witnesses of it.

For the first time since the trouble started, First Wife's eyes filled with tears, as she watched the last dove disappear into the sky. In large drops, they rolled down her cheeks. She wiped them off with the back of her hand and sat down on one of the stone benches in the courtyard. Then she took out a handkerchief from a blouse pocket to blow her nose.

Black Dog stood by, looking at her with much sympathy. He said, 'I'm sorry this is happening to you. You are a good woman and do not deserve it.'

She continued blowing into her handkerchief. The son, still muttering excitedly, was straining his eyes towards a distant cloud in the sky, to catch sight of the last dove.

'Take him to see the turtles now. I'll sit here and rest for a while,' she said to Black Dog.

There was a large enclosure at the back where the holy temple turtles were kept, some of them reputedly a hundred years old. Unlike the doves, they never took part in any temple ceremony, but ate and slept all day in their enclosure.

Black Dog got some *kangkong* for the son to feed the turtles. Still clutching his calendar, the young man threw handfuls of the leafy vegetable to the large, ancient creatures and chuckled with pleasure to watch them stir slowly to life.

There was no rest for First Wife as she sat on the stone bench. She was thinking about a lot of things, and one of them made her face harden in resolve. 'I will do anything he wants except receive her offering of tea.'

If the Old One, at the coming wedding, insisted on the

tea ceremony, and expected her, First Wife, to stretch out her hands, receive the cup of tea from the girl, take the ceremonial sip and then put beside the cup an *ang pow* or gift of jewellery, he was sadly mistaken. She could not in conscience endorse an act of folly so publicly, by means so sanctified by ancestors. She did not care how Second and Third Wife would react to the Old One's wish; she would oppose it with all her might.

She rehearsed in her mind what she would say in the eventuality of the Old One's insistence: 'I have obeyed you all my life, but if you expect me to do this, you might as well give me a rope now to hang myself. There is just so much that even the most loyal wife on earth can do. And there is just so much that ancestors will tolerate.'

'Well?' said Third Wife as soon as Black Dog was free to see her and talk to her in secret. When she heard about the offering of the doves, she shook her head and said, 'Every day hundreds of these expensive birds are released into the sky, and do you think the gods bother at all? Let me tell you this. Our gods have become neglectful and inefficient. We ought to seek the help of other gods who will not let us down.'

So Third Wife went to consult Thai Auntie. Thai Auntie was as remarkable in her appearance as in her magical powers. A huge woman who towered over the men, always dressed impeccably in a bright floral blouse and sarong, her jet black hair arranged in a single, massive roll round her head, and adorned with a bright yellow chrysanthemum, her mouth always red with *ceray* juice, she said all her magical powers had come from her mother and grandmother during her childhood in Thailand.

There she had grown up befriending gods of a lower, but supposedly more powerful order, dark hidden spirits that nourished themselves with human or animal blood and lived in tiny houses built for them. These spirits, being earth-bound, were more understanding of the secret wishes of mortals than the gods and goddesses in their lofty abodes high up in the sky. So small that they could be carried around in tiny bottles hidden in pockets, they yet possessed enormous powers to heal and destroy. They were especially adept at helping women regain their men from other women, provided that their secret instructions were carried out meticulously.

The secret instructions almost invariably involved female blood. Thai Auntie could attest to its efficacy if secretly mixed in the food or drink of the unsuspecting man. She claimed she had thus enabled at least six women to turn their unfaithful husbands into meek, compliant spouses who handed over their entire pay packets every month and never looked at another woman again.

Third Wife counted the days to her next monthly flow.

35
Ultimatum

It was a meeting so fraught with unpleasant tension that everybody wished it to be over quickly, except perhaps the old mother who had tottered up and then stood gaping at the serious faces before her. Like a child, she refused to be led away by a servant, shaking off the obtrusive arm and exclaiming petulantly, 'Stop disturbing me! I want to watch!' And watch she did, with intense fascination as her son, the Venerable One sat facing his three wives seated in a row before him, their eyes fixed on the ground or on their hands tightly clasped in their laps.

The Old One had planned for this meeting, thoroughly distasteful but necessary, to be limited purely to the giving of information and instructions, and nothing else. It would not allow a single question that could open forth a whole slew of querulous responses, especially from Third Wife, who, he could see, was clutching and unclutching a handkerchief on her lap in mounting restlessness.

'The marriage will take place as soon as her parents inform me she is ready.'

Throughout the period of the engagement and marriage, the Old One could not bring himself to mention his new wife by name to the existing three wives, in case, from sheer habit of referring to her as Egg Girl, they said, 'Who?' The insulting appellation of Egg Girl or Village Girl would of course no longer be tolerated, but he knew its use would linger on in the private conversations among the hostile women. Let them be hostile! He wanted the girl, and they could say anything they liked among themselves.

Her readiness. The three wives would glance at each other if they could. The Old One of course meant the advent of first blood. No man in the entire history of marital contracts surely ever had to wait for his bride to become a woman first. No parent in the entire history of nurturing a daughter for a profitable marriage surely waited more eagerly for the event. This much they had to say for the strange Egg Girl – she must have been born under a special concatenation of heavenly planets.

'She will live in the fifth house. Black Dog will supervise the necessary renovations and furnishing. His wife will find suitable servants.'

Indeed, the renovations had already started. They would make the fifth house the largest and best of the row of houses comprising the Great House. It would require more than the two servants allotted to each wife. So Fourth Wife, last in the hierarchy of wives, would take precedence over all of them in terms of comfort and style.

'*Sinseh* will continue to provide tuition, but in the new house.'

The Old One was taking care to give only information that would be necessary for adjustments to old arrangements. The room that the *sinseh* had been using as a classroom for the girl was now available for other purposes. Any of the wives could use it in any way.

'I expect peace and harmony to continue in my household.'

Now he had come to the most sensitive part of the meeting. It was a terse one-sentence statement, but it carried a dire warning: I know all of you are opposed to this union. Create trouble, and earn my displeasure for ever. I have chosen this young girl. Nobody treats her badly.

'I know what I am doing. I am sixty-six years old and expect to live the rest of my years in peace and happiness.'

In a flat, expressionless voice, matched by a severity of face, the Old One was affirming his total control of the present, and confidence in the future. So they were whispering about his madness? It was the closest he had come to true personal victory and happiness. He spoke without looking at anyone; he did not wish to see the reaction of his wives, which, in any case, was irrelevant. They managed to conceal their reaction reasonably well, even Second Wife, who only stole a quick look at First Wife, whose deep displeasure was shown by no more than a slight frown.

Years of peace and happiness? The disdain was written on Third Wife's face. The foolish Old One was waiting for the girl's body to become a woman's. Then he was going to wait for it to bear sons. A futile wait, twice over, for an old man with one foot already in the grave!

By now the three wives no longer showed surprise at the magnitude of his folly. They only waited to see its consequences. Distrusting each other, they would, in the coming months, gather eagerly to share information and assess the extent of these consequences.

'The wedding ceremony will be a simple affair. There will be no feast, no guests, no visitors coming with gifts. There will only be a tea ceremony.'

Tea ceremony! First Wife's external calm hid the turbulence in her soul. The other two wives were less capable of such imperturbability, and shifted about in their seats as they awaited the announcement of the greatest humiliation of this whole tragic affair. All three wives publicly required to welcome the interloper with gifts of money and gold!

'The bride and I will offer respects at the altar of the ancestors, and then offer the tea of respect to Old Mother.'

So the Old One, despite the advanced stage of his madness, could still show some decency. First Wife, who ought to have been relieved, only heaved a sigh of great weariness. She was already planning to have nothing to do with the new wife and never to step into the fifth house. She would, as soon as the wedding was over, review existing arrangements regarding use of common facilities, such as the central kitchen and the rice-grinding millstone, and change them, so that she would never once have to look upon the face of the young usurper. Second Wife and Third Wife could do as they liked; she had made up her mind.

'Ah, yes! I will receive the tea from you and your bride,' chuckled the old mother, delighted at hearing the reference to herself. 'But I can give only a small *ang pow*. We old women don't have much money, you know!'

36
Lucky Numbers

'Come here,' said Ah Bee Koh to Silver Frond. His voice had a different quality, whether instructing or persuading, to match the new status of his daughter as the prospective wife of the town's richest man.

He held in his hands a glass jar containing a number of small wooden sticks. He raised the jar and shook it, comically imitating the rattling sound to signal the start of another round of entertainment for the benefit of his wife and daughters. '*Klock, klock, klock*! Silver Frond, come here! Everybody, come and see!'

He put the jar close to his wife's ears and shook it noisily, laughing to see her frown and push it away.

The man was in a very good mood nowadays, because he had much money in his pockets, with the prospect of more. The day before, he had been summoned by Black Dog to the Great House for a face-to-face meeting with the Venerable One. It could only mean one thing: the handing over of the bride-money. All the way to the Great House, he had rehearsed his demand for the much dreamt about coconut plantation or shophouse. 'She is a very precious and rare daughter. We have had many offers for her ...'

But standing before the Venerable One, who had the sternest expression imaginable, Ah Bee Koh had forgotten the demand. He became nervous as the old piercing eyes were fixed on him and at last stammered, 'Her mother and I leave the matter of the bride-money entirely to you.' Whereupon the Venerable One, without saying a word, opened a drawer, took out an envelope of money and handed it to him. Receiving it with an effort at nonchalance, he experienced an inward thrill at its promising touch.

The Venerable One, still looking very stern, had then said, 'It is good that you have mentioned her mother. Silver Frond is a good daughter and does not want her mother to work so hard. This money is to free your wife from all that washing and to buy the medicine she needs for her illness.' He had added, never taking his eyes from Ah Bee Koh's face, 'The money is not for you to spend on your drinks and gambling.'

The Venerable One would have preferred avoiding altogether the face-to-face meeting with the despicable father, but the importance of the coming event had necessitated this face-saving procedure for the daughter. For the next disbursement of the bride-money, he had bypassed the man altogether, and got Black Dog to hand a similarly bulging envelope directly to the mother, reminding him to make clear that it was solely for her to take her daughter to a goldsmith's shop to buy the requisite wedding jewellery.

The next day, Ah Bee Soh got her foster sister to accompany her and Silver Frond to Poh Seng Goldsmith, to help with the selection of suitable bridal gold chains, bracelets and rings. The girl had fidgeted and blushed through the two hours in the shop, conscious that the shop assistants were whispering and nudging each other, and were sure to contribute to the gossip circulating in the town about the coming wedding.

The gossip-mongers seemed to know even about the private rebuke to the father handed out with the bride-money. They imitated the Old One's stern voice: 'The money is not for you to spend on your drinks and your gambling.'

Ah Bee Koh had chafed under the insult as he rode home on his bicycle, muttering, 'Does he think just because he's rich, he can ...' Between the annoyance on the one hand and the reassuring feel of the bulky envelope in his pocket on the other, he became somewhat confused. But as soon as a very pleasant picture began to shape in his mind, of paying for a round of drinks at his favourite beer shop, and being thanked profusely for the treat, the annoyance vanished and he felt at ease with the world once more, thinking affectionately of the daughter who was making all this possible.

On reaching home, he had duly handed over a large portion of the money to his wife, and then had been struck by an idea of how he might reclaim it, multiplied many times over. Excitedly, he had then gone to his friend's house and borrowed the jar of sticks.

'Quick, Silver Frond, shake them out!'

A bride-to-be supposedly enjoyed the gods' blessing, and could transmit part of it to others by shaking out lucky lottery numbers for them. Ah Bee Koh and his friends had previously used the sticks, each bearing a number carved on it, in any number of ways to procure lucky numbers – putting them in a heap on the body of a newborn baby and watching to see which fell off, getting a very old man celebrating his eightieth birthday to shake them out, getting a pregnant cat to run and knock down the jar and spill them out. It did not matter if the numbers did not strike; there was always another time.

He and his friends used to go to the cemetery in the dark of night to conjure up the dead to give the lucky numbers, but they had stopped the practice when one of the friends had suddenly and mysteriously fallen ill. Thereafter they decided to concentrate on the living.

Among the living, a bride-to-be offered the best hope.

Silver Frond laughed nervously as she put her hand into the jar and brought out four sticks, one after the other, for the Four-Digit Lottery that was her father's favourite.

'What about me? Let me try!' cried Silver Flower, and was immediately followed by Silver Pearl also crying out loudly, 'Me too! Me too!'

'No, no,' shouted their father with a great show of alarm. 'Don't you dare put your hands into the jar! Both of you are quite useless. Wait till you are about to get married, like your sister.'

'She can't get married till she gets her first blood!' cried Silver Pearl knowledgeably, and was smacked on the head by her mother who said, 'Don't talk about things that don't concern you!'

Ah Bee Soh had been brewing nourishing herbs regularly for her eldest daughter to hasten that great event. Her spirits had improved with the new freedom from hard labour, and the positive effects of the medicine from Ah Liang's shop that her daughter made her take a few times a week.

An old man's money had created much cheer among the family, who could look forward to more of it through the daughter and sister so spectacularly singled out by fortune. But it was understood that nobody, at this stage, should say anything about it. Even the free-talking Silver Pearl only dared whisper about it to her sister as they lay on their mattress on night – 'Silver Frond says she will have enough money to pay for my operation' – and mentioned a sum that she could only understand in relation to the weekly egg money or their mother's monthly pay from the washing.

Ah Bee Koh read out the numbers on the sticks in a very loud voice, playfully pulled his favourite daughter's nose, and said, 'I knew right from the time you were born that you would bring me good luck.'

Ah Bee Soh rolled her eyes, shook her head and said, 'Your father's talking nonsense as usual.' Her manner towards her daughter had changed too; she was linked with her husband in a new respect, almost awe.

Silver Flower said, 'I want the blue hairclip; you gave Silver Pearl your purse *and* your coconut shell money box,' deciding that this was the best time to claim more of the possessions her sister was generously giving away. She had already got a large stock of comic books, notebooks and pencils.

Silver Pearl said peevishly, 'You took the red hairclip *and* the pencil sharpener,' and was about to say more when she suddenly stopped. Her mouth fell open, and she dragged her mother away into a room in great excitement to communicate something of the most urgent nature.

'It's come,' she whispered, wide-eyed. 'I saw it trickle down her leg. It's come!'

And it was at this moment that Silver Frond, wondering about her sister's strange behaviour, suddenly sensed a wetness, looked down and saw the red smear on the inside of her left thigh.

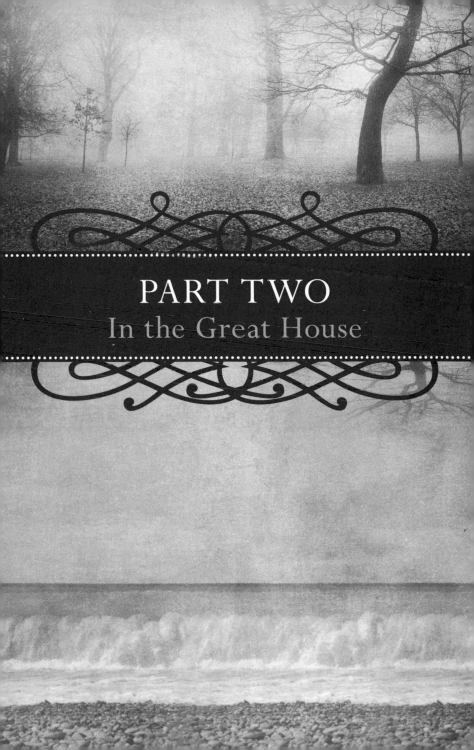

PART TWO

In the Great House

1
Has It Happened Yet?

There were four sets of spies from the three wives. (Third Wife, besides making use of her maidservant Tali-gelem, had mobilised the help of Black Dog's wife, who, in her new position as a matron of sorts to see to the needs of the young bride, was particularly useful for the purpose.) Each head spy had her own assistants, so nothing that happened in the Fifth House, so resplendently set up for the new wife, would remain unknown.

'They had porridge, salt fish and braised pork for breakfast this morning.'

'She was wearing a gold bangle.'

'Her mother visited, and went away with a tiffin carrier of food.'

'She coughed and the Old One was all tender concern. He called for some cough mixture and personally poured out a spoonful, which he gently coaxed her to take.'

'Her eyebrows have been newly plucked.'

'She said something and they laughed together.'

'This morning, he lit a joss-stick for her, and they prayed together before the ancestors.'

Nothing was too trivial to be reported. From the Great House, the ripples of curiosity about the besotted old bridegroom and the young bride whose first flow he had awaited so eagerly, spread out through the neighbourhood and the town. Oldest and youngest. Richest and poorest. Lustiest *yang* and tenderest *ying*. The wonder of the match could only be expressed in breathless superlatives.

'Watch for the rise of her belly under the blouse,' the gossipers whispered. 'If the gods are kind, it will be a *normal* male child.'

'What belly? What child? It seems he's still waiting to consummate his union with his child bride!' hooted the others.

Not even the most ingenious of the spies would have first-hand knowledge to confirm or deny the event. Of course if First Wife had been fully cooperative instead of retreating to the far edges of sullen indifference, she could have provided the white bridal trousers for the wedding night and then graciously taken them back the next morning, to wash, hang up and thus confirm not only union but the bride's pristineness. The garment would flap proudly in the air for all to see. First Wife had announced her own sister's virginal intactness with joy, and Third Wife's, years later, with enough goodwill. But this time, she had said bitterly, 'My help was not needed then, it won't be needed now,' and carried on with her life in the Great House as if nothing had happened.

So speculation on the intriguing matter of the union remained just that.

But in more general matters, it was amazing how the spies, with so little opportunity, could glean so much. The Venerable One, anticipating the assault on the privacy of his young bride, had virtually sealed off the Fifth House. It had its own kitchen, stove, stock of firewood, its own grinding stones, pounding stones and pestles. All the windows of the bridal chamber were heavily curtained; the door was kept closed at all times; a new bathroom had been built so that the bride would never have to use the common bathroom again. The village girl, who only a month ago had to walk through darkness across a stretch of rough ground if she wanted to use the lavatory at night, now had an elegant aluminium chamber pot regularly emptied in the morning by a servant. Her only contact with the outside world so far had been with her family, and the old *sinseh*, who continued to come for lessons, held in a small room adjacent to the bridal chamber.

But the Old One had unknowingly weakened this massive structure of privacy by employing Black Dog's wife as attendant for his bride. Giving the impression of total detached professionalism as she went about her work of attending to the bride's wardrobe, washing her hair with scented flower petals, cooking her favourite food, massaging her body with scented oil, emptying her chamber pot, the lady proved the most indefatigable of spies, observing, listening, and storing every detail so efficiently, that later, when she poured it all out into the eager ears of Third Wife, it was as if the latter had been a first-hand observer herself.

The bride's new exalted position was invariably coloured by her ignominious origins. Black Dog's wife, despite her suspicion of a growing affinity between her husband and Third Wife, was cooperatively going to the enemy every day to report yet another manifestation of village crudity, readily joining in the malicious laughter. The fine food, clothes, and furniture – the child-bride tiptoed in awe around them, not knowing how to react. The smell of the pig sty and the chicken dung and the squalor of her life in that little hut with the earth floor – how could she ever shake it all off ?

Once she looked so lost in her new surroundings, whispered Black Dog's wife, that she stood very still, unable to utter a sound, a forefinger pressed hard in her mouth, like a frightened child. Thus had she remained a long time. Another time, she accidentally broke a porcelain vase and, in her terror, hid the broken pieces under a cupboard. But the giveaway sign was the terrified forefinger in the mouth.

She always looked to the Old One for guidance, and he was all patience, all tenderness. Black Dog's wife would cast a sideways glance at Third Wife at this particular point in her narration, and silently revelled in the lady's jealous rage: 'Now you know how I feel when I hear about my husband spending long hours with you, and buying you *char kuay tiao.*' For it was Black Dog's wife's greatest grievance that while her husband never thought to buy her supper, he had on several occasions gone on his bicycle to the night food stalls to buy Third Wife's favourite fried noodles for her, once even in the rain. *Her husband had braved the rain to buy another woman supper.* When confronted, he had denied everything hotly and told her to shut her mouth.

Black Dog's wife had her own spies; the loyal Tali-gelem, a compulsive retailer of other people's secrets, was unaware of any disloyalty to her mistress, when, in the pleasant state induced by a delicious flow of gossip and sugared plums, she fell into the trap of Black Dog's wife's subtle questioning, and let slip a few useful items.

'Has it happened yet?'

This was Third Wife's invariable question. She would have foregone all other information for this. Jealousy had woven itself into the tight fabric of her deliberations and become textured with cool calculation: as long as consummation had not taken place, there was still hope – for what, she could not exactly tell, except that it would be a state far preferable to the hell she was going through.

'It is as if the demons have strapped me to a rice millstone and are slowly grinding up my bones!' she sobbed in a moment of unspeakable anguish, referring to that most horrible of tortures in the underworld, graphically depicted in myths and cautionary tales.

The woman who causes hell to others soon lives in one of her own, thought Black Dog's wife gleefully, remembering yet another occasion of pain, when someone had told her of seeing Third Wife actually sitting on her husband's desk painting her fingernails, while he watched and smiled.

She had every intention of unleashing all the demons of jealousy's hell upon the enemy, an assault that would be all the more effective for being done through the back doors of subtle insinuation and quiet flattery. 'You have been so good to him, cleaning his ears all these years, and yet last night, he asked her, with all her inexperience, to do it. She asked me for an ear-cleaner, and I had to go searching for it.'

The ultimate vengeance would be to report not only the consummation, but its fruitful result, to see the enemy utterly shattered and sent back home to her parents: 'Her periods have stopped. She is with child. From the shape of her growing belly, I can tell it will be a male child. I saw him touch her belly so lovingly.'

Black Dog's wife's sharp eyes sought evidence on the bedsheets and in the chamber pots, but so far, she could report nothing. 'It has not happened yet,' she would say, and add, again casting the sly glance to watch for Third Wife's reaction, 'An old rooster, ready to burst in its lust, waiting patiently for the pullet to be ready. Don't you think he has gone too far in his love for her?'

In Third Wife's desperation to know, she managed to procure a piece of the bride's used underclothing. She studied it closely and expertly, even sniffing it a few times. But, alas, the vital matter of the marital union continued to elude her.

'I promise to tell you as soon as it happens,' said Black Dog's wife whose plan of revenge centred on this single obsession of Third Wife.

The obsession sought another source. Third Wife went to the old *sinseh* after he had finished his lessons with the bride, and asked, 'How is Fourth Wife? Is she well? Did she look tired and pale this morning?' The assumption was that tiredness and paleness the morning after marked the trauma of a child-bride's first experience. The old *sinseh* muttered something and left in a hurry, more anxious than ever to avoid going anywhere near the dangerously swirling pool of women's discontent. Each time he saw Third Wife approaching, he fled.

But his much younger and friendlier assistant who came to take his place during the weeks he was away in China, was more forthcoming in the information. Mistaking Third Wife's questions for genuine concern for the newcomer in the Great House, and rather enjoying her company and the sight of the beauty-mole above the right side of her upper lip, he amiably reported on the bride's health and spirits, always finishing his description with praise of her childlike beauty and eagerness to learn. He said he had never met a female who was so interested in learning.

'So you too are captivated by the young bride?' teased Third Wife. 'I don't blame you. It seems everybody is enchanted by the village girl.'

'But she doesn't have your beautiful mole,' said the young *sinseh* slyly and looked at her boldly. He had heard about the Venerable One's attractive third wife with the self-given foreign name, and was now very gratified by her seeking him out. 'Come to think of it, her beauty is still unshaped and lacking in character. Unlike yours.'

Third Wife smiled bewitchingly, taking care that the admired mole was in full view, then gave a short laugh and walked away. He was not relevant to her purpose, at least for the time being, and she turned her thoughts elsewhere.

The past months had drained her of health and beauty. As she pondered on more effective strategies of coping with loss and the ultimate humiliation of being relieved of her status as ear-cleaner, she continued to receive information from her network of spies about the Old One's absorbing love for his young bride. In her turn, she retold as much of the information to First Wife as she thought useful for her purpose, pointedly ignoring Second Wife.

First Wife always listened intently, then said curtly, 'Why are you telling me all this? I have nothing to do with them,' maintaining both curiosity and indifference in equal measure.

The curiosity overcame the indifference at one point, for her to ask, 'Has it happened yet?'

But nobody could tell her.

2
Of Course It Has Not Happened Yet!

'Haven't you noticed?' said Second Wife excitedly to First Wife, her mouth full of half-chewed melon seeds. She pointedly ignored Third Wife, who was sitting next to her sister. Responding to the insult with cool nonchalance, Third Wife continued to play with the rings on her fingers.

In growing excitement, Second Wife stopped chewing and repeated, 'Haven't you noticed? Haven't you noticed?'

'Noticed what?' said her sister coldly. 'Why don't you speak properly?'

'She waggles her bottom when she walks,' said Second Wife, and she put down her paper bag of melon seeds and did a brief demonstration. Enormously fat, Second Wife was a natural clown. First Wife and Third Wife laughed despite themselves. 'The Waddling Duck Walk. It is because she thinks the hard thing is still between her legs and is trying to shake it off. So it *has* happened.'

'How is it you have suddenly become so clever?' said First Wife. Between habitual seriousness and present amusement, her face became criss-crossed with frowning and laughing creases, and took on a comicality of its own.

'It must be all the melon seeds you've been eating,' said Third Wife. 'And the salted plums. And the pickled leeks.

Why don't you show us the Waddling Duck Walk again? You looked so cute!' And she looked pointedly at the enormous buttocks, which were growing more enormous because of the endless snacking.

It was the only instance when resentment of the fourth wife had actually brought the other three together in laughing camaraderie.

'Ssh,' said First Wife suddenly. The feeble-minded son, his unwashed layers of jackets emanating smells as well as puffs of dust, had shuffled in. He stood still, flapping his long ungainly arms, blinking and looking at no one in particular. Some said that his father's marriage had made his weak mind even weaker, for he was not used to change, and here was the greatest change that life in the Great House had ever seen. For one thing, he was not allowed to go anywhere near the newly renovated bridal Fifth House to play with some of the grandchildren. It was all so unfair.

'Who gave you that?' First Wife's eyes had detected a comic book in the young man's hand. Everybody gave him food, toys, pencils, anything to keep him amused, as he wandered about in the Great House, going from one wife's domain to another. The comic book was different and could have come from only one person.

Usually incapable of responding to questions, the son answered promptly, 'Fourth Mother.'

The wives looked at each other, in a sharpening of alertness. Any action of the new bride to any member in the household would have to be interpreted, now that she had achieved her ambition of being part of the Great House, in the light of a greater ambition to achieve total dominance.

'When did she give you this?'

'What did she say?'

'Was Father present?'

'Did she give you anything else?'

But the feeble-minded son had lost interest and drifted away, still clutching the comic book.

Second Wife said, with a little shriek of excitement, 'Of course it hasn't happened yet! Can't you see?'

Her sister looked at her in cold severity. 'You are behaving very oddly this morning, and talking nonsense. What are you saying now?'

Third Wife shook her head, clucked her tongue and smiled with pitying superiority.

'She was not scared to face him and give him the comic book. If she were pregnant ...'

The proof was clear enough in Second Wife's head, but in the face of her sister's impatience and Third Wife's sneering disdain, she suddenly became aware of how difficult it was to put a clever thought into words for others to understand, and decided to abandon all effort at explaining further. But secretly she congratulated herself on the cleverness of her reasoning, to arrive at the irrefutable fact that it had not yet happened.

For if it had, the young bride would be pregnant, and if she were pregnant, she would have been mindful of the belief that no pregnant woman should look upon a deformed creature, whether human or animal, for fear the deformity would be replicated in the child growing in her womb, and if the young bride were mindful of this belief, she would never have come face to face with the Old One's misshapen son, and if she never faced him, she could not have given him the comic book.

Tired out by the complicated logic, Second Wife fell asleep and had a dream.

In the dream, it had happened, for the young bride was walking around with an enormous belly under her blouse. They were in the marketplace when they came upon a large wicker basket of live crabs. The crabs were huge, with long powerful claws that waved about menacingly. 'Don't!' Second Wife cried in horror, as the bride lifted one up with her fingers and said she wanted to buy it, for her mother to make crab curry, which she liked very much. 'Don't!' she screamed. But it was too late. The crab image had already imprinted itself on the child in the womb. The bride rushed home to give birth and Second Wife, who assisted in the birth, screamed to see the newborn baby waving huge claws in the air instead of arms and legs.

Second Wife woke up panting in terror. She later confided her dream to her sister who only said, with the usual impatience, 'The one who thinks nonsensical thoughts by day has nonsensical dreams by night.'

3
The Bride and the Groom Go Mor-Dung

'So we were not good enough! Only Fourth Wife is good enough to have a *mor-dung* wedding dress and *mor-dung* jewels!'

Of all Third Wife's grievances, this was the greatest, because it formed the central point of every piece of gossip and speculation. The Old One, after having observed tradition so faithfully over the years, had decided to go modern with his young bride.

It had started with the wedding photograph. There was the usual traditional one, after the offering of tea to the old mother, and the paying of respects to the ancestors at their altars, in which both groom and bride wore the formal, high-collared, silk costumes of their ancestors. They stood stiffly together for the photograph, an old, handsome, white-haired man and his very young wife, her youth undisguised by the severe hairstyle of a tight bun, an equally severe *cheongsam* with a high collar and stiff sleeves, and a massive load of antiquated earrings, chains, bangles, rings and brooches utterly alien to a young body and smooth skin.

That cache of old rare jewels, passed down the generations, meant only for progeny bearing the ancestral name, was a matter for special chastisement of the Old One for his folly. He had brought out the entire cache from an old metal safe that not even First Wife had seen, and, like the emperor who would cast his empire at the feet of a favourite concubine, had given it all to the village girl.

'Her parents are sure to pawn them!' Second Wife had shrieked.

'That is none of your business or mine,' First Wife had replied angrily, ready to vent the full load of her seething rage upon her sister.

'But it is our business; we are the senior wives!' cried Second Wife, whose lethargy seemed to have been stirred into a surprising independence of thought and spirit by the crisis in their midst. In her agitation, she began pushing and shoving her sister, while her face grew red and her voice cracked in an anguish of tears.

'Stop it! Have you gone mad?' cried First Wife. 'Has madness come to everybody in this house?'

Only First Wife, as a young bride, so many years ago, had had the honour of wearing the ancestral jewels on the wedding day; only she could have carried out a proper inventory of the glittering collection, but when pressed to do so by Second Wife and Third Wife, she had dismissed them both with an impatient wave of the hand, 'If he has the hardness of heart to thus insult his three wives, we should have the dignity of spirit to say, "So what is all this to us? Let the ancestors judge eventually." '

She would henceforth devote herself to her dim-witted, neglected son, who was becoming more confused by the changes taking place around him. The poor young man had been nothing to his proud, disappointed father all these years; now, banned from going to the Fifth House in case he did something to frighten the young bride, he had become worse than nothing. He had become an intruder in the very house in which he was born. It only added to his confusion that at the same time he was quickly led away by the servants in the Fifth House, he was plied with gifts of food and toys by the bride.

'Don't go! Don't accept anything from her!' his mother had said in exasperation. 'Don't you know when you're not wanted?'

Angry first on behalf of the ancestors, then of the cruelly treated son, First Wife continued to be selfless in her bitter struggle for redress, and could even, after the short period of a month, offer joss-sticks and prayers on behalf of the cruel husband who had caused it all.

'He is a good man. I have known him for so many years. His madness is a chastisement from the gods for some wrongdoing in an earlier life.'

Till the end of her life, she believed that the unsuitable marriage with the young village girl was a temporary aberration.

The temporary aberration was to last many years, by which time all the hair on her head had gone grey. But this loyal woman was unswerving in her belief that her husband's basic goodness had only been suspended, not destroyed, that he appreciated and loved her most of all, and would eventually show it, even if it was only on his deathbed.

First Wife, whose dignity had suffered most in the whole tragedy of the Old One's folly, would have it restored most satisfactorily in the end, when she could truly say, 'Let the ancestors bear witness: he loved me most of all. Before his last breath, he acknowledged me as the best wife of all.' Her strength had lain in her faith in the ancestors, and that faith was fully vindicated.

But that first year of the fourth wife was the worst for her, bringing nothing but pain and humiliation.

First Wife refused to hear any more about the ancestral jewels taken out of the secret safe, or about the second gift of jewels, bought from a jewellery shop just a week before the wedding, because the bridegroom wanted to go *mor-dung* to please his young bride.

As soon as the photograph with the traditional bridal clothes and old jewels was taken, the bride and groom, with unseemly haste, had put on modern attire for a second wedding photograph, to everyone's astonishment. The groom now wore the suit and bow-tie of the Western gentleman, and the bride the long white gown, lace veil, and high-heeled shoes of the Western woman. She carried a large bouquet of flowers, which almost covered the entire front portion of her dress. Her hairstyle had undergone a similarly startling transformation; the bun had been loosened into a flow of hair down her back and on her forehead rested a large kiss curl.

Whose idea had it been? How could the Venerable One have cast off a lifetime of conservative habits? But then, there was no knowing to what lengths a sixty-seven-year-old groom would go to indulge his fifteen-year-old bride.

But it was once again the matter of jewels that had provoked the strongest reaction. In the second photograph, none of the traditional jewels was to be seen. Instead, modern diamond earrings hung from her lobes, a diamond-and-gold necklace, in the latest style, adorned her neck and diamond rings her fingers.

It must have been her mother's idea, so that she could boast about it all over her village later: 'My daughter is a *mor-dung* wife, unlike the other wives!' The Old One, who had never worn a Western suit in his life, had acquiesced because of the continuing spell cast by the young witch from Sim Bak Village. Just when and how had he acquired this entirely modern set of jewels for her? How much had it cost? Third Wife had even sent her spies to the town's goldsmiths to find out, but they had returned none the wiser. There was the persistent rumour of the Old One shrewdly slipping off by himself to a pawnshop one evening and buying up a huge cluster of unredeemed gold chains and bracelets.

Third Wife had shrieked in anger at Tali-gelem for having failed her in so significant an area of information.

The two wedding pictures hung side by side on the main wall of the bridal chamber. Black Dog's wife had reported that the bride liked the modern one better: she had actually taken it down from the wall several times to have a close look at it, while the Old One, drawn deeper than ever into her spell, as if fed ten times the potent brew of secret blood recommended by Thai Auntie, had stood by her, smiling and nodding.

4
Waiting

It was nobody's business but their own. The Old One was aware of the unspoken speculations swirling around him and his bride, particularly the lubricious ones centred on the consummation. In the coffee-shops, at the food stalls in the hawker centres, at the vegetable and fish stalls in the marketplace, even in the compounds of temples, he knew the gossip-mongers were out in force. The women were the worst. His many plantations and his fleet of lorries afforded their husbands employment, and his many properties an affordable roof over their heads, but their fervid envy of the young village girl, whose fabulous fate their own daughters could never hope to have, made them reckless with their speculations. 'It is said that her mother lied about her first blood. He may have to wait longer than he thinks!'

But in his presence, they were hushed with respect. They tiptoed with breathless deference around him and his young wife during the few times they were seen together in public. 'Good morning, Ah Cheng Peh. Good morning, Ah Cheng Soh. How are you? Have you eaten?' She was far too young to be addressed as *Ah Soh*, muchless *Ah Sim*, but the unusualness of the marriage had entailed this anomaly. 'Imagine,' whispered the gossipers, 'the son who is older than her has to call her

"Fourth Mother", and the three grandchildren, who are about her age, have to call her "Fourth Grandmother"!'

One particularly bold neighbour had gone beyond the usual polite greeting to remark, 'How well you look this morning, Ah Cheng Peh! And how beautiful your bride looks!'

The Venerable One responded to this piece of obtrusiveness with a very curt 'Errmm,' while his bride smiled awkwardly, blushed deeply and looked down. The sly nudges and suppressed giggles, which he sensed even after they had left the scene, told of a continuing curiosity common among idle, mean-minded folk. Well, let them talk as much as they liked!

Once believing that the gossip-mongers would be the greatest bane of his new life, the Venerable One had very soon after the wedding, much to his own surprise, learned to ignore them, and even better, to enjoy their frustration at seeing him and his bride so happy.

He had told her, just before the wedding, 'You will not be much loved in the Great House or the neighbourhood. Unkind things will be whispered about you. But as long as you have my love, you have everything. And as long as I have harmony in my household, and everybody keeps the peace, that is all I am asking.'

That piece of advice constituted all he wanted to say on the subject, and he was glad to have done with it, and to concentrate on more pleasant matters. The most pleasant was showering attention on his beloved. It was as if a natural desire to please women had disguised itself as cold reserve through three wives to emerge as abundant generosity to the fourth. The generosity was less in the gifts than the patience. He chuckled at the thought of the ancestors' horror that the very virtue they had urged for peaceful and prosperous living had become a vice to mark the first black sheep in the long illustrious line.

How they must be turning in their tombs! Who had ever heard of a man patiently waiting for a woman to experience her first flow to marry her and then waiting further through countless nights for her readiness to do her marital duty?

It was the woman, of course, who should do the waiting. The bride should wait for the groom to start, to stop, to fall off her body at last in exhausted sleep, and then only, in the silence of the darkness, could she attend to her own body and the wonder and pain of the breaking in. Over the weeks, months and years, she should do more waiting, lying on the bed in the darkness till he came to her, and if she was lucky, the waiting would not be tinged with the fear of failure. For a husband, supported by a thousand years of tradition, could say to his wife, 'What's the use of all this, if you never give me a son?' and she would have to say, 'Then you have my blessing to take another wife.'

Silver Frond's mother, backed by the Goddess Pearly Face, had summarised all these truths in brief, terse advice: 'Let your husband do as he likes. Otherwise you will only have yourself to blame if he takes another wife.'

The advice ringing in her ears, she had been terrified beyond words on the wedding night, curling up foetally into a tight little ball, still in her rich bridal clothes, at a far corner of the bed in the darkness. There she lay, very still, hardly breathing. He had whispered, with all the gentleness he could muster, 'Don't be afraid, don't be afraid,' and waited patiently for her to uncurl, like a little frightened creature when it thinks there is no more danger. He waited a long time, and fell asleep.

Then he awoke to hear more sniffling from the refuge at the far end of the bed, under a thick blanket and a pile of pillows. He would have been much mollified to know that this time it was less the fear of a man's touch than an overwhelming sense of a dereliction of duty.

The bride had steeled herself for the crucial moment, for both her mother and the Goddess Pearly Face had told her, in no uncertain terms, what she must do and must not do. 'You can only refuse, and even then, very gently,' they had counselled, 'if you have the monthly period, since this will bring a man bad luck.' They had further advised, 'You must do the undressing yourself, to signal your readiness. Let your fingers undo the buttons ever so demurely, one by one. Let there be a smile on your face as you do so.' But when the moment came, she had failed her husband. Her blouse only half unbuttoned, she had fled to the far corner of the bed.

'Are you still making him wait?' her mother and the Goddess Pearly Face were sure to ask in the following days, and for an answer, she would have to look down and nod in shame. She could never tell her mother, but she might bring herself to confide eventually to the goddess, about that shameful dream, two nights before the wedding, of naked bodies, hers cowering in fear at the approach of his, even more monstrous than that of the horrible man at the well, not so long ago, when he had unbuttoned his trousers and lunged at her. She awoke from the dream, trembling all over.

In the darkness, the Old One lay very still and listened to the small troubled noises coming from his bride, a child suddenly thrown into the bewildering world of adult needs and duties. He wanted to move to her side of the bed and hold her tightly and reassuringly, but he chose, wisely, to remain still, and wait for her whimpering to subside.

'You must never be afraid of me, because I will never do anything to harm you,' he said finally, more kindly than ever.

He thought he detected a slight movement towards him, and then, with all tenderness, he moved towards her, to smooth her hair and pat her back, like the loving adult bent on comforting a troubled child.

One arm was bare, and he raised a hand to caress it. It met a rise of goose-bumps. The hand moved down the arm, then a leg, in slow exploration, and found that her whole body had broken out in a prickling of pure terror.

He removed his hand from her body.

'Are you cold?' he said softly, and draped a blanket over her. But he knew it was not cold, but the sheer terror of the child-bride on her wedding night. It did not displease him; on the contrary, it gave him a deeply satisfying sense of being first and sole possessor of an untouched treasure, all his to cherish and, because it was untouched, to shape to his own precise wishes.

A perfectly carved figurine in translucent jade. An opening flower waiting to surrender its full beauty and scent. A gently ripening peach on its branch, its succulence gathering to a peak.

No analogy, taken from the romantic poems he had secretly read in his youth, away from the severe eyes of his father, would be sufficient. Unlike the uncouth bridegrooms sometimes portrayed in Liang Por's stories, whose rude breath and brutal touch fell upon delicate figurine, flower or fruit before its time, snapping it, he would be patient, and await her readiness. That moment, when it came, would be supreme proof of their love for each other. Meanwhile, let the gossip-mongers say what they would!

He heard his bride say, in a frightened whisper, from her corner of the bed, 'I need to go to the bathroom.' In the abject misery of mounting terror, she was suddenly aware of the need to relieve herself and was asking his permission. The bathroom was on the ground floor; she had forgotten that a new, elegant-looking chamber-pot had been placed under the bed, precisely to spare her the trouble of going downstairs in the night.

He reminded her, very gently, of the chamber-pot. In the darkness, he listened to the sounds of her getting out of bed, of the aluminium receptacle being pulled out, of her small, bare feet crossing a whole length of floor as she carried it to a far corner, of the rustle of clothes being taken off, finally, of the relieving itself, which she did in small, well-controlled spurts, in a brave effort to suppress the sound of this embarrassing act in a man's presence.

Then he listened to the sounds of her return. Still in her bridal clothes, she resumed her curled position in a corner of the bed, and was soon fast asleep.

5
Gift

'I have a surprise for you.' Silver Frond, in an exuberance of joy, had actually come up from behind the Old One and covered his eyes tightly with her hands, a form of play she had enjoyed with her sisters, prior to the giving of surprise presents of food and toys. She liked it when the sisters pulled off her fingers, one by one, then looked round eagerly for the gifts. She had done it once with her father, but never with her mother.

There was a rich gift for her husband, tucked under her arm, which she put into his hands and said he was not allowed to see until she removed her hands from his eyes.

She preferred the day with its bustling activities, to the night, when, with the switching off of the lights and the lying down side by side on the bed, still adorned with the ornate, satin-and-velvet bridal curtains and cushions two months into the marriage, the bustle ended and the ominous silence started all over again. She would be totally still, staring at the dark ceiling, neither turned towards him, for that might falsely signal readiness when the goose-pimples were still appearing on her body, nor turning away from him, for that might provoke displeasure, which was the last thing she wanted in her married life.

No such quandary troubled her in the day. She would break out of her inhibitions, like a small creature crawling out of old skin into bright sunshine, to enjoy the many pleasures surrounding her – oh, there were so many wonderful things to eat and see and save for telling her sisters later!

During the day, touch, whether initiated by him or herself, brought no fear nor discomfort. In full view of the outside world, she actually held her husband's hand when she talked to him. She knocked his back with her fists to ease the aches, making him first sit down on a comfortable stool. Her tight hard fists, with the pugilist's ferocity, rained blows along his shoulder blades and down his spine, and she smiled to see the pleasure on his face, as he sat still with his eyes closed. She had become quite an expert at back-knocking, and had a secret ambition to become an expert at ear-cleaning as well. One of these days she would surprise him.

That dreaded desire, which arose instantly even with accidental touch, came only with the night. It was remarkable how careful she had to be, moving her hand away so slowly, by imperceptible degrees, if it happened to touch his, as they lay on the bridal bed. She tried not to use the chamber pot at night; if she had to, she moved softly out of bed, and pulled the receptacle out ever so gently. She had mastered the trick of lining it with old newspaper, so that the noise, steam and smell of a woman's urine, possibly provocative to a sleeping man, was successfully suppressed.

She wished it would always be daylight.

'You may open your eyes now!' she exclaimed excitedly. It was fortunate that no spy was at hand to report the act of playfulness. 'See, we were right. This marriage is no more than child's play. The Fifth House is no more than a doll's house where grown-ups can become children all over again. The Old One has made himself a laughing stock for ever.'

'What do you have for me?' he said, not letting go of her hand, for he liked the touch of her soft skin. She pulled the gift from under her arm and handed it to him. He surveyed it with pride and joy. 'Ah, no wonder you didn't allow me to go into the classroom!'

On a scroll of red paper, under the supervision of the young *sinseh*, she had copied out, in her best hand, a poem, which she now read out proudly to him, standing beside him and allowing him to press her to his side. He listened without the least bit of the embarrassment of the past, when he had received gifts from his wives with an uneasy 'errmm' and wished that no more acknowledgement was expected. With his young bride, he wanted the giving and the receiving to be expanded into the feast of unabashed delights he was daily enjoying. He had become a glutton at love's table. As he listened to her, he felt something of the thrill, nearly two years ago, when he had come upon her in the cemetery, a child-fairy dancing and singing to herself.

Someone had remarked that he looked twenty years younger. He had gone instantly to take a sly look at himself in the mirror, and felt immensely satisfied. Already a handsome old man, he was set to look and feel even better with the coming years. Ginseng, birdsnest, rare fungus, black chicken double-boiled with herbs – these were nothing for rejuvenescence compared to the presence of youth's innocence and joy. Already there was sly banter among the old men in the town as to how they too should avail themselves of such an elixir.

He was himself tempted to banter with that formidable August Ancestor, who still visited him in his dreams at night: 'You warned me of dire consequences. How dire can consequences be if the rheumatism in my left leg has gone, if I have energy to walk twice the distance every morning, and white hair is turning to black on one side of my head?'

'*Tchah!*' the ancestor snorted in disdain. 'You are an old fool, and that is much worse than a young fool.'

He had the delicacy to refrain from retorting, 'A happy fool, nevertheless!'

'I have a surprise for you.'

Now it was his turn to please her with an unexpected gift. Silver Frond, coming out of a lesson during which she had made the young *sinseh* search for another poem for her to read and copy, saw him waiting for her.

'Come,' he said. 'Follow me.'

Very fond of surprises, and sensing a massive one from this very generous and loving man, she followed him. Suddenly she remembered an occasion – she must have been five or six years old at the time – when her father too had said, 'Come, I have something for you,' and she had slipped her hand into his, and followed him to the back of the house where, in a cardboard box, under a tree, she saw a rabbit. He must have persuaded somebody to give it to him.

'You can have it to play with,' he said, 'or get your mother to kill it and make rabbit curry.'

'I won't eat it!' she cried, and went down on her knees to cuddle the little creature. The rabbit had died soon after, but she remembered the gift with joy.

She slipped her hand into her husband's, and together they walked down the stairs and out to the front of the house.

'They held hands! I saw them. They were holding hands as they walked together!' That detail, of course, could not have gone unnoticed in a man who had never looked directly at his three wives when he spoke to them, much less touched them.

The gift was one that could not be given in secret, and would have to be made in the presence of a hundred curious observers, both from the Great House and the neighbourhood. Indeed, it would appear that the entire neighbourhood had turned up to witness yet another offering of love by an old man to his young bride.

Silver Frond gave a loud gasp as she stood before the new, shining black Ford, parked just in front of the house, in full view of everyone. It was the most magnificent thing she had ever seen.

6
Who Taught Her This?

She remembered that when the gift of the magnificent doll arrived, more than two years ago, she did not dare touch it. She had merely stared at it, breathless with wonder. She had no idea then, as now, as she stared at the gleaming black Ford, parked on the road in front of the house, that she had the gift of making gifts, whether dolls or cars, serve a larger purpose.

A circle of keen observers, whispering excitedly among themselves, had formed around her and the car. It was a spectacle worthy of the movies that her father had taken her to see, on a few occasions, in the town's cinema – the ardent giver, the wide-eyed receiver, the fabulous gift.

The Old One, who would have preferred a private presentation, was actually enjoying the attention. He said simply, 'I hope you like it.' His words would be later variously and creatively embellished by the observers: 'I hope you will like this, the first of many magnificent gifts.' 'I hope you will have many happy hours riding in it.' 'I hope the other wives don't think I can make them similar gifts.'

She had never sat in a car before, and here she was, being presented with one, bought solely for her use and pleasure. No village maiden in the old ancestral country would have shown greater astonishment and delight at the sight of the most lavishly decorated sedan chair, carried to her door and lowered to the ground to receive her and carry her, along dusty mountain paths and across rivers, to the imperial presence.

Liang Por could have told the Singaporean version of the ancient tale of the maiden who held up a whole procession of sedan-bearers because she insisted, at each stage of the journey to the emperor waiting in his palace, to get down and admire the wondrous carvings and paintings on the sedan, especially made to commemorate her beauty. Lotus blooms, peonies, peaches on branches, exquisite birds in flight – the artisans had exhausted the range of beauty's metaphors. The poor sedan bearers, fearing their heads would be chopped off for being late, had sent an advance messenger, running with all his might, to explain.

Nobody's head would be chopped off on Silver Frond's account, but the Indian chauffeur, employed solely for her, patiently standing by the side of the car, might be severely rebuked if he drove too roughly and detracted from the enjoyment of the bride's first ride.

The bridegroom had lost all reserve, the bride all shyness, as he showed her the gift in its every handsome detail, and she exclaimed with little cries of joy, while everyone watched, nudging each other and storing up details for later telling to others. Some of the gossipers concentrated on his generosity, wildly inflating the cost of the gift, and others on her gratitude. But all were agreed on the new, glowing happiness of both, which would be all the reason needed for watching out for signs of its diminution in the weeks and months ahead. No old man who already had three wives, no village girl with such humble roots, deserved this degree of happiness. The gods, in their distribution of largesse among mortals, must show greater fairness.

'Get in,' he said, and opened the door for her to climb inside, to experience the thrill of ultimate proprietorship, for the Ford was just one of a few in the town. Everyone watched, as he helped her into the car, and said something to the chauffeur.

She sat down gingerly on the car seat, running her fingers lightly along the firm, smooth surface, inhaling deeply the smell of new leather, staring at shiny new steel. She gave a little squeal of startled delight at the sudden hoot of the car horn. The Old One laughed to see her delight and guided her hand to do the hooting herself. 'Louder!' he said, and they laughed together. The pleasure was reciprocal, and flowed in a continuous stream between them.

Later the Indian chauffeur, who had been quickly befriended by Third Wife, told her that he had never seen a happier newly married pair.

Second Wife, her expert unhusking and eating of melon seeds no longer reflecting a vacuous mind but an increasingly independent and worried one, also had a remark to make. She said that the Old One laughed more with his bride of three months than he had, over thirty years, with his three wives. 'The One with Gold in his Mouth? Why, every bit of the gold has fallen out now with all that laughter, and the bride's family has been busy picking it up!'

'Where would you like to go?'

Silver Frond thought immediately of her parents and sisters, of the wonder that would light up their faces as the sleek, black, chauffeur-driven Ford pulled up in front of the house in Sim Bak Village. Then she remembered that the paths leading to the village, overgrown with thorny bushes, would most certainly damage the new car. Or her father might be at home drunk, and say or do things to embarrass her and annoy her husband. She would have to think of some way to show her new possession to her family, and perhaps even offer them a ride. But, of course, her father would have to be sober, and on his best behaviour.

'Anywhere you like,' she said, her heart swelling in secret joy.

Then she did something that made his heart swell too, not so much in joy as relief, for he had wanted very much for there to be harmony between his first wife and his latest (the two in between not mattering at all), and here was his young bride acting in loving sensitivity to his wish.

He would not have known yet of the advice given to the bride by her mother, which had perfectly coincided with his wish for harmony in his household. Ah Bee Soh had advised her daughter, with the same shrewd understanding as when she had sent her with the eggs to the Great House: 'Remember, as soon as you become a member of the household, to show respect to all his wives, especially First Wife. Never mind the other two. Get First Wife on your side! Always address her politely first before speaking. Even if she is cold towards you, you must persist until you get her to accept your cup of tea.'

First Wife had refused to drink the tea of respect, which instantly confirmed for everyone looking on, her determination of open hostility. Now she appeared to be changing her mind. For Silver Frond, suddenly breaking away and rushing into the First House, was bringing out the important lady herself, holding her by the hand and leading her to the car. The new bride and the first wife holding hands! That extraordinary fact would not be lost on the spectators.

First Wife shook her head and waved a hand about in protest, but it was only the protest of embarrassment, not hostility. She gave an abrupt, awkward laugh and said something. The young bride responded by a show of greatest respect, moving aside some small children who were crowding round, to make way for First Wife, like an imperial maidservant clearing the way for an empress. Everyone gaped in astonishment.

Then in a loud voice the youngest and latest wife invited, indeed begged the oldest and most senior wife to go for a ride in the car. 'Dear First Mistress of the Household, do me the honour of coming for a ride with me.' The invitation, in all its humble deference, rang in the air.

Suddenly First Wife had become the centre of attention, reflecting her secure position in the hierarchy. It was as if her very presence was needed to legitimise the acquisition of the Ford, to authorise the lesser wives' use of it.

Quickly, her shrewd instincts asserted themselves once more. She had allowed the young bride to lead her out by the hand because the girl had appeared sincere enough. But that was as far as she would go. She was not to be so easily pulled into other people's schemes. So she shook her head, laughed and said, 'No, no, I am too old for this,' excused herself and was soon back in the house. No, she would never sit in that car.

But the first step in the public restoration of her dignity had been made by the bride, and must win approval from all. The Old One thought with much gratification, This young girl surprises me all the time. She is learning fast. Who taught her this?

The crowd of interested onlookers only dispersed after the car, with a loud roar and a huge trail of smoke, moved majestically down the road, the Indian chauffeur driving with self-conscious importance, the Old One and his young wife sitting close together at the back, in the continuing glow of the most improbable union the town had ever seen.

7
Severance

Silver Frond, walking through the courtyard of the temple to reach the goddess' altar at the far end of the building, could recognise the two boys staring at her, their eyes wide open, their jaws fallen loose. The Bad Brothers, who had tried to attack her in this very temple, almost three years ago.

A sudden thought came to her, thrilling her with mischievous intent. She turned round sharply, stood still and stared hard at them. For a moment, they were caught in the shock of not believing their own eyes. Fear followed shock, the real fear that hardens the body for flight or melts it to the ground for submission if flight is not possible. For her new appearance, exuding wealth and importance, also exuded the power to punish for offences, past and present. Any moment now, her servants could appear and give them the thrashing of their lives.

The brothers fled. It was their second flight of defeat, even more thrilling than the first, when they had run away in terror from a mysteriously crashing altar, because the victory was hers alone, unshared with any collaborating goddess.

Silver Frond smiled at the sight of the fleeing cowards, and saved up the delicious little episode to tell her sisters.

While the Indian chauffeur waited outside in the Ford, she took her time arranging her gifts of a big, beautiful bunch of chrysanthemums, a large bunch of joss-sticks, far larger and finer than any she had ever brought to honour the goddess, two expensive candles, a plate of six oranges, a pomelo and a packet of sweetmeats. A rich gift of gratitude to spread on the altar of the benign deity and friend who had guided her to her present prosperity and happiness.

Silver Frond sang softly to herself. Then she realised she should not be taking too long. There was much to talk to the Goddess Pearly Face about, and her husband expected her back soon. He did not like it at all that she should want to go to places he did not care to accompany her to.

'May I go to the Yio Tok Temple?'

'Don't take too long.'

'May I drop in at my parents' after that?'

'Another day, when I'm free to go with you.'

She knew he would never be free to go with her. 'It will take only a little while. I promise.'

'We won't talk about this any more.'

'I promise it will only—'

'I said we won't talk about it any more.'

She lowered her eyes and peeped timidly from under her eyelids. His face had darkened with annoyance. She never spoke about going home again.

Standing before the goddess, she said, a little tearfully, for she might as well begin with the small sorrows of her new life: 'My husband does not want me to go home to visit my parents and sisters.'

The goddess, who knew a lot of things, said, 'But they visit you at the Great House, don't they, and go away with food and money? Your husband gives you a lot of money to give to your family.'

'I want to go home on at least one visit. I want to take my father, my mother and my sisters for a ride in the car. They have never sat in a car before.'

'I wouldn't upset my husband, if I were you. Don't do anything to make him angry. So far you have not done badly. How did you get the clever idea to show the public respect for First Wife? It pleased your husband a lot. I must say, you are learning very fast!'

'But she still refuses to accept any tea from me. I asked the day after, but she shook her head and said, "No need! No need!" I know she still hates me. But I like her better than Second Wife or Third Wife.'

'Has it happened yet?' The goddess, of course, knew, but still wanted to hear it from the bride's lips.

'No. I am still scared. I try not to be scared, but the goose-bumps break out all over, and then I have to use the chamber-pot. And I have to do it noiselessly, which gives me a pain there, and everything becomes worse!'

'But when is it going to happen? A man can't wait for ever, you know.'

'Yesterday, my mother came with a flask of special soup that she says will keep the goose-bumps down. But it's the dreams –'

'What dreams?' Silver Frond began to blush and fidget. The goddess said, 'If you want my help, you must tell me.'

'It's always him. He comes in waving the comic book I gave him, with his trousers unbuttoned, but all his jackets on. I lie on the bed, unable to move and run away, and then he is on me, and in me, pushing so hard I think I'm being split in two. I am screaming, but no sound comes out.'

'You have trouble enough without any more coming from the Old One's son! You shouldn't have given him that comic book and all those gifts. Now he's drawn to you! You know that his father has forbidden him to go to the Fifth House.'

'I felt sorry for him. But I didn't think he would follow me and frighten me. Once, he came up very close to me, and then he rubbed himself against me. He was smiling and rubbing away! I was so frightened that I ran and hid myself in the bathroom. Then the horrible dreams started coming.'

'Did you tell his father?'

'Oh no.'

'Do you have the same horrible dreams about his father?'

'Sometimes.'

'Is it just as painful? Are you just as frightened?'

'It is as if there is another me, not feeling any pain, not frightened, just looking on and saying, "What a husband must do, he must do."'

'What did I tell you? You are learning fast! Good!'

'But when I am awake, the goose-bumps are still there. And as long as they are there, my husband says he will wait.'

'Don't presume too much on a man's patience. You really have to do something about your problem.'

'That is why I have come to you, dear goddess and true friend.'

'Let's start from the beginning. Are you happy in your marriage?'

'Yes! I have so much money, it is flowing from my hands, like water! I can give any amount to my parents and sisters. My father's got a new bicycle. My mother can afford the best herbs. Silver Flower and Silver Pearl have got new gold earrings, instead of the cheap silver ones. I can buy any number of books and pens and brushes for myself. I can buy presents for the grandchildren. I have a money box, for putting in spare money. One of these days, when I have saved up to exactly sixty dollars, I will personally go to Ah Hoo Chek and give it to him, for the terrible thing we did to him three years ago.'

Silver Frond was so carried away by the description of her new wealth that she waved her hands about and almost knocked down the urn of joss-sticks.

'The car – would you want it taken away?'

'Not the car! I like it for taking me far away from the Great House, where there is so much spite and quarrelling! I saw Second Wife make an ugly face at me yesterday, and then spit on the floor. Third Wife is watching me like a hawk. First Wife won't accept a cup of tea from me. I've asked three times already.'

'Well, there will be one more wife to deal with, if you still do not do what your husband wants. She will take away your fine clothes and jewels and car, and make them her own.'

Silver Frond's eyes were dilated in alarm. 'Whatever do you mean?'

'Fifth Wife. Be prepared to see Fifth Wife enter the Great House. She will be younger and prettier than you. No man waits for ever.'

'Oh no, oh no!'

'Oh yes. Within a year. Mark my words.'

'What can I do? I can't stop the goose-bumps from coming out, and as soon as he feels them, he removes his hands and tells me to go to sleep.'

'Do you detect an impatience in his voice when he tells you to go to sleep?'

'No. My husband is always patient and kind to me.'

'I say again, don't presume too much on a man's patience or kindness.'

'I have one more question to ask. Do you think my husband will give me the money for Silver Pearl's operation? It will be a lot of money.'

'Why are you bothered by unimportant things while you neglect the most important? Your husband will stop giving you money for anything if you fail in your duty as a bride.'

'Dear goddess, you are so kind and wise and powerful. You have always been such a good friend to me. I know I can depend on you for anything.'

The goddess was not above flattery, but like wary mortals, could be on her guard. 'What do you want me to do?'

'Dear, dear goddess, make my husband change his behaviour at night. When he lies down beside me on the bed, take away all his thoughts about doing this thing to me. Let him just talk to me. One night, we talked for a long time. We told each other stories. I told him my favourite story of the hunchback and the woman with a hundred warts on her face, and he laughed and laughed! Soon we got tired and fell asleep. I was so happy. I didn't have any bad dreams that night. Dear, dear goddess, please—'

'Even goddesses can't change men's behaviour.'

'Then you are not as helpful as I thought.'

'You have never spoken this way to me before.'

'You have never disappointed me before.'

'You keep surprising me! But I must say, I rather like your spirit. If I were a mortal and a woman, I would have that spirit.'

'I've got to go. But I want you to tell me that there will be no fifth wife.'

'Ah, what do I see this very moment? I see a woman standing behind the Old One. She is not you. She is very pretty. She is knocking his back with her dainty fists, and he is smiling. He turns round and takes her hand in his. Wait a moment! She looks very much like someone you know. Why, it is Mee Mee, the long-haired woman with the powdered face and the big breasts—'

Silver Frond turned pale. Her lips were white.

'I see him now pulling her round to sit on his knee. He settles her so carefully and gently on his knee because she is big with his coming son—'

'Stop!' Silver Frond's voice was shrill with mounting panic. Suddenly she felt very angry. 'I thought you were my friend. I came here for comfort and advice, and all you've done is to scold and frighten me. I'll never come to you again!'

'I see your new life has spoilt you. Well, suit yourself.'

8
The Moon on a Golden Plate

The bride was getting into the car to go shopping when she saw the youngest grandchild standing nearby, a wistful look in his eyes.

'Go and ask your mother for permission. I'll wait for you,' she said kindly.

The child, whom she recognised to be the younger of First Wife's third daughter's two sons, ran joyfully back into the house. He ran back exactly a few minutes later, wearing shoes that his mother had put on for him for the ride. The child said, 'I can come! I can come!'

Silver Frond thought magnanimously, I'll buy a toy for him in town. For the next car ride, he can bring his brother.

She came back from the ride pale and dizzy. The grandson was as bright-faced as ever, running off as soon as he got out of the car, yelling loudly about the bright blue plastic rabbit clutched in his hand. She walked a few steps unsteadily, then rushed to bend over a drain in front of the house, in time to let out a stream of vomit. She squatted on the ground, gasping and wiping her mouth on her sleeve, for she had brought no handkerchief. Moaning softly, she stood up, and puckered up her face, as if for a cry. An adult only a week before, in her shrewd manoeuvres to effect a reconciliation with First Wife, she was once more a child, terrified of her own vomit.

The Old One, who had been waiting for her return in the car, hurried up, looking very concerned. He said, 'Perhaps you shouldn't have gone. It's a very hot day. Go and lie down, and get the maid to give you some hot water.'

'Here, let me rub this on your forehead.'

It was Third Wife, who had suddenly appeared with a small bottle of Tiger Balm. Silver Frond felt too ill to resist the new offer of friendship from an enemy who had never disguised her resentment. Or perhaps it was part of a steadily developing skill in learning to survive in hostile environments, that prompted her, even as she suspiciously viewed the enemy's change of heart, to welcome it as real. She smiled weakly and said, 'Thank you.'

Third Wife was all unstinting helpfulness. She made Silver Frond sit on a chair while she expertly rubbed her forehead, neck and hands with the oil. There could have been no greater show of amity between rival wives in a large household.

'Close your eyes. I'm going to rub a little, just a little, above the lids. It won't hurt. Now your hands. Why, they are cold!' And Third Wife took the girl's hands into her own and rubbed them, to pass on her own warmth, and finally wiped, with her own handkerchief, the last stains of vomit from the mouth of the despised former Egg Girl.

Later, Third Wife made a visit to the Fifth House with a gift – a small hard pillow, stuffed with rice grains and some pungent herbs, which she said would prevent nausea in any future car ride, if placed behind the head or held close to the chest. The giving continued in an unstoppable flow. The very next day, Tali-gelem came with a tiffin carrier of nourishing soup of chicken and mushrooms, and the day after that, a new, unopened bottle of Tiger Balm.

The Old One, who would never reinstate Third Wife as the officially designated ear-cleaner, was rather pleased by her change of heart, and new show of friendliness towards his new bride. Remembering what a fellow patriarch had told him about his sixth and newest wife sowing discord among the women in his household, he credited the bride with this happy development: 'You have shown respect for First Wife and won the friendship of Third Wife. There will be peace in the Great House.' He would not be bothered by the deep undercurrents of women's rivalry, as long as there was surface amity.

She glowed with the same joy and pride as when the young *sinseh* had praised her quickness in learning by heart a very long piece of text from the classics.

The vomiting had been noted by several of the spies, who were quick to sense its possible significance.

'It's nothing,' said Third Wife dismissively to Black Dog's wife. 'I can tell you this for a certainty – she's not pregnant. You can't expect village people to ride in cars and not feel sick. They are only comfortable riding in trishaws and on bicycles.'

'Do you think she'll invite you too, for a ride in her car?' asked Black Dog's wife slyly.

'"Oooh, oooh, please invite me to ride in your beautiful car, otherwise I will die with unfulfilled desire!" For goodness' sake, don't think I have sunk so low!' said Third Wife. 'But if you want to make Second Wife happy, you may want to wangle an invitation for her. I saw her one morning looking at the car and drooling all over it.'

Later, she went to check out First Wife's reaction to the invitation.

'Why did you allow her to lead you out to look at the car? Surely you knew she was just making use of you?'

First Wife, who had an intense dislike for being dragged back into the arena of conflict once she had shaken off its dust from her feet, was almost tempted to punish Third Wife by saying archly, 'She is more sincere than many people I know!' But any argument or quarrel with the querulous, crafty woman was more than she could bear during these tiresome times. She was exhausted beyond endurance.

Besides, she had heard hints about a possible guilty liaison between that woman with her itch for men's attention, and Black Dog. The hints had come from none other than Black Dog's wife. First Wife, sighing heavily and fanning herself, had no wish to be further embroiled in the messiness of other people's lives. And things in the Great House had become messier with the arrival of the village girl.

All First Wife wanted was to be left alone in peace, to take better care of her old ailing mother-in-law and her poor, simple-minded son. She said, 'I'm tired, and have no wish to talk or listen further. So please go away.'

Third Wife would not go away till she had satisfied herself on one more point. She continued standing by First Wife's side, one hand on her hip, the other gesticulating wildly in the urgency of her questions. A lavishly furnished house. Jewels. Now a car, probably costing several thousand dollars. What would the Old One think of next? None of the wives had had the benefit of one iota of such free spending.

'Why are you telling me?' said First Wife irritably. 'Even if he gives her the moon on a golden plate, I don't want to know. It's not my business.'

9
The Vinegar Drinker

The grocer's assistant and deliveryman, Ah Kow, took his time lifting the grocery items out of his cardboard box. By naming each item as he unpacked it from the box, pronouncing each syllable slowly and carefully, he was able to stretch out his time in the kitchen of the Fifth House, all the while looking towards the doorway to see if the young bride would walk in, as she had done on a few previous occasions, or, even better, if she would walk over to see what he was taking out of the cardboard box, as she had done once.

He wanted so much to see the Venerable One's young bride, whom he had heard so much about.

'Here's the sesame oil,' said the young man whose name meant Dog or Monkey depending on whether the caller wanted to invest it with the lowliness of one beast or the playfulness of the other, both of which attributes he had in plenty. It was mainly the playfulness at work now, tinged with mischievous intent, for it was said the Old One's jealous possessiveness towards his three wives was multiplied a hundredfold in the case of the fourth. An old rooster's squawking protection of the single pullet in the farmyard was the surest challenge to younger roosters.

'Here's the second bottle of sesame oil,' said Ah Kow, unabashedly looking towards the doorway, 'and here's the rice, and here are the matches—'

Silver Frond's maidservant Ah Choo giggled and said, 'I know who you are looking out for! She's upstairs having her lessons with the *sinseh*, and won't come down till late afternoon.'

'Ah, lucky *sinseh!*' said Ah Kow with a languorous sigh, which, though intended for another woman, caused the maidservant to blush and simper. As soon as he arrived each week, she dropped all work and came to stand or sit by him, hanging on his every word, alternately giggling and simpering.

On the next delivery day, Ah Kow was luckier. The bride happened to be in the kitchen, sitting by herself at a table in a distant corner, eating biscuits dipped in Ovaltine. He took a quick sideways glance at her as he was taking out the grocery items, and saw that all the rumours were true: she had become a beauty equal to the likes of the actress Ling Ling, transformed by the appurtenances of a fabulous marriage. He noticed details, which he would be later teased about for observing: a bright yellow flower in her hair; a large jade pendant in the shape of a carp, hanging on a thin gold chain round her neck; the small swallowing movements of her very fair throat; her perfect skin.

Since she was unlikely to be enticed by the mere naming of grocery items, even in a loud voice, he searched his mind for a better enticement, which had to come quickly, before she finished her plate of biscuits and left the kitchen. He said, very loudly, to Ah Choo, holding up a small packet wrapped in newspaper, 'Now what can this be? I don't remember putting it in the box. Whatever can it be?' He shook it, felt it, smelt it, his brow knitted in an intense frown, the consummate performer determined to attract and hold his audience.

It was the perfect ruse to catch a curious child's attention, and it worked instantly, for the bride, after all, was no more than a child. Silver Frond looked up abruptly from her biscuits and Ovaltine, and stared at the mysterious packet in Ah Kow's hand. The man could not hide his delight. He greeted her effusively, all the time continuing to shake the packet in his hand.

Its contents turned out to be no more than some dried herbs, but Ah Kow's quick mind elevated these to the status of a wondrous medicine capable of curing any illness. He described their magical properties with loud, unabashed extravagance. With frowning concentration, he searched through the small heap of dried leaves, roots and bark, and finally pulled out a thin brown tendril, which he claimed was the dried entrail of a snake. He pulled out more, and then held up a cluster of the snake's intestines, draped on his forefinger like a miniature fishing net hung up to dry. He took a sideways glance at the young bride and saw, to his delight, that he was holding her attention. Indeed, she was watching him with great interest until the very end, when she finished eating and left the room.

But it was just silent interest from a distance. She had not said a word. He would have to do better next time.

He fell into a fever of planning, to spin the simple attention-getting ruse into an elaborate scheme to get the Old One's young bride right to his very side. He wanted her to stand by him and engage him familiarly in conversation, so that he could later boast to fellow deliverymen: 'Now which of you can say that you have been to the Fifth House and talked to the young bride? Which of you can say that you had the attention of the bride for a full half hour, under the same roof as her jealous old husband? I made him drink, not one cup of vinegar that day, but a whole flask! Ha, ha, ha!'

It was well known by now that the Old One was the town's greatest Vinegar Drinker. Liang Por had told many ancient tales of husbands, wives and lovers consumed by the corrosive power of sexual jealousy; the Old One would have been a most fitting subject. Liang Por told the story of an emperor who kept his favourite concubine so well hidden that, for many years, nobody saw her, except an old trusted woman attendant. One day the girl fell ill with a mysterious illness that only one physician in the whole empire could cure. The emperor sent for him, but since it would have meant admitting a man into the chamber of his beloved, he changed his mind. He sent the physician away. His jealousy was stronger than his love, and he let his favourite concubine die.

He laid her body in a magnificent jade tomb and mourned her death for the rest of his life.

'Do you know,' whispered the gossipers, 'since her marriage three months ago, she has not been allowed to visit her parents in Sim Bak Village? She has been begging him, but he is jealous even of her father!'

Tali-gelem had this to report, concerning the Indian chauffeur: 'All the man did was to adjust the rear-view mirror a little, and later the Old One summoned him, accused him of taking a sly peek at the bride, and warned him severely to keep his eyes on the road in the future.'

It was said that, taking heed of the severity as if it had been directed at her, the bride had learnt to keep *her* eyes in check, not allowing them to stray as she rode in the car, for there were always young men aplenty on the roads, walking or riding their bicycles. At the beginning, according to the chauffeur, who enjoyed a good gossip like anybody else, she would excitedly point to people, places and things she saw during a ride, and once asked her husband to stop the car for her to buy some durians she saw at a road stall. He said, 'You stay in the car; I'll get out to get them,' because the durian seller was a good-looking young man who had apparently seen the beautiful face through the car window as he was weighing some durians, and was distracted enough to let the scales wobble and drop the fruit. The Old One had returned to the car with two large durians tied in string and a surly look on his face. For the rest of the ride, he maintained a stony silence.

When they returned home, he forced himself to ask his bride, 'That man at the durian stall. Did you notice he was looking at you?'

'Yes.'

'Did you look back?'

'No.'

'Then how did you know he was looking at you?'

'I happened to look up; it was only for a very brief instant.' She was now reddening with confusion, which she hoped he would not mistake for guilt. She thought of something else to say, to save the situation: 'I didn't like him looking at me at all. I felt goose-bumps all over my body.'

'I saw a smile on your face.'

'No, no, I told you, I had goose-bumps all over my body.'

'Were they goose-bumps of pleasure or embarrassment?'

'Embarrassment.'

'What about the goose-bumps you feel when I look at you?'

She said, 'They are goose-bumps of pleasure,' and immediately felt trapped. She searched quickly for the correct answer to give her husband, casting a quick glance at him and noting the by now familiar darkened brow of displeasure. She repeated, a little miserably, 'Goose-bumps of pleasure.'

'But last night, when I tried to touch you, my fingers felt—'

'They were only small goose-bumps. Soon I won't have them any more.'

'You mean you won't have them when other men look at you? Like that bold durian seller?'

'No.'

'You mean you will get used to their stares and touch? You mean you won't feel any embarrassment and look away?'

He had become more reckless in his interrogation, as she became more confused. She blubbered, 'Oh, no. No, what I mean is ...' growing very red in the face and looking as if she would break into tears. Which she did, at last, sobbing for a full ten minutes before he said, with no softening of tone, 'All right, that's enough. We'll not talk of that again.'

She made the secret resolution, firstly, never to go near the durian stall again, and secondly, to condition her body to a fine selectivity, allowing the eruption of goose-bumps only in the presence of other men, submerging them completely in her husband's. Henceforth, his fingers would meet only the soft smoothness of a reciprocal desire.

She might need more advice and help from her mother. And from the Goddess Pearly Face. She would go and ask for forgiveness for the show of temper on her last visit.

'I'm sorry,' wept the young bride, and this time, the husband responded with silence, not tenderness, actually turning away from her on the bed. It was the first time he had used displeasure as a calculated move.

For he had felt, for some time now, that some form of reproach for the continuing aversion was in order, to compensate for the frustration he was beginning to feel. He loved her, but she must not presume too much on his love. The August Ancestor would have approved the move: 'Good. A man must not lose too much dignity by giving in to women's whims. A woman must learn not to take a man's patience for granted.'

Yet, oh! How he loved her!

He would go no further in the reproach. After all, the goose-bumps, inconvenient though they were to him, were the strongest proof yet of her innocence, and were certainly more reliable than those white bedsheets or garments for washing and showing the morning after.

With those thoughts, he fell asleep easily.

But jealousy still soured and pinched his insides where the free-talking young *sinseh* was concerned. The young man, it was noticed, took extraordinary care preening before the mirror before each lesson, and was supposed to be a temporary replacement only, but, owing to an extension of leave in China by the old *sinseh*, he was beginning to appear a permanent fixture in the Great House, clearly to his secret delight.

'You needn't ask him to search out more poems for you to copy and learn,' the Venerable One told his bride, not wanting to add, 'I know that you regard your education as my best gift to you, but I don't want people to take advantage of that. I don't want this brash young *sinseh* to talk to you unnecessarily.' His pride forbade him to say more than, 'Stick to your day's lessons. Don't ask for anything else.'

'But I want to write out those poems for you!' his bride protested. Her eyes shone and her skin glowed. She was back in the full enjoyment of her new life in the Great House. He looked at her and suddenly all pique was gone. He loved the sight so much that he took her face in his hands and held it steadily before him, feasting his eyes on its pure beauty. It was always like that. One moment, he was exasperated by her, the next completely enraptured.

'They are so beautiful, and I want them specially for you.' Her guileless innocence was the chief reassurance and consolation, the best neutralising agent for jealousy's acid. But it could irritate too, if it encouraged unwanted attention. He would not say to the rude gazers upon her beauty: 'You can look, but you cannot touch.' He would prefer his message to be sterner: 'Look at your peril.'

10
Baby Mice

Ah Choo ran to tell Silver Frond, who was in the bedroom looking at some comic books that the *sinseh* had given her: 'Quick! Come and see. There are altogether five baby mice, and he's going to swallow all of them!'

Silver Frond rushed down, and stared at a heap of newborn, furless, blind baby mice on the kitchen table, helplessly crawling over each other, making tiny squeaking noises. Ah Kow told the story of how a very sick old man in his village, covered all over with sores filled with pus, was instantly cured of his illness by swallowing half a dozen baby mice, washed down by a cup of ginseng tea. Soon his skin became even firmer and fresher than a young man's.

'Ah Choo, bring me a cup of water,' said Ah Kow with cool nonchalance. 'I have no serious illness but an occasional pain in the stomach. I need to get rid of it once and for all.'

Silver Frond stared at the baby mice. She had seen young mice in a neighbour's house in Sim Bak Village, but not newborn ones, which looked so fragile and helpless that she felt an overpowering pity for them, greater even than the pity she had felt for the poor truth cockerel in the Yio Tok Temple before its head was chopped off.

'No! No!' she screamed and made a lunge at Ah Kow. She attempted to remove the cup of water from his hand, and a small struggle ensued. This was better than anything he had expected. Attention and speech would have been enough; the bodily contact was bonus undreamt of.

'But I must,' said Ah Kow with a grave look on his face. 'That is the only way to cure my stomach ailment.'

With a great theatrical flourish, he disengaged one of the mice from the heap, and delicately held it up between thumb and forefinger. He watched the tiny creature wriggle, and made little clucking noises to it. The other baby mice, now separated from each other, began to move about weakly, sniffing the air, their baby skin as thin and transparent as paper. Ah Kow, with one hand, swept them back together into a heap.

'Oh, do be careful!' cried Silver Frond in alarm.

Five baby mice, to be swallowed, one after the other, in an act of slow melodrama that would have the young bride by turns curious, excited, squeamish, alarmed, terrified, angry, and expressing all these different emotions in a single titillating dance of protest around him. She would struggle to get the mice out of his hands, and he would turn each protesting movement into delectable bodily contact.

'What is going on?'

The noise had brought the Venerable One himself. He stood at the doorway, sternly looking on. He had been in time to catch a glimpse of hands in the air, his bride's and the young deliveryman's, briefly touching and then disengaging.

Silver Frond ran towards him, her face red with distress, crying out, 'Stop him from swallowing the baby mice!' Her instincts had already sensed trouble and told her to save herself by instantly casting the brash young deliveryman in the adversary's role. 'I tried to stop him, but he wouldn't listen.' She was now standing beside her husband at the doorway, both of them facing the evil swallower of baby mice.

Ah Kow muttered something, gathered up his mice, wrapped them in a piece of cloth and prepared to go. Ah Choo stood by sheepishly, expecting to be scolded.

The Old One never moved from his position in the doorway, and the sternness never left his face. His bride was still showing her agitated concern for the poor baby mice; in fact, she had broken into tears. Her innocence in the whole distasteful matter was clear, so his exasperation, for the time being, must be unloaded fully upon the head of the insolent young deliveryman.

'Your job is to deliver the groceries and leave,' he said with austere dignity to the young interloper. 'Pay him, and tell him he's not to come here again,' he said coldly to Ah Choo. Then he turned abruptly and left, followed by his bride.

But in his dream that night, he would be subjected once more to that hateful sight of the hands touching, as if another man had had possession of his bride's pristine beauty before he did. The Vinegar Drinker, it was said, suffered more in his dreams at night than his brooding by day, choking in the acrid fumes of his obsession in the night's stillness.

11
When Are Congratulations Due?

Ah Kow said, as he sat with his friends at the steamed buns stall in the marketplace, 'At one point, my hand actually brushed against her breast!' He made the friend sitting next to him play the part of the young bride and reenacted that delicious moment.

'Ha! Ha! That was probably more than what the Old One has managed to achieve so far. They say she hid under the bed one night in her terror. They say her mother never taught her anything.'

'Why don't you do the job for him now that you've begun so well with her?'

'They say newborn baby mice are good for old men. Why don't you present them to the Old One as a gift? Maybe he's the one at fault, not her. Ha, ha, ha!'

'Ssh, look who's here.'

They all turned to look at a man getting down from his bicycle at a *char kuay tiau* stall. He was easily the most morose-looking man in the entire marketplace.

'Good morning, Ah Bee Koh!' called Ah Kow cheerily. 'How are you this morning? Are you buying *char kuay tiau* for Ah Bee Soh? What a good husband you are.'

The man looked uneasy. He waved a limp hand at the cheerful group eating their steamed buns and drinking coffee, and muttered something about being in a hurry.

'Come and join us, Ah Bee Koh!' yelled Ah Kow. 'We must celebrate with you the joy of your daughter's marriage.' The others chorused, 'Yes, yes, do join us, Ah Bee Koh!' It was a collective malice.

Ah Kow got up, dragged Ah Bee Koh over amidst much protesting and instructed the *char kuay tiau* man to bring the noodles when they were ready.

'Congratulations, congratulations. Have you seen your daughter recently?'

They glanced slyly at each other, as they nodded amiably at the man's massive lie, uttered with betraying twitches all over his face: 'She came yesterday. As usual, she brought gifts for all of us. I tell her she mustn't spend money unnecessarily, but she won't listen!'

'Ah, how fortunate you and your family are, Ah Bee Koh. When we see your daughter in that grand-looking car, on her way to Sim Bak Village, we are full of envy!'

'We ask the gods why we cannot be similarly blessed!'

'I have sons only, alas! I would exchange two sons for a daughter!'

Each tried to outdo the other in sugared spite.

The ultimate lethal dose was reserved for the moment when Ah Bee Koh, no longer able to keep up the pretence of cheer and once more lapsing into moroseness, rose to leave.

'When are the congratulations due once more?' cried Ah Kow, and he gave a sly wink.

'What do you mean?' said Ah Bee Koh warily.

'Ah, when do you become a grandfather? You must be

eagerly awaiting the happy event! We understand that it will be soon.'

'Congratulations, Grandfather! Don't forget to treat us to a big celebration dinner!'

Ah Bee Koh fled.

12
The August Ancestor's Position Remains Unchanged

The humiliating dreams would not stop coming. In every single one, the Old One saw another man have first taste of the honey, first sniff of the flower, first bite of the sweetmeat he had been nurturing with such care for himself. In his dreams, he was presented with a large flask of vinegar, which he was forced to drink to the last draught.

In the darkness, he let out a low moan, and felt a soft hand on his brow. Then he felt a tender arm across his chest, and a face pressed on his. He knew that it was contrition for causing all the disquiet, not the readiness he had been waiting for. Contrition, concern, gratitude, awe, fear – they were all in order, to lead to a readiness too long in coming. Should he, four months after the wedding, demand its arrival?

Her words, as tender as the touch of her hand, stopped him, and he lay very still in the darkness, pretending to be asleep. She was whispering, with all the ardour of her simple, artless nature: 'I have given instructions for the deliveryman to stop coming to the Fifth House. I have asked Third Wife to sew curtains for the car, and she has kindly agreed to. I have told the young *sinseh* to stop coming, and will wait for the old *sinseh* to return.'

I have. For the first time she was asserting her authority as young mistress in the Grand House, but it was an assertiveness only to reassure him of her submissiveness. He was both surprised and delighted.

It continued as sorrowful contrition, presented as a list of concrete promises. 'From now on, I will only speak to Black Dog or any of your male assistants, through Black Dog's wife or Tali-gelem, never directly. I will leave the kitchen as soon as I see a deliveryman come in. When the old *sinseh* returns, I will ask him only necessary questions.'

It was as thorough a promise as any young wife could make, to reassure an old husband. She might as well have denounced the entire male population of the town. She might as well be that heroine in Liang Por's tale, who was so horrified when a man accidentally brushed against her hand that she wore gloves ever after.

As he pretended to snore louder, delighting in the extravagance of her avowals of wifely duty, she went on to speak about the culmination of that duty: 'I am taking nourishing herbs to prepare my body to be stronger. Today, Third Wife brought me a bowl for the sixth time. I must drink a total of twelve bowls, over forty days. After that, I will be able ...'

She could not speak explicitly of intimate matters, not even to her husband sound asleep, and contented herself with stroking his face and finally falling asleep herself on his chest. He wanted to say to her by way of gentle advice, 'Perhaps you should not be telling Third Wife everything,' but she had already fallen asleep.

Suddenly he felt very happy.

He wanted his dream that night to be about her, but it was the relentless August Ancestor who appeared, sat down magisterially in a large, high-backed chair and said, 'How long are you going to wait? I'm going to give you advice, since you need it so badly, you, the most foolish of my descendants, who allows himself to be manipulated by a wife young enough to be his granddaughter! Don't trust all that outward innocence! She is just a stubborn, crafty girl who is getting her own way, a village girl determined to exploit her fortunate marriage to the full. Say to her first thing in the morning, "Fourth Wife, if you choose to be so only in name and not in deed, I shall be obliged to bring a fifth wife into the Great House!" That will really shake things up.'

'What!' cried the Venerable One, in alarm. 'Oh no, I couldn't do that. I love her too much.'

'Love! *Tchah*!' snorted the August Ancestor. 'If your young bride does not produce a son in a year, you'll have caused the greatest grief to your ancestors. And don't try to bribe me with more top-grade opium offerings at my grave. My position remains unchanged.'

13
Snake

Silver Frond, rushing into the house, narrowly missed stepping on a squawking, fluttering chicken, but not its freshly deposited blob of dirt. The dirt flew up from beneath an elegant new sandal and splattered a dainty ankle. Only six months ago, chicken dirt and ankles had met familiarly in the daily routines of sweeping and cleaning the coops. Her mother wailed, 'Your sandals!'

She said breathlessly, 'Never mind, never mind. Where's Father? I must hurry – Third Wife is waiting in the car.'

Her mother and two sisters immediately went into a frenzy of activity to undo the damage done by the errant chicken, and to express their appreciation for the honour of this visit. Silver Flower and Silver Pearl ran to get a moist rag; Ah Bee Soh looked around for an appropriate chair to pull up for the visitor to sit on, and cast about in her mind for appropriate words to say.

For it was more than the visit home of a newly married daughter. It was a visit from a new member of the awesome Great House to which half the families in Sim Bak Village were indebted. Already, as Ah Bee Soh could see, with a mixture of trepidation and gratification that galvanized her into conspicuous activity, a dozen awed faces had appeared at the window and in the doorway, in tribute to the unimaginable height to which one of their own had been raised.

It was only months ago that she had left the village, filled with the deferential timidity towards superiors, which she was now herself entitled to receive, even from her own family. Sky and earth, with the immeasurable space between: this was the only analogy that could describe her new position and old.

'Sit down, you must be tired. Would you like tea or coffee?' gasped Ah Bee Soh, addressing her daughter with the same respect as she would the Venerable One. In the privacy of a heart-to-heart talk, she would have pinched and pressed her daughter's cheeks and arms to check for more flesh on them, smoothed her hair, inspected closely the gold studs on her ear-lobes and the bangles on her wrist, and asked, with the bluntness of concerned mothers, 'Well, has it happened yet or not?'

In full view of the peeping neighbours, she felt compelled to play the role of the humble recipient of a great favour, and keep strictly to her side of the great divide.

Silver Frond, bursting with joy to see her family again, and eager to accomplish the purpose of the visit, had no use for divides. She would not sit down but paced about, clutching her mother's arm and saying excitedly, 'Why, Mother, you've put on a lot of weight! But where's Father? I'm in a hurry.' She was about to go and look for him in his room, when her mother stopped her, flashed a worried look and said, lowering her voice, 'Don't.' Her two sisters stood by in tittering anxiety, torn between the desire to admire her new clothes, shoes, jewels and hairstyle, and a sense of looming conflict.

Ah Bee Koh walked in then. The sullen expression on his face and his slow, reluctant movement warned of trouble. It was difficult to believe that only months ago, this man was an expert in the strategy of laughter and play.

Silver Frond ran to him, crying out with the eagerness of a child, 'Father, the car is here, just parked a short distance away, and I want you and Mother to come for a ride with me – Silver Flower and Silver Pearl can wait their turns.'

It was as in those days, not too long ago, when she had made possible a sumptuous New Year's Eve dinner for them and noisily exhorted them to enjoy expensive roast duck and steamed chicken.

Completely taken up by her grand scheme to make everyone happy by offering a ride in the car, which, in its proud swing through town, would be unmatched by any treat of food or money from the Great House, she ignored the surly silence and went on eagerly talking about the magnificent gift from her husband, until her father stopped her by saying coldly, 'No. I don't want to go for any ride with you. And I don't want this either.' He took out from his pocket what remained of the money she had given him on his last visit to her in the Great House, and placed it on a chair.

It was an odd sight, the jovial father sullenly rejecting the daughter who had always been his favourite child, and the money he had always dreamt of. Daughter and money looked forlorn; she stared at him in dismay, while the notes lay in a sad, crumpled heap on the chair. Neither had brought joy and peace to him; both had to be rejected in one grand gesture, in full view of family and neighbours.

It was a double triumph for Ah Bee Koh. He stood his ground, awaiting a storm of protest and appeal, and ready to repulse it in a massive reclamation of lost dignity.

'It's your daughter's first visit home. You can't do this to her,' said Ah Bee Soh.

'Father, Father, don't do this to Silver Frond!' cried the two sisters.

'Father, forgive me,' said Silver Frond humbly, and somebody from the watching crowd at the window cried, 'Forgive her, Ah Bee Koh!' without knowing what the forgiveness was for.

It was for the shame the father had suffered, and which only he could adequately describe to them.

'Take back your money,' said Ah Bee Koh angrily. 'What's the use of all the money if you're not allowed to come home to see your family, as if we were lepers.' The analogy of disease and untouchability had its appeal, and he dwelt on it with abundant self-indulgence. 'So you will be infected if, in your grand clothes and jewels, you come close to us in our stinking hut. So if you even so much as breath the same air as your father—'

'Stop it, Father,' said Silver Frond impatiently. 'You know it's not true.'

The sympathetic voice at the window echoed helpfully, 'Ah Bee Koh, it's not true, so you must forgive and forget!'

The father brushed the money off the chair with a contemptuous sweep of the hand, and a gasp arose from the watchers at the window. The notes scattered about on the floor and brought back the errant chicken, which began pecking at them, until shooed away by Silver Pearl.

Ah Bee Koh sat down on the chair, put his face in his hands and began to speak in a voice weak with grief, taking the melodrama of loss to the next stage. 'We used to be so happy together.'

'Stop it, Father, don't behave so childishly,' said Silver Frond and wished the watching crowd would go away. But the contributing voice clearly felt it had a greater contribution to make, and cried, very loudly, this time taking the father's side, 'That's no way to speak to your father!'

Ah Bee Soh went up and stood directly in front of her husband whose face was still abjectly buried in his hands. 'Well, she's home now, so what's all the fuss about? Get up, and talk properly to her.' She who had least expected to benefit from her daughter's marriage, had had much of her health and spirits restored by a generous supply of money, whereas her husband, who had envisaged a new life of carefree drinking with his friends, was avoiding them and retreating into the most mournful seclusion he had ever known in his life.

'So your daughter has not even come home once to see you?' one of his friends had teased.

'So she's ashamed of you?' said another. He quoted a proverb about the pea that repudiated its pod, and about the lotus that forgot the mud which had nourished its roots.

'Never mind,' said a third consolingly. 'Whenever she says, "Father, I can't be seen with you now, with your dirty fingernails and your common friends in the coffee shop," you say, "That's all right, as long as you keep the money coming!" That's the way to deal with rich daughters. Ha, ha, ha!'

But all three were alarmed and clucked their tongues in genuine sympathy when Ah Bee Koh suddenly pushed away his glass of beer, folded his arms on the table, lowered his head on them and began to sob like a child.

He had stopped going to the coffee-and-beer shops since.

'You love your husband more than your father,' said the unhappy man peevishly. 'You have been my daughter for fifteen years, and his wife only for three months, yet ...' The father's grief needed to be expressed further, and Ah Bee Koh grew reckless in his desire to shake his daughter, looking so complacently distant in her new clothes and hairstyle, into the same convulsion of grieving for the happy life they had had together.

'I am not dead yet. But I might as well be dead, for all the attention you have given me. Even a dead parent gets more visits to his grave.'

'Stop talking nonsense,' said Ah Bee Soh. 'Your daughter is visiting you now, and you're behaving like an idiot.'

Desperate to hold together a situation spinning out of control, Silver Frond, in a demonstration of the skills of persuasion learnt in her new home, said with all the humility she could muster, 'Father, I have come specially to take you for a car ride. You have given me many happy rides,' she would not mention his old bicycle and its rusty pillion, 'and now it is my turn.'

The car had become the greatest gift, after the expensive private education, in her marriage, and she was excited about testing its magical powers of reconciliation once more. It had worked fairly satisfactorily with First Wife, very satisfactorily with all the grandchildren, who no longer made faces at her, and it would work with her father. She already saw him sitting beside the chauffeur, her mother, herself and Third Wife at the back, in a slow ride through the town, watched by many. That would restore both dignity and good spirits.

'Father, please hurry. Third Wife is waiting in the car. It's not nice to make her wait longer.'

She chose wisely to refrain from mentioning that it was through Third Wife's secret help that she was able to make this visit at all. Third Wife had said generously, 'If the Old One asks, you can say that I had requested you to take me to the temple for my monthly visit. If he asks me, I will say that I needed your help for the many baskets of temple offerings, and that you had very kindly agreed.'

Third Wife had thought everything through. If, if, if. Each hypothetical situation of interrogation and accounting had been carefully dissected, down to the last perilous detail, and she was well prepared.

Third Wife had, indeed, generously taken responsibility for other covert trips in the car, one of them to pick up a set of scrolls from the young *sinseh*, who, since the day he had been told to leave the Great House, had inquired about his pupil at every opportunity.

'But I promised the Old One I would never see him again,' Silver Frond had said.

'You're not seeing him again. Don't worry, you just wait in the car, I'll be the one to take the scrolls from him. He says they are the only scrolls in the whole of Singapore on the Wandering Monk poems.'

'The Old One will be so angry.'

'He won't know. In any case, if he asks, you can tell him the gift was for me, and it was I who asked you to accompany me. I have grown as thick-skinned as the durian. I can take any amount of blame! So please don't worry!' Then laughing merrily, she had stretched out an arm to make Silver Frond test the practised skin.

The young *sinseh* had been very pleased to see Silver Frond and give her the scrolls. Apparently he had waited a long time in the hot sun for the car to appear. He had said daringly, looking straight at her, 'I hope these scrolls will sometimes make you think of me,' and watched, smiling, a blush spread over her face and neck.

Back home, she had hurriedly hidden the scrolls, as Third Wife had advised.

Don't worry. Don'*t* worry. By way of further assurance, Third Wife had told three stories, all about wifely deceit, which in the end was not deceit because it had been necessitated by husbandly unreasonableness and was moreover, practised in the name of a noble cause.

Silver Frond had had a headache trying to remember her role in the whole elaborately constructed scheme, and in the end decided to leave everything to the cool, clever, quick-thinking Third Wife.

'Be careful. Be careful. The snake is waiting for its moment of victory!'

The Goddess Pearly Face would have warned Silver Frond if given a chance, and would have wept at the folly of the young bride now more responsive to a snake's sweet guile than the sound advice of a goddess. She would have added, 'Don't be impressed by her promise to pass on to you all her expertise in ear-cleaning.' For Third Wife had promised precisely that, together with a gift of the exquisite ear-cleaners she had been wearing on a chain round her neck.

The lady looked less the artful snake than the benign dove as she sat patiently waiting in the car, parked on one of the small dirt roads that narrowed into bicycle tracks in the approach towards Sim Bak Village.

'For goodness' sake, don't make Third Wife wait. She might get annoyed with Silver Frond! You're creating a commotion over nothing, everyone's watching,' said Ah Bee Soh, pushing a knee against her husband's side in exasperation, for indeed, the crowd of faces at the window had grown denser.

'Father, please,' Silver Flower and Silver Pearl begged, as much to help their sister, as to hasten their turn to ride in the magnificent car.

Genuinely distressed but still capable of enjoying all the attention it created, Ah Bee Koh said with a great show of reluctance, 'All right, just this once,' stood up and allowed his favourite daughter to take his hand to lead him outside. Silver Frond gave a little shriek of joy at the change of heart.

'Wait!' cried Ah Bee Soh in alarm. 'We are not properly dressed for a ride in a car.' She thought of the formidably dressed, jewelled and perfumed Third Wife, looked at her husband's dirty singlet and khaki shorts and her own faded samfoo, and became even more alarmed.

'Please hurry,' said Silver Frond, not at all liking the thought of Third Wife or the Indian chauffeur getting impatient.

Ah Bee Koh, for the second time, felt the need to be assertive. 'No,' he said firmly. 'If my clothes are not fit enough for the car, I shall not go near it.'

Silver Frond, agitated almost to tears, cried, 'All right, never mind!' and dragged her father out. She had no idea of course that it would be a mistake and his greatest humiliation.

For from the moment he reached the spot where the car was parked, he sensed the contempt of the Indian chauffeur, and at once set about confronting it. The man, dressed neatly in white shirt and trousers, was standing beside the car and nonchalantly chewing a blade of grass. Sneering half-smiles played around his mouth, as he looked pointedly, first at the singlet, then the khaki shorts, then the dirty sandals. He did the survey a second time, even more pointedly, his head moving up and down slowly, the blade of grass dangling from a corner of his mouth.

'Father, would you like to get inside? And this is Third Wife.' The lady had graciously got out of the car to be introduced, but Ah Bee Koh remained standing, his face turned towards the chauffeur, who was getting bolder, never blinking once as he looked with utter contempt upon the young mistress's yokel of a father, bringing to the gleaming black Ford the taints and odours of his village.

'Why is that Indian looking at me like that?' demanded Ah Bee Koh. He advanced one belligerent step towards the chauffeur, whose insolence was growing by the second.

'Father, please get in.'

Ah Bee Koh gave one last glare, turned and was about to get in, when the chauffeur shouted to him, 'Wait,' pointed to his left foot, and gestured to him to wipe it first. Everyone looked at a small splash of mud on Ah Bee Koh's left foot, just below the ankle.

His immediate response was to turn around, stride purposefully towards a small muddy puddle near a bush, plunge his right foot into it, and return to the car. Everyone gazed in shock at the mud-covered foot, which, with the perverseness of a child, he waggled provocatively at the chauffeur. Flushed with triumph, he was about to get into the car, when the man, incensed at the impending desecration of the fine interior, which he cleaned every day with a brush and rags, rushed up and stopped him.

'What? How dare you, you black-skinned servant, you.'

Ah Bee Koh lunged angrily at the chauffeur, who deftly caught him around the waist. There followed much shouting and struggling, and then a tremendous yell as Ah Bee Koh, who was no match at all for the tall, muscular chauffeur, was flung backward and sent crashing into a clump of thorny bushes. There arose a chorus of shrieks from the women. Silver Frond burst into tears.

Ah Bee Soh helped her husband up from the ground. He stood unsteadily, nursing a bruised elbow. The chauffeur calmly brushed down his white shirt and smoothed his hair. Then he walked to the car boot, opened it to get out some rags, and began to clean, with meticulous care, the part of the car that had had contact with the offensive mud-covered foot.

'All right, I want you to do it,' said Ah Bee Koh to his daughter. 'Right now. Go on, do it!'

'Do what, Father?' said Silver Frond timidly, amidst her tears.

Ah Bee Koh turned an astonished face upon the others and exclaimed, 'Did you hear that? Her father gets insulted by a black-skinned servant and she says, "Do what?"'

Never more perplexed in her life, Silver Frond refrained from asking again what she was supposed to do, and had recourse to more tears.

'I want you,' said Ah Bee Koh with savage intensity, the veins throbbing dangerously on his neck, 'to sack this man, this servant, this scum of the earth,' he pointed a quivering finger at the chauffeur, 'right here and now.'

'Oh no, oh no!' cried Silver Frond, her eyes wide open in horror. 'You know I can't do that, Father!'

'Of course you can,' sneered the father. 'You are the fourth wife of the Venerable One, the mistress of the Fifth House, the owner of this car, and the employer of this servant.'

'Oh no, oh no!'

Silver Frond began to wring her hands in her acute distress, looked around the circle of staring faces as if for support, turned abruptly and found herself in the comforting arms of Third Wife, who said soothingly, 'It's all right. Everything will be all right.'

'Let it be clear, then,' Ah Bee Koh said with great dignity to his daughter, who was trembling in Third Wife's arms, 'that I will never consent to sit in that car as long as it is driven by that black-skinned devil. And you need not trouble to come this way again.'

'Yes, let everything be clear. You have caused your father great sorrow.' It was once again the persistent voice at the window, now attached to a plump woman with a round, cheerful face, wearing a faded *samfoo* with heavy sweat rings under her arms. She had clearly followed them to the parked car and watched the entire drama, unnoticed.

Choosing to ignore her, everyone continued to watch Ah Bee Koh in his towering rage and to cast quick glances at the chauffeur, who was actually humming a tune as he bent to inspect the car for more damage.

Ah Bee Koh turned his face skywards and shouted angrily, shaking a fist, 'From this moment, let the gods be my witness! Silver Frond is no more my daughter.' He turned and walked away.

Ah Bee Soh made little agitated noises, shook her head, wrung her hands, and said to Silver Frond, 'You'd better go home now,' before following her husband, still shaking her head and wringing her hands.

Silver Flower and Silver Pearl stood around uncertainly, wondering if the unfortunate incident had dashed all hopes of their ride in the car, until their mother called to them, and they went running after her.

Silver Frond thought in anguish, Oh, why must all this happen? An image appeared in her mind and instantly dried up her tears in a chill of fear. She saw the old severe face, heard the voice: 'How many times do I have to tell you that it displeases me when you choose to disobey me?'

'Never mind,' said Third Wife, who was observing her closely. She put a comforting hand on her shoulder. 'Don't ever let the Old One know about this. I myself will warn the chauffeur—'

'Tch, tch, tch! You must ask your father forgiveness! The gods have today witnessed his shame.' The obtrusive, round-faced woman with the sweat rings was determined to stay till the very end to give advice.

'Go away!' Third Wife screamed. 'You busybody, you village riff-raff, go back to your pigs and chickens!'

14
Fastidious Medicine and the Cinnabar Gate

Third Wife said, 'Open your mouth, there's a good girl.' Silver Frond grimaced but obediently opened her mouth to receive yet one more spoonful of the black, pungent stuff from a clay bowl, placed on the table instead of held in the other hand, because Third Wife needed the hand for giving encouraging pats in the bitter medicine-taking.

It had to be clay all the way, Third Wife had explained, for the stuff to have its good effects – a clay pot for brewing it for the six required hours, a clay ladle for taking it out of the pot, a clay bowl for holding it, and finally a clay spoon, for feeding the patient, mouthful by slow mouthful, down to the last drop. Third Wife had sent Tali-gelem to the market to get these requisite agents of healing.

'Can I pay you for them?' said Silver Frond between the grimaces.

'Of course not! How could you even think of that?' said Third Wife reproachfully.

Some medicines were fastidious, like humans, and laid down precise preconditions. Like the Sticky Brown Sugar Pudding for the New Year, which refused to bubble and thicken properly over the fire in the presence of impatient inquiries – 'How much longer?' – the Cinnabar Gate Strengthening Herbal Brew refused to work with unworthy utensils. It was entitled to make even greater demands than the Sticky Brown Sugar Pudding, for its function was much nobler: to strengthen the virginal body for its first duty.

The brews that Ah Bee Soh had been bringing for her daughter had not worked, probably because they were inferior in quality or because their preparation had not been meticulous enough. Third Wife said the herbs for her brew were available only in one medicine-shop in Singapore, and the owner was extremely selective about his customers.

'Ah, one more mouthful! Good girl,' said Third Wife with soothing encouragement, as Silver Frond choked and gasped, but obediently opened her mouth. She looked into the bowl in Third Wife's hand and saw, to her relief, that there was only a little of the horrible stuff left.

All those goose-bumps, Third Wife had explained patiently, were because of a weak Cinnabar Gate. After twelve doses of the brew, spaced precisely over a period of forty days, the weak Feminine Gate would gain strength and be able to fling open in joyous welcome of the Masculine Presence. Those treacherous goose-bumps would be banished for ever, and the young bride – still called a bride after six months – would be ready at last to do her duty.

Silver Frond was already more than halfway through this marvellous programme of assistance to frightened, virginal wombs. She counted the number of clay bowls to be gone through. Four more. Then it would be three, then two, then the last one, and all her worries would be over.

She had begun to have a new subject in her dreams – an as yet unidentifiable woman, looking very much like Mee Mee, who always stood behind her husband and massaged his back with delicately knocking fists. In one of the dreams, the Old One pulled her to him and sat her on his lap, both of them laughing joyously together. In another, she was wearing a very large, loose blouse to accommodate the enormous roundness of her belly, and he was rubbing it in slow, circular, loving movements.

If Silver Frond had any grievance against the Goddess Pearly Face, it was for the detailed portrayal of Fifth Wife. As yet non-existent, it was amazing how she had so quickly become a threatening presence in the dreams.

Bad dreams, Fifth Wife, goose-bumps – they were a triad of evil that would be defeated by the Cinnabar Gate Strengthening Herbal Brew programme.

The chief beneficiary of the programme happened to pass by as the last spoonful was swallowed.

'Errmm,' said the Old One, surprised but not displeased by the strange sight of Third Wife tenderly spooning herbal medicine into the mouth of the rival wife she would have happily destroyed only a few months ago. Third Wife, who was gently wiping Silver Frond's mouth with her own handkerchief in the ultimate manifestation of the new amity, was about to say something when the Old One put up a hand to stop her, said, 'Errmm,' again and left. He had no use for women's small talk, much less the effusive explanations he was sure Third Wife was only too ready to launch into.

He would remember to advise his bride, 'Why don't you try to befriend First Wife instead? You can trust her more.'

15
Gifts From Distraught Women

Silver Frond sat in the kitchen, eating pickled olives to get rid of the bitter taste of the powerful Cinnabar Gate Strengthening Herbal Brew, still lingering in her mouth after a whole day. She heard footsteps, looked up and saw Black Dog's wife standing in front of her.

The woman looked extremely nervous. She was holding a covered bowl of something in both hands. She said, 'This is very good birdsnest. I've brewed it with pumpkin, to make it more nourishing.' The gracious words accompanying the gift were at odds with the alarming nervousness of the giver. She was a picture of wretchedness: her hair was uncombed, her voice trembled, her lips quivered and her eyes, red-rimmed with distress, darted about uneasily as if to detect a spying presence.

Silver Frond said, 'Black Dog Soh, what's the matter?'

The woman instantly burst out, 'Take my birdsnest! Don't take her brews! You mustn't trust her – I should know – I say, don't trust her.'

She broke down in a messy splatter of tears. Black Dog's wife, who had mastered the subtleties of giving and receiving secret information, was now displaying the exact opposite, talking in a voice loud enough to be heard in the adjoining house, and creating an instant audience of ears pressed against walls.

The woman became wildly incoherent: 'I have proof that he has slept with her – but what can I do – they say she gets her magic charms from a Thai woman.' As if bound by a magic spell herself, she was unable to utter the perpetrator's name.

Black Dog appeared as if from nowhere. One moment Silver Frond was gazing in dismayed bewilderment at the poor ranting woman, and the next, she was looking at her husband, sternly frowning, standing beside her. He said sternly, 'You are not well, let's go home now,' and took his wife's arm in a firm grip.

She shook off his hand. But his presence had an immediate calming effect on her. Her fury subsided into small whines, as she blew her nose into a handkerchief and wiped her eyes. 'How could you do this to me – you know I have nowhere to go – our four children ...' In the midst of the torment, she remembered to tell Silver Frond to drink the birdsnest before it got cold. 'It works best when drunk warm,' she said tearfully. 'I've put in special pumpkin. Don't drink other people's medicine. I tell you, it will harm you in the end.'

Through an elaborate silent display of head-shaking, frowning and twirling his forefinger against the side of his head, Black Dog managed to convey to Silver Frond the message that his wife had, for some time now, been unwell both in body and mind. He hinted, in a low voice, that she would not be able to come to work any more. He further hinted that her cure might necessitate a long period of cleansing in a temple, to rid her of whatever evil spirits were troubling her.

All this he conveyed in a mere whisper, but his wife heard and cried out angrily, 'Evil spirits, my foot! Is that your easy answer to the problem?' She turned to Silver Frond and spoke with great earnestness. '*She* is the evil spirit, you mustn't trust her.'

Her husband once more took her arm and said grimly, 'That's enough. Get back home now,' and pushed her roughly towards the door.

Protesting loudly, she struggled to face Silver Frond and say, 'See? See what I mean? He treats me cruelly, whereas—'

Black Dog said between his teeth, 'I say, that's enough!'

Suddenly, at the doorway, the tormented woman stopped, then squatted down heavily on the floor. 'What are you doing?' snarled Black Dog and proceeded to drag her up. Once more, she shook off his hands. She remained squatting, her arms now clasped tightly around her knees. Closing her eyes, and moaning softly, she began to rock to and fro, and could have passed for a subdued inmate in an asylum, or a temple devotee in trance, awaiting the arrival of the gods.

Her husband stood beside her in silent, helpless rage. Finally he turned to Silver Frond and said, his face dangerously white and taut, 'You see what I mean? I can't do anything with her. Please tell her to come home with me.'

Dazed by the confusion, a hundred troubling thoughts whirling inside her head like threatening bees, the young bride said weakly, 'Black Dog Soh, you'd better go home now.'

The woman continued to squat on the floor, now crying softly. Finally she struggled up, stood unsteadily and said to her husband, 'You think I don't know, but I know everything.' She added ominously, 'The gods are just. One day, everything ...' She raised her eyes heavenwards in a last, desperate appeal, blew her nose, smoothed down her hair and clothes and walked out, followed by her husband.

'Fourth Mistress, First Mistress has sent me to give this to you.'

Amazing! There was to be no end to the gifts of food from distraught women that day. Everyone seemed determined to assist her weak, inept body to perform its first duty as a wife. As soon as Black Dog and his wife had walked out, a maidservant from the First House walked in, with a gift of black chicken brewed with ginseng from First Wife. The maidservant had brought a message too, which she delivered carefully, word for word: 'First Mother says to take care of yourself and be alert at all times.'

The maid broke off with a little start of surprise, for the lady herself had suddenly appeared in the doorway. Silver Frond turned to look in utter astonishment. There was First Wife standing with silent authority, in her habitual grey silk, long-sleeved blouse and black silk trousers.

It was her first visit to the Fifth House, and it was being made in violation of previous vows never to step into the domain of the new wife who had created so much disruption. It had, moreover, been an impulsive decision, unusual for the calm, steady woman, but as soon as she had sent the maidservant with the gift of black chicken and ginseng, she had decided to follow with a personal appearance. For her message was important, and she had feared the maidservant would not deliver it properly.

'You must be alert at all times. You must not trust those who secretly seek to do you harm. I am telling you this because you are young and have a good heart. You have caused much disruption to the Great House, but it is not your fault, and you mean well.' The words were uttered slowly, with the same severity of tone as when she had stood at the doorway of her husband's room in the darkness of night, to warn and advise, impelled by the same solid decency and sense of duty to ancestors that would make her, in the end, the most respected of all the wives, though not the best loved.

Even in her bewildered state, Silver Frond was aware of an idea rapidly shaping in her head. She had to act fast, so she rose from her chair, ran to First Wife and said, in a rush of urgency moderated by respectful humility: 'Please, please, stay and sit down, and let me offer you a cup of tea.' It was an excellent idea, turning the surprise visit into an opportunity for the long desired ritual of acceptance, transforming the routine tea of courtesy for a visitor to the all-important cup of conciliation.

An angry frown appeared on First Wife's face. 'I came to advise you, that's all. Don't expect more. I will not be coming to the Fifth House again.'

In those days, the Great House was a hive of troubled activity. Everyone said the young bride was the cause of it all. Silver Frond had yearned for the stigma to be removed with a cup of tea. But First Wife was adamant. 'When the Old One informed me about his decision to take you in as Fourth Wife, I had told him not to expect me to receive any tea from you. My position remains unchanged.'

The next moment, she was gone, followed by the maidservant.

A strange day of gifts from enemies suddenly grown sympathetic, of nourishing food turned toxic because of the dire warnings that came with them! All to be shunned, except the gift of the Cinnabar Gate Strengthening Herbal Brew. It had come from the deadly Third Wife, but it was a true gift, because it was beginning to show good results.

Only the night before, the Old One, stroking her face, arms and legs, had said, 'You're improving. I can tell.'

She had a clear idea of what she would do when the whole thing was over. She would give Third Wife a handsome sum of money. How much did the medicine cost? How much her time spent in the meticulous brewing of the medicine? How much her energy? She would multiply the total sum many times over, to make it the richest compensation ever. It would be a payment, not a reward. A reward implied continuing friendly relations, which she had no wish for. A payment implied a business transaction, and signalled its termination.

How useful money was proving to be in her new life!

When the whole thing was over, she would take her husband's advice of befriending First Wife instead. Meanwhile, she depended on Third Wife's Cinnabar Gate Strengthening Herbal Brew.

16
A Happy Day On the Beach

'Come,' said the Old One. 'I'm taking you to the beach in Changi. It will only be a short ride.' His young bride was looking paler than usual, and he thought the fresh sea breezes would do her good. Besides, she had never been to a beach.

She had never been to the Grand Opera Hall and he had taken her there one evening for a dazzling performance and afterwards for supper at the grand Sin Hup Restaurant, which she had never even heard of. When she told him she had never tasted ice cream, *real* ice cream, not the kind regularly peddled in her village by a man on a tricycle, he took her to a bar with a foreign name, frequented by the foreign servicemen and their wives, and bought her a large tub of the good, expensive stuff. He did not want the foreigners to look at her, so she stayed in the car while he went inside and made the purchase.

His wealth and love converted each 'never' of her deprived life in a village into 'the best ever' of a richly memorable experience, which she was quick to share with her sisters. 'The costumes were covered with shining jewels that almost blinded me! The gongs were so loud I had to cover my ears. It was the best roast duck, with the skin peeling off in large crispy pieces, which I liked especially. The ice-cream had real milk! I could taste it! I will save some for you the next time.' Her sisters listened with wide-eyed awe.

Both were in the kitchen as she came down, with a large umbrella tucked under her arm, ready to go on a happy beach outing.

'Oh,' said Silver Frond in dismay, not at the visit itself, for she loved her sisters dearly, but at its untimeliness.

It turned out that the father was ill and in need of money for medicine. The sisters told the lie, loudly and confidently, for the benefit of any spying maidservant. As soon as the money was dissipated in drink and at the gambling table, they would be back for more, and maintain the lie with the same practised ease.

'Quick, you must go now,' said Silver Frond anxiously, after pressing the money into their hands. But Silver Flower and Silver Pearl continued standing and giggling, covering their mouths and nudging each other. Their mission for their father over, they were now ready to benefit from the visit themselves. They would not let their sister's outing rob them of the rich haul of gifts they always took back from the Fifth House – leftover chicken or duck from the food cupboard, peanut biscuits, tins of Ovaltine, tins of condensed milk, and, best of all, money from the money-box on top of a corner cupboard, which their sister seemed to be saving for the sole purpose of giving away to others.

Silver Frond gathered as much of the expected good stuff as she could find, put it into two large paper bags and said, even more anxiously, 'You must go. The Old One will be down here any moment.'

The Old One, when he appeared, stunned everyone with a generosity both abundant and loquacious. 'Why,' he said in good-humoured, mock reproach to his wife, 'you are very stingy with your sisters!' Then he himself went to the store-cupboards and brought out more tins of biscuits, more cans of milk, more packets of biscuits, to overwhelm the two sisters, who were too terrified even to greet him.

They fled with the gifts. The Old One laughed to see the joyous amazement on his young bride's face.

'Today is a day of peace and joy,' he said, playfully pinching her chin. 'You have been under too much stress recently, and look too pale. Let the good air in Changi Beach put back the colour in your cheeks.' He told her he had been there once, as a young man, and had felt very happy and carefree walking along the beach, listening to the waves and breathing the healthy sea air.

It turned out to be one of the happiest outings in her married life. The sights and sounds of the beach delighted her. Her husband said, 'Don't be afraid,' went down on his knees, rolled up her trousers, and invited her to walk into the water. She was afraid and resisted laughingly, but he insisted and together they walked along the water's edge, their trousers rolled right up to mid-knee, challenging each other, like two children, to go first into the water. Then they took a long leisurely walk together, holding hands and laughing with sensuous delight as their feet sank into the warm wet sand. They stopped and turned to look at the long trail of their footprints in the sand, and the waves erasing them and leaving the sand smooth and pristine once more.

The Old One said, looking proudly at his young bride, 'You are so beautiful. You have made me very happy,' and she smiled happily and refrained from mentioning that in a very short while, when she had drunk from the last clay bowl, she would make him happier still.

There was nobody else on the beach, except, in the distance, an old man and his young grandson. The child was digging a hole in the sand, and the old man was sitting on a mat, watching him, a coconut palm leaf draped over his head to provide shade. When he saw the Old One and Silver Frond standing together, looking out towards the sea and watching a boat bobbing on the waves in the far distance, he yelled cheerfully, 'Good morning! Have you come to enjoy the fresh sea air too?'

The Old One called back in an equally friendly voice, 'Good morning to you too! This is a very fine day for an outing, isn't it?'

But the friendly stranger spoilt it all for him when he shouted, 'There's a very large squid, or something with funny legs or claws, which has been washed ashore, just a short distance from here, near that clump of coconut trees. My grandson was very fascinated by it. Why don't you take your granddaughter to have a look too?'

The Old One muttered, 'Meddlesome old fool,' and took his young bride's arm to lead her away in the opposite direction.

His bruised vanity was somewhat assuaged when they later returned to the car, parked along the road a distance away, and the chauffeur, opening the door for them, said with genuine admiration, 'The Venerable One looks so happy and young! Sir, your skin is so fresh and rosy! I swear I could not recognise you when you were walking up just now. I had to take another look.'

17
A White and Stricken Face

Second Wife stood before the mirror and carefully combed her hair and put on a fresh layer of rice powder before making her way to the front part of the Fifth House facing the road where the Ford was parked. The unusual care with her appearance, together with the absence of the melon seed packet in her hands announced a clear purpose, despite her attempts to hide it, and the small grandchildren, who were hanging around and closely watching her, were ready to tease her about it. They skipped around her, crying out boldly, 'Second Grandmother, we know! We know! Shall we tell Fourth Grandmother you want a ride in her car?'

'*Choy*! Do you think I am so hard up?'

The more spirited Second Wife's denial became, the less convinced were the children. They circled her, becoming bolder in their teasing, for of all the grandmothers, she inspired the least fear. Behind her back, they imitated, with gross contortions of face and limbs, her walk, her habit of scratching her armpits, the expert ejection of melon seed husks from her mouth, but in her presence they contented themselves with mere verbal teasing. Second Grandmother was their favourite.

'Go away,' she said angrily, shooing them away with both plump arms. 'I've just come to have a look around. Is there a rule against that?'

'Don't bluff, Second Grandmother!' cried a particularly bold little girl, who was the youngest daughter of one of First Wife's daughters. 'Why else would you comb your hair and put powder on your face?'

'I've been twice in the car! We went to so many shops!' proclaimed the grandson, who had in fact been given a ride only once, and been taken to only one shop, where Silver Frond had bought him a bright blue plastic rabbit.

'I've been many times,' lied the third of the grandchildren. He turned to Second Wife and said spitefully, 'You've never been even once. That's because you've never been invited by Fourth Grandmother. Everybody says you're the only one who's never been invited by Fourth Grandmother.'

'Of course I have!' exclaimed Second Wife hotly. 'But I don't wish to ride in her car. Do you think I am so hard up? I told you, I've just come to have a look around!' She made an angry lunge at the children, who ran off giggling. They hid behind a stack of crates by the road, and prepared to watch her every move.

A silly adult being manipulated by disrespectful children in noisy play – First Wife would have frowned in disapproval and delivered her heaviest sarcasm: 'Since the Great House has been taken over by a child-bride, it is most appropriate for all of us to behave childishly!'

Nettled by the tittering children, Second Wife was more aware than ever of the need to get an invitation. The need became excruciating. An invitation no less public and as clearly articulated as the one made to First Wife. Like First Wife, she would decline and demur, and provoke the young bride to persuade and coax, forcing her to go up and up a dizzying spiral of flattery, for all to witness, cancelling out all the insults she had ever suffered in the Great House. This public demonstration of her importance should last for, say, ten minutes, and then she would make a great show of reluctance and finally accept the invitation. She would enter the car with cool indifference, and on her return, she would say, 'Oh, it's not really that different from a trishaw ride. Come to think of it, I prefer trishaws.'

Thus in one fell stroke, she would silence those noisy, troublesome children, command the respect of Fourth Wife, shut Third Wife's scornful mouth once and for all, claim an experience that First Wife had never had, and find out for herself what a ride in a car was like.

Poor Second Wife's plans went awry from the start.

Her jaw dropped in dismay when she saw Third Wife appearing and taking a position of command beside the car, speaking to the chauffeur in a voice of shrill authority, followed by the young bride, who had apparently placed herself under the authority. But no, she would not let Third Wife deter her from her purpose. She shifted about and coughed a little, trying to get the bride's attention. But two more people had appeared on the scene, taking all the attention.

Old Mother, tottering on her small bound feet, and the feeble-minded son, chattering excitedly, were being led towards the car by a maidservant.

Third Wife, who had apparently seen Second Wife watching with open-mouthed astonishment, said in a very loud voice to Silver Frond, 'I told them not to worry; I have the Tiger Balm ready, and we'll open the windows and draw the curtains if it gets too hot.' Then she said to Old Mother, who was as excited as a child, 'You'll sit between Fourth Mistress and myself,' and to the son, who was peering at his reflection in the shining metal of the car door, 'You'll sit in front with the chauffeur.' Finally she turned to the chauffeur and said with much imperiousness, 'Go by Wan Kee Road, and not Jalan Anak, as you did the last time.'

She capped the list of instructions, delivered with relentless precision, with a fitting posture of authoritative hands on hips. It was a flawless performance, watched by many, most of all by Second Wife, still gaping stupidly. Thus had Third Wife established, for anyone who still might have doubts, her position of complete responsibility for this excursion, down to the last details of passenger seating and car route.

The young bride had apparently relegated all authority to her, being too busy seeing about the comfort of Old Mother, who was making excited little noises, and of the son, who was examining the steering wheel with intense concentration.

The car had become the means by which the young newcomer to the Great House was announcing to the world that far from being a threat, she was its truest exemplar of goodwill. A bringer of harmony. She could, at least for the time being, fulfil this role desired by her husband.

A small crowd had gathered. The car was about to start. And still Silver Frond had not noticed Second Wife, who was timidly edging closer, looking extremely fearful in the face of a massive public humiliation. She stopped and looked even more timid, as she saw one of the small grandchildren suddenly run up to the car, knock on the window pane for Silver Frond's attention and jerk an urgent thumb in her direction.

She made to hide behind a pillar, but Silver Frond had already got down and was running towards her. 'Second

Mother,' she said breathlessly, 'I'm sorry I didn't see you. Would you like to come with us?'

Second Wife hesitated. Then, her original intention of displaying lofty indifference returning quickly, she managed to compose her features, and focus her thinking. She said, with a great attempt at nonchalance, 'Actually, I'm quite busy this morning—'

'Please do me the honour.'

This was exactly what she wanted. She trembled with secret delight and, to provoke Silver Frond to a louder repetition of the invitation, said with convincing casualness, 'Well, I don't know whether I will get sick. It's a very hot day, and I'm quite busy—'

'Hurry up!' Third Wife's impatient yell was followed by a chorus of echoes from the watching children: 'Hurry up! Hurry up!'

'Please, Second Mother.'

'I'm not suitably dressed. I should—'

In a later recapitulation of the events that had led to so much misunderstanding and pain, Silver Frond was convinced that the starting point had been this moment: Second Wife's announcement to go for a change of clothes. It had been uttered so softly that it was easily drowned out by the impatient yelling from the car, especially the children's shouts. Silver Frond had then seen the lady turn and leave, and concluded that she had decided not to come along after all. With much relief, she had run back to the car, where Third Wife was fanning Old Mother and the chauffeur was trying to stop the son from bouncing up and down on his seat.

But as the car sped off, Silver Frond realised her mistake. She turned round sharply to see Second Wife's shocked face staring at her. It was the most stricken face she had ever seen, and would subsequently appear to haunt her – a ghostly visage, covered with white rice powder, with two black staring holes for the eyes, and a larger black cavernous hole for the mouth. Not even in the most fearful illustrations of demented female ghosts in her comic books had she seen anything like that.

She gazed at the face until it was out of sight, and noticed, for the first time, the children prancing round it, small figures in an unmistakable dance of mockery. Even from the distance, she could feel the cruelty of the jeers, the pain of the victim standing in the centre.

'Stop!' cried Silver Frond in a panic.

But it was too late. She had to leave Second Wife, dull, fat, despised, but with the same keening need for acceptance and respect, standing in the arena of a public shame.

18
Tea of Contrition and Forgiveness

Third Wife said, 'It's her own fault. Why couldn't she accept the invitation graciously, like everybody else, instead of making a big fuss?'

First Wife said, 'I don't know how long all this childish play will go on, but don't make me part of it!' For Silver Frond had tearfully begged her to go to Second Wife, and convey, on her behalf, a sincere apology for that terrible infliction of shame, since all attempts to do so personally had failed. Second Wife had fled at each approach, locking herself in her room, refusing to come out of the lavatory, running to a neighbour's house to hide.

Once Silver Frond ran after her up a staircase, and she turned round and threatened to throw herself down if not left alone. The maidservants and grandchildren reported that she had been so distressed by the incident that she had actually stopped eating, awakened in the middle of the night to cry, and threatened to kill herself by swallowing detergent.

Third Wife said, 'Ha! Behaving like a spoilt child. Trying to get everybody's attention. I'd ignore her if I were you. One more dose to go, and you're stressing your body instead of preparing it for the final strengthening! What will the Old One say?'

It was fortunate that the grandchildren were too much in awe of the Venerable One to tell him, the chauffeur too unsure of the exact placement of his loyalty, at this stage, to be involved in the messy business of the four wives.

It was the feeble-minded son, of all people, who made the discovery, and alerted everybody. Red-faced and hoarse with excitement, he raised a tremendous howl, like a wild animal, in the middle of the night, about a week after the incident, and woke up everyone in the Great House. The Old One was the first to come down the stairs and check on the hullabaloo. Silver Frond followed timidly; already she knew, with a sinking heart, that the wild howl must be connected with the miserable Second Wife, whose white, powdered face, stricken with shock and shame, she had once more seen in a dream. First Wife and Third Wife followed, with dishevelled hair let loose for the night, and then the servants came running in, one after the other. Everybody stood staring at the son, who was wildly gesturing and trying to say something.

Suddenly, the young man, still blubbering, ran out of the house. Everyone watched the Old One, from beneath lowered eyes, to take the cue for their next move. He was looking extremely displeased to be in the centre of what promised to be a most ludicrous situation. 'Let's see what it is all about,' he said tersely to Silver Frond, and together they walked out, following the trail of wails. The others followed, faces taut with anxiety.

The son stopped in front of the Ford parked, as usual, on the road, directly in front of the house, and pointed a trembling finger at it. It was too dark to see inside the car. The Old One took several steps forward, but the son suddenly leaped ahead of him, opened the car door and then, in a voice hoarse with excitement, pointed to a huge, crumpled heap on the back seat.

Even in the dark, the plump fair arms, the enormous buttocks were recognisable. As everyone rushed to look, the crumpled heap stirred a little, and then let out a low moan.

'Oh my God,' cried Silver Frond, as she saw a pile of small empty bottles scattered around on the seat and floor. It was exactly as she had seen it in a dream, except that they were not the large bottles for the liquid detergent regularly brought by the deliveryman for the daily laundry. They were small bottles by comparison, but equally deadly-looking. There were two bottles emptied of Tiger Balm, three of Windy Stomach Oil, and two of Dragon Embrocation.

Third Wife would later remark with a contemptuous laugh: 'Oil doesn't kill! I told you she was only trying to get attention.'

It turned out that she had ingested only one third of the Tiger Balm and a quarter of the Windy Stomach and Dragon Embrocation oils. She refused to be rushed to hospital, and insisted she would be all right, which she was, after two bouts of vomiting and a long rest in bed.

The Old One, livid with rage, had only one question: What had started it? For a while, his rage hushed the entire Great House into a deathly silence.

'Please, Second Mother.'

Silver Frond knelt before the lady, who looked very pale and weak as she sat in a large cane chair, attended by a maid who was massaging her temples. The young bride knelt with utmost humility with the tea of deepest contrition, in a small porcelain cup, which she held in both hands. Second Wife turned her head away.

'Please, Second Mother,' said Silver Frond with tears in her eyes. 'Please forgive me for causing you all this pain.' The lady continued to keep her face averted.

First Wife, who was sitting in a chair nearby, said, 'Take the tea. Don't make a fuss.'

Second Wife whimpered, 'I have never been so humiliated in my life. Even the children mocked me.'

First Wife said again, 'For goodness' sake, take the tea. The girl has shown enough contrition.'

Second Wife pressed a handkerchief to her eyes, and sobbed, 'I wanted to die. You all should have left me to die!'

Her sister gave a snort, got up, stood before her and said with authority, 'I say you should receive the tea.'

Second Wife put the handkerchief back into her blouse pocket and received the cup of tea grudgingly.

Silver Frond burst into tears.

She was about to leave the room, when First Wife said, 'Stop,' and ordered a servant to prepare another cup of tea and to give it to the distressed girl. Then she sat down again, assuming the unmistakable magisterial air of the senior wife about to acknowledge obeisance.

Tremblingly, with tears of joy this time, Silver Frond knelt and offered her the cup. With a grave expression, she received it, took a sip and said, 'You are a good person. I have looked into your heart, and have seen that it intends no harm to anybody.'

First Wife's act of conciliation was the only good that came from the incident. In other aspects, it was painful, indeed, one of the most painful experiences in the Great House. For it meant the permanent loss of the car.

'It has brought more trouble than I will tolerate,' said the Old One testily. 'I have already given instructions to Black Dog to sell it to Towkay Lam.'

Towkay Lam had acquired a new wife too, some months back, and the car, it was rumoured, was less to please her than to placate the other wives.

19
Tremblingly, in Shadows

Third Wife and Silver Frond had a question for each other, which both were holding back till the moment when the last drop had been drunk from the last bowl, to end a period of uneasy truce and extraordinary collusion. For both knew that after that moment, their lives would pass into a new phase when such questions would no longer be relevant.

Why do you trust me?

Should I trust you when I have been warned against you?

If the Old One were to tell the story of his four wives and the intersection of their four lives as they fought for influence under his sheltering roof, the narrative would pivot on this amazing cooperation between these two wives. His question to both would dispense with the whole matter of trust and concentrate on practical realities: *Why did you have to go through all this fuss and nonsense on my account?*

But perhaps such questions would never be asked because they could never be answered. For in the Great House, the truths of the heart, fearful of tradition, had hidden themselves, or dared to appear only as half-truths. In the Great House, everyone lived under some form of fear, and moved warily, tremblingly, in shadows.

The need to discharge the saddest truth of Third Wife's overburdened heart took on a desperate quality, contorting her features into a mask of pure virulence and infusing her body with so much new strength that the bowl she was grasping between her hands cracked in two. The gentle dispenser of healing medicine had become its destructive agent.

Third Wife, quivering with dangerous energy, subjected Silver Frond to a long, slow, withering scrutiny. Here was a girl, a mere village girl, for whom the Old One – fool that he was! – had distorted truth beyond all imagining.

'Do you think,' she sneered, 'that the happiness you're going to give the Old One tomorrow night, can even match the happiness *I* have given him so many nights?'

Silver Frond, as usual sucking on a piece of pickled leek to get rid of the bitter taste of the Cinnabar Gate Strengthening Herbal Brew, instantly took it out of her mouth, to say the appropriate words for placating an adversary. 'No, no, no,' she said humbly, and shook her head vigorously.

Placatory gestures had become an essential part of the strategy of survival in the Great House, and watching Third Wife's sudden transformation, she was ready to unleash as many as were necessary. She had come a long way.

'Let me tell you this,' said Third Wife, her eyes flashing fire. 'When the Old One lies on his deathbed and asks himself which of his four wives brought him greatest happiness, it will not be First Wife, nor Second Wife, nor you, who will come before his eyes. It will be me! And if he dies with a smile on his lips – may the old fool die with a smile on his lips! – it won't be because he's thinking of First Wife's total devotion, nor Second Wife's laughable stupidity, nor your young beauty. *Tchah!* None of these matters as much to a man as a woman's skills in bed. The old fool knows this better than any man, I can vouch for that. As his decrepit old body approaches the grave, he will remember how my skills revived it night after night. "You are amazing," he once said to me, sitting up in bed and looking at me. "No woman has given me or will give me so much pleasure." His very words, I swear!'

The living proof of the hollowness of that avowal stood solidly before her, still childishly sucking on the piece of leek, and drove her voice to a higher pitch of frenzy.

'False! False! He as good as promised he would never take another wife, and here you are, Egg Girl from Sim Bak Village—'

The old exasperation at the insult had, during the months of intense learning in her new life, been successfully tamed to achieve the harmony so sternly demanded by her husband. Thus was Silver Frond able to respond to the insult with calm acknowledgment: 'Thank you for all you have done for me.'

'Egg Girl,' said Third Wife, 'you might be interested to know that First Wife hates you most of all for your causing the Old One to desecrate the memory of his ancestors. Second Wife hates you chiefly because of the good things that the Old One has lavished on you – the car, the jewels, the fine food. And do you know what I hate you most for?'

Silver Frond had no ready answer of placation, and merely looked silently at her. The piece of leek having been fully sucked and swallowed, she had recourse to the biting of a forefinger.

'For your education!' screamed Third Wife. 'For all the learning under the *sinseh*, so that your simple village mind can fill with knowledge and your roughened village hands can hold a pen and write beautiful words! I was never allowed to have a *sinseh*, though I begged and begged the Old One.' The pain of the discrimination stung Third Wife to angry tears. 'I would have made a better student than you! I've got much more up here than you!' She repeatedly jabbed her forehead with a sharp forefinger. 'Even as a child, I could memorise whole poems. I could repeat any proverb or wise saying. You know how I felt when I first walked past your classroom and saw the *sinseh* teaching you how to read and write? I ran off and hid in the bathroom to sob my heart out!'

Silver Frond opened her mouth to say something, but Third Wife said sharply, 'Don't say anything, village girl! And take that finger out of your mouth! That's right, a mere village girl, and me the daughter of a much respected man, and he chose to give you the education.'

'I'm sorry,' blurted Silver Frond, and was not sure she was.

'I said not to say anything, but just listen to my story! Nobody listens to my story.'

Gratitude, apology, praise, blame, argument, agreement – suddenly none of these mattered any more. All Third Wife wanted was a pair of ears to listen to the secret tale ready to burst from her bitter heart. The dim-witted son, the old deaf mother, the youngest grandchild as yet incapable of comprehending adult talk – she would have caught hold of any of them to listen to her tale.

'Come with me,' she said to Silver Frond, taking her by the hand. 'I want to show you something.'

Third Wife led her all the way to her house, and up the staircase to her bedroom. She locked the door, to emphasise the enormity of the secret about to be revealed.

20
Third Wife's Astonishing Tale

Silver Frond listened wide-eyed. It was the most marvellous tale of passion and intrigue, deceit and pleasure, jealousy and triumph. Liang Por, at his best, could not have told a more spellbinding tale.

Third Wife's face, pinched and darkened with bitterness, cleared wondrously with the telling of her magical tale. She looked younger, more beautiful.

The tale began with sex.

As soon as she arrived at the Great House as a young bride, the Old One established a routine by which each of the three wives was entitled to two nights a week with him, leaving him free to give the remaining night to whichever wife he wished. As expected, she was the one who had privilege of the extra night, to the intense annoyance of First Wife and Second Wife.

Things became worse for them when the Old One, totally enamoured of the new wife's charms and skills, desired to spend *all* his nights with her. His desire was only exceeded by the need to maintain harmony in the household, something strictly enjoined by the ancestors, the best exemplar being one who had eight wives and never witnessed a single fight among them.

Now the Old One was not a man to submit easily to the strictures of tradition. Harmony among wives and respect for ancestors, on the one hand, and total private self-indulgence, on the other – he wanted them all. He soon developed the simple ruse, on his two nights each with First Wife and Second Wife, of claiming to have a stomach-ache, a backache, a headache, or any illness of the mild kind that had no need of fussy ministrations from women and could be easily cured by simply going back to one's room to rest and sleep alone.

First Wife knew of the subterfuge right from the start, but understood and appreciated its face saving grace. Second Wife never did, and till the end of her life believed her husband to be one of those lucky few whose perfect record of good health was marred only by occasional attacks of stomach-ache on the marital bed.

Once happily back in his room, the Old One would swing into exciting action. He would send a trusted servant to go secretly to Third Wife and bring her to him. The escapade was usually in the still, silent hours between midnight and dawn, before the servants woke up. The clandestine nature of the trysts between two lawfully wedded persons only heightened the excitement, appealing to the Old One's sense of boyish mischief and her own delight in outwitting the other two wives, who showed their jealousy in any amount of spitting, mouth-twisting and snide comments.

'He dreaded to see the first light of dawn,' said Third Wife, and for the first time, her eyes filled with tears of tenderness, not anger. '"Must you go?" he would say, and my heart would break to leave him. Once we overslept. The servants were already awake and making a great clattering noise preparing the morning meal. They were all spies for First Wife and Second

Wife. One of them would soon come with the Old One's morning tea and towels. You know what he did? He locked the door and said, "Don't worry! I'm going to keep the door locked all morning and shoo everybody away. Now why don't you take out that ear-cleaner again?"'

Third Wife's eyes never sparkled more brightly than when she spoke about the ear-cleaning in those deliriously happy days, before the Old One lost interest and the ear-cleaning lost its sexual role, and became just that. The climactic point, said Third Wife, was when she carefully and slowly brought out a long, thin curl of wax from his ear, dangling delicately from the tiny bowl of the exquisite little instrument, showed it to him as he lay on her lap, and watched him go into a frenzy as he sprang up and was all over her.

'I like your story,' said Silver Frond, and meant it. 'It's even better than Liang Por's.'

'It isn't over yet!' cried Third Wife. 'Now I want to show you something, as I promised.'

She picked up a chair, carried and placed it in front of a tall cupboard, stood on it and managed to reach the topmost shelf from where she brought down a small flat tin box.

'Look,' she said and opened it to reveal a small pile of ear-cleaners, ordinary ones of plain metal, not the exquisitely crafted ones of silver and gold that she wore in the small cylindrical locket on a gold chain round her neck.

Silver Frond gazed wonderingly at them.

'Ah, the memories, the memories!' said Third Wife, and soon she was lost in tender recollection. 'Every secret visit in the night, commemorated by each of these precious things! As I watched them grow, how happy I was!' She poured out the tiny instruments on to the palm of her hand and arranged them in a row on a table, touching each lovingly with her fingers.

'I'm very unhappy,' she said quietly, the tears flowing freely now. 'I've been unhappy for a long time. Even when I'm laughing with Black Dog. I know all those rumours about us. Don't believe them. You think I want any man after the Old One?' She touched the ear-cleaners again. 'They used to give some comfort. Now they give only pain.'

The frenzied anger was returning. She rose, breathing heavily, a wild look in her eyes, like a tigress about to spring. Then, with a little cry, she fell upon the ear-cleaners and swept them off the table with both hands.

Silver Frond instantly rushed to rescue those instruments of pleasure and remembrance and return them to their owner.

'Oh, don't bother,' said Third Wife wearily. 'Let Tali-gelem sweep them up and throw them into the dustbin later. I don't want them any more.' She turned to Silver Frond and gave her one last long scrutiny. 'Egg Girl from Sim Bak Village, why do you trust me?'

Silver Frond had not yet reached the stage of unrehearsed placation. She opened her mouth to say something, but was instantly stopped.

'No. Don't say anything,' said Third Wife. 'Whatever you say now will be a knife cutting into my flesh.' She looked at the enemy and continued, slowly and reflectively, 'You're no longer that simple village girl everybody takes you for, you know. You've grown up since coming to the Great House. Oh yes! I've been watching you. You might well turn out to be the cleverest of the four wives.'

Silver Frond's strategies did not go that far into the future. She stood hesitantly at the doorway, not knowing what to say.

'Your big night tomorrow, eh?' said Third Wife. 'Let me give you some advice. Have a good bath first. Clean yourself thoroughly. The Old One is fastidious. Don't talk too much. Don't move too much, but don't stay still and unresponsive, like a log of wood. Don't touch his ears. That's the part he can't bear touching, outside the ear-cleaning. When you're in a sitting position, press your arms against your sides – like this – to push your breasts together – like this. He seems to like the sight of breasts pushed to bursting point against each other. See how much I know? Now go and get ready.'

'Thank you for—'

Third Wife raised an imperious hand of dismissal. 'Your story is beginning,' she said. 'Mine hasn't ended yet. Oh no, don't you for one instant believe my narrative is over. And don't you for one instant feel sorry for me.'

21
Fastidious Preparations

Make sure her hair is shampooed with scented water, oiled and dressed beautifully, with a large yellow chrysanthemum pinned over the right ear.

Make sure her skin is free of all blemish, her breath sweet and pleasing.

Make sure her ears are adorned with the ancestral Empress jade ear-drops, her fingers with the ancestral Mountain Cloud diamond and jade rings, with the largest on the middle finger of her right hand, her ankles with the Golden Sky Ribbon anklets.

Make sure her left wrist is adorned with the Bamboo Green jade bangle and her right wrist with the Phoenix Purple Jade bangle, her right shoulder with the Moongate Pavilion brooch, her neck with the Three Golden Dragons chain and pendant.

Make sure the bridal blouse and bridal skirt are free from the smallest crease, sweat stain or camphor smell.

Make sure her eyebrows are plucked cleanly and finely, her cheeks delicately rouged, her lips lightly coloured.

Make sure her ears are cleaned thoroughly, her fingernails and toenails trimmed, her navel and the area around and below it cleaned with warm water mixed with a little brandy.

It was the longest mental check-list for Suan Choo Sim, most trusted matchmaker, who also doubled up as Preparer-of-the-Bride-for-the-Important-Event. She had been summoned to the Great House six months ago for the latter purpose, and was once more, to her surprise and delight, entrusted with the task. Her experience in that special role was well-known, as was her meticulous observance of the rituals to ensure that the evil spirits were kept away on that most auspicious occasion, and the good spirits attracted to come with their full load of beneficence.

So Silver Frond was made, at different stages in the preparations to meet the bridegroom in the bridal chamber, to turn and face the doorway, turn away from it, cast a handful of rice grains in the air, light a joss-stick, hold on to the end of a red ribbon, take a sip of blessed temple water. She heard Suan Choo Sim's voice blaring instructions, like a stern teacher, and obeyed automatically, like a wooden doll she saw once, moving stiffly, impassively, to commands.

But inside the stiff wooden exterior was all excited expectation. Her thoughts were wildly pounding about almost giving her a head-ache, and came together in the overpowering realisation that the twelve bowls of the Cinnabar Gate Strengthening Herbal Brew were certainly working: their power was beginning to permeate her body, beginning with the neck, and working down to the shoulders, the chest, the stomach and that vital part that would no longer shrink in timidity but open gently, delicately, like the welcoming lotus.

She subjected that vital part to a quick mental test, imagining it to be touched and caressed and finally invaded. She closed her eyes tightly for a better visualisation, then ran her fingers lightly over her arms. To her relief, not a single goose-bump had appeared.

Suan Choo Sim led the bride to the bridal chamber. As they stood before the groom with bowed heads, she held out to him the neatly folded ritual garment of testing, as pristine as the bridal body it would test. The Old One took it from her with an 'Errmm' and a slight cough of embarrassment, and put it aside casually, as something both redundant and irrelevant.

Then Suan Choo Sim, still with head bowed and lips discreetly sealed, took a few steps backward, and left the chamber.

22
Acceptance

'Come,' said the Old One, and led his bride to a room that she had never seen in her six months in the Great House.

It was a small room but lavishly furnished, because it was given entirely to the August Ancestor alone. It was a tribute to his unique position among the ancestors. His huge portrait, massively framed in gold, hung on the wall, above an ornately carved teak altar replete with ancestral tablets and urns, and gleaming plaques, statuettes and ornaments of gold, jade and ivory.

An ornate chair with inlaid mother-of-pearl stood on one side, a fitting seat for the most illustrious member of the ancestral line, if he deemed to present himself. If he chose to appear in dreams instead, it was always on this magnificent chair he sat and no other, his arms laid magisterially on the carved dragon arm rests.

The Old One lit two joss-sticks, one for himself and the other for his bride. Together they stood before the August Ancestor, clasping the joss-sticks with utmost respect and humility. Together, in perfect unison, they bowed three times.

'August One,' said the Venerable One. 'Today I present to you my new wife.'

He had already done that, six months ago, but today was a new and necessary beginning, to erase all the absurdities and messiness of the past months, and put bride and groom truly and at last on the path of conjugal union and happiness.

He asked for no blessings and made no promises of male progeny, to be conceived that very night to ensure the earthly mortality of the illustrious family name. Instead, he dealt with the immediate problem of acceptance.

'You see her here,' said the Old One, looking straight into the eyes of the ancestor staring back at him from within the massive gold frame, 'a young girl whom, against all expectations and wishes of family, against even my own better judgement, I have grown to love dearly. It must be Fate, to whom we must all submit in the end, as even you, August Ancestor, will agree. But I have rejoiced in, rather than resisted that act of Fate, which brought us together at a cemetery that strange morning. My bride has worked very hard these months to find acceptance with my three wives, and I believe she has succeeded. Therefore I beg you, the ancestor I have highest respect and regard for, to receive her too, into the family, and to give me a sign of your acceptance.'

The nervous inability of his bride's body to receive his — could it be because of the August Ancestor's refusal to receive her? The logic was somewhat convoluted but had its appeal. A sign from the ancestor would banish those troublesome goose-bumps for ever.

The Old One led his bride to two chairs placed close together at the opposite end of the room, also with inlaid mother-of-pearl, but much smaller and less grand-looking than the ancestor's. Both sat down and waited for the ancestor's sign.

It came within minutes. There was a clattering sound that made Silver Frond start up and give a little gasp. A gold-plated goldfish glued on a white porcelain plate on a tall stand, had come unstuck and fallen among an assortment of small urns on the table, knocking them over.

The Old One would have preferred a roll of thunder reverberating on the rooftops of all the five houses of the Great House, or the appearance of a white temple dove flying in through the window and circling three times over their heads, or the powerful scent of some unidentifiable flower filling the room.

But he had to take what was available.

'The Ancestor hears,' he said to his bride. 'Come, let us go to our room.'

23
Knife, Saw and Pestle

Her teeth were clenched, her eyes were tightly closed in the darkness, but she saw very clearly the knife, its blade shining with menace, about to descend on her frightened flesh. She closed her body against its deadly advent, screaming silently.

Next she saw the saw, even more terrifying in the menace of its sharp metal teeth, approaching the petrified log of her body, like a marauding shark, sniffing for the spot between her legs, to sink in the teeth and rip her into two.

Last, before she finally fainted and lay inert on the bed, she saw the giant stone pestle, with its massive rounded end, smooth and gleaming through constant pounding, approaching the mortar receptacle of her poor unresisting body, for a demonstration of its immense pounding power.

The Old One withdrew hastily and with a little weary sigh, fell off the cold, terrified body, and lay beside it. He covered its cold, pristine nakedness with a warm blanket and noticed under it, the crumpled white cloth of confirmation, crumpled but unstained and still waiting to perform its function of confirming.

The Old One sighed again. The waiting was beginning to be tedious. Suddenly he had an idea. He was sure it would work better than any amount of gentle persuasion, any amount of nonsensical women's brews.

The Old One smiled to himself, in the pleasing sensation of a self-congratulatory glow. He believed he had come a long way in his understanding of women, and of the strategies of managing them.

24
The Time For Behaving Like Children Is Past

The first day of her husband's absence was frightful, the second day was unbearable and on the third day, she locked herself in the bathroom and howled out her misery.

On the first day itself, the news had already spread through the entire sprawl of the Great House, causing everyone to converge upon First Wife for the most reliable confirmation, given her position and the fact that the young bride was assiduously avoiding everyone and keeping tight-lipped about the mysterious event.

The servant who had gone up with the early morning hot tea and towels had found the bride alone, red-eyed, and then had sped breathlessly through the Great House with the news: the Venerable One was gone from the Great House. Such a thing had never happened before. The servant told everyone, 'I asked Young Mistress very politely where Master was, and she just shook her head and cried.'

There arose a swirl of intense emotion and speculation that concentrated all activity in the Great House into a single relay race, as servant ran to whisper into servant's ear, and each of the three senior wives rose quickly from chair or bed to seek or give views about what could only be seen as the impending fall of the junior wife.

It was a matter too serious to be left to guesswork alone, and First Wife, at last rising from her chair in a clear show of leadership, decided to confront the bride. She had little use for wild gossip beyond their initial provocation, and was now determined to channel it into a specific number of responsible questions: Why had the Old One suddenly left the Great House? How long would he be gone? Did he leave any instructions for any action during his absence? Did he look ill? Did he take with him the special Po Chai Yin Stomach Disorder pills that he had been using for forty years?

The sudden departure, coupled with the young bride's obvious distress, could only mean one thing: the trouble that everybody had expected in this strange marriage had begun, and everyone in the Great House ought to be fully aware of its nature and development in order to prepare for a proper re-assertion of their former roles. The young girl's coming, like a pebble thrown into the tranquil surface of a pond, like an intruder disrupting the harmony of hive or nest, should be quickly followed by her departure, to restore peace all round. The first hopeful signs were appearing. But until everyone was sure what was happening, they had better suspend hope and feeling.

The bride would provide no answer to their questions.

Silver Frond, her eyes very red and her face puffed with crying, would only shake her head and say, 'I don't know. I don't know anything. Please leave me alone.'

Misery could not afford defiance; there was none of that cool confidence, nearly three years back, when she, Egg Girl from Sim Bak Village and recipient of the gift of the most magnificent doll, had defended herself as she stood in the midst of a circle of accusing, abusing women. Now they did not stand in a circle around her; having followed First Wife all the way to the young bride's house, they were content to stand behind their leader and watch her perform the first act of destroying the upstart, who for the first time was left without her protector.

The abjectness of her state, as she continually blew into her handkerchief, and kept her eyes averted from their faces, like a guilty child about to be punished, was a gratifying beginning. Second Wife stood with a supportive daughter and a maidservant, all four linked by a collective smile of gleeful expectation. There was no smile on Third Wife's face as she too stood with a daughter and the maid Tali-gelem, only an expression of taut neutrality poised to swing either way, depending on how the drama unfolded.

First Wife said, with an effort at gentleness, despite a rising exasperation against the girl who was bringing endless trouble to the Great House: 'It is not possible that you don't know why the Old One is gone. He has never been gone from the Great House even one day in his life. As First Wife, I have the right to know.'

Second Wife screamed, 'Tell us quickly, you wretch! You have brought nothing but trouble. You must be responsible for this strange behaviour.'

Nearly three years ago, it was Third Wife who, in her anger, would have inflicted physical injury upon the Egg Girl as she stood coolly before them with the Old One's gift. Now she was actually restraining Second Wife who, encouraged by the sight of the girl shorn of all protection, made a lunge at her, and lacking any weapon, flung a packet of melon seeds at her.

'Stop it,' said First Wife severely. 'The time for behaving like children is past.' Once again she turned to Silver Frond and continued the interrogation: 'A man does not leave his house and family suddenly like this without a reason. Only you know.

You may be the newest and favourite wife, but we are still his wives, and need to know whether he is well and safe. He has many enemies who may seek to do him harm.'

Silver Frond burst into loud tears. When she was a little girl, she had one day made her father angry about something, and he had walked out of the house, saying, 'Since you don't need your father any more, he will go away.' He had lingered, waiting for a sign of relenting, but she had remained sullenly silent. He then said, 'I will go into a dark jungle where a tiger will eat me up, or throw myself into the first river I come across and be swallowed up by a crocodile.' The emotional blackmail succeeded beyond his dreams, for when he did not return by nightfall, she fell into a screaming terror, told her mother she had killed her father and was all sobbing contrition when he at last returned.

The Old One, in his neat clothes, with his air of self-assurance, would be the last to die in a beast-infested jungle. But the terror she now felt at the possibility of enemies lying in wait for him was no less devastating. She saw him successively lying dead on the road with knife wounds, ground under the wheels of a massive lorry, flung to the bottom of a well.

She was so overcome by the horrendous images that First Wife had to wait a full three minutes before continuing the interrogation.

'The Old One is much respected,' she said, unaffected by the sight of the sobbing young bride, who looked a total wreck, 'but there are people in this town whose eyes are red with jealousy watching him grow in prosperity and influence. As his wife, I have always advised him to be careful. Now he has gone away mysteriously, and you will not tell me anything. How can you behave in this way to me?'

Silver Frond never felt more miserable in her life. The sobbing terror had subsided into the heaviness of despair and something like bitter regret: *I wish I had never come into the Great House.*

She felt a hand touching her shoulder, then moving to touch her cheek, a kind, papery dry hand that could not belong to any of the accusers surrounding her. Once again, Old Mother had appeared to offer comfort, once again, she was saying, with the same gentle concern, 'Why, poor child, she'll get sick with all that crying. She needs a clean handkerchief. Does anyone have a clean handkerchief ?' Putting her face very close to Silver Frond's, she peered into her eyes, stroked her cheek and said with so much kindness, 'You are upset. Which bad person has upset you?' that the girl let out another loud burst of tears.

Behind the kind old face, Silver Frond had a glimpse of another sympathetic one, less demonstrative but no less kind.

The dim-witted son, making little reassuring sounds, came forward and offered her something he was carrying in his hand, one of the many small nondescript objects he carried around, like a lonely child never without the companionship of a worn toy or piece of clothing or food saved for solace rather than eating. She shook her head, he murmured something, and put the proffered gift back into his pocket.

Together, he and Old Mother stood anxiously before the crying girl, until First Wife instructed a maid to lead them away. Then she continued to speak to Silver Frond, maintaining her severity of face and expression: 'I tell you it is your duty to tell us exactly what happened.' She waited for a response, and getting none, increased the severity: 'I have said that you are a good, sensible girl who has behaved well towards her superiors.

Now I take back my words. I will call you the most ungrateful young person if, despite my consenting to receive tea from you, you refuse to answer my questions.'

Silver Frond said miserably, 'I told you I don't know anything. I woke up and saw him leaving. He said he would be away for two weeks or longer.'

This was limited but valuable information, inviting a barrage of questions. They fell upon her, like so many shafts of a relentlessly pelting rain, that she crumbled to the floor in a heap of confusion and distress. Two weeks or longer? Did he say where? Why? How did he leave? Did he take a lot of clothes? Trishaw? Car? Did he get Black Dog's help? How was it that no servant saw him? What were his last words to you? Was he displeased about something? He must have been displeased about something. Why aren't you telling us?

Silver Frond whimpered, 'I've told you all I know. Please leave me alone.'

And that was the point when Third Wife knew she had to step in, to take over the entire process of the interrogation. It was also the point when her face could abandon its expressionlessness; suspended between hostility and friendliness, it now chose the latter and instantly softened into a look of utmost concern and caring. She had decided, in an instant, that it would serve her purpose better to publicly take her place on the side of the young bride.

She stepped forward adroitly and stood beside the girl, facing the others.

'All of you leave her as she says,' said Third Wife authoritatively. Then she bent down and helped Silver Frond up from the floor. 'She is very upset. There's no point asking her more questions. Go on, leave her.'

Everyone looked to First Wife once again to lead them in their response. The lady said, 'I have done my part in asking.' She looked at Third Wife, who was actually wiping Silver Frond's brow with her own handkerchief, allowed herself the most contemptuous smile she could manage and said, 'May your true intention match the kindness of your actions,' adding, in a voice raised for all to hear, 'Heaven sees into all hearts.' The next moment she had turned and left, followed by the others.

By themselves, Third Wife said to Silver Frond in an urgent whisper, '*I* know why the Old One has gone away.'

The girl lifted her face to ask sharply, 'Did he tell you?'

Third Wife said, 'I know. I know everything!'

Silver Frond said sullenly, 'You don't know everything. You told me everything would be all right after the last bowl.'

'The medicine was all right, *you* were not,' said Third Wife with righteous indignation. 'What's wrong with you? The Cinnabar Gate Strengthening Herbal Brew has worked in all cases except yours. Ask the physician at the Tong Ting Medical Hall if you don't believe me! Why are you so different from other people? Do you think I would waste all that money and time if I hadn't been sure? What's the matter with you?'

The bullying rhetoric, the aggrieved tone, the sheer barrage of words – they were the classic ploy to throw the already confused person into greater confusion. Silver Frond opened her mouth to say something, stopped, opened her mouth again, and finally lapsed into a troubled, frowning bewilderment. Third Wife, watching her closely, decided to extend the use of the ploy. She had one more tactical manoeuvre, which she was saving for last – to plant, ever so carefully, the seeds of doubt, suspicion and fear in the fertile ground of the young, confused mind.

'Fifth Wife,' she said softly, as if talking to herself. 'Of course! He has gone away on some secret visit to look at the young woman who will be his fifth wife.'

Silver Frond stared at her in horror, and cried, 'No, no, no!' The unspoken reason was louder even than the protestation: *He loves me best of all the wives. Everybody knows this, everyone in the Great House and the neighbourhood and the whole town. Everybody's been talking about it.*

'When he got dissatisfied with Second Wife,' continued Third Wife, still in the hushed tones of someone caught in awesome recollection, 'he went away for a week to meet my parents for secret negotiations.' She spoke softly and slowly, in a melodrama of momentous recollection.

'But First Wife said he's never gone away before!' Silver Frond almost screamed out her protest. The terrifying image of the beauteous interloper in the dream, sitting on the Old One's lap, was returning and sending a chill through her.

'*Tchah!*' snorted Third Wife. 'You believe First Wife too much. You know, I am sometimes jealous that you like her so much better than me.'

'I know he loves me,' insisted Silver Frond. A look of wild desperation had come to her face. Six months ago, the love had been only an abstraction, only a part of the wondrous, bewildering world she had been thrown into. Now it was taking on the force of desperation and hope. It had become her very salvation in a confusing, threatening world.

A new resoluteness appeared on her face. She had to please her husband as soon as he came back, and make sure he never went away again. She would go to the Goddess Pearly Face to get help. All her troubles had stemmed from the day she had parted company from her closest friend and confidante, when she had become unreasonably angry and stormed out of the temple. She would ask forgiveness. The goddess was kind and helpful. She would forgive her readily and help her recover the love of the Old One.

25
Goddesses, Ghosts and Real Women

It was the strangest dream in her life, thrown up by the greatest fear in her marriage. 'You get off his lap this instant!' In her dreams, she had always been more assertive than in real life, standing up to the Bad Brothers, the men who had approached her with their lust deliberately exposed, her father, her mother, the senior wives, but now she was a dynamo of furious energy, running up like a whirlwind to the interloper perched on her husband's knee. The woman would have fallen off, but for the Old One's protective arms circling her tightly. He was laughing and enjoying the sight of women fighting over him.

'You get off, I say!' she screamed, and raised her hand to slap the woman's face before she saw that it was not that of the detestable Fifth Wife, but the Goddess Pearly Face. 'You!' she heard herself shrieking in shock, while both the Old One and the goddess turned calmly smiling faces upon her. 'How can you do this to me, you who call yourself my friend?'

'Not any more,' said the goddess, settling herself even more comfortably on the Old One's lap, and putting her arms around his neck. 'Not any more! Besides,' she added, with a provocative wink at the Old One, 'we goddesses can be real women too, you know. We like a man's touch, and we know how to make a man happy.'

The next moment, she was watching the goddess making the Old One happy. The fair pearly body never recoiled from his; instead it was like the lotus, welcoming, fresh, fragrant. She heard them laughing together, saw her fair legs curled around him, saw him, at last, roll off with a tremendous sigh of satisfaction. They lay very close together, their eyes closed, smiling. Then she saw him open his eyes and peep at her from beneath the goddess's fair, silken underarm, which he had playfully draped across his face, and heard him say to her, with undue cruelty, 'Why don't you go use the chamber pot? It has seen more of you than your husband ever has! Ha, ha!'

In her rage, she grabbed the utensil, which was half-filled, and flung it at the offending pair on the bed. It crashed against a bedpost, and spilled its contents over an entire carpet. The pair were now sitting up together, naked, and laughing at her. She heard a voice saying sternly, 'Stop behaving like a child. That's the whole trouble. You haven't grown up when you should,' and turned to see Old Mother.

'So you too have stopped being my friend?' she cried in anguish.

'We have never stopped being your friends; you are your own enemy.' It was the Goddess Pearly Face standing beside Old Mother, shaking her head and clucking her tongue. She stared at the goddess, then turned in bewilderment towards the bed. She saw the Old One once more on top of the white, silken body, but it was that of Fifth Wife, not the goddess. The Old One was saying, amidst the grunts of pleasure, 'You promise?' and Fifth Wife was saying in reply, 'I promise. Before the year is out. A healthy male child.'

There arose a commotion, and she turned now to see her father storming into the room. He was wearing a dirty singlet and khaki shorts and had mud-splattered slippers. He rushed to her, took her by the arm and tried to drag her away. 'Come home!' he roared, looking more ferocious than any temple warrior god. 'Come home to your father who loves you! Leave all these vultures who will destroy you!'

'I did love her!' protested the Old One, sitting up in bed. 'But how could I go on waiting? No man can wait that long. I went away because I thought that she didn't love me after all. I went away heart-broken. Then Third Wife came to my help.

I'll always be grateful to her. She helped me through a full week's negotiations to win this woman who indeed loves me. Her body never protests with goose-pimples.'

She did not know whether he was referring to Third Wife or Fifth Wife, for both were now on the bed with him, naked, one on each side. Together, the trio faced her, linked by a smile of utmost power and triumph.

'I promise you I will be a good wife. Please come back,' she said humbly.

'Oh ho! Promises, promises!' chortled the Old One.

'No, you come back with me,' said her father. 'I am a poor man, but rice porridge with soya sauce is better than all that rich food seasoned with tears!'

'I promise you I will be a good wife,' she repeated solemnly, her heart ready to break. 'If you don't believe me, I will swear by the truth cockerel. We will go to the Yio Tok Temple tomorrow, and I will chop off the head myself.'

'No truth cockerel can save a woman from her false promises,' said the Old One spitefully, and the two women with him giggled and said, 'As for us, we never made any false promises.'

'I've got the car,' her father whispered into her ears. 'Don't tell anyone, but I've taken the car back from Towkay Lam, and sacked that arrogant chauffeur. I rubbed chicken dirt in his face. We'll leave in the car. It's ours now.'

'Your bride is truly sorry,' said the Goddess Pearly Face to the Old One, 'so please accept her tea of contrition. I will prepare it now myself, if you like.' The goddess's face was a blur, sometimes taking on her own features, sometimes Fifth Wife's, and once, those of an unknown woman who looked foreign, with a dark complexion, deep-set eyes and a daring dress that revealed half her breasts. But the goddess's voice remained the same throughout; clear, steady, persuasive.

'Yes, yes, the tea!' exclaimed Old Mother. 'Nothing solves problems better than the tea of genuine feeling. I would have given you a rich wedding gift, but an old woman has no money.'

'Will you or will you not come with me?' roared her father, and the next moment he was joined by her mother standing by his side, shedding tears and saying, 'You have brought us endless trouble. But it is our fault. We should never have allowed you to leave our humble village for the Great House.'

Her voice faded away, as did everyone else's. Soon there was total silence. Where had they gone? She would have run after them or called out to them, except that she felt a tremendous weight on her body, locking up all movement, and a tremendous constriction of throat, stopping up all speech. Like an animal caught in a relentless net, she struggled to be free, but it seemed that the more she struggled, the more the net tightened around her. She was about to give up when she felt someone coming to her aid and gently pulling her up. She was conscious of only one thought: Why, I can't have grown up very much if I'm always in trouble and depending on people to rescue me.

'Who are you?' she asked her rescuer, a tall, pale-looking woman with a huge mass of matted hair, which fell untidily over her face.

'Look again,' said the woman smiling. 'You know me. I know you know me.'

'I'm sorry,' said Silver Frond politely, 'but I don't think I've seen you before.'

'You should have then,' said the woman. 'I've been wandering this earth for a long time now, maybe one hundred years, well before you were born, before your parents were born.'

'I know! I know!' cried Silver Frond excitedly. 'Is it true what they tell me – that you hanged yourself from a rafter in one of the Old One's houses, because you were too ugly to get married?' Death erased ugliness; the woman, though not beautiful, was certainly presentable.

'I don't wish to go into that,' said the woman petulantly. Death did not erase the pain the living carried with them, not even after one hundred years.

'Well, thank you for lifting that awful weight from me,' said Silver Frond.

'Will you lift the awful weight I've been carrying?' said the woman.

Silver Frond was about to say that she was only a simple, ignorant girl with many problems of her own, when the first cockcrow summoned the woman back to her home. The woman, in apparent distress, began to moan and to swing her huge, heavy mass of hair, slowly and rhythmically, from side to side. *Swish, swish.* She began to swing faster, and the hair, like unruly black curtains, like the wings of some giant black bird, flapped back and forth, back and forth, across her face and neck. She stopped only when the third and last cockcrow came, loud and insistent, then died away in the night's silence. The next moment, she was gone.

Alone by herself once more, Silver Frond looked around the dark and silent room, and realised how fearful it was to be alone. She listened for sounds to come out of the darkness. Even the tiniest would be reassuring – a small cough, a footstep, the rustle of clothes – to connect her with the world of the living. Even the presence of that ghost woman would have been better than nothing, so excruciating had the sense of desolation become.

Then she heard sounds, small scratching sounds coming from outside the locked door. She listened intently. Somebody was at the door, and asking urgently to be let in. She heard a voice, which she recognised to be her husband's, and felt a great lightening of heart and uplifting of spirits. He had come back! She cried out joyfully, 'You have come back to me! I knew you would never leave me.'

'Yes, I have come back,' he said, but his voice was lost once more in the small scratching sounds. The sounds became more insistent, building up into a harsh crackle, before subsiding into a soft, contented gurgling, as if the Old One had transformed himself into a small child happily playing by himself. When she strained her eyes through the darkness, she saw small things being slipped under the door, one by one, as if the child were enticing her to come out and play with him.

She heard a loud thump, and sat up with a start. She saw herself sitting up in bed, clutching a pillow. She looked around. So it was a dream after all. But no, it was not a dream, because by the light of a street lamp coming in through the window slats, she could see the objects that had been pushed under her door – a piece of paper, a length of string, some rubber bands, a pencil, a circlet of beads, a sweet in its wrapper – the friendly overtures of the child in her dream, now transformed into a real presence outside her door.

She got out of bed, walked towards the array of gifts, and saw one more, a flattened cigarette box, being pushed through with some difficulty. She bent down to take a closer look, caught a glimpse of fingers and heard, once more, the scratching and gurgling sounds of the giver.

She knew it was not her husband, and was afraid to open the door.

'Who's that?' she cried out. The barrage of gifts increased, now pushed under the door with furious energy, and it was only when she saw and recognised a comic book that a new fear invaded her and made her say urgently, 'Please go back. Please go back to sleep.'

But the dim-witted son, worked up to a manic generosity by the novelty of gift-offerings pushed under the door, would not go. He had apparently been drawn to the Fifth House, then to the bedroom by a recollection of the crying face that morning, which he had so much wanted to comfort, and no locked door between that face and himself was going to deter him. He began to mumble something.

'Please go back,' begged Silver Frond through the door. 'Your mother will be worried about you.'

The sound of her voice only fired him to a greater urgency of purpose, a stronger convergence of energy in that determined body. He began to shout and kick the door.

Silver Frond ran back to her bed, and hid herself under the blankets. She pressed her hands to her ears, against the horrible noise, and closed her eyes tightly against the even more horrible image of the extravagant impulses of generosity turning into uncontrollable lust. She knew for a certainty that if she should be so foolish as to open the door, that lust would leap upon her and work itself out with brutal energy.

She lay in petrified silence for a while. Then she heard someone approaching, speak softly to the son and lead him away. She recognised both the footsteps and voice of First Wife. She listened for the last sounds of that night's terror to die away completely before daring to move under the blanket.

Her last thought, before she fell into a troubled sleep with the first faint light of dawn, was how she would get rid of the mess of gifts piled on the floor around her door.

26
The Stone of Truth

'What is it?' said Silver Frond, as Third Wife showed her something wrapped in a small white handkerchief in her hand. She felt better and was able to get up from bed, but her heart was as heavy as ever and the tears never stopped filling her eyes and flowing down her cheeks. She missed her husband unbearably.

'I bought it yesterday from a holy man in the market,' said Third Wife. 'It cost me three hundred dollars.' Instead of removing the wrapping, she tightened it around the object, showing the outline of something small, hard and round.

The sum was staggering, and would normally have provoked surprise and curiosity. But Silver Frond was too despondent to do more than look on listlessly.

'It is the Stone of Truth,' said Third Wife, taking off the handkerchief and revealing the object at last. It looked like an ordinary pebble, but the reverence accorded it, and its very high price, attested to its uniqueness.

Third Wife continued, 'I bought it specially for you,' and still provoked no response. It was just another mundane claim. 'I bought another black chicken for you,' or 'I got Tali-gelem to buy another bottle of Tiger Balm for you.' The girl in her misery was unimpressed by the promise of magic stones.

She said, looking into the dully staring eyes, 'Aren't you going to ask me anything? I should think you would want to know,' and for answer, the staring eyes once more filled with tears.

'I went to the Sin Min temple yesterday,' said Third Wife. 'You must have heard of this temple, built a hundred years ago? The monks, when they die, do not rot, but are kept in large, earthen jars. Their hair and fingernails continue growing in the jars. Did anybody ever tell you that? There are rows and rows of these jars in an underground room in the temple. I consulted the wisest of these monks there about your condition. He said a demon is inside your body, causing you all these troubles. It has made your body its home, and will not go away. It is an extremely jealous demon and will harm any man who competes with it for possession of your body.'

The long speech was unrehearsed. Third Wife would disdain to rehearse any claim, any lie, whatever its magnitude.

She rather liked her description of the demon residing inside a woman's body, and duly embellished it. 'It is supposed to live here,' she pressed an intimate part of Silver Frond's abdomen, 'and it lives, eats, sleeps here, giving no trouble until it smells a man coming, and then it turns mad with fury. You know what it lives on?'

She whispered it into the girl's ear, and had the satisfaction of seeing a flicker of interest in her eyes. The flicker turned into a sceptical smile. A demon needing the sustenance of monthly blood. Even Liang Por, at his most imaginative, could not have come out with a story like that.

When Silver Frond was a little girl, she had listened enthralled to stories of mischievous demons, living inside mortals' ears and making them deaf, so that they wandered straight into exploding firecrackers or the dens of lions; blocking their nostrils so that they could not smell and walked straight into stinking cesspools.

But it was no laughing matter when a demon inhabited one's private bridal body and denied access to one's husband. Silver Frond's instinctive response was angry denial.

'There's no demon inside my body. I'll be all right as soon as I go to the goddess to ask for forgiveness and help.'

'The monk has never been wrong before.'

'I tell you there's no demon inside me. I'm just being punished for being rude and ungrateful to the goddess.'

'I hope you are right. But you could be wrong. And you mustn't take chances. This kind of demon is vicious and will leave you raving mad. The monk told me there was a woman who was possessed like you, and she ended her misery by throwing herself into a well.'

'Did he tell you what I should do?'

Third Wife once again opened her hand to show the Stone of Truth. 'This stone has the power of truth only, not of cure,' said Third Wife solemnly. 'It will tell you if you have the demon, and that's about all it can do.'

Stones, the bark of trees, bamboo sticks shaken out of an urn, pieces of potato laid on a fevered brow, the tiger's name written on indigo dye – simple, humble things of the inanimate world were used by gods, goddesses and ancestors to convey truth to mortals as well as to cure them of their ailments. The little stone had cost three hundred dollars but was worth its weight in gold.

'How can it tell me the truth?'

Third Wife went to get a cup of water. She gave the stone to Silver Frond and said, 'Drop it into the water.' She did so. The pebble dropped to the bottom of the cup and lay there. She looked at Third Wife, as if waiting for more instructions. Third

Wife was looking into the cup and saying, 'Oh no, oh no,' with so much alarm that with a little shudder, Silver Frond turned to look herself. She gasped to see a cupful of black water, a dense, ugly, malignant black. The water seemed to rise a little, then fell back, leaving a rim of black on the white interior of the cup.

Third Wife turned a horrified face upon Silver Frond. 'Oh no, oh no,' she gasped again.

Silver Frond got out of bed, got another cup of water, placed it in front of Third Wife and said, 'I want you to do the same thing. You do exactly the same thing.' Third Wife picked up the stone with two deft fingers, wiped it on her blouse, then dropped it into the cup. The water stayed clear and unstained.

Silver Frond had turned a ghostly white.

'Don't worry,' said Third Wife soothingly. 'I will have to think of something to help you. There must be monks whose special work is to help people like you.'

Silver Frond began to cry, in the bitter knowledge that both the world of spirits and the world of mortals were working together to destroy her. What had she done wrong, in this or another life?

Third Wife said, 'Do you remember what happened to Black Dog Soh that day when she came to give you some brew?' Silver Frond looked at her wonderingly. 'Do you remember how strangely she was behaving, as if she were possessed by a spirit? Well, she *was* possessed, and it must have escaped and found refuge in you!'

It was getting worse and worse. So she was the choice of homeless spirits. It was all so unfair! With a little scream, Silver Frond covered both ears with her hands.

'There is a monk I know who can drive out the most stubborn demons. But he won't agree to help you.'

'Why not?'

'He will take one look at you and say, "She's only a girl, with a girl's weak body. She can never survive the pain of the treatment."'

'What's the treatment like?'

'The most painful. This kind of demon never gives up without a ferocious fight. Your body will be the battleground. It will twist and turn, heave and thump as monk and demon struggle for possession. Once, according to the monk, the battle was so furious that the poor woman's body rose two feet into the air before it fell back to the floor with a loud bump. There will be one moment of the most acute torture, precisely at the moment the demon is expelled, and then it will all be over.'

'Take me to the monk tomorrow.'

'Why, aren't you afraid? I would be terrified to go through this kind of treatment.'

'I am not afraid. Take me to the monk at once.'

'First you have to cleanse your body by fasting. But you have just recovered. You are in no condition to fast.'

'Take me to the monk tomorrow.'

'He may not agree. Yours is a frail-looking body. You may not be able to survive the torment of the cure.'

'I say, take me to the monk tomorrow!'

Silver Frond was shouting now, but the voice in her heart that whispered to the absent one – oh, how was it possible she could miss anyone so much! – was soft and tender with longing: Old husband, I will go through any pain for you.

27
In the Sin Min Temple

It was the longest and most uncomfortable car ride in her life, though Third Wife, who was sitting beside her at the back, rubbed Tiger Balm on her temples and massaged her hands and feet, and Black Dog drove as carefully as he could. Black Dog never once looked at her. In fact, he was looking utterly ill at ease, as if he had been dragged into this secret venture – they had all slipped out of the house in the darkness of night – and wishing with all his heart it would be over quickly.

His unease soon settled into a heavy sullenness. Third Wife gave instructions to him to do this and do that – to go by that road instead of this one because it had a tree growing beside it that sent out evil emanations, to avoid going too near a roadside offering made to some wandering spirit, comprising a plate of food, a candle and some joss-sticks in an empty cigarette tin – and he obeyed silently and sulkily. It was as if he had realised, too late, his folly in having allowed himself to be dragged into a thoroughly worthless undertaking, and could do nothing to express his regret except by a show of bad temper.

The Sin Min Temple was hardly a temple, more a ramshackle wooden building on the edge of a jungle. Silver Frond, weak through lack of food and sleep, but strong in purpose, was taken by Third Wife to meet the monk with the promised powers, while Black Dog was told to wait outside in the car, for as long as it would take for the monk-healer to do his job.

But the monk refused to see Silver Frond until she had first cleansed herself. She was led to a small room at the back of the building by Third Wife. There she was required to put on a white loose blouse and trousers. The cleansing process was simple, involving a full ablution from a large, brown earthen jar full of blessed water, a drink of more blessed water mixed with the ashes of a piece of prayer paper on which the monk had written some words, and an hour's meditative silence, with both legs and arms crossed, before the altar of the temple's presiding deity. After this preparatory process, which would take two hours, her body would be ready for the envisaged battle between the demon and the monk himself, a burly man with a shaven head bearing small burn marks and arms with tattoos that were said to have appeared spontaneously, as a result of a lifetime of such cosmic battles.

Throughout, Silver Frond kept up her courage by a series of happy images – her husband returning home, his happiness at the change in her, his satisfaction on the marital bed, his wellbeing and hers at last restored, her happy visits to the temple of the Goddess Pearly Face, and to her home in Sim Bak Village, perhaps even in the beloved car bought back from the businessman to which it had been sold amidst so much vexation – it was sweet restoration many times over.

This was the bright, happy world she had embraced in her marriage, to be regained only after a necessary but hateful passage through the dark worlds of demons and monk warriors.

She was aware of a numbing heaviness creeping into her limbs, and upwards into her eyes, ears and tongue, so that she could move about only very slowly, see only very dimly, hear sounds as if they were coming from a distance, and struggle to give life to the words lying inert on her tongue. But the images of a restored peace and happiness remained remarkably clear, and made her smile a little in the midst of all the anxiety of a strange experience in an unfamiliar place.

She thought, The battle is not so bad after all, for she felt little pain, as she lay on a mat on the floor, apart from the little pricks on her shoulders and abdomen, as if tiny needles were being poked into her, and a slight burning sensation on her right thigh as if melting wax from a lit candle were falling in drops upon her skin, through the thinness of the white cotton trousers. In the dimness of the room, she saw the lit ends of joss-sticks moving about rapidly in front of her eyes, like a small agitated swarm of fireflies, and smelt the pungency of their smoke. She waited for the terrifying convulsions of body that Third Wife had warned her about, but none came, to her relief. She heard a low growl from the monk, a dark shape moving around her, as if he had read her thoughts: 'The worst is yet to come. Do not expect an easy victory. The demon is lying low, conserving his energies for the worst.'

Then he led her to a huge cauldron from which flowed huge billows of dense, grey smoke. Her nostrils were filled with the acrid fumes of joss and incense, her eyes smarted with tears and she began to cough violently. 'Do this,' commanded the monk, and he showed the action of gathering up the holy smoke with both hands and splashing the face with it, as if it were water from a wash basin. The smoke was indeed so thick as to appear capable of being touched, carried, put in a bag or basket for taking home to comfort and heal.

She obeyed the monk readily, gathering up the smoke with her hands and spreading it on her face. Though she continued to suffer the stinging tears and choking cough, she knew this was but a prelude to the real battle. She had no doubt the monk, whose ferocity of expression only added to the reassuring impression of his competence and dedication to the task at hand, would help her win it.

'More! More!' cried the monk, and she bent down and gathered up an armful of the thick smoke and spread it on her face and neck.

'More! I said more!' cried the monk with brutal insistence, and this time, she put her face into the dense, swirling grey clouds in the cauldron, breathed deeply and felt their cleansing power.

For a fleeting moment, as she lifted her face and saw him, through the thick smoke, facing her and swaying from side to side, she caught sight of a clustering of deep, ugly pits on each cheek, and a neck creased with sweat. And yet all the time, she thought she never opened her eyes even once. A violent throbbing had appeared inside her head, clouding her thoughts, and yet there was one part of her brain that lay outside all this turmoil of smoke and noise, allowing her some clarity.

Money – money was never far from her mind in her new life where she could use it to please family and friends, and pay off enemies. Third Wife was not really an enemy, neither was this fierce, ugly, expert monk, but she would be very happy to pay them handsomely when all this was over, and never see either again. She made a mental note to ask both how much she owed them.

She was led back to her mat on the floor and made to lie down again. Then began the real battle with the demon, as she felt her body take on a life of its own in the grand battle to drive away the intruder. It had broken free from her and become a separate entity, twisting, turning, heaving, as she watched helplessly. 'Stop,' she said, but it would not. For one shuddering moment, she thought of the headless body of the truth cockerel, thrashing in torment on the ground. The more she tried to stop her body from doing violence to itself – she could see her fists, aiding the monk's, pummelling at her abdomen – the more it demonstrated its fierce independence. She heard the monk yell angrily to her, 'Stop it! Can't you see your body's trying to get rid of the demon?'

Strangely she felt no pain.

'Help me,' she moaned with a sense of mounting terror that something was going wrong, and the monk ripped off her blouse and thrust a cluster of lit joss-sticks on her left breast. There was still no pain. She heard him mutter, 'It's gone elsewhere. Ah, here it is!' and felt the joss-sticks thrust on her right breast. 'It's moved again! It's going to hide! Here it is! It's moved again!' Her body was now both battleground and playground, as monk and demon played hide-and-seek. She was exhausted but felt no pain.

'I've got it trapped! This is the moment!' roared the monk, and all of a sudden, her mind now a dense fog like the smoke around her, she felt a massive weight on her body, and a tearing, searing pain inside that she had never experienced before. She caught a glimpse of a face very close to hers, so close she felt its hot breath and saw the ugly nests of pits, deep and black, on the cheeks. She tried to push away the face with a feeble hand, but it came closer, with increasing brutality, which exploded with a roar and then eased itself out in a series of soft moans. The brutal face, totally spent, laid itself gently on hers, in a luxuriousness of relief and ease, now that the enemy had been vanquished. The pain inside her body had come and gone suddenly, leaving no distress. She lay very still for a while, neither feeling nor thinking anything, for sensation and thought had blended hopelessly into a big grey blur, like the surrounding smoke. Then she was aware, vaguely and distantly, of the resting face detaching itself from hers, and the massive weight slowly lifting itself and moving away.

Her body, stretched out on the mat on the ground, wet and shivering, was once more free.

She heard a voice, which she recognised easily, saying softly, 'It's over. You are saved. We can go home now,' before darkness and silence suddenly overtook her, and she saw and heard no more.

28
Clear and Pure Water

Third Wife put a mirror in her hand and said, 'Look! See how well you have recovered!' She did not think she looked well at all. The memories of the past few days were still dim in her mind, and she badly wanted to know what had happened.

'What happened? Is everything all right?' she murmured. 'Is my husband coming back?'

'He will be back in two days,' said Third Wife reassuringly.

Silver Frond stared at her with eyes wide with excitement and trepidation. 'How do you know?'

'Ah, I know, I know! People never believe me, but I watch and know everything!'

Mixed in the thrilling anticipation of her husband's return was the bitter taste of jealousy. So it was Third Wife he had chosen to trust with the information about his return. What else had he told that least trusted of wives, that he had withheld from her, his favourite? It was a painful thought, but she would not be bothered by it for the present. All she wanted now was for her husband to come home. 'Don't ever leave me again,' she would say to him, as she had said to her father when he at last returned and she clung to him in a frenzy of relief and terror, and her mother had to give her a cup of hot water and rub her chest with Tiger Balm to calm the choking fit.

'The demon in my body. Is it truly gone?' she asked nervously.

'You think that everything I undertake is a failure?' cried Third Wife reproachfully. 'Why don't you trust me more? Now let me show you something.' She was clearly in exuberant spirits.

She brought a cup of water, took out the Stone of Truth from her pocket, and handed it to Silver Frond. The girl took it nervously. With trembling fingers, she dropped it into the cup.

'See? I told you!' cried Third Wife triumphantly.

Silver Frond's eyes filled with tears of relief and joy. For the water remained clear and pure.

'I will tell you something else,' said Third Wife. 'I saw the demon precisely at the moment it was forced out of your body.'

'What was it like?'

She wished she had never asked the question. Third Wife took out of a paper bag the cotton trousers she had worn at the cleansing ritual in the Sin Min Temple, turned them inside out and exhibited what must be a sample of the terrifying evidence of a mighty battle, whether between men, gods or beasts – blood and vomit and the blackened faecal smear of sheer terror.

'Ugh! Take it away!' cried Silver Frond. 'Take it away and burn it!'

'It was a particularly savage demon,' said Third Wife and continued, in the most comforting of voices. 'But it's gone now. It will never trouble your body again.'

29
The Old One Returns

He had left in stealth and secrecy, but he reappeared with all the pomp of a chieftain returning to his village in full regalia, stern of mien and resolute in the purpose of commanding even more respect and adulation than when he left.

The Venerable One, dressed in a neat white suit, sat upright and austere in his chair of command, while around him stood the three wives, summoned to his presence, expecting to hear his explanation for the sudden and mysterious departure from the Great House more than a fortnight ago. The fourth wife had clearly not been summoned; her absence could be an indication of her imminent downfall, and that surmise alone was enough to keep the heart of each of the three senior wives palpitating with hope, as they stood with respectful silence before their august husband, and avoided looking at each other.

But they should have known better than to expect explanations from a husband who never believed he owed them any. Just as he had summoned them, almost a year ago, to tell them of his intention to marry the girl from Sim Bak Village and to warn them against any discord in the household, he would now divulge only the least of whatever little information was necessary about his sudden absence, once more warn them against creating trouble, and then dismiss them back to the routines of their life under his sheltering roof.

'I went away because it was my wish to go away. I have come back because it is my wish to return, and nobody else's. I expect everyone to speak no more of the matter and to maintain harmony in the Great House.'

He was godlike, sitting in the chair of authority with its inlaid mother-of-pearl, his calm, austere voice filling the room and striking awe in the hearts of his subjects ranged before him. Godlike, he could have spent his leave from home in the company of deities or wise sages or illustrious ancestors, in the noble precincts of temples, monasteries or sacred mountain caves, far away from the sorry, messy world of mortals.

But the truth – the Old One revealed it only years later – was that he had spent the entire fortnight catching fish, prawns and crabs.

He had a trusted business friend who owned a *kelong* in a fishing village, more for pleasure than adding to his large business, which included the import of fish. The *kelong*, with its many bamboo and net traps laid all along the wooden pier, yielded substantial quantities of fish and other sea creatures, including a strangely shaped and coloured cuttlefish that the friend swore was even better than the prized Chinese New Year *soon hock* for bringing good luck. The friend, born into a proud and wealthy family, had never been allowed as a child to dirty his hands or feet and certainly not to join common little boys looking for fish or frogs in muddy ponds. When he grew up and made a lot of money in his own business, he defiantly bought a *kelong* to which he could secretly go during his free time and enjoy himself as much as he liked, catching fish, getting wet and dirty, eating food that would have horrified his wife, playing with the ragged village children.

There was a serious taboo connected with *kelongs*, which fitted in perfectly with his wishes: no woman could be allowed anywhere near a fishery, in the belief that an unclean, menstruating woman would offend some presiding deity of the sea and drive away the fish for ever.

The Old One, himself curbed in the simple joys of boyhood by his stern father, had always felt an affinity with this friend. He had yearned to join him in one of these secret joyous expeditions, and one night, exasperated with his young bride and feeling the need to get away, he suddenly realised he could kill two birds with one stone.

During his fortnight at the fishing village with his exuberant friend (who chose to wear only old sarongs and tattered straw hats, and eat with his hands from banana leaves), living in a simple wooden hut, with the roar and smell of the sea outside, far away from home and contentious women, he was very much at ease and felt happy.

He had meant to stay away for a whole month, but one night woke up, missing his young bride acutely. He wanted badly to see her again, to hear her voice and feel her warm presence on the bed. So the next morning, he told his friend he was going back home, and instructed the servant who had been entrusted with all the arrangements for his departure, to make similar careful arrangements for his return.

He had not summoned his young bride to his presence, meaning to see her privately and quickly assess the whole situation (which he had confided, despite the embarrassment, to his friend). He had a rather pleasing image of her waiting for him in their room, fretfully pacing the floor and biting her fingernails, not daring to disobey him by joining the other wives.

Now, as he was preparing to dismiss the three senior wives from his presence, he caught sight of her at the door. She was staring at him and moving about like a little bewildered lost animal. She looked pale and distraught and showed all the signs of a child struggling desperately to keep her promise to obey.

Disobedience won. With a little cry from her overcharged heart, Silver Frond ran to where the Old One was sitting in his chair, ran pantingly with the fearful expectation of being stopped and dragged away. As soon as she reached him, she threw her arms around his neck and burst into tears. She sobbed as if her heart would break. It was a sight unseen in the Great House, watched in astonishment by the wives and the peeping servants, and would be the subject of intense discussion for a long time to come, as had been the many extraordinary events since the Old One brought this strange, intense village girl into his life.

More astonishing still was the reaction of the Old One. He took her into his arms, settled her on his lap, laid her head on his shoulder, close to his, and began comforting her. Someone later whispered there was a glistening of tears in his eyes.

One by one, the senior wives left the room.

30
Consummation

Pain? There was no pain. A demon inhabiting and inhibiting her body? It was as if her body had never known any obstacle in its smooth passage to be ready for his. Knife, axe, pestle? There was only a sweet sensation as she welcomed him home.

In the darkness, as she curled up in his reassuring warmth, she said, with a sob, 'Please don't leave me again. I promise I will never be any more trouble to you.'

He said, loving her more than ever, 'Everything's all right now.' His hand, as it caressed her, felt the cumbersome presence of the white testing garment, now crumpled and twisted, under her, and moved it out of the way.

31
The Secret In the Clothes Cupboard

He distrusted the sight of Third Wife in her confident posture of uplifted chin and one firm hand on hip, and he distrusted even more the sight of her with bowed head and eyes humbly downcast.

It was precisely this posture she adopted when she approached him, the morning after, as she looked around nervously to ascertain no one was watching.

'What do you want?' he said tersely, and for answer she thrust into his hands the testing garment.

'You must know the truth,' she said, her eyes reddening with the distress of having to perform so painful a task. 'You no longer care for me, but I have a duty to give you the truth.'

Now she spread out the garment, to show the truth it contained. Its pristineness proclaimed the stain on the honour of its user, and of the man, too, if he chose to ignore it.

'What is this?' said the Old One angrily. But of course he knew what it was, as the tightening of the lines on his face, and the suppressed ferocity in his voice so clearly told.

Many a husband in the old ancestral country must have looked at the garment of indisputable proof, stared at the proof of the bride's plundered virtue, and demanded instant retribution. An unstained garment stained not only the bride but her entire family for ever.

The sight of the growing anger, even though it was unfairly venting itself on her, encouraged Third Wife to say, in the most urgent tones she could manage, 'Go to her clothes cupboard, to the topmost shelf and look into a small white bundle hidden under the clothes.'

'What are you talking about?' the Old One hissed in his rage.

'You'll find some scrolls. A gift from the young *sinseh*. She has been secretly meeting him. Your old chauffeur knows. You can ask him,' cried Third Wife in a series of gasps and fled.

32
Rage

His bride came to him again, in the soft darkness of night, but this time the sight of her bare white shoulders and the young white body eager to please him, gave him no pleasure. Indeed, it was giving him as much pain as the sight of the secret gift scrolls, which he had found in the clothes cupboard, as Third Wife had said, hidden under a heap of clothes in the secrecy of the guilty liaison. He had stared at them, the veins throbbing dangerously on his temples and neck, and then returned them to their secret hiding place.

It was amazing how one often recalled, too late and with perfect clarity, those incidents that should have set the alarm bells ringing. The Old One now remembered coming into the room one morning, at exactly the moment when his young wife was pushing something under a pile of clothes in her cupboard, and turning to greet him with a little guilty start. He remembered the incident clearly because she was standing on a stool and almost fell as she scrambled down from it.

At that time of course he had thought nothing of it. Love blinded a man to all evidence of the beloved's treachery, and made him a fool and laughing stock. Indeed, he remembered asking her about how she was progressing under the young *sinseh*, said to be a much less capable teacher than the old *sinseh*, who was taking far too long to return from his visit to China. The irony of it! The flood of recollections became relentless, pouring over him, mocking him. The flush on his wife's face and her nervous fidgeting with the rings on her fingers – how could he have missed all the signs of guilt?

He had been amazed at his own calmness, as he returned the guilty gift to its hiding place. He had even been able to sit down with Black Dog to go through some business accounts, make the relevant checks on the management of his many properties, and sip a cup of hot ginseng tea as if nothing had happened.

That night, he had a fitful sleep in which he saw the young *sinseh* and his bride, sitting side by side on a bench in the classroom, reciting poetry together. Then they turned to look at each other and laughed joyously together. He could not hear what they were saying, but was enraged to see their improper playfulness, as they threw paper pellets and bits of chalk at each other, like children. At one point, the young scoundrel held a scroll high above his head, inviting the girl to reach it. She jumped up and down, her arms outstretched, laughing shrilly. He saw an amorous dance of hands in the air, coming together to touch and tease, moving away and coming back together again, with increasing boldness. He looked again and saw that it was not the young *sinseh* but the brazen young delivery man called Ah Kow who was engaged in this noisy dalliance with his bride. He was about to advance upon the interloper when he heard a loud, angry voice and felt a sharp *thwack!* on his head, as something descended on it. He turned and saw that it was the August Ancestor, who was getting ready to deliver another knock with a wooden ruler held tightly in his hand, like an angry schoolteacher.

The August Ancestor was saying, 'You fool. You brought all this on yourself. Don't blame anybody! Now kneel down.' He knelt down obediently. 'Now slap yourself three times.' It was the ultimate humiliation – the self-administered series of sharp slaps across the face, on bended knee, reducing the offender to an idiot and a buffoon, a fit object of laughter and derision.

The Old One woke up with a start. The pain returned with full force, and he let out a low moan.

If he did not fly into a rage now, grab her by the shoulders and roar for an explanation, it was because there was something stronger than the rage, which he could not as yet define or give a name to – something akin to sadness, an engulfing sorrow, which he had never experienced before. It was the kind that did not permit the relief of tears, but instead dried them up and made his eyeballs burn in their sockets. Anger and sadness – they were about the worst combination for a proud man, locking him into a paralysis of helpless confusion.

With great difficulty, for the heaviness inside was making speech difficult, he said to his bride, not looking at her, as he got up from bed, 'I'll be in the August Ancestor's room for a while.' She looked at him with intense anxiety, stretched out a hand to touch him and was about to say something when he stopped her abruptly and said more harshly than he intended, 'I said I will be in the August Ancestor's room for a while,' before walking out of their room.

There was no wish to confer with the ancestor, only the need to be alone, to deal with the turmoil in head, heart and soul, as he stood, a lone figure in a boat on the vast heaving sea of a horrible new experience, buffeted by a hundred waves, pelted by sheets of sharp wind and rain.

He heard the soft sounds of footsteps outside the room, and

was about to turn and say sternly, 'I told you to leave me alone,' when he saw Third Wife standing at the door, head still bowed, saying, in the trembling tones of the reluctant teller of secrets: 'Forgive me, but I have to tell you something more.'

Third Wife's mind had been very active, sorting out the many incidents of the past weeks, and seeing how all these could be used to confirm and reinforce each other, to fit together into a coherent and convincing narrative of the young bride's treachery. The incidents had floated about in her head, like the many separate pieces of cloth cut into squares, triangles and hexagons, for fitting together into a patchwork pattern.

The biggest piece to fit in was her role in the administration of the Cinnabar Gate Strengthening Herbal Brew. She had decided that a second visit to the Old One was necessary to account for this, and at the same time to reinforce the suspicion created by the first visit, thus pushing the Old One's anger to full-blown retribution.

'She had urgently asked me for some strengthening brew. I had no idea then that it was her guilt that was causing all those goose-pimples. Please forgive me.'

Third Wife wanted to ensure that the mammoth task she had singled-handedly undertaken would roll on to a successful completion. Anytime now, she was expecting the youngest wife to be sent home in disgrace to her parents.

'Go away,' said the Old One, clenching teeth and fists in rage, and Third Wife went quickly, glad to see that rage.

33
The Ancestor Who Said 'I Told You'

'I told you,' said the August Ancestor with savage glee. Normally the Old One liked a good argument with the irrepressible ancestor, whom he liked best of the entire pantheon. But now his heart was heavy with sorrow, and his spirit darkened by ominously gathering clouds of hurt and rage that threatened to swamp out the sorrow.

In this state, he actually welcomed the gleeful taunts of the ancestor. Proceeding only from a genuine concern for him, they might detract from, rather than add to, his pain.

'I told you from the beginning,' said the ancestor, 'that it was the height of folly to take as wife one so young, so inexperienced, and so vulnerable to the wiles of flatterers, as one would expect of poor village girls.' The young *sinseh* was now cast as the worst of flatterers, seducers, traitors.

'I could have warned you against him if you had cared to listen,' continued the wise ancestor. 'Did you not sense something when he was so eager to teach her new poems, and she to learn from him? When she asked to be allowed to use the car for visits she never cared to fully explain on her return?'

The Old One sat slumped in his chair and let out a groan of anguish.

'How could you bear even to look at those words he wrote for her on those scrolls?' fumed the ancestor.

The Old One once again saw in his mind not only the words of love, but the delicate pictures of flower blossoms and flying birds. At that moment, suffering the ultimate anguish of the Vinegar Drinker, who had been forced to drink a whole keg of the bitter stuff, he wanted to lay his hands on the throat of the young miscreant.

The ancestor was not finished yet. 'There was a very respected man by the name of Teo,' he said with the consummate ease of the accomplished story-teller Liang Por, 'who, when he found out that his young wife had been secretly meeting her lover in the dead of night, set a trap for them. He surprised them in bed together and got his men to drag them out of the house naked. Then he paraded them through the whole village.'

The Old One groaned, 'No more, no more.'

'There is more!' said the ancestor savagely. 'In our ancestral country, they did the right thing. They stuffed the adulteress into a pig basket and threw her over a cliff!'

The Old One could only say weakly, 'That was in the past. People don't do such things nowadays.'

'The past? Nowadays? There is no past nor present for the values that our ancestors hold dear. They are for all time. A woman who deprives her husband of his right to her virginity should be duly punished, whether then or now!'

The Old One said, 'What do you expect me to do?'

'Expect?' exploded the ancestor. 'Expect? Why, you annoy me more with each passing second! You do what you are bound by honour to do, not because you are expected to. Where is your sense of honour?'

The Old One remembered a story his father had told him

about the first step in the reclamation of honour: sending a dead pig to the bride's parents, with its snout hacked off. The image of a mutilated carcass carried in parade through the streets of the town and the paths of Sim Bak Village, accompanied by a crowd of giggling children, suddenly appeared in the Old One's mind, and would have raised a smile if his heart had not been so heavy.

'Remember,' said the August Ancestor by way of a parting shot, 'that if you don't intend to heed my advice, you might as well stop coming here and wasting my time.'

34
Disgrace and Expulsion

Silver Frond, who had fallen into a tearful, fitful sleep, woke up with a start to see her husband standing by her side. He said, 'Get ready to leave the Great House and return to your parents.'

He had earlier gone to First Wife and said, with the same terseness of tone and tautness of face, 'Get ready to help Fourth Wife leave the Great House and return to her parents. Give her whatever money she needs.'

Get ready. Leave. Take whatever you need. He hated lengthy explanations and the noise of women's protests or pleas, and hoped that his orders, brief, stern but clear, would spare him all the odium.

First Wife had looked at him with a frown of puzzlement, and waited a full minute for an explanation, but he offered none, as usual, only the reassurance that instant, discreet compliance would please him greatly.

His young bride had sat up and stared at him in total incomprehension as he said, 'Go quickly and without fuss. First Wife will see what you require.'

But there was to be none of the quiet acquiescence of First Wife. Silver Frond let out a shriek and made to throw herself at her husband in a panic of mounting terror. 'What? What did you just say?'

The fear sought confirmation, and when he repeated, with the same calm authority, 'I want you to leave the Great House at once, quickly and without fuss. I have instructed First Wife to help you,' Silver Frond let out another shriek, fell sobbing at his feet, and was incapable of asking the one vital question: Why?

The chilling reality of her husband's rejection of her froze out all questions, and all feelings except the terror of losing him all over again. It deprived her of speech and convulsed her body in a prolonged torment of sobbing. He remained unmoved.

Suddenly a thought forced itself into her mind: The demon had returned and taken possession of her husband's body. There could be no other explanation for his strange behaviour. The evil spirit had not left her after all. In her act of love with her husband, it had simply passed from her body into his, just as it had passed from Black Dog Soh's body into hers. The world was full of demons. The Great House had more than its share.

She fell down on her knees and embraced his tightly, sobbing, 'Please don't send me away. I almost died when you left me.'

Once more, he heard the August Ancestor's contemptuous laugh. *A soiled woman who is insulting you by touching you with her soiled hands. Shake her off.* He was glad the sadness was being rapidly dispelled by the rage, so that he could obey the ancestor. He flung her off with violent energy and said, 'You have shamed me. I don't want to have anything more to do with you. Now leave.'

35
If You Don't Believe Me

The Old One said impatiently, 'Who is it? Who can be calling at this hour?' His servant, who had come to him in a hurry with the urgent message of the dawn caller, said, 'He says he is from the Sin Min Temple, and that he has something very important to tell you.'

Still grappling with the nasty events suddenly broken upon him, the Old One was certain the strange visit was one more piece in the unfolding drama, like a nightmare continuing into broad daylight.

He looked at the visitor from the Sin Min Temple with great distaste. The man did not have any of the respectability of a temple resident, being dressed in a loud shirt and trousers, and wearing a thick gold chain around his neck. The ugly pits on each cheek were particularly repulsive. The Old One's contemptuous eyes moved upwards and spotted the equally ugly burn marks on his bald head, then sideways to take in the amazing tattoos of ferocious dragons and cloud swirls on his arms.

'What do you want?' he said coldly, and the man's face and entire demeanour suddenly assumed the earnest purpose and cautious cunning of someone about to enter into hard negotiations with an adversary.

The man began by saying, in a tone of deep respect, 'You are well known and respected in the town. You are the Venerable One and everybody looks up to you—'

'What do you want?' said the Old One even more coldly.

'You want to protect your good name, don't you?' said the man, abandoning the respectfulness for sly insinuation.

'Tell me what you want, or I'll get my servants to throw you out this instant,' said the Old One grimly.

'All right, all right,' said the man, smiling amiably and raising both hands in a gesture of peace. He could afford affability in the face of the contempt, for the cards were stacked in his favour, and he meant to go away with victory and a lot of money in his pocket.

Out of his monk's habit, he was also freed from the need for respectable language, and he duly went into a detailed and raw description of how, mistakenly possessed by a demon instead of a deity, he had ravished the purity of Fourth Mistress from the Great House, and was now come to report everything to the Master, and to promise discretion, so that nobody would know of the unfortunate incident, which could have the whole town talking for years.

The man said he was partly to blame for the incident. He had not gone through the full process of purification, allowing a weak spot, which the demon, a particularly alert and powerful one, had quickly taken advantage of and thus entered his body. It was also an extremely lustful demon, with a partiality for young, beautiful, virginal bodies.

The man was impatient to name the price of the promised discretion. He mentioned the sum and watched closely the reaction of the Old One.

It called for supreme self-control, but the Old One managed

to keep his voice calm and ask for a clearer explanation. 'Tell me exactly what happened,' he said, and surprised himself that he could still face that most despicable of creatures, a bogus monk, and listen, all over again to his lurid tale, of treachery twice over, by his young bride. So she had been despoiled *both* by the young *sinseh* and this scum. What else would be revealed of her depravity?

In his narration the second time, the man, to prove his credibility, mentioned names: 'If you don't believe me, ask Third Mistress and Black Dog.' He had chosen to ignore the promise of silence she had enjoined upon him in return for some money; the money, he had concluded, was a pitiful amount compared to the rich prize of direct blackmail, and that was when he had the idea of going to the Great House.

'She and Black Dog brought Fourth Mistress to my temple in a car, and Black Dog waited outside, on the small lane in front of the temple. It was about ten o'clock at night, on Thursday.' The proof needed embellishment, and the man, closely watching the gathering intensity on the Old One's face, was ready to provide all the details of time, place and action.

It was exactly at this point that Third Wife, who had been alerted to the presence of the monk by Tali-gelem and had come running over to peep and watch and listen, burst in and screamed, 'Lies! Lies! This man is lying! Don't believe him!'

The situation was proving too difficult for her. Unable to think on the spot how she could fit the new development into the smooth fabric of her story, she could only denounce him shrilly.

'Call Black Dog. He will prove that this man is making it all up!' she shrieked, resorting to her well-tried stratagem of calling for witnesses among subordinates and servants in the full knowledge that they would be intimidated enough to cooperate with her.

But she was making a fatal mistake. For the Old One took up the challenge and instantly sent for Black Dog, who, as soon as he arrived, saw at once the position he should take. His best hopes for keeping his adopted father's favour and having a share in the vast fortune clearly lay in confession and contrition, rather than a continued loyalty to Third Wife. Indeed, he was beginning to believe that his infatuation with her was the result of a secret charm provided by her good friend, the Thai sorceress. Therefore he broke down in an extravagance of confession and contrition, and after that, an equal extravagance of blame, as he pointed a quivering finger at Third Wife. Yes, he had driven the car to the Sin Min Temple, yes, he had waited outside, but that was only because she had forced him to. Indeed, all the way to the temple, and while he was waiting in the car, he had experienced a strange numbness, as if he were not himself, but another being, under the influence of a powerful charm.

Third Wife, her mind working feverishly to salvage whatever she could from a situation spinning perilously out of control, clung desperately to the strategy of aggressive and loud blaming. She faced the Old One, pointing an accusing finger at Black Dog, and unable to go beyond his minor culpability in the whole affair as a passive accomplice waiting in a car, she began to rake up his wrong-doings of the past. 'He has been secretly taking your money from the locked safe, and falsifying accounts! He has secretly bought a coconut plantation in Johore. He managed to rent out the haunted house but pretended to you that people were frightened off by the stories of the long-haired ghost.'

She stood panting and trembling in the fervour of her accusations, and as soon as she paused for breath, Black Dog began shouting in a very loud voice. It was his turn to go the whole way of the desperate defendant and rake up all the dirt against the accuser. He adopted the accuser's stance, facing the judge boldly and yelling out the accusations. 'She cast a charm on me, making me quarrel with my wife. She spread all kinds of malicious gossip about you and laughed at you behind your back! She hates Fourth Mistress and has sworn to harm her and drive her out of the Great House! She spread all sorts of stories about Fourth Mistress and the young *sinseh*. She got Fourth Mistress to accept a gift of some scrolls from the *sinseh*. She—'

'Enough!' roared the Old One, livid with rage. The anger resisted the intrusion of a remorse that rose with the shocking realisation of a grievous injustice committed against innocence, because pure, unmixed anger was so much easier to deal with.

He looked with withering scorn at the three culprits before him, now turned upon each other, shouting accusations, and thought, How I despise them all. I will make sure that each worm is crushed into the ground.

The Old One, looking upon the repulsive man with the pitted face, concluded that he was the vilest worm of the three and deserved total annihilation in the bowels of the earth. He looked away from the man's brutal visage, from Black Dog's cowardly paleness, from Third Wife's frenzied, darting eyes, and thought, They will all be duly punished. I have no wish to see any one of them again.

Then he was confronted by a different image that had suddenly appeared in his mind, of a young gentle face, wide-eyed with terror, also with a love and need he had never seen before. Other images followed, of the wild joy on his return, the loving response on the bed, the complete bewilderment at his accusation, all surely not compatible with deceit and guilt, all reflecting innocence, even if the innocence had been plundered by a conniving and wicked world.

The sorrowful remorse had managed to push its way into the heart swollen with rage, only to be expelled by it.

For the truth was that the innocence was no more.

Nothing could change that truth. The pure flower that was his to pluck had been rudely plucked by others, the fragile branch snapped, the delicate jade figurine broken. There could be no consolation in attenuating circumstances: his bride had not gone virginal to the marriage bed, and he must act by that truth alone. He owed that much to his ancestors.

He would make himself go to the August Ancestor's room, and say, in all humility, 'Forgive me. You were right all along. Taking a young village girl was asking for trouble. I have been suitably punished.' The ancestor might be spiteful enough to suggest a greater punishment for the young wife, to make it commensurate with her heinous crime, and he would say, again with all humility, 'You know best. I will heed your advice this time.'

If that part of him rose to defend her, 'But she was the victim,' he would beat it down, stand solidly with the ancestor and say, 'That does not change the truth. *The truth is that she dishonoured me on our marital bed.*'

Deep in painful thought, he was unaware of a slight clothes and her favourite books, and none of the money that First Wife had offered, was hurrying past and leaving by the back door.

36
Friends Again

'Tch, tch, tch, what a mess you are in.' The goddess sounded sympathetic enough, but could have been more. Perhaps she had not pardoned her for the quarrel. 'Please forgive me. I behaved badly. Can we be friends again?' 'I have never stopped being your friend. I have been keeping watch over you.'

Silver Frond wanted to say, 'Then why didn't you prevent all those terrible things from happening to me?' but being afraid of annoying the goddess and starting another quarrel, merely said tearfully, 'I have been kicked out of the Great House.'

'Do you know why you have been kicked out of the Great House?'

'My husband says I have brought shame to him.'

'And how have you brought shame to him?'

And it was at this point that Silver Frond, instead of saying impatiently, as she was tempted to do, 'Why are you always asking me about what you already know?' burst into angry tears and cried out, 'It's all so unfair, so unfair! I have never done anything bad to Third Wife, and yet she has done this cruel thing to me! Why does she hate me so much?'

The goddess wanted to say, 'I told you so. I warned you that she was a snake.' But this was not the time for recrimination, but reconciliation and comfort. She said, 'You know, you have learnt a lot and grown up since you went to the Great House.'

Silver Frond said petulantly, 'Everybody tells me I've grown up. But what's the use? I wish I had never gone to the Great House!'

'Do you wish you had never met the Old One?'

She hesitated, then said 'Yes.'

'You're hesitating, see? That means you still love your husband.'

'I don't love him any more.'

'Suppose he asks you to go back to him?'

'He will never ask me to go back to him. I have brought him shame.'

'Are you blaming yourself?'

'How can I blame myself when everything I did was for love of him? I was prepared to go through any amount of pain to cure myself for him! No, I don't blame myself, only those wicked people who sought to harm me.'

The goddess said, 'You know, I'm beginning to like you very much. If I were not a goddess, I'd like to be a woman like you.'

Silver Frond thought that mixed into the goddess's wisdom was a lot of nonsense, as if she, like a mortal, grew old, became senile and indulged in much nonsensical prattle, like a very old and talkative woman in Sim Bak Village who used to live next door.

'What are you going to do now?'

'I don't know. I'm going home. My parents and sisters will be shocked, but they will understand, because they love me. I only want to be among people who love me.'

'Do you think your husband still loves you?'

Silver Frond said bitterly, 'He loves my virginity more than me. That's not love.'

'Where are you going?'

'To the Great House.'

'What? I thought you said you had just been kicked out of the Great House.'

'I'm going back only for a very short while. To see my husband. To tell him something. The last thing. Because I don't ever want to see him again.'

'What are you going to tell him?'

'Something important.'

'It's very late.'

'I don't care. I'm just going to force myself into his room, stand by his bed and say what I have to say.'

'I'll tell you again: if I were not a goddess, I'd like to be a woman like you. Did I ever tell you that mortals are sometimes stronger than the gods and goddesses they pray to?'

Here was her strange friend talking nonsense again. But it had been a rather comforting visit.

She rose to go.

37
The Wife At the Doorway

A wife on a mission, to entreat, warn, advise, offer love, standing in the doorway of his room, her form ominously dark against the light, speaking to him as he lay on his bed. It had happened with each of his wives, so many times in his life, as if that was their chosen method of approaching him when all other approaches had failed.

This time, instead of remaining on his bed in indifferent or cautious silence, he sat up and faced the visitant at the doorway. For it was none other than the youngest and favourite wife, who had brought the greatest upheaval in his life.

Her diminutive, slender, almost child-like form belied the damage she had done. She stood very still at the doorway, like a statue, and spoke in a voice that did not seem to be her own, so charged was it with reproach and foreboding.

'I would have gone through any amount of pain in the temple for love of you. I would have sacrificed my virginity ten times for you, but that would only make you despise me ten times more.'

The words of a girl-bride transformed beyond all recognition by a single trauma, they would haunt him ever afterwards. But now they only fed his confusion. He wanted to say to her, 'I've been in torment. I've been thinking of you. I'm sorry I asked you to leave,' but her purposefulness of tone and posture in the doorway forbade all response. 'I would have gone through a hundred knives or axes or stone pestles for you, but that would only make you despise me a hundred times more.'

Even at her most serious, he thought, she was capable of the most peculiar and incomprehensible language, like an imaginative, talkative child imitating adults in their use of colourful analogies. Knives? Axes? Stone pestles? He recollected the strange tales, some of a violent nature, that she had heard from that irrepressible story-teller Liang Por, and passed on to him in those happier times – how distant now, yet how recent – when, in the darkness of night, she forgot her fears in story-telling and curled up against him, like a happy, secure child.

Magic stones. Herbal brews. Blessed smoke that you could gather up in your hands, put in your pocket, and save for loved ones. She was indeed talking strangely.

But what had stuck in his mind, and would burrow into it, like so many tiny thorns, were her words about her love for him. There was nothing incomprehensible about them. In his despair in the coming days and weeks, they would return to haunt him in both his waking and sleeping hours.

He heard her say, 'Thank you,' in a softened tone, and wondered once again about the peculiar swings of mood of this strange, intense girl he had brought into his life. She was saying, 'I thought your gifts of money and jewels and clothes would make me happy. I don't wish to take away any of these. I've already told First Wife. But thank you for the education you have made it possible for me to have. I take it away with gratitude in my heart.'

The next moment she was gone, like a ghost or like one of the shadowy beings that inhabit dreams. He got up from his bed and went outside to look, but she had vanished.

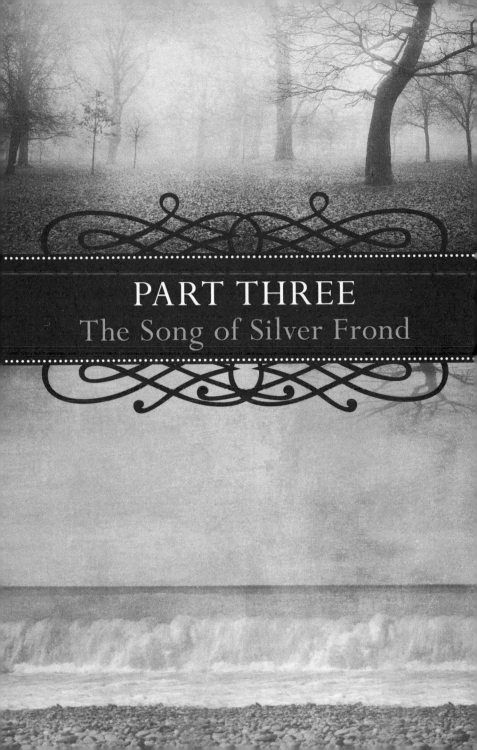

PART THREE
The Song of Silver Frond

1
A Stranger In Their Midst

Ah Bee Soh whispered to Silver Flower, 'Go and see what she's doing,' and Silver Flower whispered back, after walking past her room and taking a quick look inside, 'Nothing. She's still lying on the mattress, staring at the ceiling.'

On another occasion Ah Bee Koh murmured to Silver Pearl, 'She's been in the bathroom a long time. See what she's doing,' and Silver Pearl returned, after a minute, to mutter, 'Nothing. She's still staring at the water in the tub.'

Happily, the period of seclusion and staring at nothing did not last, but while it did, the whole family tiptoed nervously around the returned member, watched her moods from lowered eyelids, and refrained from the questions they only dared to bring up among themselves, in the secrecy of family meetings after they made sure she was fast asleep.

Who would have thought that in the short period of a year she would take them all on a dizzying journey through the brightest hopes and the most bitter shame?

In the ancestral country in the old days, a married daughter sent home in disgrace by her dishonoured husband could have the door shut in her face by irate parents, or even beaten and thrown into the well if the parents too felt the sting of the dishonour. Ah Bee Koh and Ah Bee Soh would never do that to their daughter, whether or not she had been guilty. They merely submitted to a cruel fate that gave them a beautiful daughter to build dreams on, and to see those dreams brutally smashed.

Ah Bee Koh stood outside the house on a rainy day, when thunder rumbled across a dark sky and called upon the Lightning God to strike him dead with a single bolt if his curse against the Great House was unjust: May the Old One and his three wives and their progeny never know a day of peace again.

Ah Bee Soh dragged him out of the rain and said, 'You fool. Don't you know he has spies everywhere? He could throw us out of this house any moment!'

She confided sorrowfully to a friend, 'The fortune teller was right,' meaning that when her firstborn was taken to a temple for a blessing, an old holy woman had looked at the baby, grabbed her little hands for a closer look, and then predicted that she would grow up to affect the lives of those around her in the most spectacular way.

The aura of her erstwhile wealth and status still clung to her, as she moved among them, and made her a stranger in their midst. Superimposed upon the pale, subdued face was the bright, confident one of not so long ago, upon the humble plain village suit of blouse and trousers, the finely tailored silk *samfu* whose buttons alone cost much more than the entire village suit. The sheer nakedness of the earlobes, fingers and wrists now shorn of jade, diamonds and gold was a startling sight that needed getting used to.

So she stood in their midst, stripped of the astonishing abundance of an old man's fickle love, but not of its memory, so that even as she squatted down and washed clothes by the tub or stood by the stove, fanning the coals, she inspired feelings of awe. Her sisters stood some distance from her, clinging to each other as they stared at her, remembering their visits to the Great House when she dispensed money and gifts freely. Her mother snatched the broom from her hand or instantly relieved her of the slop-pail for taking to the henhouse, crying out, 'No, no, you don't touch any of these,' as if her short stay in the Great House entitled her permanently to a life of luxury and ease.

As for her father, he never stopped murmuring to her, in a mournful voice, 'Your father is so happy to have you home,' the mournfulness being for the loss of the money that he needed for his beer and the occasional treats he liked to give his friends. He never referred to the ignominious incident when he had been publicly humiliated by the Indian chauffeur, but in the liberality of mood and tongue after a few glasses of beer, he spoke with bitterness about the humiliation and confided to some close friends that his daughter's marriage to the Old One had brought more pain than benefit.

'My favourite daughter,' he would say with a smile, clasping his beer glass with both hands. 'It is better for her to eat plain porridge and be happy than dine on all that fine food and suffer their insults!'

The reference to the fine food was but a small step to the painful recollection of all the lost wealth. 'You know,' Ah Bee Koh would say, shaking his head sadly, 'I should have insisted on one of the Venerable One's coconut plantations and one of his houses. What a fool I have been!'

'No, no,' said Ah Bee Soh to her daughter, 'don't go to the well. I'll draw up the water for you,' and again, 'No, no, don't go out to hang the clothes. I'll do it.'

For even after Silver Frond had come out of her seclusion, and was ready to have her share of duties in the household, her mother did not like her to be seen by the neighbours. Like a fallen heroine, or the favourite concubine sent back to her village from the imperial palace, she provoked the strongest gossip and elicited the wildest speculations, which her mother disliked intensely. She was aware, while doing simple chores such as feeding the chickens or plucking the jasmine flowers from the small bushes near the well, of faces peeping from behind window curtains or doors, of hands held up to hide whispering mouths, of staring children who forgot adults' instructions and said loudly to each other, 'Ssh, that's the one they chased out of the Great House!'

A little girl of about six, carrying her baby brother on her hip, came up to her one morning as she was drying some clothes, tugged at her hand and asked, 'Why did they kick you out of the Great House?'

A woman came one afternoon with a gift of four rice cakes, which was quickly revealed to be no more than a cheap ploy. Silver Frond instantly recognised her as the obtrusive commentator who had looked through the window on that day of her visit home, and had later witnessed her father's humiliation by the chauffeur. The woman had lost none of the impertinent inquisitiveness.

'Tell me,' she said to Silver Frond, her eyes wide with excitement. 'Is it true that your husband kicked you out because you had an affair with your *sinseh*?' For answer, Silver Frond held her firmly under the elbow and showed her to the door. She protested, laughing nervously and saying that she was merely repeating what everyone was saying. 'Please don't be offended with me, I'm just a simple, ignorant woman,' she said goodnaturedly, as she took her leave and had her rice cakes flung after her.

Silver Frond said, 'Mother, I want you to tell me what people are saying about me.'

Once, not too long ago, in a quiet cemetery, the man who was to become her husband and destroy her quiet, peaceful life for ever, asked her what people were saying about him, and she had obliged, upsetting him with truths he did not wish to hear. That was the burden of the rich and influential. The truths of the poor and the humble were not worth gossiping about. She had straddled both worlds, and would be worth gossiping about.

Ah Bee Soh said nervously, 'There's no point knowing. What is past is past. You are back home with us. That is all that matters.'

Silver Frond said, 'Mother, I want the truth.' She needed to know, even if they were lies or half-truths.

The Venerable One's fourth wife was seduced by the young sinseh, *who had cleverly got himself to replace the old* sinseh *and had done everything to delay his return from China.*

The Venerable One's fourth wife was seduced by the young sinseh *because the old man could not satisfy her young body. When he still proved impotent after three months of marriage, she went straight to the bed of the young* sinseh.

The Venerable One's fourth wife could not satisfy her husband's lust. He wanted sex every night and, exhausted, she asked him to take a fifth wife. Then she chose to leave the Great House, but not after securing a coconut plantation and a house on her father's insistence.

Third Wife was the mischief maker and schemer who fed the Old One all kinds of untruths about the innocent village girl.

Third Wife had caused all the trouble, which was why the Old One had kicked her out too. She was now living with her parents, who allowed no visitors. She had completely lost her mind, a pitiful lunatic confined to one room in the house. A beauty once, she looked like a witch now.

All the misfortunes could be traced to the car that the Venerable One had bought as a love gift for his bride. It gave off evil emanations, and even lured Second Wife to commit suicide inside it one night.

The real reason for bringing the village girl into the Great House was First Wife's desire to find a suitable wife for the dim-witted son. But First Wife's plan backfired when the Venerable One fell for the girl. So she had no choice but to create trouble for the girl and drive her out.

A curse had been put on the Great House for some terrible sin committed in the past by an ancestor, who for some reason was the most revered, because he had a room all to himself in the Great House. The curse would continue to affect the lives of all those living in that house for the next seven years. The young bride's departure was a blessing, because it meant escape from the curse.

A demon from the Sin Min Temple had taken residence in the Great House, and was causing all the trouble. If the Venerable One took a fifth wife, the demon would create trouble for her too.

The young bride, on the wedding night, was found to have a strange disease, which appeared as harmless-looking goose-pimples, but which was really very contagious and deadly.

The young bride was proving too intelligent for the Old One, as a result of her education. She would not obey him, like his other wives, and he was so upset that he actually left home and went into seclusion for a while. Then he decided to return and kick her out.

'Why are you laughing?' said Ah Bee Soh. She wanted to say, 'It's no laughing matter for parents when their daughter is sent home in disgrace,' but checked herself, this being no time to quarrel with her strong-willed, difficult daughter while so many vexing questions remained unanswered.

Silver Frond said, smiling, 'Liang Por could not have thought up such stories.'

Since the departure of his young wife, the Old One has not been well. Indeed, they say he is deeply unhappy and pining for her. They say he has lost his good looks and walks with an old man's stoop of defeat and sorrow.

This was no laughing matter. Silver Frond felt a little frisson of pity. Suddenly she remembered his kindness to her. It was not a single act of kindness, but a continuous stream, sparkling in the sunshine of an old man's lavish love, flowing to benefit every member in her family. But she quickly dismissed all such thoughts and feelings for a firm resolution of forgetting. To begin anew, she must forget every single moment of each day of her life in the Great House.

She had just turned seventeen and felt a resurgence of energy and purpose, so that after exactly six months of quiet moping at home, she was ready to step out of it, like the butterfly wriggling out of old, cracked skin into the freshness of a new world. She knew exactly what her new world would be, because all the time that she was moping at home, a dream had lain latent, not dead, and was now stirring to life, banishing the paleness from her face, the dullness from her eyes.

It would not depend on men and their conditional promises of love and wealth.

She tested the butterfly wings of the secret, exciting dream, and soared on a new song of hope.

2
The Scented Water
of Forgetting

'More!' cried Silver Frond, as she bent her head for her mother
to pour more water on her hair. 'Are you going to use up all
the water in the well?' grumbled Ah Bee Soh, but she happily
obliged, sensing the new energy and purposefulness in her
daughter, which was certainly better than the morose dullness of
the past months. She dipped a small pail into the large bucket of
water beside the well, and brought up, together with the water,
the blessed flower petals of cleansing and forgetting. As the water
fell slowly on Silver Frond's hair, it allowed the healing touch of
balsam, rose, chrysanthemum and jasmine to course down from
the wet strands on her head to her face, neck and shoulders.

Silver Frond caught the petals with her fingers, pressed them
to her cheeks and smiled.

Throughout her childhood and girlhood, her mother had
insisted on the power of water scented with flower petals blessed
in a temple, to cleanse her of any evil influences, as when she
came back one morning from a cemetery, carrying the odour of
death on her skin and clothes. She had always resisted the rituals
by the well, but now she demanded them, as the final stage of
forgetting and renewal, before moving on to the fulfilling of her
cherished dream.

She stood up, her wet hair dripping on to a towel draped around her shoulders, and smiled at the small group of children who had gathered to watch.

Her mother looked at her anxiously. *What will you do now?* The question had been on the tip of the anxious maternal tongue for weeks, and now perhaps her daughter was willing to talk about her future.

The future of young brides sent home in disgrace was not necessarily bleak. Already, someone had secretly approached Ah Bee Soh through a mutual friend to sound her out on the possibility of a connection with a rich businessman from Indonesia, called Tjoei, who kept homes in Singapore and Malaya and was now looking for a young mistress. This Tjoei was richer than the Venerable One, and a few years younger. He would be mesmerised by Silver Frond's beauty, which, at seventeen, showed promise of even greater flowering. He was said to be extremely generous when he was pleased.

The condition of virginity would be waived by this liberal old gentleman. But if insisted upon, and provided of course her daughter agreed, Ah Bee Soh was prepared to take advantage of that rumour about the Old One's impotence, build an elaborate tale upon it, claim pristineness for her daughter and persuade the girl, when the time came, to have recourse to that harmless deception of chicken blood, indistinguishable from human blood, upon the garment of proof. If the men made all that fuss about first claim to a woman's body, then the women should humour them with whatever means available. Ah Bee Soh knew of an actual instance when a woman thus helped her niece pass the crucial test on the marital bed.

Ah Bee Soh should have known better of course. She watched her daughter's look of grim determination and knew dependence on a man could never be a part of the plan hatching in her head.

'Just what are you planning to do?'

'I have a dream,' said Silver Frond, 'but it will mean spending some money. I have no money.' She regretted now her proud rejection of a packet held out by First Wife, which must have contained quite a lot of money because it was wrapped in newspaper.

The situation was actually bleaker, for there was no possibility of earning any money for the time being. Her mother and sisters were making a little by selling eggs, and her father was, as usual, peering into cigarette and biscuit tins inside cupboards and under beds, in the hope of securing even a small handful of coins to buy him a cup of coffee in his favourite coffee-and-beer shop.

Soon, whatever savings they had would be used up.

'If you will lend me some money, Mother,' said Silver Frond, 'I promise to repay you as soon as I can. It may take a while, but I promise. And it's only a small sum I'm borrowing. Just for some benches, chalk, pencils, books.'

Her mother heaved a huge sigh and said, 'I don't know what you're talking about. But if you need money, I'll give it to you. After all it's yours. There's quite a bit in a place where your father will never find it. Your mother is cleverer than you think!' Ah Bee Soh proudly tapped that part of her head where cleverness was supposed to reside. She put a finger to her lips to signal total secrecy, took Silver Frond by the hand and led her outside.

3
The Wonderful Secret of a Filthy Hen-House

'Do Silver Flower and Silver Pearl know?' 'No,' said her mother. 'They are two silly girls who can't be trusted with secrets.'

Ah Bee Soh made straight for a special spot in the henhouse, a dark corner filled with rotting planks covered with chicken dirt, and rusty nails sticking out, close to a row of beams that provided, on the outside, a resting place for the less active roosters and hens, and on the inside, a permanent home for a whole colony of cockroaches and other insects. It was the perfect spot to deter even the most determined hen thief, but not the burglar in search of a rich loot, and certainly not Ah Bee Koh, if he knew of it.

A wonderful secret it was, comprising two biscuit tins, one square and the other round, which Ah Bee Soh pulled out, slowly and carefully, from their hiding place under the dirt and rot. Before she opened the tins, she made sure that she and her daughter had their backs turned to the entrance of the henhouse, blocking out all sight of the secret from any curious eyes. In any case, she was prepared for the intrusive question.

'We'll say we're trying to get some eggs that had dropped through the planks.' Ah Bee Soh pointed to two eggs that she had craftily placed under a small pile of rotting wood, and once again said in self-congratulatory fervour, 'Your father used to say I had nothing but dead shrimps in my head for brains! Now see how I have outwitted him!'

Ah Bee Koh's eyes would have gleamed at the sight of the treasure. The square tin was filled with notes, in different denominations, tied up in rubber bands, the round tin with a small assortment of gold jewellery.

Silver Frond recognised both the money and the jewellery. She had refused to take the bundle of money wrapped in newspaper that First Wife had offered, as well as the wedding gifts of necklaces, chains, bracelets and rings that First Wife had tied up with a piece of cloth. For she had thought then, in lofty defiance, that having come into the Great House with nothing, she would leave with nothing.

Now looking at the hoard that her mother had pulled out of its hiding place, she remembered that her husband's generosity had not been limited to the wedding jewellery and cash gifts, but had spread, like the tributaries of a river in rich flood, dispensing money and gifts freely, almost on a daily basis, which she had been only too happy to pass on to her father, mother and sisters when they came on their visits.

She had no idea what wealth had decked her body and passed through her hands.

Silver Frond picked up a gold chain, and looked at it closely, immediately recollecting a visit to Sin Hin Goldsmiths, which her husband had insisted on making with her, simply because she had happened to mention that the chain she was wearing was not to her liking, being too elaborate and heavy. The shop assistants had brought a tray of gold chains, her eyes had lingered over one longer than the others and her husband had instantly pointed to it and said to the assistants, 'That one. We'll have that one.'

Silver Frond next picked up a gold ring, which also carried pleasant memories. Her husband had bought it from a friend who was doing a quick sale of his wife's jewellery to raise cash. But the ring had proved too big for her and she had given it to her mother, together with large paper bags of tinned food, dried mushrooms, biscuits and other good stuff.

Then Silver Frond's eyes alighted on a gold bracelet, yet one more gift from her husband, which had proved too small, and which she had given to her mother for either Silver Flower or Silver Pearl.

The collection was modest, compared to the one left behind, but together with the rolls of notes tied in the rubber bands, it was a treasure unseen and unheard of in any house in Sim Bak Village, much less in a hen-house.

'It's all yours,' said Ah Bee Soh. 'I don't need it. You have been extremely generous to me in providing money for all those expensive medicines, which have cured me.'

'I don't need so much,' said Silver Frond, feeling very happy. 'Just for some benches, a chalkboard, some boxes of chalk, pencils and copying books. I brought back a lot of books from the Great House. They have no use for these things there.'

He is deeply unhappy and pining for her. They say his good looks are gone, and he walks with an old man's stoop of defeat and sorrow.

In her dream that night, she saw him, very old and stooped and sickly. He was holding her hand and saying, 'Don't leave me,' and she was saying, 'But I can't fulfil my dream in the Great House. I have to leave!'

He said, 'I've spoken to the ancestor again on your behalf. But he says his position remains unchanged. You are disgraced for ever, because what is lost is lost for ever. He says you cannot be brought back to the Great House. But please give me time. I can persuade him.'

She said, 'No, don't go to all that trouble. I don't care any more. People can laugh at me if they like, your ancestor can condemn me as much as he wants, but I don't care. I can be happy on my own, because of my dream.'

He said, 'I looked for you. I looked everywhere for you, and even shouted your name. But you had vanished.'

She said, 'Goodbye. But thank you once again for my education. I will never see you again, but when you are dead, and lying in your coffin, I will come and pay my respects and say thank you to you for the last time.'

When she woke up, she found that her eyes were wet with tears, and she did not know whether they were tears of compassion, sadness, or joy, or all three.

4
A Song of Triumph

The ideal was a real classroom with rows of desks and chairs facing a chalkboard and the teacher's table, which should be big enough to hold the many piles of copybooks to be marked and have at least four drawers with good locks to keep the teacher's books, pens and chalk. The table top should, preferably, have a long groove in front to hold the teacher's marking pen or pencil when not in use, so that these would not roll off.

She had seen such excellent furniture in the better schools during those days of selling eggs when she liked to pause by a school to peep in or listen to the sounds of teaching and learning. But this kind of furniture was probably expensive and she wished to spend her money carefully. So she made do with a large square table that the carpenter Ah Siak Chek made for her at a good discount. The table was large enough for at least four pupils to spread out their copybooks and write and read comfortably. Ah Siak Chek also made for her, again at a generous discount, four wooden stools, which were less comfortable than chairs, but which young learners should not mind in the noble cause of acquiring knowledge. Her mother had made available to her two low stools for additional pupils, who could either write with their copybooks placed on their laps, or take turns to use the table. Lastly, there was a mat for laying on the floor, which could seat two more, should her class grow over the months.

To pay for the new furniture, she made use of a small roll of notes from the square biscuit tin. The hiding place continued to be the hen-house, and her mother continued to be alert and vigilant each time she made a visit to the precious hoard on her behalf. One evening her father had asked her mother, 'Why are you always going to the hen-house? Do you like the smell of chicken dung? Ha, ha, ha!'

She had to be careful with the secret money, to let it put food on their table and clothes on their backs for a long time to come. The jewellery would only be pawned or sold in the last resort, and could well serve the long cherished goal of an operation for Silver Pearl, whose harelip was growing more pronounced. The poor girl had never reminded her of that grandiose promise, made on her marriage, when money promised to flow as abundantly as water from her hands. As for the father, who claimed a debilitating disease that forbade even the very occasional odd job, he would have to make do with whatever she or her mother could spare.

She was beginning to hate the sight of her father's outstretched hand, and even more, the sound of his voice in whining self-pity: 'Whatever your father has suffered, he has suffered on your account!'

The necessary financial arrangements made, Silver Frond launched upon what would turn out to be one of the happiest periods of her life. She had loved being a pupil; she loved being a teacher even more. She had left the Great House with a store of knowledge and skills assiduously picked up from both the old and the new *sinsehs*, which now, in the new capacity of educator, she was only too happy to share with her pupils.

It was a curious store, a mixture of the peculiar preferences of two very different personalities, the old *sinseh* having concentrated on the old classics and the younger *sinseh* on romantic poetry (much of which he had obviously written himself in sly tribute to his beauteous student), but both believing in the supremacy of learning by rote. This teaching method had fitted in well with Silver Frond's special talent and inclination, for she had a very good memory and learnt with ease, reciting long poems or pieces of text effortlessly and flawlessly. It did not matter that she mostly did not understand what she recited; the sound alone, rebounding on her ears, filled her with pride and confirmed her status as a true scholar.

From her modest classroom then, in the front portion of the house, swept very clean and kept clear of wandering chickens and their dirt by a small barricade at the door (a few still managed to fly in through the open window, squawking and being a nuisance), Silver Frond dispensed the wisdom of the classics and the romance of enchanted poet-dreamers to her charges. They comprised her two sisters, their friend, an earnest girl of eleven who looked to be the most promising, their friend's small brother of seven, whom her mother insisted she take along, a girl of fourteen, who would have gone to school but for her poor health, and a small group of cousins of mixed ages, who had begun by curiously peeping in through the window during a lesson and had been invited in. It was a motley class, displaying various degrees of cleanliness, which, in the more serious cases, might result in a slight classroom crisis, as when one of the cousins failed to prevent a large wet blob from falling from her nose on to one of the precious textbooks as it was being passed round.

One afternoon, a woman with a baby on her hip asked if she too could be educated and was duly welcomed. She was only sixteen, and wanted to read and write, so that her in-laws would not look down on her.

Their voices raised in unison, Silver Frond's pupils bellowed out sonorous quotations, which even their teacher did not understand, but which sounded very grand and worth learning by heart. Sometimes, they sang the songs that Silver Frond had learnt years back, when she stopped by schools to listen to songs being taught or sung. The songs were always sung to martial music played on a gramophone record, which she replicated rather convincingly by using two stout bamboo sticks to beat out the rhythm.

She enjoyed in particular correcting her pupils' pronunciation and guiding their hands in the penning of characters. How she loved to see beautiful strokes flowing out of brushes!

The old *sinseh* had been particularly strict about handwriting, once or twice hitting her knuckles with a wooden ruler. She imitated his stern pronouncements as she looked over her pupils' shoulders to watch their progress: 'It is an insult to the brush when you do not use it properly. The pen is a noble instrument. Do not abuse it.'

Their heads bent over their copybooks in frowning concentration as they copied out row upon row of words written on the chalkboard in their teacher's fine hand, they presented a very convincing picture of serious scholarship, and their teacher of conscientious mentorship. She carried a wooden ruler to knock the heads or knuckles of recalcitrant students, as she had seen the old *sinseh* do to the Old One's grandchildren, but had so far applied the ruler only on her own sisters. They treated it as part of classroom fun, shouting 'Ouch!' and grimacing clownishly to make the other pupils laugh.

Back home, when asked by their parents what they had learnt from their young teacher, the other pupils would instantly and proudly recite the impressive quotations and poems, but when asked the meaning, could only scratch their heads and giggle.

For her work as teacher, Silver Frond wore a white short-sleeved cotton blouse and black cotton trousers, a uniform for lady teachers she had seen in a Chinese school, and had her hair tied in two tight plaits.

She charged no fees, but later required the pupils to make a small contribution towards the reading and writing materials. Some of the pupils brought homemade cakes or homegrown vegetables in place of the fee.

The less charitable in Sim Bak Village whispered about the dreadful fate of the jewel-bedecked, chauffeured mistress from the Great House reduced to teaching pupils who could not afford to pay fees in an improvised classroom still smelling of chicken dirt.

A teacher! She *was* a teacher. It was a dream come true. She sang a song of triumph.

She had left strict instructions not to be interrupted during a lesson, unless absolutely necessary, and was once extremely annoyed when her father, reeking of beer, strolled in and stood watching her, smiling and nodding his head in approval to each word she said. Vexed, she had signalled to him to leave, and when he still went on watching her and grinning at her pupils, she abruptly left her place by the chalkboard and led him away.

Ah Bee Soh came hurrying, in the midst of a writing practice exercise, to tell Silver Frond that somebody wanted to see her, and was waiting in the kitchen. 'From the Great House,' she whispered.

Silver Frond, in her best schoolteacher voice, told her pupils to continue their copying diligently, asked the sixteen-year old mother-pupil to report any misbehaviour, and went to meet the visitor.

5
Singing a Louder Song of Triumph

She had heard that Black Dog had been dismissed in disgrace, but clearly he was still in the employment of the Old One and still entrusted with errands. Perhaps he knew too many family secrets to be dismissed.

He stood awkwardly, not looking at her as he muttered something and pointed to a pile of paper bags on the table, bulging with presents. Not too long ago, he had been sent with other gifts, which had set in motion the events that had done so much damage to her young life. A messenger from the Great House with gifts – she should ever be wary of that. She stood looking at him and waited for him to speak.

He was almost startled by how much she had grown and matured. Eight months ago, she had left the Great House a frightened child-woman; now she faced him with the calm confident bearing of a woman who could never be frightened again. He also noticed her fresh beauty, which must have derived from the new confidence. He remembered that in the days of the Old One's ardent courtship of her, when people spoke of her beauty, he had responded with a contemptuous laugh. '*Tchah!* You call that beauty? She's a mere child, with *every* child's prettiness!' Now, without daring to look at her directly, he surprised himself by thinking, She is the most beautiful woman I have seen.

She said, 'How is the Venerable One?' and went on to inquire about the health, in order of seniority, of the rest of the residents in the Great House. The Old Mother, First Wife, Second Wife, Third Wife, the son.

Black Dog muttered, 'Very well,' to each inquiry, clearly impatient to get over the courtesies and go on to the business of the day. He had been told to deliver the gifts in the paper bags together with a gift of money, in a large pink envelope, which he now took out of his pocket and placed beside the paper bags. He had also come with words carefully learnt and rehearsed: 'The Venerable One would be very pleased for you to accept all these gifts, which are for your good health and the health of your family.'

Ah Bee Koh came in then, and would have greeted the visitor from the Great House with hearty amiability, but for the air of stern formality in the room that had been set by the unsmiling courtesies. Ah Bee Koh went to stand beside his wife, and was about to say something to her when she frowned, said, 'Sssh!' and silenced him completely. Together they stood and watched the proceedings in intense but polite silence.

Peeping out of a paper bag was a box of expensive ginseng and a packet of nourishing herbs, which Ah Bee Soh's sharp eyes immediately recognised as the most costly in town. She cast quick glances at her daughter, and saw only indifference. Her daughter said, 'Please thank the Venerable One for his generosity. But I don't need or want the gifts. So I will ask you to take them back.'

Her mother's eyes said, I'm sure it's all right to keep the ginseng and herbs, and her father's eyes, which had just alighted with great interest on the bulging pink envelope said, almost pleadingly, Keep that. You are entitled to it. After all, they kicked you out.

There appeared two faces at the window, peeping in, and as if that justified their presence as spectators at a most interesting happening, the entire body of pupils left their work and gathered round to take a look at the magnificent offering of gifts. They were particularly interested in the tins of biscuits, the packets of dried mushrooms, the large pomelo, the oranges and apples, the tins of Ovaltine, and what looked to be a tub of ice-cream. They stared, and speculated among themselves in intense whispers about the contents of packages whose shape and size and wrapping gave no clue. Then they looked at the person before whom all these gifts were laid, like offerings to a goddess in a temple, and their esteem for their young teacher rose immeasurably.

But she was adamant. She said firmly, 'Please tell the Venerable One not to send any more gifts. I am well. I have enough,' rejoicing in her proud independence. The song of triumph was complete, but looking upon the face of the man who had participated in the plot against her, she had a sudden urge to sing it louder in his ears.

'Wait,' she said, and to everyone's surprise, disappeared quickly into her room. She emerged just as quickly carrying something, which Black Dog recognised instantly, despite the intervening years, because he had brought it to her himself.

'I have no need of dolls,' said Silver Frond, 'so please take it back.'

The magnificent doll, still in its box, had lost its brightness of hair, eyes and clothes. It had lain in a cupboard these past years, the ultimate toxic gift because it had caused all the wives in the Great House to swarm around her like a pack of savage animals. It was best returned to its giver, through its original deliverer. It was her last link with the Great House. She wanted not the slightest reminder.

Black Dog's face went pale with shock and humiliation.

Silver Frond next calmly gathered up the paper bags to put into his hands. He got up to go. He looked confused and wretched. And still there was something she had to do, to take advantage of a visit that she knew would never be made again.

'Those rumours about Third Wife,' she said. 'Are they true?'

And Black Dog, who had planned on simply delivering the gifts and resisting all attempts to elicit information about any resident in the Great House, was forced to confirm the rumours. Yes, Third Wife had left the Great House. Her two daughters had left with her. She was unwell and was being cared for by her parents. Yes, she had lost her mind and had to be confined to a room. No, her life was not in danger, but she had lost a lot of weight, had refused to have her hair or nails cut, and was virtually unrecognisable.

And once more surprising himself, Black Dog voluntarily divulged his most private thoughts on the subject: 'I think she is faking the madness, for her own purposes. She is better than any actress.'

6
The Wife Who Would Be Swallowed Up By A Python

The old *sinseh* and the young *sinseh* had seldom told her stories, but she believed that story-telling was the best form of instruction for the young. In any case, she had always enjoyed both telling and listening to stories, and if her pupils had been obedient enough and done their work well for the day, she would reward them with her favourites.

'The one of the Monkey God and the peanut-seller!' cried the cousin with the offensively dribbling nose. They had all heard it three times, but she loved it and always yelled for more.

'No! The one of the woman with one hundred warts on her face!' cried another cousin, glaring at her.

'We've heard that one before,' said the eleven-year-old girl, who was turning out, as Silver Frond expected, to be the brightest of her pupils. 'Let's have a new one. Our teacher has so many stories that there will always be a new one to tell.' The girl simpered in the self-consciousness of a brilliant piece of flattery, which was clearly working on the teacher, for she was smiling and looking very pleased.

'Liang Por recently told the story of a woman who walked through forests and mountains looking for her husband,' said the mother-pupil, who sometimes missed part of a lesson to go into a corner to breastfeed her small son. 'But when she found him, he was already dead. He had been eaten by a tiger. She saw his bones scattered on the ground, picked one up, pushed it down her throat, choked on it, and died. That showed she loved her husband very much.'

Suddenly aware that she had told a story instead of requesting one from the teacher, she laughed and apologised for her presumptuousness.

'That's a sad story!' cried Silver Pearl. 'I want to hear a happy story!' And Silver Flower echoed, 'Yes, a happy story!'

'All right,' said their teacher. 'Here's a story with a happy ending.'

So the woman wandered through the most dangerous forests looking for her husband. 'Oh where can he be?' she moaned, and asked everyone in the villages she passed through. Thus did she search in agony for thirty days. After that time, she gave up hope. He must have been eaten by a wild beast. But surely there would be some bones she could recover and take back with her? She wanted to lay the bones lovingly in a grave and be buried beside him when her time came. Then someone told her that he had seen a huge python swallowing him up. He had simply disappeared into the python's body. There were no bones to take back in loving remembrance. The woman was very distressed. She was determined to look for the python and plead with it to give back her husband's body, or whatever was left of it. At last she found the beast. It lay under a tree, unable to move, because of the man's body struggling inside it.

'Help! Help!' yelled the man. 'Let me out! I want to return to my wife. I know she is looking for me! We love each other very much!'

Now, the python would have obliged the man by vomiting him out, as he was more trouble than he was worth. But the problem was that, try as it would, it could not expel the man from its body. It could swallow people, but not release them if it changed its mind.

'Oooh,' moaned the man, 'I'm going to die! I feel death coming in minutes!'

And the woman said to the python, 'I command you to swallow me.'

'What?' said the python. 'No human being has ever volunteered to die in this way.'

'It's the only way for me to be buried with my husband,' said the woman, and with a smile, forced open the python's mouth and climbed into it.

'Ugh!' said Silver Pearl. 'It is not a happy story.'

There arose a noisy debate about whether a woman could love her husband so much as to want to be swallowed by a beast in order to be with him.

'Let me tell you another story,' said Silver Frond, delighted to see that even the shyest of her pupils, a pale-looking girl with a large purple birthmark on her right cheek, was coming out of her shyness to join in the animated discussion.

But she was prevented from telling the story, for once more, her mother had hurried into the classroom and whispered urgently, 'You have a visitor from the Great House.'

It was amazing. The Old One was persisting in his gifts of placation and reconciliation. Her sense of triumph in rejecting them outright was sweet. She wondered how he could keep improving the wondrous scale of his gifts.

She said to her pupils, 'Go on with your discussion, but don't make too much noise,' and went with her mother to meet the visitor.

7
First Wife Makes a Proposal

'How is the Old One?' said Silver Frond. It was not a mere courtesy as on the occasion of Black Dog's visit, but a genuine inquiry, expressed with the deep respect that First Wife had always commanded. Although no more under the same roof and therefore under no obligation to acknowledge her authority, Silver Frond found herself giving her all due deference, including bringing the best chair in the house for her to sit on and asking her mother to prepare some tea.

First Wife, as stern of mien as ever, responded with her usual no-nonsense terseness. 'He's not at all well. He has lost his appetite, and does not sleep well at night. He is being attended by a Western doctor, as he has not responded well to the medicine from the Lam Tong Medical Hall.'

It would be only a small step, from describing the Old One's illness, to blaming the one responsible for it. First Wife chose to delay the blame, in her need first to clarify her role in the whole sorry business.

'The Great House is no longer the same. A curse has fallen on it. I tried my best to warn everybody, but nobody would listen. Never in my life had I ever thought such a tragedy could befall one of the most respected houses in Singapore. I went to the temple many times to discover the truth behind all the folly and sorrow, and each time I was told the same truth: the ancestors have been dishonoured and must punish the transgressor.

Yesterday I went to the temple again, and was told that the Old One's punishment is nearly reaching its end. The ancestors are satisfied. By the next moon, his illness will be gone.'

Silver Frond murmured, 'I am glad.'

First Wife now turned to face Silver Frond with the special purpose of her visit.

'The Old One will be well only on condition that you return to him,' she said, in a demonstration of that strange logic whereby gods and dead ancestors claimed total power, yet depended on mortals in the exercise of that power. They could restore the Old One to health, provided they secured the cooperation of the one who had caused the loss of health in the first place.

A faint flush appeared on First Wife's face as if her intelligence were embarrassed by the absurdity that governed the relationships between gods and mortals. A second flush appeared with the very disagreeable realisation that neither god nor mortal could shake the Old One out of his mad love for the village girl.

'Did he ask you to tell me to return to him?'

The question displeased First Wife by its bluntness: her word should be taken on trust, and not be subject to any questioning.

'I know exactly what is good for him,' she said with cold hauteur. 'I have been his wife for more than forty years now, and have always acted for his good. And his alone.'

'Is it your wish then, and not his, that I should return to the Great House?'

The impertinence should not go unrebuked, and First Wife turned upon Silver Frond a look of cold displeasure.

'You dishonoured the Venerable One,' she said grimly, 'and you cannot expect to be accepted back into the Great House, which has never known such dishonour. All the brides, in the long history of the family, went virginal to the marriage bed.'

None of the brides had been so unfortunate as to be tricked and robbed of their virginity. I did everything out of love for the Old One, and he knows it. Only he can't bring himself to acknowledge it because of the ancestors, Silver Frond thought angrily. I'd like to go into the room of the August Ancestor and throw some chicken dirt on his august portrait!

'We women must know our place,' said First Wife, making a great effort to speak calmly, preparatory to laying out her proposal, which had to be presented with a clear head and a calm voice. 'When a man is deprived of his honour on the marriage bed, and is confronted with the proof, he has every right to drive his bride away.'

'Hasn't the Old One already done that? Isn't he satisfied?' Tears of anger filled Silver Frond's eyes. Through them she saw her mother and two sisters in a corner of the room, nervously watching.

First Wife took a sip of tea, and decided to put an end to all the disagreeable argument, which she had, indeed, not expected in the first place, by laying out her proposal, in clear, precise terms so that there would be no misunderstanding. She was sick of misunderstandings.

'I want you to return to the Old One not as Fourth Wife, but as mistress. That means you will not be allowed to enter the Great House again. You will be set up in a very comfortable house in another part of town, and given everything you want.

All the money and jewels owed to you are still in my keeping, and I will hand them over as soon as you agree to the proposal. The Old One will visit you whenever he wants. But you will no longer be Fourth Wife. If you give birth to a son, he cannot have the same status as my son. When you die, you cannot be buried in the family burial ground. As you must know, the tomb next to his will be mine.'

The absurdity of the whole situation – of the proposal in all its meticulousness of detail, of the sheer effort that must have gone into its crafting, of the complete confidence that it would be accepted – almost deprived Silver Frond of speech. She gathered her thoughts for a suitable response.

Two passing neighbours looked in through the window then, and witnessed the strange sight of a young village girl in plaits and school uniform and an elderly woman in fine town clothes facing each other in an ominously brewing storm of opposing wills. They paused to look and listen.

Silver Frond decided to repeat the question that First Wife had adroitly avoided answering: 'Did the Old One ask you to come to me with this proposal?' and at once knew the truth when First Wife, with an impatient gesture of the hand, said, 'I've already told you it's for the best. He's at present unwell, and I have to act to restore him to well-being.'

Her love for the Old One had always been the protective and defensive kind. Perhaps that was the most difficult kind of all.

There was much less temptation to be defiant and ruthless with her than with the others, particularly Black Dog and Third Wife, but Silver Frond was annoyed enough to retort with sharp contempt: 'If I do not wish to return to the Old One as his wife, what makes you think I will return to him as his mistress?'

First Wife thought, This village girl – who has taught her to speak in this way? Then she stood up to her full height and said, without looking at anyone, 'I have done my duty. There is no more that I can do. From this moment, I wash my hands of the entire matter. The gods will bear witness to this.' If there were thunder and lightning then to endorse her vow, it could not have sounded more awesome.

Ah Bee Soh rushed forward to say timidly, 'Please finish your tea,' but the lady, without looking at her, was already walking towards the door. Outside was a waiting trishaw, with a maidservant inside.

8
What Was It Like?

Silver Flower gave Silver Pearl a push towards their sister's room and whispered, 'You ask her.' Silver Pearl said, 'No, you,' and gave her a shove that made her fall down. Both girls sat on the floor in an explosion of giggles, rolling their eyes and covering their mouths. 'What was it like?' they asked, and once again covered their mouths to hide the uncontrollable giggling.

'Nothing,' said their sister.

Nothing? They could not believe it was nothing. They had heard that a girl bled, screamed, fainted. In one of the stories told by Liang Por, the bride was found on the marriage bed the next morning, a white and cold corpse, unable to survive the trauma.

Both had thought about how they would react when their time came.

'I will ask Mother to brew me a lot of strengthening medicine so that I can bear the pain,' said Silver Flower.

Silver Pearl said, 'I will tell my husband to be gentle. The pain is only when he is rough and thinks only of his own pleasure!'

Silver Flower said tauntingly, 'You needn't even bother thinking about it. You will never get married because no man wants to marry Miss Split-Mouth!'

It was a reflection of the sisters' closeness that even the grossest insult melted away in a wash of laughter and playfulness. 'Miss Split-Mouth! Miss Split-Mouth!' they repeated together boisterously.

'It was nothing', said Silver Frond, meaning there was no pain, none of the brutality of knife, axe and pestle. Indeed, the body melted away and felt nothing, in the sheer happiness of giving joy to the man she loved. What had that tiny piece of pristineness to do with the vastness of a woman's loving?

She had long decided to banish from her memory that recollection of the awful weight on her body as she lay on the mat in the temple, the terrible proximity of the ugly pitted face breathing on hers, and the suffocating smoke of incense in her nostrils and throat, and to cling, instead, to that image of the closeness – oh, so short-lived – on their warm, secure bed, when wife and husband never felt so relieved or so happy to be together.

The fearful dreams had not completely left her nights, despite the peace and contentment of her new life. In one of them, the joyous closeness on the bed was rudely interrupted by a grim intruder who came to them in the darkness and pushed them apart, muttering, 'No, no, she is defiled, and you must never forget nor forgive that,' and she knew exactly who he was.

9
Oh, How Can I Bear All This?

A ghost, she thought, in a chill of terror. He has died, and his ghost has come on a visit. One part of her mind said, 'Quick! Put your hands together and bow three times to show respect, if you don't want to be harmed,' and the other said, 'Quick, give him a chair to sit on. He is no ghost but a very weak old man!'

With a gasp, she guided the Old One to a chair and asked him, in a voice faint with shock, 'Would you like some hot tea?'

Her mother, who had just entered, wiping her wet hair with a towel, stopped and stared, the towel suspended on her head. Her father came in next, and her sisters, all frozen into dazedly staring statues.

The Venerable One had not, in anyone's memory, stepped even once in to Sim Bak Village. Neither during his courtship of one of their own, nor later during his marriage to her, had the villagers expected that the esteemed personage from the Great House would be seen in their midst. And now, after he had driven his young bride out of his house and started the most rabid rumours that ever circulated in town and village, here he was, sitting on a chair and taking a cup of tea from her with trembling hands.

What was one to make of this? Neighbours peeping through the window would speak of that strange sight for years afterwards.

To the many rumours would be added one more: *The Venerable One had been told by his ancestor that he would die soon. So he came to make his peace with the young wife he had kicked out. She forgave him, and offered him the tea of reconciliation.*

The Old One took the tea and said weakly 'Thank you.' Less than a year ago, they were in the intimacy of a shared room, the backseat of a car, a long walk along a beach, struggling together, in the privacy of their bed, to overcome the quandary of his need and her unreadiness. Now they were like strangers; he might as well have been any old man who had lost his way and stumbled into their hospitality of shelter and hot tea.

She asked in a gentle voice, 'How are you? I hear you have not been well,' and regretted the question instantly, for it brought a faint glistening of tears into the old proud eyes right in the midst of a growing crowd of inquisitive observers. The eyes seemed to tell her, in a mixture of sorrow and anger, Why do you ask? Can't you see? I have been in hell since you went away!

The situation was getting intolerable, and perhaps the Old One had anticipated it, for he said, getting up from the chair, 'Come outside with me. I would like to show you something.' The business-like briskness of tone saved the situation; the tears receded, from both his and her eyes.

Black Dog had brought gifts, which she had rejected; First Wife had put forward a proposal, which she had rejected even more vehemently; now the Old One, his visit climaxing the strange procession from the Great House, was going to show her something she was likely to turn down too. No gift or proposal from the Great House should be allowed to tempt her to return.

Outside she saw Black Dog, who avoided looking at her. As soon as he saw the Old One walking out, he rushed forward to help him. The Old One stumbled a little and Black Dog held his arm tightly to steady him. As she watched, she thought, in a rush of pity and sadness, how strong and upright that old body had been, delighting in long morning walks, walking up whole flights of stairs without the least sign of exhaustion. She looked at the old face, and thought it looked old now, a marked contrast with the face, warmed by sun, sea breezes and love's special joy, that only a short while ago, the chauffeur had complimented him on, as they made their way back to the car from the beach.

She walked beside him with a growing sense of unease, wanting to hold his arm but afraid to break the air of formality that he seemed intent to maintain in their first encounter after the terrible estrangement. She did not even dare ask, 'What is it? Where are we going?' but continued to walk in silence, with Black Dog leading the way.

They approached a narrow dirt road, and even before the Old One said, 'I bought it back from Towkay Lam,' she knew what he had taken her to see.

The car was parked by the road, in the shade of a tree, and was already, by its rarity, attracting the attention of some village children, who were gathering round to look and admire. It gleamed as brightly as ever. The protective window curtains were gone.

The Old One said, 'I bought it back from Towkay Lam for you, because it gave you so much happiness.' This was the closest to a humble declaration of contrition, love and longing that a proud old man could make to his estranged wife in full view of others.

Silver Frond thought, Oh, how can I bear all this? She let out a sob, turned and ran all the way back home.

10
Sweet Song of Revenge

Now that they were friends again, the Goddess Pearly Face was more inclined to tease than to advise. 'What else did you reject, to impress your family and pupils?'

'Not to impress anyone! I was simply doing the right thing. The third paper bag contained a tin of good quality biscuits, grapes and I think a packet of dried plums, the expensive kind for putting into herbal soups. I could see Silver Pearl's eyes wide with longing! But no, I told Black Dog to take them all back.'

'A big house in town, maybe even bigger than any of the five in the Great House. All your wedding gifts of cash and jewellery returned. A car to take you around. And you turned all that down?'

'I have my pride. I don't want to be anyone's mistress. Do you want to hear again what I said to First Wife when she put forth the proposal?'

'All right. I know you enjoy repeating it.'

'*If I don't wish to go back as wife, what makes you think I will go back as mistress?*'

'Bravo!' exclaimed the goddess. 'And I enjoy repeating this: *If I were not a goddess, I would like to be a woman like you. You have come such a long way I can hardly believe it!*'

A rebuke from the goddess always elicited spirited self-defence, lavish praise its exact opposite, so Silver Frond said, suddenly looking doubtful and a little remorseful, 'I could not sleep last night because I kept seeing his face. Oh, how old and sad he looked! And when I would not get into the car, and turned to leave, he looked even older and sadder.'

The goddess asked, 'How long will you be singing your song of sweet revenge?'

Silver Frond said sullenly, 'They were so cruel to me.'

The goddess said, 'The song of revenge ought to be short and sweet. Yours looks like it's going to be very long and extended! Do you mean to continue singing beyond his grave?'

'What do you mean?' said Silver Frond in alarm.

'He's very ill. An old man does not recover from illness like a young man. An old man without hope never recovers at all.'

'He should have thought of all that before he acted so cruelly! He treated me worse than he could have treated any servant in his house!' Silver Frond was almost shouting, in a growing confusion of triumph and self-pity, anger and compassion, certainty and self-doubt, the worst possible maelstrom to drag a woman down screaming.

'He's been sorry for it ever since. Can't you see that his visit to you was the greatest act of contrition he could ever make? What else do you expect him to do?'

'Did it cost that much to come in a chauffeured car to see me?'

'Now you're being sarcastic and nasty. Think of the enormous sacrifice for one whose meticulous sense of hygiene has never allowed him to risk stepping on chicken dirt and smelling pig dung. He never visited you once when he was courting you. He visits you now when he has lost you. For some men, love is greater with loss.'

'I know I don't want to go back to him. I am happy being a teacher.'

The goddess said, somewhat spitefully, 'You are not a real teacher. Real teaching goes on in the proper schools set up for it. It means you instruct your pupils how to do sums and write letters and petitions and pass examinations. Real teachers have to be properly trained. Did you know that?'

Silver Frond said with some hauteur, 'Well, I'll be properly trained then. I know Madam Leong Fah, who teaches in Hwa Hin School. She is very good and experienced. I'll ask her to tutor me!'

'Do you intend to return to the Old One or not?'

'No.'

'For goodness' sake, what more do you expect him to do?'

'I want him to stand with me in front of the portrait of the August Ancestor and say, "*I was right and you were wrong. This girl from Sim Bak Village loves me more than the rest of the wives combined, because none of them would have gone through the same fire and pain for me.*"'

The goddess let out a shrill peal of laughter. 'You have listened to too many romantic stories, that's the trouble!' Then returning to her serious tone, she said, 'If the Old One dies of a broken heart now, as is likely, considering his advanced years, the remorse you feel for not heeding my advice will be ten times what he felt for heeding his ancestor's.'

11:
Third Wife Does Not Offer Tea

She found the house easily, although it was in an unfamiliar part of town, and almost totally hidden from sight by *rambutan* and mango trees. From one of the trees hung a swing, or what was left of it, for one of the rope supports was broken and the swing seat, a rectangular piece of wood big enough to seat an adult and a child, hung limply, almost touching the ground. A stick broom, much used and worn down, lay amidst a small pile of fallen *rambutan* twigs and leaves.

There was an air of desolation about the whole place, which probably reflected the present state of Third Wife: every rumour told of her utter misery and that of her ageing parents and two daughters devoted to caring for her.

One of the daughters, whom Silver Frond recognised as the more hostile of the two during her brief stay in the Great House, was at her most hostile then, for as soon as she saw Silver Frond at the door, she said angrily, 'My mother does not receive visitors. Go away.'

She was joined by the other daughter who was of a milder temperament. The girl actually addressed her as 'Fourth Mother', probably out of habit, and contradicted her sister by indicating, with a swift turn of her head, her mother's presence in the room.

Third Wife had appeared at the bottom of a staircase, at the end of the room, and was watching the visitor with great interest. Frowning intently, she walked slowly forward and said, 'Who is it?' She stood before Silver Frond, scrutinised her closely and said, 'Ah, of course! For a second, I could not recognise you because of your new hairstyle and your plain clothes.'

The rumours had exaggerated both her appearance and the state of her mind. Silver Frond had expected to see a dishevelled, unwashed woman with wild tangles of hair, like the female ghost in the abandoned shophouse belonging to the Old One, wandering the earth for a hundred years. But apart from the paleness, caused mainly by the absence of the familiar make-up of bright rouge, lipstick and darkly pencilled eyebrows, and the strange apparel of some loose, ill-fitting clothes that looked like pyjamas, which she would have thoroughly disdained at the Great House, Third Wife did not at all look alarming. And apart from the tendency to frown and put her face very close to other people's faces when talking, as well as to mutter to herself and now and then let out a short, sharp laugh, she did not at all appear unsound of mind.

In fact, her mind became very focused on certain issues, which she would not let go of, dangling them excitedly before her visitor, like an overactive puppy repeatedly shaking a dead rat in its teeth.

'*Did he see you secretly? Was there some secret agreement between the two of you? Did he ever talk about me? Did he go to bed with you? Did you like it?*'

It was some time before Silver Frond realised that she was talking about Black Dog.

'He loved me,' she said plaintively. 'I told him I was not sure of my feelings, but he said he would wait. He despised his wife

and loved me. He would do anything for me.' Her face softened
in the recollection of his tender, loving attention to her. 'He
would even go out in the rain on his bicycle to buy me *char
kuay tiau* from my favourite stall in the market,' she said softly.
'"Make sure it has plenty of cockles and bean sprouts," I would
say, and he would nod his head and say, "As if I didn't know
your preferences!"'

Then her features hardened again. Silver Frond was not
prepared for the outburst that followed. Her face contorted with
rage, all ten fingers tensed to strike and scratch, the unhappy
woman rushed at her, shrieking, 'He betrayed me! And all
because of you!' Her daughters moved forward to restrain her,
and she collapsed in their arms, her fury spent as quickly as it
had arisen. She began to cry softly. 'You already had a man who
loved you,' she whimpered. 'Why did you have to steal another
from me?'

'I did not steal any man from you,' said Silver Frond,
unafraid of the long fingers that quivered with restless energy
and might rise to strike again.

'The Old One loved me best of all. Then you came, and he
never looked at me again.'

'He loved me until you came in with your plot to destroy
me.'

The hostile daughter shouted, 'Don't you dare talk to my
mother like that! She hasn't been well, and must not be upset.'

Third Wife said to her, 'Keep quiet, and don't interrupt
us while we are discussing important matters. Why don't you
go and get some tea for our visitor?' The girl fell into silent,
sullen muttering and Third Wife began stroking her face and
smoothing down her hair. 'My poor Ai Ai!' she said soothingly.
'You know, you're the brightest of his granddaughters, but he

never gave you the expensive education he chose to give some people!' Still stroking her daughter's face, she cast an arch look at Silver Frond and said, 'No, I will not offer you any tea. Tea is offered only to friends, not enemies!'

Silver Frond said with grim determination, 'I've come to ask you why you did such a cruel thing to me.'

Black Dog could have been right about the lady's artfulness, which used insanity as strategy for both attack and cover. Frowning in greatest puzzlement, Third Wife said, 'What are you talking about?'

Or perhaps it was a selective sanity that erased some things completely and concentrated on others obsessively.

'He loved you so much,' she said with a sob. 'Everybody could see it, but I saw it most clearly, because I have the sharpest eyes and the brightest brain. When you stole him from me, I wanted to die. And then you stole Black Dog from me, and I wanted to die a second time. Let me tell you something.' She moved closer to Silver Frond and whispered in her ear, behind a cupped hand, to prevent her daughters from hearing, 'Upstairs in my room is a long rope, which I can easily tie round a rafter and hang myself with, when the time comes. If that doesn't work, under my bed is a large bottle of bleach, which I can swallow and be dead within hours. Stupid woman!' From her store of memories of the Great House had floated up the image of Second Wife curled up in the backseat of a car, with the pathetic half-finished bottles of embrocation oil that only caused retching, not death. 'Stupid woman! She was not serious about dying, that was why.'

Death became the obsessive topic. 'You are a witch,' she said to Silver Frond, smiling. 'You came to the Great House taking advantage of an old man's love, and you left it, with a great deal of his wealth to benefit your family. He will die soon of a broken heart. You will come to his funeral pretending to shed tears for all to see. All you care about is his money. I know about your good-for-nothing father and scheming mother!'

Silver Frond remained silent. The time for argument, refutation and recrimination was past. The Goddess Pearly Face was right about the need for the song of revenge to be short and sweet. Looking at the tormented Third Wife, she could not have wished for a greater punishment for her. As her mother would say, the gods were just in the end.

Suddenly she remembered that she had brought a gift of a packet of biscuits and some oranges, the usual visitor's courtesy, even for someone not particularly liked.

'It's for your mother,' she said tersely to the daughters. 'I'm leaving now.'

'How kind!' cried Third Wife. Then she said excitedly, 'But wait, wait, don't go yet. I have a gift for you too!'

She turned to present the back of her neck to the hostile daughter and said, 'Quick, take it off.' The daughter hesitated and she said, 'Never mind, I can do it myself,' and struggled to undo the hook of the gold chain round her neck. She managed at last, and held out to her visitor, on the palm of her right hand, the chain and its cylindrical locket. She began to smile, in the recollection of the happy ear-cleaning days, and threw the gift at Silver Frond, laughing heartily, 'Much use this will be to either of us now. Ha, ha, ha!'

12
Return

The Old One was glad that, at the moment of her coming into the room, he was about to take his medicine from an array of bottles on his table, so that pointing to this or that bottle, explaining these or those instructions from the Western doctor, whom he was beginning to trust more than any of the traditional physicians, he could keep a calm exterior.

For his joy was of the bursting, shouting kind, tolerable in children but not in old men.

Besides, someone might appear in the doorway then. First Wife, who came to his room regularly with nourishing black chicken and herbal brews, would certainly frown upon such unbecoming behaviour. So the Old One, ignoring her timidly uttered announcement, 'I have come back to you,' fell instantly to talking volubly about the many bottles of medication ranged before him. He said to her, 'Doctor Bala – he's better than any of our Chinese doctors! – told me to take these for my heart,' holding up a bottle of white pills, 'and these,' pointing to a bottle of brown pills, 'for the stomach pains, and these,' pointing to a very large bottle of small grey pills, 'for general health and energy.'

She was less inclined to hide her feelings. The sight of so much medication, from so knowledgeable a doctor, confirmed the seriousness of his condition that she had been told about and personally witnessed only a few days before. Third Wife's prophetic words 'He will die soon' rang in her ears. As she moved towards him to touch his hand, she burst into tears. 'I've come back,' she sobbed, 'I've come back to take care of you.'

'I'm all right,' he said, as his trembling hand moved to receive hers. 'Doctor Bala says that for my age, I am doing very well.'

'Who recommended this doctor to you? Is he really good?'

She understood his lifelong habit of managing and checking emotion, and was content, for the time being, to go along with his strategy of heroic control.

The doctor became the topic of intensive talk for the next half hour. This doctor had actually been educated and trained in Great Britain. He was certainly competent. He knew the most modern methods of cure. He had cured Towkay Lam of a kidney ailment. Ah Kiong Peh's daughter-in-law had almost bled to death in childbirth, but the doctor had come in time to save her and rush her to hospital for proper treatment.

They talked about the good Dr Bala as if their lives depended on it. Then, still unwilling to allow their feelings, swirling ferociously like a powerful underground stream, to break forth, they went on to talk about the merits of Western medicine and wondered whether it would eventually supersede traditional medicine in Singapore.

She saw the unmistakable glow of joy on her husband's cheeks and in his eyes. By the minute, he was coming out of that image that had so saddened her, of an old man stooped with defeat and sorrow. She had crept out of her own cocoon of defeat and confusion, to flap her butterfly wings confidently in open blue air, and would patiently wait for him to emerge fully, like her, to sing together their song of freedom.

The last confining segment of his cocoon cage was his fear of showing the truth of his feelings, so offensive to the ancestors. He had overcome this fear once before, when he had returned after the terrible absence of more than a fortnight, and she had climbed on to his knees like a child and sobbed on his neck. He had tried to suppress his joy and failed, for the joy had simply crept into his eyes and coated them with a film of tears. Desperately, he had tried to blink them back, aware that his wives were watching him. She had never loved him more than during this moment of his surrender to the truth of his heart.

In the end, after all the confusion and pain, that was all that mattered.

And it came soon enough, for not all the diversionary power of Dr Bala and his genius could stop the truth of the heart from breaking forth, the underground stream needing to bubble up into the bright sunshine, and leave its dark, silent confines for ever.

She was at his feet, pressing her face on his lap and sobbing loudly, and he was saying, again and again, 'You have returned! You have come back to me!'

13
See How They Love Each Other?

In 1948, a year after Silver Frond's return to the Great House, the old mother died, and for some reason, First Wife used the opportunity of the visit of a relative who had come from Malaysia for the funeral, to take a long leave of absence from the Great House, following the relative back and taking both her son and sister with her. Second Wife was only too glad to go away for awhile.

It was a most unusual move and was generally understood to be a reflection of her displeasure at the return of the disgraced fourth wife, and the Old One's display, once again, of that maddening madness, which would surely turn back the tide of the ancestors' readiness to forgive and sever all ties for ever. When asked if she would stay away permanently from the Great House, she had responded with much spirit, 'How can that be? I am First Wife and will be around to claim my ultimate right as First Wife. On his deathbed, the Old One will acknowledge at last that he loves me best of all!'

For years, she had darkly hinted of this irrefutable truth of the deathbed, though it was contradicted daily by the Old One's unabashed love of the youngest wife. The trauma of the disgrace, the exile and the final reconciliation seemed to have strengthened his devotion to her, and completely obliterated his awareness of the existence of First Wife and Second Wife under his roof (he never spoke about Third Wife). They were mere shadows on the edge of the bright core of his new life, centred on the return of the favourite wife. Second Wife, who was capable of brief bursts of mental activity in a long dull life, would say, at least once a day, 'We are nothing. She is everything.'

Against all proof of their being nothing, and the young wife everything, First Wife kept up her self-delusion: 'I know he loves me most of all.'

Many events occurred in that year of Silver Frond's return, and in the year after.

The Old One suffered a mild stroke, but under the devoted and tireless care of his young wife, and the dependable Dr Bala, he recovered completely. He said he never felt better, and claimed he could take even longer morning walks without feeling tired. He asked Dr Bala to tell him frankly about his condition, and was gratified to hear the good doctor say, 'I wouldn't be surprised if you lived to a hundred!'

He was also learning to drive, so that he could take his wife anywhere she wanted, anytime she wanted, and not have to depend on the chauffeur.

As soon as her husband was well again, Silver Frond interested herself in a project, which was the building of a small village school. She contributed generously and had secret dreams of returning to her work as teacher. But her life with the Old One was too busy to allow her to pursue her dream. She did not feel the loss, however, and was satisfied to make occasional visits to the school and acknowledge the gratitude of the two teachers running it. The school closed down after a year, because one of the teachers had absconded with a substantial amount of money, and the enrolment had dropped to three pupils.

Some months later, Ah Bee Koh died. He had been ill for a while, and Silver Frond had been paying for the best medical treatment. For a while, strangely, the old jocularity returned, and he talked of being completely cured. But even Dr Bala could not save him. On his deathbed, he asked to see his favourite daughter, consoling her for her misfortune, for his mind, in the last days, had become locked in the past. He told her, between sobs, 'I would never have allowed you to go to the Great House if I knew how they were going to treat you! Please forgive your father who only thought of himself.' Then he would turn to his wife and say, 'Make sure you give nourishing food to our daughter. She is so thin!' When she assured him that she was well and happy with her husband, he still insisted on seeking her forgiveness for the serious dereliction of parental duty.

The following year, with the help of Dr Bala, who had become the family doctor and trusted advisor on many matters, Silver Pearl underwent a successful operation on her hare-lip. Silver Frond wept to have fulfilled a long-kept promise.

About the same time, Black Dog suddenly left Singapore, and was never heard of again. His distraught wife at first connected his disappearance with that of Third Wife, who was reported missing by her family at about the same time. But later it was confirmed that Black Dog had been secretly meeting a Thai dance hostess and had eloped with her to Thailand.

Each event, tragic or happy, significant or trivial, shocking or mundane, whether involving the Venerable One and his young wife in a major or minor way, was, strangely, remembered not for itself but for the way it served to show, once again, the extraordinary devotion of the couple towards each other.

See how they love each other? the guests at the old mother's funeral whispered to each other, less interested in paying their respects to the body lying in the coffin than in observing how the young wife bustled around her old husband, solicitously urging him to take one more sip of ginseng tea and how he, in his turn, insisted on her taking a rest and sipping the tea with him.

See how he loves her? the servants whispered to each other, when Black Dog Soh came to the Great House in the middle of the night, after the discovery of her husband's flight, and created a hue and cry. The Old One's only concern was that the noise should not wake up his wife, who had not managed to sleep well the previous night because of a fever. 'His adopted son has disappeared, and all he can think of is his wife's need for a good night's sleep,' the servants said in both amazement and reproach. The Old One told First Wife to give Black Dog Soh whatever money she needed so she could leave at once. Then he went upstairs to see that his wife was still sleeping peacefully.

And then there was the incident of the fish porridge, which the servants could not stop whispering about.

The Old One had one morning, during a breakfast of fish porridge, got a fish bone stuck in his throat. His young wife immediately sent for Dr Bala. For once, the doctor was helpless – and failed to dislodge the bone. Crying to see her husband in pain, she persuaded him to allow her to get the help of an old woman from Sim Bak Village well-known for her ability to remove fishbones from children's throats through special prayers and holy water sprinkled down the throat. The Old One with his new dependence on Western medicine, was too embarrassed to return to the superstitions of his ancestors. Silver Frond begged him, saying, 'Fishbones have killed adults and children,' and he was so moved by her loving concern, that he consented to see the old woman, and was duly cured. He later told Dr Bala, by way of face-saving, that the bone had actually been a very small one only, and had been easily dislodged by a tightly pressed ball of boiled rice slowly pushed down the throat.

Thereafter the young wife took it upon herself to ensure that any fish porridge for the Old One was totally free of bone. She used a spoon to scour the porridge for even the tiniest fragment.

There was a stall at the market in the centre of town selling Silver Frond's favourite *laksa*. The stallholders and their customers at the busy market soon got used to the sight of a handsome, gleaming black car, driven by an Indian chauffeur, stopping a short distance from the *laksa* stall, and of the Old One and his young wife, stepping out and walking hand in hand to the stall to sit there at a rough wooden table and wait their turn to be served the delicious noodles in curry. No couple had ever been seen walking hand in hand. 'Old Man coming with granddaughter!' some of the more spiteful observers would whisper. They would often hear the young wife's voice raised in clear instructions: 'Please don't put too much salt in the curry. My husband does not like salty food. Please take away this bowl. It has a little stain on the rim. My husband eats only from very clean bowls.'

My husband. My wife. First Wife shook her head when told. That was not proper. Husbands and wives never referred to each other as such, or used each other's names. Instead they made oblique reference only, through using their children's names. 'So-and-so's father has gone to Malaya. I will consult So-and-so's mother on the matter.' At the most, they would say 'My male-person', or 'My female-person', and avoid using those terms that only the very coarse, or the very shameless, used publicly, in the full hearing of others.

I love you. If the direct reference to "husband" or "wife" was bad, the explicit declaration of love was shocking. Husbands and wives showed their love by deed, not word. A wife would go to any degree of sacrifice for love of her husband, but if asked to say those words openly, she would faint from the embarrassment.

When told by a servant that the Old One had actually been guilty of that misdemeanour – the servant said she could not have made a mistake, as he was saying it quite loudly to Fourth Mistress, when they were walking down the stairs together – First Wife shook her head even more vigorously. She permitted herself a sad smile: 'The Old One is reaching senility. He is behaving more and more like a child.'

Then she said wearily, 'If they want to flaunt their love to the whole world so shamelessly, it is their business!' and added cryptically, 'A man's true love for his wife is not shown in such a way. It is expressed only at the end, on the deathbed, when all folly makes way for truth.'

The deathbed was far from Silver Frond's thoughts. She had never been happier. The only cloud in the new radiance of her life in the Great House was not First Wife's ominous claim, whatever it meant, but the absence of the signs of an heir.

Her return to the Great House had yielded great happiness for the Old One, but no heir. That might be the August Ancestor's last laugh.

Her husband said, holding her very close to soothe away her fears, 'Last night, when you were asleep, I stood before the August Ancestor's portrait for the last time. I said, "I was right and you were wrong. I have never been so happy in my life.

My health has never been so good. So what if my wife does not produce a son. I love her for herself, not for anything else!"'

Loss of virginity. Barrenness. A woman was valued by the condition of her body. He had long repudiated all that, and learnt to value a woman by her capacity for loving and bringing joy.

He did not tell her that the August Ancestor had responded with a roar of anger, 'So you choose to go against me once more! You will have much to answer for, when you draw your last breath on earth and face your ancestors at last!' But he told her, with a return of the boyish sense of mischief, 'I locked the door, threw away the key and said, "Goodbye, we part company for ever here!"'

14
Laughing Song

'Here come Old Man and granddaughter!'

The comment from an assistant at the *laksa* stall was too loud not to be overheard by Silver Frond as she and her husband made their way to one of the tables. She cast a quick glance at him as he pulled out a stool, and saw a faint reddening of his ears, and a slight frown on his forehead.

She went to the offender, and over the rich steaming smells of the *laksa* curry bubbling in a pot, shook an angry forefinger at him. 'It's none of your business,' she said in a voice that carried and was heard by everyone around. 'If you have a daughter and she grows up to marry a man like my husband, you can thank all your temple gods for her good fortune.'

The owner of the stall came up then, sensing trouble and ready to apologise to the valued customers from the Great House. Silver Frond turned to him and said coldly, 'Don't count on us ever coming to this stall again.' Then she went to the Old One, took him by the arm and led him back to their waiting car.

Inside the car she was still fuming. 'Let people say what they like,' said the Old One. 'You can't stop them anyway.' He took her hand affectionately in his.

'That wasn't the first time you were mistaken for my granddaughter,' he said, smiling. 'Think. Think hard.'

She looked at him and smiled back, glad that the irritation had disappeared in the exuberance of spirits which had been his since her return.

'I'll give you a clue,' he said. 'Sand. Sea. Dead cuttlefish or what-not that you never got to see.'

She gave a little shriek of sudden recollection.

'You were very annoyed then. I remember you hurrying me away from that offensive man.' The incident came back in every vivid detail – the old man, with a palm leaf shading his head, watching his small grandson playing on the beach, yelling friendly greetings to the Old One and receiving friendly responses until that rude remark.

He said, 'I wish I had gone up to him and said, "This is not my grand-daughter. She is my wife," and watched the shock on his face.'

She laughed heartily with him. Then he told her what he knew she must have wanted to ask for a long time.

'I saw not only strange-looking cuttlefish, but crabs and fish and prawns that are too strange to be put into the cooking pot.'

It was a good enough starting point to reveal the truth of that mysterious absence from home for more than a fortnight, when she had suffered the greatest anxiety in her life. He told her about the *kelong*, and how he and his good friend had spent their days like carefree schoolboys. He told her he had returned earlier than planned because he missed her so badly.

She said simply, not of course expecting him to follow up on a simple wish expressed for the sole purpose of giving him pleasure: 'Then I wish to go on a *kelong* with you.'

'It's decided then,' he said. *Kelongs* did not allow the contaminating presence of women; his good friend would have been shocked if he had suggested an extension of the invitation to his wife. So he bought a *kelong* to please her.

As it turned out, she was able to visit it only a few times. But the rumour that provoked more gossip than any other rumour about this fascinating couple concerned the *kelong*. It had the same romantic aura as Liang Por's tale about the emperor who ordered a whole hill to be denuded to build a summer palace for his bride, because she had expressed a wish for that particular spot.

When told, First Wife said, 'Let her ask for the moon next. The old fool will present it to her on a golden plate!'

15
The Anxious Womb

He was seventy-one, she was nineteen, they had lived as husband and wife for three years, and still there were no signs of an heir.

The August Ancestor and First Wife, his staunchest ally on earth, must be gloating together, although neither could, as they did in the old days, directly confront the Old One about his folly and its dire consequences.

Ah Bee Soh came regularly with herbal brews to strengthen her daughter's womb, but it remained unproductive.

'It's not for want of trying,' whispered the servants. The most delicious gossip concerning the closed bedroom door, even during the day, and the unabashed sounds that came from it, was saved for the most secretive sharing, well out of the hearing of the grandchildren or the minor servants, who might spread it round.

Dr Bala was consulted, very discreetly. He recommended a specialist. Even more discreetly, a consultation and examination were arranged. The specialist said, 'Nothing is wrong with either of you. Indeed, both of you are very healthy. You have to keep trying.'

Both Western and traditional expertise had been commandeered for the all-important goal, so that after a visit to the specialist, Silver Frond drank her mother's brew, and wore a temple amulet blessed by a holy woman.

Ah Bee Soh said, 'Why don't you ask Ah Lian Soh for one of her sarongs?' Now Ah Lian Soh, who lived in Sim Bak Village, had had eleven children, eight boys and three girls, and her fertility could be passed on to less fortunate women through the sarongs she had worn during pregnancy, birth and the thirty-day confinement. Indeed, no fewer than six women had conceived after wearing Ah Lian Soh's sarongs. And they all bore sons. They even claimed they could feel the parturitive power of the sarongs *seeping* through the cloth into their wombs.

Silver Frond wore one of the amazing *sarongs* for six months but nothing happened.

She decided to go to her closest friend for help.

'Dear goddess,' she said beseechingly, 'how can I give my husband a son?'

'You are too anxious. An anxious womb cannot conceive.'

'How can I not be anxious? My husband is already seventy-one.'

'Ah,' said the goddess, 'I know just the trick,' and she told Silver Frond.

16
The Fulfilled Womb

She approached her husband to tell him of her plan, and he said, 'If it makes you happy.' She wanted to say, 'But the whole idea is to make *you* happy!' It had become a very odd situation indeed, where each had become anxious about an heir on the other's account. There were still some aspects of tradition that love, no matter how strong and defiant, had to submit to in the end.

She went ahead with the plan. To her surprise, First Wife, who must have heard about it, as she heard about any plan hatched in the Great House, no matter how secretive, offered the name of a very reliable woman who knew the right people to approach for the adoption of a baby boy, preferably a newborn, straight from the mother's womb into the arms of the adoptive mother, so that he would never have memory of the truth of his origins.

The woman was brought discreetly to the Great House to discuss the matter, and within a month, the baby boy was secured, the fifth child of a poor seamstress, who had also given away for adoption the previous child, also a boy.

When Silver Frond, holding the baby, went to thank First Wife, she said graciously, 'Don't mention it,' adding, 'I have nothing personally against you, as I have told you before. It is just that in this life, one must do one's duty.'

The Old One could not be expected to show enthusiasm over the new arrival, not of his blood, and as long as the baby was taken care of by a servant and did not encroach on his time with his wife, who sat down with him for every meal, joined him for every outing in the car, and went to bed only when he did, he was satisfied with the arrangement.

But he had cause to be grateful to the child, when only four months later, Silver Frond told him, her eyes shining with joy, 'I am pregnant.'

The next day she went with her mother to thank the Goddess Pearly Face and to make a huge offering of roast pig, roast duck, steamed chicken, and the most expensive joss-sticks. The goddess said nonchalantly, 'It is common knowledge. An adopted child calms the anxious womb and prepares it for bearing its own child.' She told the story of a woman who was barren for eight years, adopted a child, and then bore five children of her own.

Silver Frond gave birth to a healthy son – she never had any doubt that it would be a boy – and Ah Bee Soh not only offered another roast pig to the Goddess Pearly Face but sent a big *ang pow* to Ah Lian Soh even though her sarong had not contributed to the success.

The following year, Silver Frond gave birth to another son, and if the Old One was tempted to tell the August Ancestor once again, 'I told you I was right and you were wrong,' he never gave in to the temptation. Indeed, he had mellowed in his new happiness, and was prepared to unlock the ancestor's room and renew the rituals of respect.

But the ancestor, who did not forgive and forget as readily, had appeared in a dream, to say, with a very cold look on his face, 'You had made it clear that we should go our separate ways. Let things stay as they are.'

17
A Dream That Is Not To Be

In 1954, when he was seventy-five, the Old One suffered a second stroke, and this time Dr Bala was less optimistic. Old age, he said. Old age is unavoidable and takes its toll. One cannot expect to recover that fast. The Old One fretted for a while. For he was supremely happy in his life and did not want it to end too soon.

Dr Bala confided in his colleague, whom he had recommended to the Old One to take his place, since he was leaving the country, 'The old man won't last a year.' Of course, he did not tell the young wife. She had put on weight since the birth of her second son, but still looked very beautiful. The fulfilment of motherhood enhances the beauty of an already beautiful woman, it is said, and at twenty-three, Silver Frond, as she went out to the shops and the market with her little boys, provoked the same intense speculation as she had when a young girl-bride. 'She will be a very beautiful and desirable widow. And an extremely rich one.'

There was another rumour, which gathered intensity as it rolled on through the Great House, the neighbourhood, the market, the coffee shops. 'The servants hear loud, angry voices coming from their room, which is a very strange thing, considering how devoted they are to each other.'

She had never thought she would raise her voice to her husband, especially as he lay ill on his bed. But if there was a voice raised from pure love itself, it was hers.

She said to him, her voice angry and pleading by turns, 'Can't you grant me this? It is my dearest wish!'

He looked at her sadly and said, 'I wish I could. You know very well that I will do anything for you.'

She said sharply, 'Then why can't you just tell her you have changed your mind? You have every right to do so!'

She wanted him to tell First Wife that the tomb next to his would not be hers. The instructions of the dying carried the weight of divine ordinance, and could never be disregarded. First Wife would protest and say, 'You are going against tradition!' But love was greater than tradition, and First Wife would have to divest herself of the consolation that had supported her these many years, and accept her place in the hierarchy of the Old One's love.

'You love me most and I want my grave next to yours!' Silver Frond stamped a foot with the petulance of a spoilt child.

'We'll not talk of death,' said her husband calmly. 'I am still alive, and I have you. That makes me very happy.'

The servants had remarked that for someone who had longed for a son through three wives, the Old One was amazingly indifferent to his two sons in his obsession – yes, it remained an obsession – with his young wife. The old belief about a supernatural power she carried with her, even if she was not aware of it, persisted, and even if he lived to be a hundred, he would be as enamoured of her as on the day they met.

Silver Frond had an idea. She was not sure it would work, but she would give it a try. She went to First Wife, who was sitting on a chair, offered her a cup of tea, and said with all reverence and humility, 'First Mistress, I have a great favour to ask of you.'

Sensing what was coming next, First Wife said with the determination of one who could never be prevailed upon to grant a favour that would destroy a lifetime's dream, 'Say what youhavetosay.'

Silver Frond offered her entire share of inheritance, to dispose of as she liked, to children and grandchildren if she would forego all claim to that coveted place beside the old man's grave in the cemetery. First Wife shook her head and Silver Frond pleaded and argued. A strange competition by two women, brimming with life, for a position of honour in death!

First Wife said, 'You are talking nonsense. You are now a mother, but you are talking nonsense like a child.'

'Please,' said Silver Frond. 'Not for my sake but for his. You know he loves me most of all.'

She had made an error, for First Wife suddenly stood up from her chair and said haughtily, 'There you are mistaken. A man proves his love by deeds, not words, in death, not life. He may say he loves you ten times a day, but he has proved it to me by his act of commitment to our sacred traditions. He may spend his years of life with you, but he will spend longer years in death with me beside him in his resting place.'

18
In the Belly of the Python

As he lay dying, she told him a story. He liked to hear the sound of her voice, whether in story-telling or song, and he loved her presence at all times, so that when she left to go for a meal or to the bathroom, even for a few minutes, he grew impatient and asked for her.

A python entered a village and swallowed a man. Just as it was gliding away, the man's wife ran after it and said, 'Please swallow me too.'

'What?' said the python. 'What a strange request to make. And why, may I ask?'

'So that I can be together with my husband,' sobbed the woman. 'I had meant to be buried with my husband and lie beside him for all eternity. Now your belly will have to be our resting place together.'

The Old One smiled, though he wanted to weep. But he still could not grant his wife's wish. He knew she loved him so much she would go into the belly of the python ten times for him, just as she had gone through the unspeakable horror of a demonic cleansing ritual in a temple for him.

'Please,' she said and sobbed afresh.

A terrifying picture had floated up in her mind. She saw two tombstones side by side in loving closeness, with handsome offerings of suckling pig, roast pork, pink buns, fine noodles, cups of fine tea, surrounded by burning candles and joss-sticks, then watched, with pain, as two figures emerged from the tombs, the Old One as neatly and impeccably dressed in death as in life, and First Wife in her finest grey silk blouse and trousers. She watched them talking in low voices to each other, their heads close together, before they sat down and partook of the feast. And she saw herself, inferior ghost because of inferior location of tomb in a distant corner of the family burial plot, move forward timidly, not daring to break in upon the intimacy of the Old One and his first wife as they dined and drank together, two ghosts bound together for all eternity.

Oh, it was unbearable!

The Old One said, stroking her cheek, 'I am going to face the August Ancestor very soon. I have been disobeying him these many years. I want to be able to say to him when I see him at last, "My last act was one of obedience to the ancestors. I have come home."'

19
Bittersweet

At the funeral, people watched all four wives. Third Wife, accompanied by her daughters who stood on each side and held her arms protectively, looked well enough, and sane enough, though people wondered why, when the Old One had completely repudiated her, she had bothered to come at all.

First Wife had no expression on her face. Second Wife, who moved about with difficulty because she had grown grossly fat, wore a frown that seemed to suggest grief, or puzzlement or anger, or all three. But it was Fourth Wife whom everybody was watching most closely.

Silver Frond was sobbing uncontrollably, and people whispered to each other, 'Those are genuine tears. She must love him a lot. But then he loved her most of all the wives. Anybody could see that.'

And in response, if she had heard, she would have turned to First Wife and said, 'See? I told you. His last promise might have been to you, but his last *word*, his last *touch*, his last *look*, were all for me!'

And indeed, it was true.

It is said that if a man dies without being able to close his eyes, and keeps them resolutely open as he lies in his coffin, it is because he has not seen, for the last time, the woman he loves best of all. People looking at him will be terrified and try to close his widely staring eyes in the coffin. But he will resist, and wait until the loved one appears. Then his eyes will close in peace at last.

If, for some reason, she had been away at the moment of the Old One's death, there would be no doubt that his eyes would stay open to wait for her arrival. He would wait for her in death, as he had waited for her in life. And if they were not joined together in the closeness of twin graves on the earth, why, that did not matter, because they were already joined together in supreme awareness of that love.

Epilogue

Silver Frond died in 1961, aged only thirty. Her mother Ah Bee Soh outlived her by fifteen years. Her three sons (including the adopted one who did not know about the adoption till adulthood) were still very young, and were brought up by an aunt, one of First Wife's daughters, First Wife having died only a few years after the Old One.

I am the daughter of Silver Frond's youngest son, which makes me her natural granddaughter. That means some of that marvellous woman's blood flows through my veins! How I yearn to be able to claim a little of that defiance and indomitability of spirit, that amazing eagerness to learn, that radiant generosity of heart, that remarkable capacity to give and inspire love, which guided her along the perilous pathways of her life during a period when pathways could be particularly perilous for women.

And of course I would love to be able to claim a little of that famed beauty. My favourite photo of her shows her at eighteen. She has the luminous beauty of the actress Gong Li, and indeed could be said to be even more beautiful, with her large pensive eyes and wistful smile.

One of these days, I will get a friend of mine who is an excellent artist to do a portrait of Grandmother based on this photo. It will have pride of place in the little apartment where I live alone with my cat.

I first became fascinated by Grandmother's story when one day (I must have been sixteen or seventeen), quite by chance, a visiting relative told me about the terrible rape by the bogus monk in the temple. Such a thing did not happen to one's mother or grandmother! I was shocked. I checked with Dad, but he could tell me nothing. He was only three when Grandmother died. Nevertheless, I pestered him with questions. Even very young children, I insisted, have memories of remarkable parents. And Grandmother, surely, was a most remarkable person.

What did she look like? What did she wear? How did her voice sound? Did she spank you when you were naughty? What was she like as a mother? How did she and the Old One behave when they were together? Did they laugh a lot together? Did you ever hear anything about her from the servants, that upset you?

The relative swore, in an awe-stricken whisper that the horrible story was true, but the family had kept the truth hidden, or had dressed it up with so many false stories that in the end it seemed like just one of the unsavoury rumours one would expect the envious to circulate about the wealthy and prosperous.

There was no stopping me now. I just had to find out more. My research took the form of countless interviews of relatives and servants still alive, and extrapolation from old documents, photographs, artefacts, anything I could lay my hands on. A niece of Silver Frond (one of the four children of Silver Pearl, who married a businessman; Silver Flower never married) provided valuable information, as did one of the Old One's great-granddaughters, the daughter of Third Wife, who had gone to live in Malaya. I managed to track this cousin down, and was thrilled by the many things she remembered.

My fascination with this ancestor continued through my years at the university, Silver Frond having become the subject of some short stories, a poem and even a play, which explored the whole issue of tradition's obsession with virginity, and the terrifying impact on a woman's life. In my play (which never made it to the stage), three generations of women, in a country somewhere in Asia, suffered the punishments meted out by society for the loss of virginity, and although the forms seemed less severe with the passing of time (the grandmother was almost beaten to death by her husband), the social stigma remained the same (the granddaughter was constantly taunted by her in-laws as 'secondhand goods').

Indeed, for a while, after I completed a degree in sociology, I was tempted to do a post-graduate thesis on the issue of virginity, and trace the development of the related concepts of sexuality, male ownership of female bodies, first rights, social taboos, empowerment, etc, until I realised that what I really wanted to do was simply write the life story of this wondrous, unforgettable ancestor.

I wanted in particular to write about how this forbear, a young ignorant village girl, made an old, experienced, tradition-bound businessman with three wives, love her so much that he virtually upset the old order on her account, and how she returned his love by rejecting for ever her own childlike world of innocence and security. They had leaped across incredible barriers – of age, background, temperament, social convention – to reach each other. It was an inspiring love story, and all the more remarkable for being seen as the exact opposite in their time – an improper, shameful union, frowned upon by family and society.

What lay behind this extraordinary triumph of love? It could not be her beauty or his desire alone.

I took a long look at their wedding photograph, the one where they wore traditional dress. There is something about the expression on their faces that might help explain their love's special magic. Beneath the restraint and the reserve of formal wedding photographs in those days, there is a hint, on both faces, of irreverent playfulness, defiant obstinacy and a sparkling eagerness to claim their share of life's pleasures. It must have been this extraordinary need to live life to the full that made the Old One become like a child again, as First Wife would remark contemptuously, and the young village girl become a shrewd and alert woman overnight, as her own family would observe with astonishment. In the end, despite the more than fifty years difference in age, they had achieved an enduring soulmateship. It would be some years before I could write the novel. I was busy in my work, and went through a difficult time in a relationship, which finally ended in the most painful way. For a while, I tried to forget my broken heart in a frenzy of activity, which included going into another relationship, with someone who had nothing in common with me. It too ended, much to my relief (and his). Then I thought writing a novel about Grandmother could absorb the restless energy that was being expended so uselessly or relationships.

As I worked on the story, I became more and more captivated by this ancestor. I was aware – and profoundly moved – that this woman who exemplified the Cinderella dream of rags to riches, obscurity to privilege, was in reality a very sad woman, because her greatest dream – to be buried next to her husband – had remained unfulfilled. It was true that she would have given up all her share of the vast wealth of the Great House in exchange for that dream. This bright, intense, beautiful woman had only two desires in her life: to be educated, and to be buried beside her husband. In a way, neither dream had been fulfilled.

Midway through writing, I paid a visit to the cemetery, to see where she was buried and where she had wanted so dearly to be buried. The tombstones of the Old One and First Wife were identical: they were no different from the many Chinese tombstones in this old cemetery, with the portraits set in oval engravings, and the inscriptions of name, date of birth and date of death, and a large paved cement enclosure for the laying out of food offerings and the burning of ghost money during the Cheng Meng festival. Silver Frond's tombstone was the same in size and structure, but, as she had feared, it was some distance away, separated from her beloved husband's grave by many others. (I could not find the tombstone of Second Wife; Third Wife was buried in another cemetery.)

In a strange dream I had as I was working on the novel, I saw Silver Frond sitting desolately on a small earth mound near her grave. She had no reason to be a despairing, wandering ghost like the poor woman who had hanged herself in one of the Old One's houses in Choon Kiah Street. But she looked desolate enough, because the triumphant song of her life was not complete. In the dream, I walked up to her and addressed her as 'Lai Ma' (the Hokkien term to indicate the superiority of the grandmother on the paternal side, as opposed to 'Gua Ma', indicating the inferiority of the grandmother on the maternal side), and she turned to me and gave me a smile.

In 2000, I saw a government notice in *The Singapore Times* gazetting the exhumation of the graves in the cemetery, to be completed over four months. This was part of an ongoing exercise of the government to reclaim land for residential and industrial use. The old Chinese cemetery was certainly valuable land, marked for the development of a Science and Technology Park. And it was precisely at this moment, as I held the newspaper in my hand and stared at the notice, in its dry officialese, that I made a decision. Or perhaps, as I am sometimes inclined to believe, though I do not believe in the existence of ghosts, my grandmother Silver Frond appeared then, whispered something in my ear, and inspired that decision.

I asked Father if I could take over the responsibility of overseeing the exhumation of our ancestors' graves. He looked at me with surprise but was clearly glad to be relieved of a tedious duty. It was also characteristic of Father that he showed little curiosity about my interest beyond saying, 'Why? Oh, I see. You've always been fascinated by your grandmother's story.'

It was a very cold and dark morning when I went to the cemetery to represent my father at the exhumation – exhumations, never a pleasant sight, with none of the cathartic solemnity and poignancy of a burial, always take place before the first light of dawn, while the world is still asleep.

The sight of the bones, covered with mud, darkened by time, brought up one by one from coffins still intact though waterlogged, took up less of my attention than the need to make sure that they were placed in their separate receptacles. I watched the workmen closely to make sure that there would be no mistake. As I took charge of the three boxes of bones, I whispered an apology to First Wife's: 'I am very sorry, First Grandmother, but I'm going to give all my attention to Grandfather and Fourth Grandmother.'

I made arrangements for the cremation of the remains, and went to collect the ashes the next day, for taking away to place in a columbarium. The ashes were in jade-green urns. I had brought along a larger urn. I took the urns containing the ashes of the Old One and Silver Frond, and *mixed them together in a single urn.*

Silver Frond had dreamt of togetherness in the cemetery, and even, in her desperation, of the gruesome togetherness in the belly of a python. She would have appreciated this reunion most of all.

I went away in the joy of having enabled a wonderful ancestor, more than thirty years later, to finish singing her song.

About the Author

A prolific writer, Catherine Lim has written more than 19 books across various genres – short stories, novels, reflective prose, poems and satirical pieces. Born in 1942 Malaya, Lim was a teacher, then project director with the Ministry of Education and a specialist lecturer with the Regional Language Centre (RELC) before dedicating herself fully to writing in 1992.

Lim has won several national and regional book prizes for her literary contributions, including the National Book Development Council (NBDCS) awards in 1982, 1988 and 1990; the Montblanc-NUS Centre For The Arts Literary Award in 1998; and the 1999 regional Southeast Asian Write Award. She was conferred an Honorary Doctorate of Literature by Murdoch University, Australia, in 2000, and a Knight of the Order of Arts and Letters by the French Ministry of Culture and Information in 2003. Lim was also Ambassador for the Hans Christian Andersen Foundation, Copenhagen, in 2005.

Many of Lim's works are studied in local and foreign schools and universities, and have been published in various languages in several countries. She was the first Singaporean author to pen an electronic-novella over the Internet, which has since been adapted into a movie.

Besides writing, Lim guest lectures at local and international seminars, conferences, arts/writing festivals and cruise ships worldwide. She has also appeared on radio and television programmes in Singapore, Europe and Australia.

Other books by Catherine Lim

The Catherine
Lim Collection

Miss Seetoh
in the World

Following the
Wrong God Home

The Teardrop
Story Woman

The Bondmaid